Between The Rivers

By Carolyn R. Booth

Between the Rivers
Carolyn R. Booth

Coastal
Carolina Press
www.coastalcarolinapress.org

Second Edition

Cover and book design by Maximum Design & Advertising, Inc.
Cover illustration by Natalie Schorr
Interior illustrations by Katie Anne Rawls McKendry

Printed in the United States of America
Library of Congress Cataloging-in-Publication Data

Booth, Carolyn R. (Carolyn Rawls), 1936-
    Between the rivers / by Carolyn R. Booth.--1st ed.
      p. cm.
    ISBN 1-928556-29-9
    1. Onslow County (N.C.)--Fiction. 2. Women teachers--Fiction. I.
Title.
    PS3602.O66 B47 2001
    813'.6--dc21
                                        2001047561

10 9 8 7 6 5 4 3 2

Acknowledgements

Many of the events retold on these pages are true; many are not. Facts have been rearranged and names changed to suit my purpose. To those of you who might be offended by a character's similarity to someone you knew and loved, I ask you not to look so closely. This is a work of fiction.

I could not have written this story without the love and support of two women in my family: my sister, Katie Anne McKendry, who drew the houses, gave me great insight into the characters and encouraged me to keep going until I came full circle; and my mother, Mildred Smith Rawls, who instilled confidence in me when she asked, How did you know that? You weren't even born!

To my husband, Dick Booth, who tirelessly researched my genealogy and put on paper those names that I had only heard the old folks talk about; to my friend and mentor, Georgann Eubanks, who urged me to go way beyond the truth; and to my editor, Emily Colin, who held my hand through the lengthy revision process, I give my love and gratitude.

To my youngest sister, Elna Rawls Averitte, who died July 4, 1995, I dedicate my story.

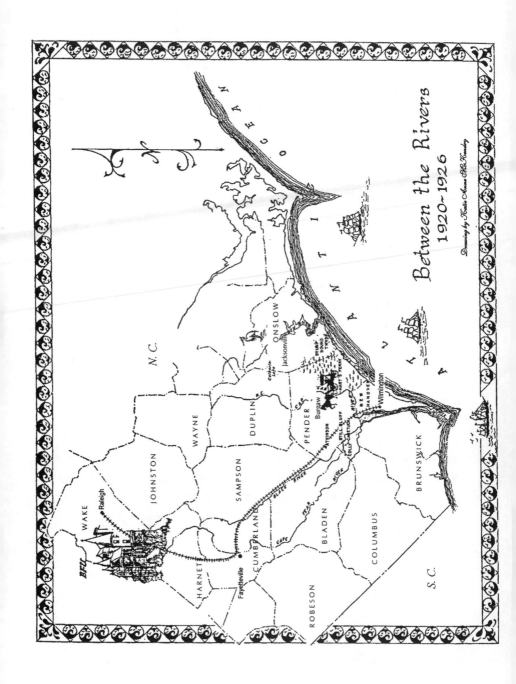

Between the Rivers
1920~1926

Drawing by Kadie Anne McKinley

Prologue

Bladen County, North Carolina
May 1924

Lizzie must've smelled the smoke. She was running across the field, her long feedsack gown pulled up high around her waist. Barefoot, she leapt like a deer across the newly planted rows of corn, her black skin glistening in the moonlight.

Leaning against the smokehouse, his breath coming in short raspy huffs, Tate Ryan watched the fire roar up, licking and splitting through the attic, rolling the old tin roof back like a sardine can. *No need to come running,* he thought. *There's nothing nobody can do now—not even God Almighty Himself!*

Maggie and the boys were huddled in their nightclothes beneath the shelter of the oak grove, their eyes wide and unbelieving as they watched the house sputter and cough up great clouds of black smoke. Ashes rained down on the canopy of ancient trees, covering their moss-bearded limbs with a peppery dust. No one said a word or moved until the old colored woman who had brought Maggie and her children into the world gathered Maggie in her arms, turning her away from the flames. "Don't look," Lizzie cried. "It don't do no good to look."

William and Lenny, Maggie and Tate's two teenaged sons, stared at the flames, mesmerized by their savage roar. "P-p-papa. M-m-my b-b-books, Papa," William said. His stuttering had started when his little brother Yancey died two years ago, but tonight there was an added tremor of fear in his voice.

"It's all right, son," Tate said, reaching out and pulling the boy beneath his arm. "Papa'll get you some more books."

Lenny, the younger of the two boys, gaped at the burning house, the flames reflected in his frightened eyes. "This is gonna kill Mama. It's just gonna kill her."

"Hush up now, Lenny. Don't let your mama hear you," Tate said. His second son was almost as tall as he was, but Lenny still lowered his eyes and shifted his feet when his father spoke sternly to him. "Come over here," Tate said, catching hold of Lenny with his other arm.

Lizzie tightened her grip on Maggie, fixing her eyes on the burning house. "There now, ain't no need to cry, Missy. I seen more'n one old house go up like dat. It be a mean thing to watch, but you and Mr. Tate and the chil'ren is safe, dat's alls matters to me."

Maggie sobbed. Her muslin nightgown was streaked with soot, and her long red hair, let down and brushed smooth at bedtime, had been singed and bobbed by the greedy flames when she crawled across the hot floorboards and pulled her trunk to safety. "It wasn't just any old house, Lizzie, it was Aunt Mag's house that Uncle Archie built for her."

"Hush now. Jus' hush. It don't matter whose house it was. Mr. Tate can build you 'nother one, can't you Mr. Tate?"

"I'll build it back, Maggie," Tate said, touching her on the shoulder.

Maggie whirled around in Lizzie's arms, glaring at him. "You can't build Aunt Mag's house back!"

"Me and the boys can build us a better house, can't we?" He looked to his sons for approval and they nodded, their tear-streaked faces brightening.

"We will, Mama," William said.

Before Maggie could protest again, Lizzie took her arm. "C'mon now, Missy, you can talk about that in the mornin'. Right now the boys need a place to get some sleep. We'll jus' go back t'my house and be back over here with some vittles and things when it gets light." She took Maggie's hand, pulling her along like a child. Stopping abruptly in front of an old steamer trunk, Lizzie stared hard at an old Olivetti typewriter sitting on it. "Is that the onliest thing you gots out, Mr. Tate?" she said, her dark eyes flashing.

Tate looked away, watching the fire blister and melt the old piano and gobble up the rose damask settee. He had tried to stop Maggie from going after the trunk, but she had wrenched away from him, crawled through the smoke, grabbed the trunk's handle, dragged it out, and shoved it down the steps, toppling the typewriter into the sand. "Maggie pulled the trunk out, Lizzie. The typewriter was on it. Everything else is..."

"I should've known. Why'd you let her go in dere, Mr. Tate? She could've been burnt up."

"I couldn't stop her."

Lizzie held Maggie's face and strained to see it by the light of the fire. "Here, lemme look at you, chile." She ran her hand over Maggie's hair. "It'll grow back, Missy. Ain't nuthin' won't grow back 'cept your life. Don't look so worried now, Lizzie'll take care of you, jus' like always."

When the flames had licked all resistance and burned steady like a banked stove, Lizzie and the boys took the cart path towards her cabin with only the moon to light their way. Tate walked slowly around the smoldering heap, stopping now and then to stare as a tardy flame shot upward. He had gotten the boys out, knowing that Maggie was on one of her late-night rambles outside. Unable to sleep, she'd often leave the house, walk around the yard and fall asleep in the gazebo swing. He'd found her there many a morning.

Under the oaks, Maggie shivered, more from her thoughts than from the damp night air. Wrapping her long nightgown tightly about her knees, she braced her heels against the trunk and reached out for the Olivetti. She pulled it in close to her, pressing it hard against her thigh. Tate would never say it, but others like Lizzie would—how it was funny that once again everything they possessed had been destroyed by fire except the old leather trunk that Uncle Archie had given her to keep her things in when she was just a child. Yes, by God, when Tate refused to even try, she went straight to her things, the things she cherished most in this world, and dragged them out with her bare hands.

Maggie reflected on how he'd just stood there, saying *let it burn, let it burn.* She'd thought he meant the trunk, but now she was beginning to wonder if he had meant the house, too. She watched him poke among the ashes with a long stick. Tate had hated Aunt Mag's house as much as Maggie had loved it. All the pretty things she'd cherished signified nothing to him. But it had been their home, where they'd raised their children.

She closed her eyes. Aunt Mag had come yesterday and told Maggie that she wasn't going to put up with her anymore, she wanted her house back. She'd told Maggie that she wasn't a good wife, and much worse, she'd accused her of not being a good mother. Aunt Mag was like everyone else; she didn't understand why Maggie still suffered so. They all thought she had gone mad since little Yancey had died. Maybe she had. She still tried to think of things she might have done to save him. There must have been something.

———

The moon still shone in the early morning sky as dawn broke across the sandy fields. The barn and the smokehouse seemed out of place without the house towering over them.

"I found your wedding ring, Maggie. It was in the postage cup." Tate was standing over her, his outstretched hand coated with thick white ash. He was wearing his nightshirt tucked into an old pair of work pants that had hung on a nail in the packhouse. Maggie stared at the blackened ring. "Here, take it," he said, thrusting it towards her.

The ring had belonged to Tate's mother. Her great-grandfather had first given it to her great-grandmother when they were married in Ireland. The two hands, clasped together in a silver circle, were supposed to signify eternal love. Maggie had put the ring in the postage cup when she was pregnant with Yancey, her fingers too swollen to wear it. The circle of love had been there ever since.

She pushed his hand aside. "You keep it. I have nowhere to put it."

"You could put it in your trunk," he said without meeting her eyes.

Standing up, she reached out and grabbed the ring. "Yes, I could put it in my trunk, Tate. I could put it there and never take it out and it would never be in danger of getting lost again, would it?"

"Maggie Lorena, it's yours to do what you will, but the boys should have it when you're done with it."

Rubbing the blackened ring on her nightgown, she tried to polish it. "Well, I should hope they'll have enough money someday to buy their own wedding rings, unless they get stuck in this hellhole for the rest of their lives like I have," she said, holding the ring up to the moonlight.

"You shouldn't be talking like that, Maggie Lorena. You always said you wanted to live right here, between the rivers."

"That was before Aunt Mag's house burned down."

"Don't say that. You don't mean it."

"I do mean it. I do! There's nothing here for me with Aunt Mag's house gone. She gave it to me so I would always come back here. Now it's gone. I might as well go away and never come back."

Tate fell to his knees in front of her, taking her hands in his. "No, don't say that, Maggie," he pleaded. "I can build us a bigger, better house. You'll see."

"I told you, I don't want another house." She lunged at him and he reached out to steady himself, upsetting the Olivetti and tumbling it into the black sand again. "Now look what you've done," she cried, stamping her bare feet. "My typewriter is all I have left and it's ruined." She went rigid, her arms tight against her sides and her fists clenched. "You did it on purpose."

Tate picked up the typewriter and placed it on the trunk. "You did it yourself. Don't go blaming me."

With the hem of her nightgown, Maggie began to brush the sand from the tangle of keys, whimpering at first, then letting out long sorrowful wails. Tate reached for her arms and pulled her to him. "Don't. Please don't. I can't take no more. We'll start over. I swear I'll build you the best house there ever was, one better than Aunt Mag's." She stopped crying and looked at him. "We can do it, Maggie," he said. "I know we can, if you'll just..."

But she pushed him away and stared at the smoking rubble. "You're a fool, Tate Ryan. You can't build a house like Aunt Mag's. Not in a hundred years could you build that house back like it was—not Aunt Mag's house."

"I didn't say I'd build Aunt Mag's house back. I don't even want to. I said I'd build you another house—your own house, right here between the rivers—like you always wanted." His voice was eager, his arms holding her tightly again.

But she pulled away and walked towards the remains of the house, stopping at the wire fence that surrounded her vegetable garden. "There's nothing I want here anymore. Everything I ever wanted is gone. A new house can't bring it back."

In the daylight the ashes seemed to grow hotter, with the sun beating down and a soft breeze fanning the coals. Beyond the clearing where the house had stood, Maggie's bantam hens scratched in the mud around the rusty hand pump.

Tate had begun to collect some things, pulling them from the rubble and placing them on a makeshift table. He had found a chair in the barn for Maggie, who was rummaging in her trunk. "Haven't you got something in there you can put on?" he asked, walking towards her. "You don't look decent if Lizzie comes back with some help."

Maggie looked down at the muslin gown, as if aware for the first time that she was still in her nightclothes. She was forty-four years old and had lost her figure after their third child, but Tate still loved her large breasts that bulged against the thin fabric. Even when she was like this, he wanted to reach out and take them in his hands.

"There's nothing in here I can put on," she said, slamming the lid shut.

"You must have something, Maggie, an old dress of some kind."

"There's nothing in here I can wear."

"Fine," he said, walking away, "but it don't look right, you in your nightgown."

"For heavens' sake, Tate, we just lost everything we own in a fire and you're worried about things looking right? I don't care who sees me in my nightgown."

"Well, I know you've got some clothes in there. I saw..."

She glared at him. "What did you see?"

Tate looked away, wishing he'd kept his mouth shut. "Nothing. I didn't see nothing."

Maggie opened the lid and lifted the wooden tray, shielding the contents as much as possible. She pulled out a pink satin corset and her wedding dress, a crumpled bundle of white embroidered batiste. Unbuttoning the rough cotton nightgown, she let it slip first off one shoulder and then the other. Her singed red hair fell over her heavy breasts in uneven ringlets.

"Not here, Maggie Lorena!"

"If not here, where? I've got nothing to hide."

"Are you crazy? Stop it. Go to the barn."

He reached for her arm, but she pulled away from him. "I'm not going anywhere. Now help me with my corset."

"You *are* crazy, Maggie," he said, grabbing the corset and wrapping it around her.

―――

Aunt Mag thought she'd die when she rode into the oak grove and saw her house nothing but smoking ruins and Maggie sitting on the trunk in her wedding dress. Lizzie's brother, Freddy, had found her in the garden pulling onions when he came in the wagon to tell her about the fire. She was still wearing her heavy boots underneath a long skirt. "My God, how did this happen?" she said, jumping from the wagon, spry as a chicken despite her age.

She stared at the chimneys that stood like sentries over what little remained of the house her husband had built for her some thirty years ago. Swallowing hard, she looked at Maggie, feeling ashamed that she had come down so hard on her the day before. "Oh, Maggie, honey, I'm so sorry. Come here."

Maggie fell into her aunt's arms. "It's gone, Aunt Mag. Your house...all your things...gone."

"Now, now, it's all right," she said, patting Maggie. "Nothing matters except you and Tate and the children. It was just an old house when I gave it to you. I didn't really want it back. Nothing in it mattered to me anymore," she said, the lie making her voice crack. "You've been wanting to build her another house, haven't you, Tate? I'd say this is your chance."

"I told her I would," Tate said, hanging his head.

"See there, I knew he would. Why, he's been talking about building you another house ever since you two came over here from Onslow County."

Tate was beginning to feel a little better. "Could we build it right here on the same spot?" He'd had his eye on another place near Colly Creek, but now he was trying to please Maggie.

"Why, sure," Aunt Mag said. "I don't see any reason why not." She gestured towards the ruins, choking back the tears.

Maggie turned on them. "I don't want another house, I'm telling you both!"

"Straighten up now, Maggie Lorena," Aunt Mag said. "You've got a right to be upset, but there's no need to take it out on us. Here, I brought you something to put on. You look like a pure fool in that wedding dress."

Maggie had tried to stuff herself into the dress and many of the tiny pearl buttons that ran up the back remained undone. Aunt Mag had made the dress for Maggie's college graduation and she could recall every stitch that had gone into it. But it had served another purpose then, and now—another.

Aunt Mag slowly circled the ruins of the house, staring deep into the ashes for some trace of what had once been hers. She'd been seventeen when she'd married Archie MacFayden, a widower twenty-two years her senior. His first wife died childless, and at first Archie had hoped that Mag would bear him children, but despite a lot of wallowing about in bed, she had never conceived. Archie was a government man, settling claims and such after the Civil War. His business took him all up and down the Seaboard Coast from Boston to Florida. She traveled with him when she could, but she tired of it and asked him to build her a little house right there in Colly where she could be near her only sister, Ellen. Their father, John Moreland, had given each of his two daughters a section of his best land as wedding presents and Mag intended to build a house on hers, even if Archie wasn't a farmer.

It seemed everyone was poor in those years after the War—everyone except people like Archie who had kept their money in the banks up North. Coming home from the War to his Bladen County farm, Maggie's father G.W. Corbinn was a broken man. Not only was he overcome by the loss of the cause and so many good soldiers, he found his parents in failing health and the fields overrun with sawgrass and sandburrs. Every bit of his family's livestock had either been stolen or sold to make ends meet. He said the Yanks didn't personally take one thing off that farm, but they robbed them, sure as the world, of just about everything they had. They took G.W. too, but he said he survived that hellhole of a prison at Fort Delaware to spite them.

G.W. Corbinn had gotten hold of a piece of prized Moreland land when he married Mag's sister, but he always said the best piece had gone to Mag. There'd been a lot of talk about that, how she'd gotten the best tract of land and her husband not the least bit interested in farming.

The little house Archie had built for Mag looked like a dollhouse back then, sitting there all shiny and new in the moss-draped oak grove. Archie found the plans in *Bicknel's Village Builder* and had parts of the house ready-made up in Raleigh so it could be put together in no time.

Most folks in the country didn't bother to paint cypress siding, but she had her heart set on a little painted cottage like one she'd seen up in Richmond. Archie painted it white and trimmed it out in pale blue on the shutters and all the little bric 'n' brac along the porch rails and posts. The picture showed the roof made out of split shingles, but Archie knew how much she loved the sound of rain on a tin roof, so he told them up in Raleigh to leave off the shingles and send tin and some silver paint to keep it from rusting. It was as fine a house as any between there and Wilmington. Everybody said so.

How she came to give her house to Maggie was another story. G.W. and Ellen didn't get married and start raising a family until ten years after the War. They'd courted before the War, but it took G.W. a long time to get his mind straightened out. They'd had eight children—five boys and three girls—the young'uns coming every two years, just like clockwork. Jasper, George, Zeb, Ernest and Mary Ellen came before Maggie; then Raymond, Katie and baby Ralph.

Georgie went to Agricultural College up in Michigan, married Ada, and never came back home. He was eight years older than Maggie, and used to carry her around on his shoulders so she could reach up and pull the long Spanish moss off of the trees. Ellen and G.W. sold it by the bushel basket for packing pears and grapes to ship up north.

Jasper was a wanderer of sorts who left from time to time to work in the shipyard in Wilmington, but he always came back home to farm. Zeb, the one most like G. W., was drawn to the soil in the same way his pa had been. They were both hot-headed and hard-driven. Maggie felt closer to Zeb than to any of her other brothers. They shared a love of writing poetry and he often asked Maggie to read his work. Although he teased her at times, he was always the one who took up for her if she got in trouble.

After Zeb came Ernest, who was so peculiar that he never married, then Mary Ellen. Maggie was born between Mary Ellen and Katie. Her two sisters made life easier in a houseful of boys who seemed naturally bent on teasing and taunting. The girls stood up for one another and seldom had a cross word among them. Aunt Mag said you could tell they were all tarred by the same stick. Mary Ellen was the most striking, with glints of auburn in her dark hair. She had the Corbinn eyes, piercing and blue, but her nature was gentle, like Ellen's. Maggie and Katie could have passed for twins. Both had red hair, freckles, dark brown eyes and the Corbinns' little crook in their noses. Last of all was Ralph, whom they all still called "Baby" because he looked the part, if nothing else.

When G.W. and Ellen named Maggie Lorena after her, Aunt Mag felt she and Archie had been handed a child of their own. Maggie would come and stay with them for weeks at a time and they fussed over her like she was a little princess. Archie even fixed up the storage room off the back porch for her to play and keep her things. When she was a little older, he bought Maggie the Olivetti typewriter because she was always writing stories and saying she wanted to be a writer. So when Archie dropped dead on the front porch of a heart attack, it seemed perfectly natural for Maggie to live with Aunt Mag permanently.

When Maggie came of age, Aunt Mag wanted her to go to college more than anything. As much as she would miss her, Aunt Mag knew that college was a chance for Maggie to get her education and see more of the world than the swamps on either side of the rivers. G.W. had managed to send the oldest boys off to college, but Maggie and her sisters each only got two years of high school at Salemburg Academy. He figured that was all his girls needed. After Archie died she'd opened up a little one-room schoolhouse across the road, and that was where Maggie and her sisters followed in Aunt Mag's footsteps, helping her teach school.

But things were changing. The Legislature was talking about making it mandatory for teachers to have some college education. She tried to talk to G.W. about it. "You're a county commissioner, you know what they're saying up there in Raleigh. Old schoolmarms like me aren't going to be able to teach school just because they want to," she'd said. "Teachers are going to have to go off to college, get certified."

G.W. wouldn't listen. She just couldn't get through to him, until the idea came to her about giving her house and land to Maggie.

Mag had picked a good day—it was Monday and she felt he would be at his best, rested up over Sunday. She'd found him shucking corn, throwing the ears into a pile in the corner of the corn crib. They chit-chatted a little about the weather before she lit into him. "G.W., Maggie wants to go to the new Baptist college up in Raleigh."

He stopped shucking and heaved a sigh before he glared at her. "Now look here, Margaret, it's all I can do to keep food on the table for this crowd. I can't afford to send Maggie off to college. She's gonna have to find her a husband, just like you did."

She'd picked up an ear of corn herself then, pulled the white husks back, gathered them in her hand and shook the corn at her brother-in-law. "You think that's all she wants—to get married? Just because she's a woman doesn't mean she can't get her education!" She threw the ear of corn as far as she could towards an old sow. Six or eight little piglets ran for the corn, squealing in unison.

G.W. stood up and wiped his forehead with the back of his sleeve. He pointed a long gnarled finger at her. "You get off my back, Margaret!" Picking up a half-dozen ears, he walked towards the hog lot, leaving her standing red-faced. "What's got into you?" he called back. "You know money is tight. I do the best I can for my children. You can't get blood out of a turnip. Besides, we need all our girls nearby," he said, his tone softening a little. "You don't understand how it is to have your health failing and no one to look after you."

Mag knew he was thinking of his own parents making it on their own, their sons gone off to war. Without their daughters there to help, they would have lost everything. She'd followed him to the fence then, confident that she was beginning to get to him. "I've been thinking about something. You know, Archie left me a little money. I can help out a little, if you'll let me. I talked to the preacher last Sunday and he said the church could help, too."

"What do you mean, 'help'?"

"Well, he said they'd pay her train fare, for one thing." She dreaded his reaction. "And he said they'd take up a collection to help with her tuition."

G.W. snapped to attention, his eyes cutting right through her. "You know how I feel about charity. The War took just about everything I had 'cept my pride, and I don't ever intend to let that go."

"Don't be a stubborn old fool, G.W. There's such a thing as too much pride. You're not the only one that's poor, you know."

"Listen here, woman, Maggie Lorena may be your pet, but I've got two other daughters to consider."

"Mary Ellen and Katie are dear to me too. You know that. But Maggie Lorena is like my own, living with me since Archie died, helping me teach school." There was a little quiver in her voice. "She's talented, too, playing the piano at church and all. You've read her stories and poems. I know you have."

He had stomped away and avoided her for the next few weeks. Then, one Sunday after church, she'd followed him to the cemetery where he always went to pay his respects to his mother's grave. The preacher had made mention again that the new Baptist college in Raleigh was calling for young women from all over the state to fill its halls. There was also a notice in *The Biblical Recorder* challenging the churches to help with tuition. Mag carried it in her hand. "If I find a way for Maggie Lorena to work her way through school, will you accept that? She'd come home a real teacher. You'd be proud of her, wouldn't you?"

"What makes you think Maggie Lorena would ever come back here to live once she gets as far away as Raleigh? You've put some big ideas in her head. She won't ever be content with what you and Archie had."

"Oh, she'll come back, all right." She knew she was being haughty, but G.W. had to be dealt with on his own terms.

"What makes you so sure? You're just wishful thinking."

"No I'm not, because I'm giving her my land and my house and everything in it and I'm not waiting until I die to do it." G.W. didn't say a word, just studied her as if trying to figure her meaning. "If she goes off to college, I can't live there alone. It's too lonely."

He spat between two gravestones. "And where are you figuring on going?"

"Ellen needs me. She's really going down and you don't seem to mind my cooking." Aunt Mag smiled. "I thought I'd just close up the house and come live with you, if you'll have me." She knew he couldn't refuse her, not with an offer of giving Maggie her house and her land, too. Straightening her hat, she waited for her words to sink in.

G.W. put his hands in his pockets and rocked back on his heels. His jacket looked as if it could use a good brushing and his shirt was a dingy gray. "I wouldn't object to that a'tall, Margaret. But you can't just lock a house up like that. Everything in it will be ruined. The rats'll get into it and what they don't eat up, the colored folk'll haul off."

"Don't you go worrying about my house. I know what I'm doing. Lizzie will keep an eye on it. You just wait, Maggie will find her some nice young man up there in Raleigh who'll be proud to have a place like mine to start out."

He leaned over to straighten a vase of asters he had placed on his mother's grave. "Now, what kind of nice young man from Raleigh is going to want to come down here and live in the backwoods of Bladen County?"

He might as well have added, *in that prissy little house of yours*, because she was sure that's how he felt about it—but the land was a different matter. She held her shoulders back, feeling triumphant, her eyes on Maggie in the distant churchyard. "Maybe a lawyer, or even a doctor," she declared.

G.W. had roared with laughter. "You are something, Margaret! No wonder Maggie is so goddamned uppity. You put all these ideas in her head."

She hadn't known then how far the ideas in Maggie's head were from the likes of hers. Maggie did come back to live in the little house, but not the way Aunt Mag had planned.

Everything that surrounded the house—the barn, the smokehouse, the laundry shed, the gazebo and the garden—was just as it had been the day before the fire. Nothing had changed, except that the house was no longer there. Tate had taken the boys to feed the livestock, and Maggie was curled up on the cypress settee he had built for her last year beneath the grape arbor. Her wedding dress was laid out across her lap.

Lizzie moved the washpot and built a fire on the mound of ashes left from the last washing. Aunt Mag remembered the day she had first seen the scrawny ten-year-old black girl at her sister Ellen's house. She had been only twenty herself then. Now the years between them had melted away and they were both old women.

"I reckon I'd better go gather the eggs, Lizzie. Doesn't look as if Maggie is going to do it," she said.

"Yes'm, I reckons you better." Lizzie was barefoot and wore a long white starched apron and a scarf tied neatly around her head. She filled a coffeepot with water at the pump and placed it on the fire to boil. Spreading a cloth on a bench beside the smokehouse, she set out a pan of cold biscuits and smoked ham, going about her work as if fixing breakfast in the yard was the most natural thing in the world.

Aunt Mag returned from the henhouse with a half-dozen eggs. "I declare, you'd think it was the chicken house that burned down. Look at this, only six eggs from that whole passel of chickens."

"They's skittish all right, Miss Margaret. Mos' d'time dey'd be over here looking for a scrap of somethin'. I ain't seen a one of 'em all mornin'. But I'm not studyin' chickens right now. I gots my mind on other things."

"I know. Me too, Lizzie, but life will go on. You and me, we know that, don't we?"

"Yes'm, I reckons we do, but I jus' can't get my mind offen Miss Maggie and how her mind gone be now. T'was bad 'nough already."

"Law me, I know what you mean. I'm hoping this might shock her into straightening herself out. This is just about the worst thing that could have happened right now. Thank God they all got out."

"Me and Troy smelled smoke and saw d'flames, Miss Margaret. They was as high as them pine trees over there. I gots here first—then Troy came with every bucket he could find, but we couldn't do nuthin' 'bout it. Miss Maggie and the young'uns was all tore up and Mr. Tate tried to beat out d'flames, but it won't no use. He say she gots pas' him and went in there with d'house burnin' like d'devil and she pulled d'trunk out herse'f! When I gots here her eyes was all red and wild and her hair still smokin'. As tore up and all she been since Master Yancey died, I don't know how in d'world she got d'strength to pull dat trunk out all by herse'f."

"Now, don't you go making a lot over that, Lizzie. People do foolish things when they're scared."

"Yes'm, I reckons they do. But if you ask me, Miss Maggie put too much store in dat trunk. Me, I ain't got nuthin' dat impawtant." She stirred coffee into the boiling water and pulled the pot off the fire.

Aunt Mag watched Maggie start to move about, carefully folding her wedding dress and putting it in the trunk. There was bound to be talk, she thought. It was the second time Maggie and Tate had been burned out, and the second time that Maggie's trunk was the only thing salvaged. When the first fire over in Onslow County had taken everything except the trunk, Aunt Mag hadn't thought much about it. Tate said his pa, Bill Ryan, told him that the house was going up like fat kindling when Maggie screamed at him to get her trunk out. She told him right where it was and Bill had raced in with the roof falling. All the talk then was how devoted he was to his daughter-in-law.

"Mr. Tate, he found her wedding ring," Lizzie said. "It was still in d'postage cup where she always kep' it—right there in her special room that nobody but her was 'llowed in," she said, cutting her eyes towards the chimneys.

"Now listen here, Lizzie, that room had always been Maggie's and you know it. Even when she was a little girl, she played in there. I remember Archie buying her that old Olivetti typewriter from the preacher. It was just a quiet place for her to do her writing, that's all. There's nothing wrong with that. Don't you let me hear you talking against Miss Maggie, you hear me?"

"Yes'm, Miss Margaret."

The old trunk had always been a repository for Maggie's things. Once, out of curiosity, Aunt Mag had attempted to lift the lid and found it locked. She had a trunk of her own, full of her treasures, but hers held no secrets. She had emptied it many times for Maggie, sharing mementos of the far-off places Archie had taken her. But the contents of Maggie's trunk had been off-limits to everyone, including her.

"Didn't you ever save anything, Lizzie? Something you could take out and look at that would remind you of something, or somebody special that was lost to you?" she asked.

Lizzie straightened up and wiped a thin trail of brown snuff juice from the corner of her mouth. "The onliest thing I saves is scraps in a lard stand t'make my quilts. Everythin' else I has was ha'f used up when I gots it—don't do no good to save somethin' ain't got no use lef' in it."

"Didn't your mama pass anything on to you when she died?"

"Yes'm, I has her Bible and a chair her daddy made, but I don't keep it locked up in no trunk." Lizzie squirted a small stream of snuff juice into a rusty tin can.

"What about little Noxema, didn't you save something of his when he died?"

Lizzie straightened up again, wiped her hands on her apron and reached up to tuck a wiry curl underneath her cap. Her eyes filled with tears, and she bowed her head and placed her hand over her heart. "No'm, nuthin' you can see. Everythin' that b'longed to that li'l chile is right here in my heart where no fire or nuthin' can ever touch it."

Aunt Mag remembered the day they had found little Noxema in the drainage ditch near the river. His brothers had run off to play, thinking the baby was tagging along right behind them as usual. When they went to look for him, they found him facedown in a foot of water. All the white folks had attended his funeral. His mama had brought a lot of them into the world.

Lizzie set the coffee aside and placed a black iron spider on the fire. She fried fatback crisp and brown before adding the eggs and stirring them around in the hot grease. Lured by the smell of food, Tate had left his chores, pulled up a wooden crate to the makeshift table and was waiting for his breakfast. "The boys said they ate at your house a couple of hours ago, Lizzie," he said.

"Dey did, and dey sho was hungry."

"I'll go get Maggie," Aunt Mag said.

"She just told me to leave her alone," Tate said.

"Well, then that's what we'll do for the time being." She cut her eyes over to Maggie and saw that she had turned her back to them.

Tate looked up at the sun in the morning sky. "I'm perished. It must be after nine o'clock."

Aunt Mag held a plate for Lizzie to heap with eggs and bacon. She reached into her pocket and pulled out a tiny watch on a ribbon. "You're not far off, Tate. It's at least two hours past your breakfast time."

Tate was black and dirty from sifting through the ashes and sweat rolled off his forehead, making little stripes down his broad cheeks. Aunt Mag had always thought him to be a handsome man, not at all like Archie who wore a good suit of clothes every day of his life, but handsome just the same. Tate was tall, with a large rugged frame. Just the way he walked—with those long strides, swinging his arms side to side—said he was content to be himself.

"I'm sorry about your house, Aunt Mag," he said.

"I know you are. Do you have any idea how it happened? Maggie doesn't seem to remember much."

Tate stared off into the distance, unable to meet her gaze. "I don't know either. She said she was hot, went outside and fell asleep in the gazebo swing. If the wind picked up...maybe the lamp...I don't know. I was half asleep when I smelled the smoke."

"I don't remember a cloud coming up last night. It sounds a mite strange, a little like what happened when your place burned over in

Onslow County." She studied Tate for a moment, but the comment failed to get a rise out of him. "You know, when she was a little girl, she used to stay with me and Archie a lot and she wanted to leave a lamp lit in there all night long. She didn't like the dark one bit. I used to go in and blow it out after she went to sleep."

"She says she hates the dark even more since Yancey died," Tate said. He raised his hand to wipe his brow with a soiled rag and Aunt Mag saw that his hands were charred and blistered.

"My God, Tate. Your hands are burned. Let me go to the barn and get some salve."

"No, I'm all right. I can't stop now. I keep finding things that we can use to start over."

"Well, you won't be much good if your hands get infected. I'll fix you up and then I'll take Maggie Lorena back over to my place. You and the boys can come on when you're ready."

"I believe I'd better stay here and sleep in the barn, but I'd be much obliged if you'd take the boys. I don't want them poking around in the hot ashes. It'll take a day or two before they cool down."

"I'm sure Zeb and Jasper will be over here as soon as they hear. I'll get word to them," Aunt Mag said.

"I reckon we ought to send for her sister. If I know Katie, she'll try and come."

"No, she's got no business over here with that baby she's carrying so near. And I'm not going to bother about Ralph and Ernest. They'll hear about it soon enough." Aunt Mag folded her arms and set her chin. "Wouldn't do any good. Neither one of them would come unless someone died. Ernest, he's living like a hermit over there near Lyon Swamp. No one sees him for days on end. And Ralph's so poor he and Myrtle can't afford to close up their little store."

"I don't want anyone to feel like they have to come help us. We'll make it all right."

"Well, Maggie can just stay with me as long as necessary."

"Aunt Mag, there's something I want to ask you. I mean, you know how Maggie's been acting since Yancey died." He ran his sooty hand through his hair, stopping at the back of his muscular neck, rubbing it, and shaking his head. He closed his eyes. "Is she crazy, I mean really crazy?"

Aunt Mag pursed her lips and tried to think of the right words. "No, Tate, I don't think so. I'm as fed up with her moroseness as you are, but I don't think she's crazy. Dr. Bayard calls it melancholia. You know, it's like hysterics, only worse."

"I don't understand," Tate said. "She's always had those little fits, flying off the handle when things don't go her way, but I've tried everything I know how and..."

He knows there's more to it, Aunt Mag thought. She had gathered some new peas from the garden and she began to shell them furiously. "I declare, Tate, she's just high-strung. You know when Ellen was carrying Maggie, little Georgie—he was only six years old then—got lost in the woods for five whole days. Ellen about went out of her mind. That might have made Maggie the way she is."

"No, it's more than that, Aunt Mag. I can put up with her temper, but it's more like she hates me and I've never done anything but what she wanted." He looked towards the chicken yard where Maggie was throwing out corn. "She probably wishes she hadn't married me."

Aunt Mag was at a loss for words. She knew too many hurtful things. Reaching out, she put her hand on his arm. "Don't dwell on that, Tate," she said. "Come on. I'll doctor those hands."

It was late in the day when Aunt Mag pulled the wagon up to the old house where Maggie had been born. Maggie stared at the dark windows. If Papa and Mama were still alive, everything would seem better. But they were long gone from this earth, and no matter how hard she tried, Maggie could barely see their faces in her mind's eye. So much had happened in her life since she had called this old house home, yet there was still something comforting about the sight of it. Comforting and lonely at the same time. It was Aunt Mag's home now, empty except for her, left to her because she had been the one who cared for them right up to the last.

"You go on in, Maggie, and get the fire going in the stove while I gather the eggs," Aunt Mag said. "William, you unhitch the mule and put the wagon away. Lenny, help your mama. Y'all get that trunk inside, too." Maggie sat as if in a trance, staring at the house. "Maggie Lorena, did you hear me?"

Maggie looked at her. "What?"

"I said go on in the house."

"Oh, all right. I'll go."

Aunt Mag watched her climb down off the wagon, wondering if her mind had really snapped. "It's turning cool. Maybe some flapjacks would be good for supper."

"Yes, the boys would like that," Maggie said, dragging herself up the back steps. Every bone in her body hurt and her head was swimming, but all she could think about was the fire. She hadn't even smelled the smoke. If she'd been in the house when the fire started, she would have seen what was happening—could have done something. She stopped on the porch and put her head in her hands.

"Mama, don't cry," Lenny said, slipping his arm around her and helping her into the kitchen.

Maggie sat down in the nearest chair. "Mama's lost everything."

"You got your trunk out."

"Where is it?" she asked, panic-stricken.

"Me and William'll get it," he said, racing out the door.

Oh, dear God, what if I had lost them, too? She reached for the dishtowel to wipe her tears, wishing she could take back all the unkind things she had said to Tate. He was like a child, wanting to make it better, wanting to build her a new house. But she couldn't bring herself to want a new house, not now. All she could think about now was everything that had gone up in smoke. Everything they owned—except her trunk.

Maggie tried to remember what had happened yesterday afternoon, before supper. Something important. She'd gone to Katie's after Aunt Mag had accused her of letting the house go to rack and ruin...said she was going to take it back...give it to Lizzie. Maggie had left everything spread out on the floor. When she got home, Tate was in the barn. He was upset. Had he seen something?

Later that night after she had put her things away and Tate and the boys had gone to bed, she had gone out to sit in the gazebo swing. Uncle Archie had built the little latticed enclosed room in the middle of Aunt Mag's flower garden. Maggie hadn't kept the flower garden up for several years, but she loved to sit out there in the evening when she couldn't sleep. Last night there had been the scent of new clover on the cool night air.

Had she fallen asleep? She tried to remember, but all she could recall was Tate's firm hand on her arm, pulling her out of the swing and yelling, *Maggie, the house is on fire!* Flames had already been leaping out the back door. *Did you get my trunk out?* she'd asked. *Just stand here beside the boys and I'll try,* he'd said, but she saw right away that he didn't intend to risk his life for her things. So she'd gone in after the trunk herself, with him right behind yelling, *let it burn!*

———

Lenny and William trudged into the kitchen, one on either side of the trunk. "Where do you want it, Mama?" Lenny asked. But Maggie was still lost in her thoughts. Tate had said the door to her room had been open and he'd closed it. What had he seen?

"Mama?" William was standing over her. "Are you all right?"

"What?"

"Where do y-y-you w-w-want your trunk?"

"Put it in Grandpa's room for now. I might need something out of it."

The boys struggled past her. The oily smells of kerosene and woodsmoke wafting from the old leather trunk made her sick to her stomach.

Part 1

Bladen County
September 1906

Chapter 1

The old funnel-topped train engine puffed and sputtered in the early morning mist, as if anxious to be on its way. Aunt Mag sat primly beside G.W. in a black leather-topped buggy at the edge of the loading platform. Through the train's lighted window, they could see Maggie arranging her bags in the seat beside her. Ellen had wanted to see her daughter off in the worst way, but her infirmities had gotten the best of her in the last year and she wasn't even able to leave the house to go to services on Sunday. Besides, Aunt Mag had made all the arrangements. For her, seeing Maggie off to the new college in Raleigh was like a dream come true. She could see that G.W. wasn't near as excited.

Maggie wasn't surprised that Aunt Mag would take any steps necessary to get her off to college. They had talked about it many times. Aunt Mag said Maggie would end up just like her mother, with a house full of children and her health ruined, if she didn't get out of the county and meet a man with some education and refinement. "But you've got to have more to offer than a pretty face," Aunt Mag had said. "This house will be your dowry. Mark my words, some nice young man will see it like that."

At first Maggie had been concerned that Mary Ellen and Katie would resent Aunt Mag's offer, but both of her sisters assured her that they didn't care in the least. By that time, Mary Ellen was already married to Cyrus Devane and living in Burgaw. Cyrus had been left a widower with three children when his first wife died. He was right well off, owning a hardware and feed store in the small town that had become the county seat when Pender County was carved out of New Hanover. To G.W.'s delight, he'd swept Mary Ellen off her feet with his promise of a fine home and a ready-made family. Katie was riding on the coat-tails of the old law, teaching school without a certificate long enough to find a husband. She'd been close once or twice, but the right suitor hadn't come along yet.

Aunt Mag had had to work with the preacher to convince G.W. that allowing the church to help send Maggie to Baptist Female University wasn't accepting charity. "They're begging us to send girls up there, Capt'n Corbinn," the preacher had said. "Why, it's like the good Lord himself putting his blessing on you and your family. Think about it as some compensation for what you tried to do for the Confederacy." That was more than enough reason for G.W.

Then Aunt Mag had written a letter to Mr. John Pullen, a benevolent trustee at BFU who helped indigent students find ways to stay in school. She told him that Maggie could be a teacher's assistant. *Why, she's practically a schoolteacher already, Mr. Pullen. I trained her myself.* John Pullen had written back that he would be most happy to help Maggie get settled and he'd certainly see to it that she found work at the University to pay her board and tuition.

The loading platform at Atkinson was deserted except for two hefty men loading milk cans into a boxcar. From the train window, Maggie saw Aunt Mag point to another buggy coming into the train yard at a fast clip. The driver pulled up beside G.W., and a young man in a gray pinstriped suit stepped out. There was something familiar about him, but before Maggie could inspect him more closely he shook G.W.'s hand, tipped his hat to Aunt Mag, and stepped out of sight into the station.

Maggie had settled comfortably in her seat when she heard footsteps approaching her from the rear of the train. Even so, she felt a slight start when someone touched her shoulder. "Good morning, Miss Corbinn."

She blushed, recognizing the young man she'd seen earlier. Now she remembered—she'd admired him at the reunion of the North Carolina 18th Regiment at Point Caswell the previous summer.

"I'm Wash Pridgen from over at Frenches Creek. Weren't you at the 18th's reunion last year?"

She smiled. "Yes, I was."

He removed his hat and made a slight bow. "I believe you were wearing a light blue dress and violets pinned in your hair."

Maggie extended her hand. "If you say so." Yes, she recalled vividly how Katie had teased her because she couldn't take her eyes off the Pridgen boy who had come to the reunion. She had caught him glancing at her several times, too, but she had been daunted when she saw him holding hands and walking along the river with another girl. Today he looked older in his gray striped suit and string tie. "I guess you know my pa," she said.

"Oh, yes, ma'am, everybody knows Captain Corbinn. He's a hero." Wash smiled, his dark eyes taking her in. His curly black hair was parted in the middle and flattened by his hat in little ringlets against his forehead. He dabbed at his face with a folded handkerchief.

"Was your pa in the War?" Maggie asked, tucking the heels of her high-buttoned shoes against the trunk under the seat. Seeing him up close like this, he was even nicer-looking than she remembered.

"Yes, ma'am, he was. Pa didn't make it home, but he was at Chancellorsville with Captain Corbinn." He dropped his gaze reverently. When he looked up again, he was smiling. "I understand you're going to BFU. I'm at Wake Forest College—my last year in law school. I told your aunt I'd keep an eye on you."

He was like a kid, grinning and flirting with her, and she was enjoying it. In the past, she'd had few chances to be with a young man without everyone looking on. "Aunt Mag shouldn't have bothered you, but please, won't you sit down?" She adjusted her skirt to make room for him to slip into the seat across from her, noticing the white spats above his dusty black shoes. Zeb and Jasper would have laughed and called him a Fancy Dan. Wash Pridgen was certainly the opposite of her rough-cut brothers, who dressed in suits only for church. He was pretty enough to be a girl, with his shiny black hair and long lashes.

When he had seated himself opposite her, she tried to avoid his steady gaze by looking out the window. The sun was rapidly climbing above the horizon. "Maybe you could raise that window. It's a mite stuffy in here," she suggested to take his attention off her for a second. Wash leaned across her, stretching his arms out of his sleeves, straining against the balky window. He smelled of sweet soap and bay rum.

When the window gave and he was able to raise it, Aunt Mag waved frantically at him. "You'd better not let that window up, Wash Pridgen, or Maggie will look like a darkie before she gets to Raleigh," she yelled.

"Oh, it's all right," Maggie said.

"Do you suppose I should do as she says? She told me to look after you."

Amused, Maggie nodded her head. Wash settled himself in the seat again and wiped his brow.

"So you're going to be a lawyer. I hear they turn out a few preachers up there, too," she said.

"I sure don't want to be a preacher," he said, laughing. "What about you?"

"I want to be a teacher, a certified teacher."

"Well, you're going to a good place. BFU is our sister school. Twice a year we have BFU Day and all the girls from BFU ride the train up to Wake Forest for free."

Looking down at the skirt of her dark blue suit, Maggie wondered what girls wore on BFU Day. Aunt Mag had worn the suit home from a trip to New York City with Archie. It was a beautiful tissue wool crepe, with black soutash braid along the hem and on the edges of a small capelet that encircled the shoulders. There was a wide-brimmed hat to match, and her mother had given Maggie the candy-striped silk taffeta blouse with a stand-up ruffle at the neck. She tucked a stray red curl behind her ear and smoothed her skirt.

Wash fidgeted with his hat, tossing it round and round in smooth clean hands. Maggie tried to think of some clever conversation, but she was at a loss for words, something unusual for her. He crossed and uncrossed his legs, checked his watch, glanced out the window, back at her, then at the back of the train. They both started to talk at once. "Go ahead," Wash said, laughing.

"No, you," Maggie said, and they both laughed.

"I was just going to ask if I might call you by your first name."

"Yes, it's Maggie—Maggie Lorena."

"Well, Maggie Lorena, I don't suppose you've been away from home too much, so I'll be glad to keep an eye on you—for your aunt's sake, that is."

"My stars, I've been away from home lots of times. Why, I go to Wilmington with Papa almost every year on the steamer to sell cotton and tobacco. We stay two or three days at a time."

"Raleigh's a lot different from Wilmington, it being the capital city and all. There's not as much riffraff in Raleigh, for one thing." He smiled. "I wish I was going to practice law in Raleigh."

"Well, why can't you? If a man's got gumption, he can do anything he wants. It's not that easy for a woman." She blushed, knowing she must sound like a suffragette.

"I'm going into practice with my uncle in Wilmington. He's a judge and he's getting on up there in years. He doesn't have any sons, and he wants me to take over his practice eventually. He's paying my way to school, so I guess I can't rightly refuse."

"I suppose that won't be so bad. You'll have more work in a town like Wilmington with a lot of riffraff," Maggie joked.

Wash let out a deep guffaw and Maggie looked around to see if everyone was staring at them. "I like you, Maggie. Maggie Lorena," he said, assuming a more serious tone, rolling her name around like the bowler he twirled between his knees. Their eyes met and Maggie felt the connection. She thought he felt it too. There had only been a few boys in her life, stealing kisses in the barn, grabbing for her breasts, but Wash was different, with his sharp looks and nice manners. She'd dreaded the long train ride; now it might not seem long enough.

The car was full of passengers. From their loud talk and laughter,

Maggie imagined that most must be students. Wash spoke to several young men and introduced them to Maggie as his classmates. She'd heard a lot about lawyers—how they wrangled and argued. Wash Pridgen didn't look like a wrangler, and neither did the other fellows.

"Is that the only reason you decided to be a lawyer, because your uncle offered you a job?" she asked.

"Gosh no! I just love law. Justice is the backbone of our nation. We have rights that don't exist in other countries."

"Some of us don't have the same rights as others."

"Oh, you mean the vote!" Wash grimaced. "That's gonna be changed someday, Maggie. I'm sure of it. You'll be hearing a lot of talk about it in Raleigh. That woman Helen Lewis will probably be on her soapbox there at the capitol grounds. Sometimes I think she does more harm than good."

Maggie knew about Helen Lewis and her suffrage league. "Pa says women don't need to vote. He says it's their responsibility to provide a Christian home for their husbands and children as God intended and they should leave voting to the menfolks."

Wash studied her face. "And how do you feel about it, Maggie Lorena?"

"Now, don't you go putting me on the witness stand. I have my feelings about such things, but it's too nice a day to talk about politics." She forced a smile, all the while thinking about how G.W. had not allowed any such talk about women voting. But when someone came through Colly looking for women to sign a petition sponsored by the North Carolina Equal Suffrage Association, she and Aunt Mag went behind his back and signed it. She had a copy of the petition in her trunk, signed by Helen Morris Lewis.

After a while Wash became quiet, looking out over the flat countryside, then dozing off. The train stopped now and then at a crossing and picked up a passenger and some mail. Each time it started up again, it jerked and jostled Maggie against Wash. She pretended to sleep, watching him when she could, taking in the way he breathed so evenly. Occasionally he took a deeper breath, almost a sigh, and she felt he was watching her from beneath his long lashes. What was he thinking? Would he ask her to BFU Day? He wasn't a Fancy Dan at all. Just a nice fellow, with a lot more on his mind than raising tobacco and cotton. She hoped she was on his mind, too.

Wash stretched and yawned. "Pardon me. I guess I fell asleep."

"Me too," Maggie said. She secured the roll of hair at the nape of her neck and brushed off her shoulders. Despite the closed window, little flecks of soot dotted her jacket. "I'm a mess."

Wash stood and pulled out his pocket watch. "There's a toilet at the end of the train if you'd like to wash up. We'll be stopping in Fayetteville soon, and there are some boys who always get on there with sandwiches and fried chicken. I'd like to buy you some lunch."

"No need for that. Aunt Mag packed me a box lunch, up there on the luggage rack. I'll share it with you, if you'll be so kind as to hand it to me." Wash reached above her, standing so close that they touched. When he brought the box down, his face was only inches from hers. They gazed at one another a moment before she took the box and placed it on the seat across from her.

"Look, I'll get something. I don't want to take your lunch."

"I'm sure there's enough in here to feed two or three hungry fieldhands," she said. "Aunt Mag's not skimpy. I'd be much obliged if you'd help me with it after I wash up."

He steadied her as she squeezed by him on the way to the toilet. Swaying along the aisle, she felt his gaze following her. Her skin tingled where he had touched her, and her heart was racing. Aunt Mag had warned her: *Don't fall for the first man who tips his hat to you.* But this was far more than that. She had felt something between them as long ago as the picnic at Point Caswell. That something had brought them together again. She could hardly wait to get back to her seat.

When she did, Wash had moved into the seat beside hers. "I thought it might be easier if we sat together," he said. Maggie smiled and opened the box he had set in front of her. There were two thick biscuits with slabs of cured ham poking out the sides, a jar of crisp green water-melon rind pickles and an oatmeal box full of scuppernong grapes. Wash fashioned a table out of his book satchel and tied the napkin Maggie offered him around his neck. "I declare, Miss Maggie, this is a real treat. My brothers Jeff and Samuel do all the cooking at home and I don't get victuals like this very often."

"Save room for Aunt Mag's grape hull cake. You'll say it's the best thing you've ever tasted."

When they had finished their biscuits, Maggie opened a round cake tin, letting out the dark spicy smell of a cake made with cane syrup and the large amber grapes that grew in an arbor behind Aunt Mag's house. The cake was her specialty and Aunt Mag refused to share the recipe with anyone.

"Ummm, this is good. Sort of like gingerbread," Wash said, wiping his mouth with his handkerchief.

After they had finished, his eyes drooped and he began to nod his head again. Maggie settled back in her seat and closed her eyes, drift-ing into a light sleep. She dreamt that she floated high above the train. Her arms were feathered wings, and her legs and feet stretched out behind her like a great white heron's. Looking down, she saw the train, a black caterpillar on a thin branch slowly making its way north to-wards Raleigh. To the south was Colly, a wedge of woodland between the Cape Fear and the Black Rivers. In the distance another bird flew, darting here and there, calling back to her, *follow me, follow me.*

At the edge of the city, the train slowed and released a long high-pitched whistle. Maggie peered out the window at the rows of tiny houses that lined the tracks. On every porch children waved franti-cally at the passing train, and the engineer responded with two short blasts of the whistle. As it approached the station in the heart of the city, the train slowed again, taking a side track, bell clanging, puffing and spewing steam, until it finally came to a stop at the rear of the

Union Passenger Station. Aunt Mag and Uncle Archie had been there the day of the dedication, in 1892. Aunt Mag said there was no finer station on the Seaboard Airline Railway.

On either side of the track, a covered portico the length of the train extended out from the two-story building. Pulling narrow painted wagons on metal wheels, young Negro boys rushed towards the train to unload freight and goods shipped up from Wilmington. Under the cover of the other shed, a few passengers waited to board another train. Maggie was spellbound, watching the activity.

"You're going to love it here," Wash said. "You wait, you'll be an old hand at riding trains before you finish school."

Maggie smiled at him. She had no doubt that she would rapidly become accustomed to life in the city. She had longed for the excitement of it, making new acquaintances, going to plays and concerts. Meeting him on the train was only the beginning. She tugged at her gloves, adjusting each finger. "Will you be getting off here, too?"

"No. Wake Forest is another seventeen miles up the line, but I've got a few minutes before the train leaves. I can help you off with your bags." He stood and stretched his arms over his head and she resisted an urge to tickle him. "Is that your trunk under the seat?" he asked.

Maggie lifted her skirts to the side to reveal the trunk. "Yes, I didn't want it thrown into the baggage car."

"It's no problem, I'll take it off for you and put it on a dolly. But before you go, there's something I'd like to ask you." He slipped into the seat beside her and touched her arm. "I'd like to write to you. Would you mind?"

"I'd like that, Wash. I really would." His hand lingered on her arm. "I'll write back. I'm pretty good at that," she said with a little laugh.

Wash beamed. "I'd hoped you would."

"I've found that it's the only way to get letters." She knew she sounded silly, but he was taking in every word.

"I'd like to see you too," he said. The train lurched forward slightly and he brushed his cheek against hers.

Maggie felt that he had almost kissed her. If he had, she was sure she would have kissed him back. "I should go. Mr. John Pullen is meeting me. I'll look forward to your letter," she said.

He reached for her trunk and hefted it to his shoulder. "You must have a lot of pretty dresses in here, Maggie."

Chapter 2

Watching the train pull out of the station, Maggie was sure that Wash Pridgen would become a part of her life. She missed him already. There was something about him that reminded her of Uncle Archie, but she'd never mention that to Papa. G.W. didn't cotton to lawyers and legislators, whom he said were all in cahoots with the carpetbaggers that came down to the South after the War.

Realizing she was the only passenger left standing on the platform, Maggie rummaged in her bag for the letter she had received from her sponsor only a few days earlier. Mr. John Pullen was not only a BFU trustee, he was also a deacon at the Fayetteville Street Baptist Church, her co-sponsor with Bethany Baptist Church in Colly. Preacher Mizelle had sent Mr. Pullen fifty dollars for Maggie's first semester. It was up to Mr. Pullen to see to the rest of her needs in Raleigh.

She looked up and down the platform and through the dirty windows of the station. A young colored porter was picking up newspapers and sifting out the remains of cigars and ashes from sand-filled buckets. There had been two other girls on the train who looked as if they might be students, but they had disappeared while she was talking to Wash. Anxiously, she scanned the letter. Mr. Pullen had said that he would meet her at the station. What if he had forgotten?

"You want me to get dat trunk for you, lady?"

"What?" Maggie jumped, startled, when the porter spoke to her. "Oh, someone's meeting me. A man from BFU." She glanced towards the station.

"That'd be mastuh Pullen. I saw him down d'way gettin' his wagon loaded. He be meetin' you out front, I reckon." He slipped the dolly under the trunk and placed her satchel on top. "C'mon, I'll show you."

Maggie hurried along behind the porter, who wheeled her bags through the station and out the front door. Wagons were parked along the curb and the sweaty smell of horses seemed out-of-place in the city.

"Jus' wait right here while I goes to fin' him," the porter said, leaving Maggie while he went around towards the back of the building.

Suddenly Maggie felt very alone. There were people walking by, a streetcar clanging along on the track, but no one paid her a bit of mind. Across the street was a large park where two women with baby carriages were strolling along a sidewalk. Maggie ran her hand over the edge of her trunk and thought how someday she might fill it with baby clothes.

Pacing up and down, she wondered what could be keeping Mr. Pullen. The late afternoon sun was hot and she was exhausted from the long train ride. She was about to take hold of the dolly and go look for him herself when she saw a stout, red-faced man hurrying around the corner of the building towards her. He was dressed in a tan suit with a black-and-white houndstooth vest that seemed ready to pop open with each stride. "Hello!" he called out. "Miss Corbinn?"

"Yes. You're Mr..." Maggie said, extending her hand.

"Pullen, John Pullen. Oh, Miss Corbinn, I do apologize for being late. I was unavoidably delayed by a shipment of oysters I had sent up on the train from Wilmington. Please forgive me!" He removed his hat and wiped sweat from his brow and neck before bowing and extending his hand.

"Oh, that's all right, but I was getting a little worried. At least I'm out in the fresh air. The train was a mite stuffy."

"Ah. The air agrees with you. You certainly look refreshed to have arrived only so recently by train. If you'll forgive me, I had expected a younger girl. You look more like one of our teachers."

Maggie smiled. How well Aunt Mag's suit had served her thus far. "Thank you very much, Mr. Pullen. I'm twenty-four and I *am* a schoolteacher, but I've never been to college. I'm much obliged to you for sponsoring me."

"You are so welcome, my dear. There could be no greater pleasure in the heart of an educator than to see a fine young woman like you at BFU." He picked up her satchel and motioned to a young Negro boy who had followed him, waiting to take her trunk. "Mrs. Pullen has asked that you have supper with us this evening and be our guest on your first night in Raleigh. You've had such a long day. A fine meal and a good night's rest will get you off to a good start tomorrow."

Maggie tried not to show her disappointment. She'd imagined herself spending her first night in Raleigh in a small room at the top of one of the Gothic towers of the new college. It would have suited her just fine to hire someone to take her straight to the school. But Mr. Pullen was already loading her things into a green wagon with *B.F.U.* painted on the sides in gilt-trimmed red letters. When he had the trunk and satchel situated, he flipped a coin to the porter and removed his hat, making a slight bow. "The BFU chariot awaits you, Madame."

Taking his hand, Maggie placed her foot on the small step and slid onto the bench seat, thinking that the wagon *was* a chariot compared to the rough board wagons she knew, with their wheels smeared with axle grease and their smell of hay and manure. "We'll take a little tour first and I'll show you some of the highlights of the Capital City." He took the reins and flicked the horses' rumps with a small whip. "We can't dilly-dally too long with these oysters."

Maggie glanced over her shoulder at the baskets covered by a dark green tarp. The smell was unmistakable. She hated oysters. "That would be nice, Mr. Pullen. I've never been to Raleigh before."

He threw up his hand to a group of young boys who had congregated on the park corner across the street. "Those boys are from the Raleigh Male Academy. Most of them are in my Sunday school class." Maggie looked over at the boys, who whistled and waved wildly at her. "Don't pay them much mind," he said. "They're whippersnappers, still wet behind the ears."

She raised her hand slightly, but she was thinking of all the things she needed to say to Mr. Pullen. "The preacher said you helped girls like me who couldn't afford college, but I can pay my way if there's work to be done."

"There'll be plenty of time to talk about such as that this evening." Straining against his large belly, he reached under the seat to pull out a red silk parasol. "Whew! It's hot as Hades out here today. You'll need this." He snapped the parasol open with a flick of his wrist. "Now, just sit back and enjoy the sights, my dear." He clucked to the team of horses and they started up towards the town, the briny smell of the oysters drifting along with them. "First I'll show you our church, Fayetteville Street Baptist. There are other Baptist churches—First Baptist Church is only a stone's throw from the university—but I think you will find our congregation more to your liking. Pastor Fields is also a trustee and the chief financial officer for BFU. So you see, our ties are very strong." Maggie reckoned she would like Mr. Pullen's church as well as any other, but she knew this was what Pa meant when he said accepting charity made you beholden to people.

The Fayetteville Street Baptist Church was a large brick structure with a tall steeple sitting directly over the front doors. Maggie thought it looked just like the First Baptist Church in Wilmington that she had seen from the river. Mr. Pullen hopped out of the wagon and tied the horses to a well-worn hitching post under a group of trees. "We'll take a moment and go inside. There's something I want you to see." He took her hand, helped her down from the wagon, and escorted her briskly through the center door and down the aisle to the back of the pulpit. A heavy velvet drape the color of grape wine parted in the middle when he pulled a long cord. Steps led down to a oversized tin-lined tub. "There," he said, "I thought you might like to see the baptismal pool, Miss Corbinn. I imagine you were dunked in the river."

. Maggie smiled, remembering the day Preacher Mizelle had washed her sins away at Still Bluff on Black River. She had worn a white dress and slip that clung conspicuously to her maturing twelve-year-old body. "Why, yes, I was. I suppose that's pretty countrified to city folks."

"Oh, no, my dear, that's the way our Lord would have done it."

As they continued up Fayetteville Street, Maggie took in the sights, but her mind was on Wash Pridgen. She thought of a dozen things she should have asked him. Where would she write to him? Did he live in a dormitory? She had heard that some of the Wake Forest students lived as boarders in private homes.

"And here we have the Wake County Courthouse," Mr. Pullen said. He had stopped in the shade of a four-story red brick building. Five stone-trimmed dormers were set like jewels into the mansard roof. On top of the central dormer, a marble figure of Justice held a balancing scale out at arm's length. "When they remodeled the facade a few years ago, the statue of Justice was added," he said, looking up and shading his eyes. "Can't say that I like that statue there, but the birds sure do."

Maggie studied the statue and wondered if Wash Pridgen had stood under it. She smiled, remembering the kiss he had blown her from the window as the train pulled out of the station. "I like it," she said.

In the distance, Maggie could see the dome of the Capitol. They passed one store after the other—Briggs Hardware and Woolworth's Five and Dime, Boylan-Pearce and Efird's department stores, and a candy shop called Royster's. The street was crowded with well-dressed shoppers carrying boxes and bags, and she imagined herself among them. Mr. Pullen seemed to read her mind. "You'll have an opportunity to shop downtown every Monday, with a proper chaperone, of course." Maggie fingered her purse. She had managed to save up five dollars, and Aunt Mag had given her five more. The money would have to last until Christmas and include her train fare home.

Mr. Pullen kept the wagon to the side, avoiding the trolley tracks set into the cobblestone street. Every so often a trolley car passed them, making the overhead wires crackle and spark. At the top of Fayetteville Street, he pulled up in front of a large dome-topped granite building that sat in the middle of a park. "Ah, the great Capitol of North Carolina." All around the square there were benches and fountains, bronze statues of men on horseback and huge artillery cannons. They stopped again in front of a statue of Zebulon Baird Vance, commander of the

North Carolina 26th Regiment and one of her father's heroes. G.W. had named a son after him.

A flock of pigeons rose up from the dusty path and landed on the green tarp covering the oysters. Maggie ducked as they skimmed over her head. "What are they doing?"

"They won't hurt you a bit, Miss Corbinn. In fact, they'll eat right out of your hand. You'll soon get to know this park and every pigeon in it. Our girls are required to exercise every day before supper. This is a favorite spot."

In the block beyond the Capitol, Maggie saw a building with Gothic towers and turrets reaching for the sky. "That must be it!" she exclaimed. "I mean BFU—that or a fairy castle," she said, laughing and remembering how her sisters had called her 'Aunt Mag's princess.' They had been teasing, but she knew there must have been times when they resented Aunt Mag's devotion to her.

"Yes, that's it. A fairy castle it is, but of God's kingdom, built by the sacrifice and toil of the good Baptists of North Carolina. We opened our doors for the first time in 1889. There have been many obstacles to overcome, and there is still much to be done, but with the prayers and faith of our people, we will excel as the greatest institution of Christian education in the nation."

Maggie thought he sounded a little like a preacher or a politician, but he had such a look of devotion on his face that she knew his eloquence must be sincere. "It's even prettier than the picture in *The Biblical Recorder.*"

"The trustees are mighty proud of the university, Miss Corbinn. We built it for you girls—a home away from home, you know, and a Christian education to boot."

Approaching the school, she marveled at the large oak trees that lined the streets. They were huge and already had begun to drop some of their leaves. Along the sidewalks, children played marbles and hopscotch, and women strolled with babies in their carriages. The houses they passed were white, yellow and brown two-story homes with gray slate roofs and long porches.

When they stopped in front of the university, she looked up in awe. There were three-story towers flanking either side of the building. In the center, curved granite steps went up on either side to the second floor where a landing formed a wide balcony. Several girls leaned out over the rail and called to Mr. Pullen. He smiled broadly and waved back. Maggie waved too, thinking how happy she was. This beautiful castle was going to be her home.

Inside the building, Mr. Pullen showed her the classrooms and offices on the second and third floors. Maggie scanned the familiar titles of books on a cart in the hall. "The dean and some of the faculty have their quarters here as well," he said, leading Maggie into a wide parlor with sofas and chairs along the walls and a grand piano at one end. Maggie sat down at the piano and ran her fingers over the keys. It was finely tuned. She looked about and imagined the room filled with students for a concert.

Mr. Pullen pulled out his pocket watch. "Oh, my, look at the time. You'll have to see the art studio and the infirmary on the fourth floor some other time. I must get those oysters down to the kitchen."

"Could you just show me where I'm staying? You said it was in a cottage?"

"Oh, my dear, I do hate to disappoint you, but Mrs. Pullen will have a fit if we are late for supper. That will have to wait until tomorrow morning. I'll see to it then that you are duly registered and settled good and proper in your own room."

The Pullen home was only a few blocks from the university. Mrs. Pullen was waiting on the back porch, a thin woman dressed in a lavender flowered dress. Seeing them, she called out, "John, at last you're home. I see you have Miss Corbinn with you."

Mr. Pullen helped Maggie down from the wagon and escorted her to the porch. "Yes, dear, I'm home and this is the lovely lady we've been expecting. Maggie Corbinn, my wife Charlotte."

Charlotte Pullen's graying hair was swept up in the latest fashion, piled loosely above a plain face. "Welcome to Raleigh and to our home, Maggie." She took Maggie's hand, then put her arm around the girl's shoulders and showed her into the house. "John, I'm sure Maggie is exhausted. I'll take her to her room and we'll get acquainted while you secure the horses. Don't forget the oysters, dear."

Charlotte took Maggie's hand and showed her into the kitchen, where she poured a glass of cool water from a pitcher. The kitchen was very modern, with a long white enameled sink boasting hot and cold water faucets. A massive gas cookstove had several oven doors, and in the center of the room was a large work table. Bowls and pans were stored underneath.

"You must be famished, Maggie. I'm sure John dragged you up and down Fayetteville Street. He always does it—wants his girls to see everything at once. I declare, I don't know what I'm going to do with him."

"His intentions were good, Mrs. Pullen, and I'm so excited to be here, I don't want to miss a thing. I can rest up tomorrow."

The Pullens's home was lit by electricity, something not entirely new to Maggie but a comfort she had never known in her own home. The high-ceilinged rooms were furnished in polished dark woods with rich velvet upholstery. All of them had wallpaper, wide stripes and large florals in rich colors. Above the carved wooden mantels in every room, mirrors extended to the ceiling.

Mrs. Pullen showed Maggie to her room. Like a painting, everything was perfect—from the rosebud wallpaper to the pink velvet counterpane that covered the high-posted bed. Ruffled white organdy curtains covered the windows. Off to the side was a tiled bathroom with a white china sink and toilet, and a clawfooted tub big enough for two.

"I'll leave you to freshen up," Mrs. Pullen said as she closed the door. "Supper is at seven o'clock."

Pulling the curtain aside, Maggie looked out across the backyards that were separated by tall fences into patchwork squares. In one she saw a small collard patch and a few chickens pecking near a tiny henhouse. She slid the window up and let in a breeze laced with the aromas of food and woodsmoke. Suddenly she felt homesick. Aunt Mag would be waiting to hear all about the train ride and the Pullens's house. Maggie couldn't wait to tell her about Wash Pridgen. She opened the door to the bathroom and smiled as she lifted her skirts and sat down on the toilet, delighted that there would be no slop jar to empty in the morning and no water to fetch from the pump. She laughed out loud.

At supper that evening, Maggie was thankful for Aunt Mag's training. *Pretty is as pretty does* ran through her head as she placed the napkin in her lap. While John Pullen asked a blessing that rivaled any Preacher Mizelle had said on his best Sunday, she squeezed her eyes shut to keep from looking at the delicate handpainted china and starched cut-work linen tablecloth.

Charlotte Pullen sat at the head of the table. She had changed into a simple black broadcloth dress with a white lace collar and cuffs. At her throat, she wore a jet black cameo pin that she fingered from time to time as if it were some secret source of strength. "Our cook, Mrs. Hagan, has been with us a long time, Maggie. Try the oysters, dear. Mr. Pullen is very fond of oysters. He has them sent up from the coast every week."

John Pullen smiled. "Would you care for hot pepper vinegar?"

Maggie nodded and doused the oysters generously with the sauce. Holding her breath, she slipped one into her mouth. A remark her brother Jasper had made once came to mind. *Go ahead, Maggie Lorena. Taste them. They taste like snot!* It was all she could do to eat the one in her mouth, much less finish those remaining on her plate. But she smiled and vowed not to show her true feelings. Getting her education was too important.

When the meal was over, they moved into the parlor. "Mr. Pullen and the other trustees have worked so hard to get the university on its feet," Charlotte said. "We're sponsoring several other girls this session. You'll meet them on Sunday when we pick you up for church. I expect you'll want to teach Sunday school and sing in the choir. All of our girls love church as much as they love the university."

"I suppose I will, Mrs. Pullen. I'm anxious to do whatever the other girls do. I expect to do a lot of studying, that's for sure." Maggie thought it was sounding more and more like she was up here to go to church instead of college.

"You'll be staying in South Cottage," John Pullen said. "This is the first year for the cottages. The Baptist State Convention purchased them to use until we can build another dormitory. The trustees decided that the girls who couldn't afford full board and tuition would live there, cook their own meals, and do their own cleaning. You won't mind that, will you?"

"I'm not above doing anything for the opportunity to get my education," Maggie said. Working for her tuition was something she had no call to resent, but being set apart from the rest of the school was another matter. She'd adjust, she knew she would. Entering college at twenty-four, she was already different from most of the girls.

"You'll have a housemother, of course. Someone has to rule the roost in the henhouse, you know," Charlotte tittered. "You cottage girls will have a few more responsibilities than the girls in the main building, but in every other way, you'll be the same."

No, not the same. If we were the same, we'd all be living in the dormitory, Maggie thought.

"We've arranged for you to teach piano in the preparatory department, and you can work in the library if need be," Mr. Pullen said. "With that and whatever your family can send, you should be able to pay most of your tuition. Our congregation has agreed to pay the remainder."

"I'm much obliged to you folks, but if it comes to that, I mean your church having to help out and all, I hope I can count on you not to mention it to my pa."

"As you wish, but you know, Maggie, it's not a sin to accept charity."

"It may not be a sin in God's eyes, Mr. Pullen, but it is in my pa's."

Chapter 3

When Mr. Pullen delivered Maggie to South Cottage the next day, he was apologetic about the house's condition and the housemother's absence. "I had no idea things were in such a mess. Dr. Vann, our dean of student affairs, stopped by and warned me this morning. He said he thought everything was arranged, but the housemother's mother died recently and yesterday she was called home to care for her ailing father. We'll have a replacement in a few days, I'm sure." He fidgeted with his collar, sweat forming on his forehead. "My wife suggested that you might be willing to keep order for a few days, you being an older student and all."

"I expect I could, Mr. Pullen. If it's only for a few days," she said, hiding a feeling of indignation. *He's expecting me to go to church, sing in the choir, teach Sunday school, work in the library and teach piano. Now, he's asking me to be a housemother!* She looked around at the boxes of food and household things that had been donated by the Raleigh Baptist churches. "I could straighten things out a bit until she gets back. You'll explain to the other girls, tell them it's only temporary?"

"Of course, of course. Thank you, Miss Corbinn. That would be such a big help. I'll tell Dr. Vann." Mr. Pullen bowed and his hair fell away from his bald spot, causing Maggie to stifle a laugh.

———

Ella Bradley, Maggie's roommate, had been the first of the cottage girls to arrive and had claimed the best bedroom in the house. Right away she asked Maggie to share her room. The daughter of a Baptist preacher, Ella had also been sent down to BFU at the expense of her church's congregation. Maggie liked the perky little nineteen-year-old mountain girl with her heart-shaped face and hair pulled back and braided into a tight bun. When Ella laughed, her cheeks bunched up like rosy crab apples and her eyes almost disappeared behind them. Thin and wiry, she barely came up to Maggie's shoulders.

The two girls worked together in the kitchen, unloading pots, pans and old silverware in need of polishing. There were kettles and crockery bowls, a wooden churn, and a heavy black spider for frying chicken. "I declare, Maggie, I've never seen so much stuff. Where in the world are we going to put it?"

"We'll take what we can use and the rest we'll put in the cellar or up in the attic," Maggie said. "I can't stand this mess all over the place."

"Well, Mr. Pullen brought another load of canned vegetables this morning and I had him set it out on the back porch until we can make some room in the pantry. This isn't exactly my idea of fun. How about you, girl?"

"I can't rightly say I'm having fun, Ella, but the sooner we get this house straightened out, the sooner we can get on to being regular college students. Help me take these dishes into the dining room, please."

"I can't wait for my mama to come down here and see where I live," Ella said. "Look at these. Did you ever see the likes of it, how people give away the prettiest thing just because of a little crack or a chip? Why, I've never in all my life!"

"What in the world are you talking about, young lady? Mr. Pullen promised some good Baptist matron stars in her heavenly crown for donating that fine china," Maggie said, laughing.

"Yes, and I'll bet the preacher took them down there to the Fayetteville Street Baptist Church and baptized them in that tin tub right behind the pulpit."

They fell over themselves laughing, Ella strutting around like John Pullen, bowing deeply, sweeping the floor with her pretend hat. Finally, Maggie was able to speak. "Hush, Ella. Someone might hear us. Mr. Pullen might stop by." She tightened the strings on her apron and smoothed her hair.

"All right, all right," Ella said. "Just let me get my breath."

At the end of the week, Dr. Vann sent word for Maggie to come to his office. Maggie waited in the outer office with a silent, dull-faced secretary. She had worn the blue serge jumper that Aunt Mag had insisted would be the mainstay of her college wardrobe. With her hair piled loosely on top of her head, she thought she looked as young as any of the other girls.

Dr. Vann opened the door to his office. "Miss Corbinn, won't you come in?" His tone was formal, almost cold. Maggie was nervous as she stepped into the dark-paneled office surrounded on three sides by shelves of books. His desk sat directly in front of a large oval window that overlooked the street. "Please sit down," he said, offering her a stout leather chair facing the desk. Ella had warned her that Dr. Vann had an artificial wooden arm as the result of a childhood accident. She averted her eyes as he passed her chair, only to have him sit down in front of her, promptly displaying both of his hands on his desk. To her surprise, the wooden fingers looked almost identical to his real ones.

"Miss Corbinn, I'm sure you have no idea why you're here."

"No sir. I hope nothing's wrong."

"No, my dear, nothing's wrong. In fact, everything is very right. I apologize," he said, leaning forward on his elbows, his good hand crossed casually over the painted wooden one. "Let me explain. Last evening, Mrs. Vann and I had the pleasure of dining with John and Charlotte Pullen, and your name was mentioned." He paused. "Well, it was more than mentioned. John and Charlotte sang your praises no end." Maggie blushed and looked down, ashamed that she had made fun of Mr. Pullen.

The dean walked around the desk and stood beside her. "I have an idea and I'd like to present it to you before I delve into it further. As you know, our housemother for South Cottage is indisposed right now because of a death in her family. We've advertised for another, but there seems to be a shortage of women suitable for the job. I've prayed endlessly over the situation. This morning, in Chapel, it came to me:

Because of your age and maturity, you might be willing to assume that position for this session, or at least until the housemother, Mrs. Murphy, has settled her affairs."

"I-I don't know, Dr. Vann. I have my schoolwork and a job in the library. I'll be teaching music to a preparatory student on Saturdays. I just don't know how I could do it."

Dr. Vann returned to his chair, sat down and leaned back, the lifeless hand on his lap and the other grasping his bearded chin. "Yes, I thought of that. Do you think you could manage if it was your only job? We'd have someone come in to do the janitorial duties." He hesitated a moment. "It would provide full tuition."

Maggie was stunned. "But sir, the other girls, what would they think? I'm not sure they'll like me as a real housemother."

"Of course they will. You'll be like a big sister."

He was asking a lot of her. Still, she was intrigued. Being a housemother might be fun. "I wouldn't have to give up any classes, would I?"

"Of course not."

"Not even for full tuition?"

Dr. Vann stood behind his desk and looked her in the eye. "Miss Corbinn, you will be a tremendous asset to the school. It is the least we can do."

"It's only temporary?"

"Yes dear, unless it works out otherwise and you like the situation."

"I guess I could give it a try, Dr. Vann."

⸻

"I declare, Maggie, you are the luckiest thing I've ever seen," Ella said when Maggie told her later that afternoon. "He's going to let you be housemother and you'll get your tuition free. If that don't beat all. Why, that's like letting a hog wallow in slops."

"Now don't be a smartypants, Miss Ella, or I'll put you on restriction," Maggie teased.

"Yes ma'am! But there ought to be some advantage to being your roommate. I reckon you'll be wanting me to turn down your covers at night and such as that."

The last thing Maggie wanted was to be set apart even more. "Oh, no, Ella. I know you're joking, but what if the other girls treat me like that? I couldn't stand it."

"Pshaw, honey. Nobody's going to do that. I was just teasing you." She put her arms around Maggie's shoulders and hugged her. "It'll be fun. You love being in charge of things and you know I'll help you."

It was true, Maggie did love being in charge of things. Maybe she'd gotten that from Aunt Mag. Turning the little cottage into a real home would be fun, just a matter of putting to use all the donated furnishings—a pretty quilt over a tattered sofa or a picture here and there.

All the girls liked to cook. She'd have them plan meals and take turns cooking and doing the dishes. They'd elect officers like in the campus clubs, have someone in charge of daily devotionals, things like that. Within a few days Maggie had the house schedule worked out, and she found herself sitting in the big horsehair chair in the parlor every now and then, thinking about what it would be like to live in a house like this with a man like Wash Pridgen.

When classes began, Maggie was relieved to find that she was able to do most of the work without difficulty. She had chosen elocution, rhetoric, American history and music theory. Her favorite class was elocution, where the professor, Dr. Abigail Adams, applauded her reading of Poe's The Raven.

"Maggie, I think you could act," Dr. Adams said. "Have you ever been on stage—you know, in school plays or what have you?"

The thought of the small stage at Salemburg Academy brought a small chuckle from Maggie. "No ma'am, but I like to write poems and stories. Once I wrote a little Christmas play for the schoolchildren, but I've never acted out a part myself."

Dr. Adams listened, leaning on the podium in her classroom, one of her high-topped shoes propped casually on the foot of the stand.

She wore her graying hair cropped short, and dressed in tailored suits and starched white shirts. She could have passed for a man except for her heavy bosom and long skirt. "In my department, we study the effective use of language in every form. There will be plenty of opportunities for you to write. The college has a literary magazine for the best stories and poems that come out of our classrooms. I'm sure you'll be seeing your name in print before long."

Maggie was elated. Although teaching had always been her forte, what she wanted to do more than anything was to write novels like Jane Austen. Dr. Adams was going to help her. She thought of Zeb, who did his share of writing too, mostly poetry. He never sent anything off, saying he just enjoyed reading his work out loud to the family. Maggie dreamed of more—she wanted to have a novel published.

In the following weeks, Dr. Adams encouraged Maggie to write short stories and poems outside of class. "It's the best way to develop your style. The longer things will come later, but while you're here, we'll address your writing on a smaller scale." She gave Maggie her personal copy of a collection of short stories by Henry James, her favorite contemporary writer. "Be a good reader first, my dear, and you'll learn, learn, learn."

Dr. Adams was widowed and lived with her widowed mother, Vanessa Burchart, in a home near South Cottage. According to Dr. Adams, her mother had been a popular actress before she retired. "She was in over fifty plays in her heyday. My father was an actor too, but you won't hear Mother even mention his name." Dr. Adams handed Maggie a large book with a red leather cover. "Here, I have her scrapbook. You may look at it."

"Why won't she talk about your father?"

"It wasn't always a happy time," Dr. Adams said. "Mother had some disappointments. Read the clippings. You'll see."

Maggie read them all, but the one that intrigued her the most was captioned: *Actress retires after suspicious fall.* The article was laced with innuendos—*Burchart reported for rehearsal with a badly bruised eye...might have been the cause of her imbalance.* The article went on to read that the actress's husband, who had the lead in the play, had not reported for rehearsals...*probably another bout with the bottle, hmmm?*

——

Maggie often walked home along the same path as her professor, and despite the ten-year difference in their ages, they became good friends. In some ways Dr. Adams was like Aunt Mag, always telling her about books she had read and places she had been. But Abigail Adams was only forty-two, and knew so much more than Aunt Mag did about what was going on in the world today.

On one of their walks, Dr. Adams encouraged Maggie to get more involved in campus life. "You mustn't let being housemother at South Cottage keep you from doing other things," she said. "Tryouts for *Twelfth Night* are coming up very soon and I think you'd make a wonderful Viola."

"Oh, I don't think I could do that," Maggie said.

"Look, there's Mother on the porch. Let's ask her. Mother, don't you think Maggie would make a wonderful Viola in *Twelfth Night?*" Dr. Adams leaned over her mother to give her a kiss on the cheek.

"Oh, please don't listen to her, Mrs. Burchart," Maggie said, touching her affectionately on the shoulder. "You know I'm not shy, but I'm no actress either." She perched herself on the porch rail, swinging her feet up and leaning against the post.

"If Abigail thinks you have a good chance of getting a part, you should do it, Maggie," Mrs. Burchart said, setting her rocking chair in motion. She was in her seventies, still a beautiful woman, with skin the color of a ripened peach. On the vine-shaded porch, with her thick white hair piled up in a stylish pompadour and her burgundy silk dress draped over the chair, the older woman reminded Maggie of Lady Catherine in *Pride and Prejudice.*

Abigail excused herself to go inside. "I'll see if Joella's made any cookies, and we'll have a cup of tea. Mother, you talk Maggie into being in the play." '

"I could never, Mrs. Burchart."

"One never knows until one tries, Maggie Lorena. Abigail says your elocution is excellent. Why don't you try out for Viola? You'd make a good Viola."

"I'd make a fool of myself," Maggie said.

"*'Alas, it is the baseness of thy fear that makes thee strangle thy propriety,'*" Mrs. Burchart said in a resounding stage voice. "*'Fear not, Ceasario. Take thy fortunes up. Be that thou know'st thou art, and then thou art as great as that thou fear'st.'*" She closed her eyes and paused. "I played Olivia once, but it was a long time ago, before I broke my hip."

"Oh, that was beautiful, Mrs. Burchart," Maggie said. It was the first time the older woman had mentioned her acting or her infirmity. She walked with great difficulty, using a wooden frame that she pushed along in front of her, grimacing with each painful step. But, as a rule, once she sat down her face was radiant and she dismissed any inquiries about her health.

"You mustn't miss a single opportunity while you are young. Things change very quickly. You must take advantage of everything while you are here at BFU."

Maggie slipped into the chair beside her. "Tell me about your life, about being an actress."

"That was a long time ago, Maggie. Let's talk about you. What do you hear from that fellow of yours over in Wake Forest?"

Maggie blushed. She wasn't quite sure she was ready to reveal her feelings about Wash to anyone. "I'm not sure that I should call him my fellow. We've just been writing to one another."

"Well, I'd say that's a step in the right direction. But you must invite him here after the Music Department's recitals next Sunday. Abigail and I will see if he passes inspection."

Maggie's face lit up. "Would that be all right? I mean, I'm not sure he would even come."

"Well, we'll just see about that. You write and tell him about the recitals. Ask him to come here afterwards. Joella will make a little cake and we'll have tea. Abigail and I will see if he's worthy of your attention."

"Oh, that would be wonderful," Maggie said, throwing her arms around Vanessa Burchart's neck.

"Now, now, don't get your hopes up. We might not like him, you know."

"Yes, you will, you couldn't help but like him," Maggie called out as she cut across the yard, anxious to start a letter before supper.

Sunday tea with Mrs. Burchart and Abigail Adams became a regular occurrence, providing coveted opportunities for Maggie and Wash to be together. The rules on dating at BFU were strict. Boys were not allowed to call on freshmen girls except on Monday afternoons; on weekends, concerts, recitals, and sometimes plays were open to other colleges, but a BFU student was not allowed to date to these affairs. Abigail Adams's Sunday teas were popular with many members of the faculty, and she always gave her guests an open invitation to drop in between two and four o'clock. If Maggie and Wash were always there, greeting visitors from the porch swing or serving tea at the table, no one remarked upon it. No one except Ella Bradley.

"What's that Wash Pridgen doing with his hands under the table all the time, Maggie darlin'? I declare, you two make me sweat just looking at you."

"Oh, don't tease. We're just holding hands and you know it. We never have enough time for anything else."

"Yeah, but let me tell you from experience where that hand-holding leads," Ella said, nodding her head. And she did tell Maggie, almost every night, about the kissing and things she did with her boyfriend before her daddy found out and sent her off to BFU. "I declare, once you get a taste, it's like that first piece of candy you ever had—it just makes you want some more."

Chapter 4

On the last Sunday in October, to Maggie's surprise, Wash was waiting in the cottage parlor for her when she returned from church. She had told him that she couldn't see him that weekend; she needed to study for a test. *It's just one weekend out of a lifetime,* she had written to him. *I need a little time to catch up.*

"Maggie, I'm sorry, but I need to talk to you. I brought a picnic. I thought we might take the streetcar out to Bloomsbury Park." He took her hand, pulling her close.

"Wash, please! I'm not allowed to go off-campus without a chaperone. You know that." She pulled away, afraid she'd get in trouble. "You have to leave. Someone's always checking on us."

"Maggie Lorena, you are too much! *You* are the housemother here, you can do whatever you please. Besides, I know girls who've done it before."

"You may know some girls like that, but I'm not one."

Wash realized that he had said the wrong thing and he reached for her hand. "I know, I just meant that girls do it all the time. Ask Ella. School wasn't meant to be a prison. I'll have you back before supper."

"I can't. I have things to do. I need to study."

Her plea was half-hearted and he took advantage of it. "You can't work all the time. You have to take some time for yourself. Please, just go tell Ella you're going with me."

Maggie ran upstairs and found Ella on her bed studying. "Ella, Wash has brought a picnic. He wants me to go to Bloomsbury Park with him. Tell me honestly, should I go?"

"Why not? All you have to do is go out the back way, cut across that little park and you'll be up on Hillsborough Street way past the

Pullens's house. Who's gonna know?"

"I don't like sneaking around," Maggie said. She was changing her clothes, knowing that she was going no matter what Ella said. "But Wash won't take 'no' for an answer." Looking into the mirror, she saw that her hairdo was slipping. "Should I wear my hair down?" she asked, pulling out the pins at lightning speed.

Ella watched her, laughing. "Well, I see you really didn't need my permission."

Maggie put on a brown serge skirt with a light blue calico waist, trying to look more like a young matron than a college girl. She looked in the mirror and decided to tuck her hair beneath her brown derby hat.

"All you need now is a baby hanging off your hip," Ella said.

"That'll come soon enough," Maggie laughed. "I should be home before dark, but just in case, leave the back light on, please."

The trolley to Bloomsbury Park was crowded with families taking their children out to the end of the line. The year before, a large park had been built on Crabtree Creek near Lassiter's Mill pond, and the main attraction was a German-built carousel. Maggie and Wash boarded the trolley several blocks from the university, intent on avoiding the attention of any members of Mr. Pullen's congregation who might be along for the ride. Wash wore a soft white shirt without a collar and suspenders attached to a pair of striped cotton pants. It was the first time she had seen him without a coat and tie, looking a lot less like a young lawyer.

He slid into the seat beside her, pressing close. "I love you, Maggie Lorena," he whispered.

"Wash, people will see."

They had taken the last seat facing the rear and Wash reached over and lowered the striped awning to shield them from the sun and the traffic behind them. "Let them see I love you."

"What was so important that you had to come today when I told you I needed to study?"

He took both of her hands and pulled them to his chest. "I'm tired of having to share you with everyone at concerts and receptions. I just wanted to be alone with you."

She took her hands away and looked out the window. Hadn't she felt the same way? Hadn't she longed to feel his arms around her, lay her head on his shoulder? "You know the rule about public displays of affection. They're just not done by university girls."

"Can't you just pretend for today that you're not a university girl—you're my girl? I'm in love with you." He took her chin in his hand and turned her face to his. "Can't you see how much I love you?"

"Wash, I know people are looking. Please. Wait until we get to the park."

He lifted her hand peevishly and placed it back on her lap. "All right, you win, but watch out when we get there," he said, whistling and looking about. A young boy chased a rubber ball down the aisle, and Wash retrieved it and tossed it back. "There you go, kid."

Maggie smiled. What had gotten into him? He was feeling frisky as a puppy today. She had planned to wait until they got to the park to tell him about the play, but she couldn't. "I won the part of Viola," she said. "I was going to write to you tonight."

"What has *that* got to do with me loving you?"

"Wash! I just thought you would be interested, that's all."

Before she could turn away, he put his arms around her. "I was only teasing, darling. That's the best news I've heard in a long time. You'll be wonderful." He tried to kiss her on the cheek, but she resisted.

"Wash, I told you, not now!"

When they reached the park, he led the way to a grassy bank far downstream from children and families. It was a bright October day, the sky deep blue and the sun hot, despite frost that had already brushed the trees with shades of red and gold. Wash spread a quilt on the soft grass and pulled Maggie to him. She dropped to her knees, and he pulled again until she lost her balance and fell against him. He rocked her back and forth in his arms, kissing her lightly at first, then again more fervently. She closed her eyes and her mind to everything except the velvety softness of his mouth, his breath filling a long aching emptiness within her.

"Maggie, I love you with all my heart." He kissed her hard, his breath quickening, his arms encircling her shoulders, taking her down beneath him. "I've dreamed of holding you like this." His hand slid across her breast, down her thigh, then up beneath her skirt. She heard Ella Bradley say, *once you get a taste of it, you want it again and again.* A shadow passed over them. A bird, a cloud? She opened her eyes and grabbed his hand. "Please, don't."

He sat up, his hair tousled, his face scarlet. "I'm sorry, Maggie. I shouldn't have...I lost control. It's just that holding you is all I can think about."

In the distance, the Bloomsbury carousel organ piped its colorful wooden horses round and round, and children laughed and shouted in the shallow water of Lassiter's mill pond. Wash couldn't possibly know how much she thought about being alone with him. "I know. Me too."

After the picnic Maggie wrote to Wash every evening, running down to the train station before her first class to post her letter. The mail clerk said he could set his watch by her better than he could the train.

As captain of the debating team at Wake Forest, Wash was in a position to schedule matches between the two schools, and he did so with great regularity. BFU's debating team was one of the best on the college circuit, and the debating rivalry was lively. Since Abigail Adams was faculty advisor for the BFU team, after a debate she and Wash often discussed the issues at great length. Maggie knew that on those days she would find Wash with Abigail and Mrs. Burchart on their porch.

Sometimes Maggie envied the time Wash took with Mrs. Burchart and Dr. Adams. They were both well educated in the classics and music, and Wash never seemed to tire of their company. She told him how she felt. "If I didn't know better, Wash Pridgen, I'd think it was two widow ladies you're courting instead of me."

They were sitting on the back steps of Abigail's house. Wash put his arm around her. "Maggie, you're jealous, and I'm glad because that must mean you love me."

"Oh, Wash. You deserve so much more than I can ever give you. I'm just a backwoods girl up here trying to get an education, and you're so smart. You need a woman who can talk to you the way Mrs. Burchart and Dr. Adams do. They're from up there in New England where they've had colleges for women for years. Why, I'll never match the likes of them."

"Don't say that." Wash stood, took her hands and gathered her into his arms. The November air had chilled rapidly as the day grew shorter and she snuggled against him. "Don't ever say that. Mrs. Burchart and Dr. Adams are my friends just as they are yours. I guess they both remind me of what my mother might have been like. I was so young when she died."

"Oh, I'm just feeling sorry for myself. I never knew college would be so hard. I'm worked to death on the play and school will be out in a few weeks. I wish I could just stay here during the holidays and catch up."

Maggie rehearsed daily with Mrs. Burchart, her patient but demanding coach, who expected Maggie to show up promptly on her porch at prearranged times to say her lines. Memorizing had come easy for Maggie, but she dreaded being up on stage in front of so many people. "What if I panic? I might forget..."

Mrs. Burchart put up her hand to shush Maggie. "That isn't going to happen," she said. "If you know your lines, you won't forget. Just pretend that there's no one in the auditorium but you."

"I'd rather write a play."

"Come now, you're not getting cold feet, are you? I know you can do it, Maggie Lorena."

The older woman took all of the other parts, saying most of them by heart. "Remember, you are in disguise, Maggie. The audience knows that, but Olivia does not. She must think of you as Caesario. Be Caesario! Be a man! There's humor in it: She falls in love with you instead of heeding your plea on Orsino's behalf. Now, once again in Olivia's garden."

———

As rehearsals became more intense, Maggie's nerves became increasingly frazzled. There were not enough hours in the day for her lessons and the play. She longed to spend time with Wash, but that seemed hopeless as well. Each night before she said her prayers, she wrote him a short note telling him of the day's events. In turn, he wrote to her, declaring his love in flowery language. Sometimes she had to laugh at his expressions. *You are my Diana. I look at the moon and there you are...my goddess...my love.*

She'd written Aunt Mag about meeting Wash on the train, but she'd been careful not to reveal too much, avoiding Aunt Mag's certain reprimand. In her letters to her sisters, Maggie told them everything she could think of about him. Katie wrote that she remembered Wash— *Wonder what happened to that girl he was holding hands with along the river? Did you ask him?* Mary Ellen's return letter was full of advice. *Maggie, dear, first love is a wonderful thing, but be careful. These young boys off at college think they're on holiday. When they go back home it's business as usual, often with a girl they've already promised their heart to.*

Aunt Mag was concerned about Mary Ellen's health. She'd written that Mary Ellen had been down with consumption several times, each time a little worse than the other, but Dr. Bayard was treating her and she'd been responding until recently. Cyrus had been over to the house to talk to G.W. *I wasn't allowed in on the conversation,* Aunt Mag said in her letter, *but I suspect it was about Mary Ellen because your pa hasn't been the same since.*

Chapter 5

The entire school was caught up in the production of *Twelfth Night*. For weeks, the Sewing Club and the Drama Club worked on costumes for the play, stitching day and night under Maggie's direction. Ella Bradley was a member of both. "I declare, Maggie, if it don't beat all how you know how to do everything. You'd think you'd been in plays all your life."

"It doesn't take much to sew costumes, Ella. They're just regular clothes, but you don't have to take so many pains, and a safety pin here and there can take care of the fit."

"*Nay, I prithee,* these gowns will *make thee believe thee art Sir Topas!*" Ella could hardly get the words out for laughing. She had won the part of Maria, Olivia's maid, and although her lines were few, she repeated them incessantly.

"Well, *prithee* get these costumes out of my sight. I've been having terrible headaches the last few days and I'm sure that it's from all this sewing. Maybe I need some glasses."

On opening night, Wash escorted Mrs. Burchart and Dr. Adams to see the play. They all came backstage among the props and ropes after the final act.

"Maggie, you were wonderful! I never saw Viola played better. I am so proud of you," Mrs. Burchart said. She had tears in her eyes and dabbed at her cheeks with a lace handkerchief.

"She's a natural-born actress, isn't she, Mother?" Abigail Adams was elegant in a black velvet evening coat. She had her arm through Wash's, and Maggie felt a twinge of jealousy. "Wash, I'm afraid Maggie will have stars in her eyes after this," Abigail said, squeezing his arm.

Wash politely removed her hand and embraced Maggie. "You were beautiful, Maggie. I'm so proud of you," he said, kissing her on the cheek, feeling her tears. "Why are you crying?"

"It's my eye, it really hurts."

"Let me see. Did you get something in it?"

"I don't think so."

"It's awfully red," Mrs. Burchart said. "Come, let's get your makeup off and let me look at it." She led the way to the dressing room. "Just wait for me, Abigail. Wash, Maggie will meet you at the stage door."

Vanessa Burchart soaked a sponge in warm water and helped Maggie remove her makeup. She peered into Maggie's eye. "If it were just a headache, I wouldn't worry. Stage fright can do that to you. But your eye is terribly bloodshot. I'll ask Wash to take you over to the infirmary and let the school nurse look at it." She hugged her protégé and said again, "You were wonderful."

"Thanks to you," Maggie said to Mrs. Burchart's reflection in the mirror. "I don't know how I did it, but I couldn't have done it at all without you."

Vanessa Burchart grasped her walking apparatus and smiled at Maggie. "I'll tell Ella to leave the light on for you."

Outside the stage door, Wash took her aside and wrapped his arms around her. "Now I'll tell you properly how wonderful you were, Miss Viola." He kissed her until she pulled away, shivering. "What is it, Maggie?"

"I'm glad it's over. I was so scared out there in front of all those people. I guess I'm not cut out to be an actress."

"What do you mean? You were wonderful. Mrs. Burchart said so. Everyone said so."

She tried to smile. "Thank you. But I had this awful headache...knew I had to go on or ruin everything. What if I'm going blind?"

"Hush, hush, now. I'm sure it's nothing that bad. Come on, Mrs. Burchart said I should take you to the infirmary."

Miss Nettie Oldham, the school nurse, was reluctant to let Wash into the infirmary. "You run along, young man. I'll take care of this girl."

"Please, madam," Wash said in his most gracious tone, "the young lady will require an escort back to her cottage."

"Oh. Well, come on in. What's the matter with you, son?" she asked Maggie. Maggie had warned Wash that Miss Nettie called all the girls 'son.' The nurse was still in her starched white uniform, despite the late hour. There wasn't a wrinkle in the long apron that covered her large bosom and buttoned at the back of her narrow waist. She studied Maggie through thick bifocals as she seated her on a tall white metal stool.

"Looks like you got stuck in the eye, son. How'd this happen?"

"I was in the play. Nothing happened. My eye just started burning and hurting."

"And you didn't get anything in it?"

"No ma'am."

"Has it ever hurt before?" Miss Nettie was right up in Maggie's face, peering into her eye with a magnifying glass. She smelled like liniment, a smell that made Maggie think of her pa's barn.

"No ma'am. I think I would remember if it had ever hurt like this before." Miss Nettie continued to peer into Maggie's eyes, first one and then the other. "Tonight, before I went on stage, I had a terrible headache over my left eye, like someone was sticking a knife in it. Everyone was sitting there, just waiting for me to go on. I didn't think I could say my lines, but I knew I had to, or ruin everything."

Miss Nettie put her hands on her hips. "Well, it don't look right to me, son, but we'll let Dr. Norwood take a look at you in the morning. Do you want to stay here with me tonight?"

"No, ma'am. I think I'd better go back to the cottage. The girls will be worried about me."

"Who's that fellow out there? He shouldn't be here so late."

"Oh, he's a friend of Dr. Adams," Maggie said. "He was kind enough to escort me to the infirmary."

"Well, you tell him to move along after he gets you back to the cottage. Dr. Vann doesn't like young bucks hanging around this late at night."

The following morning, Maggie waited in Dr. Norwood's office. She had seen the doctor around campus and had heard her rail at the students in assembly about not wearing their high-top shoes and long underwear. Before she left her room that morning, Maggie had slipped into the long underwear that she kept folded in her drawer. She hated long underwear, and out from under the watchful eyes of her mother and Aunt Mag had refused to wear it. Aunt Mag warned her about catching pneumonia, but Maggie had never seen longjohns advertised anywhere except in the Sears Roebuck Catalogue. Surely the women in the ladies' magazines didn't wear longjohns under those beautiful dresses.

Dr. Norwood marched into the office like an army general. "Where's Miss Nettie?" she demanded of the receptionist. "Miss Nettie!" she shouted.

Miss Nettie opened the door to the reception area and stuck her head in. "What in the world is it? I'm right here!"

"Where's that girl with the eye pain? Was she wearing her long underwear?" She followed Miss Nettie into the examination room, checking the instrument table, then washing her hands. "Probably not. Over there prancing around in those flimsy costumes. It's no wonder." Miss Nettie escorted Maggie into the room. "What did you do to your eye, girl?" the doctor asked. Maggie hesitated near the door. "Come here. I'm not going to bite you."

"I didn't do anything to it. It just hurts, and now everything is blurred." She began to weep. During the night she had awakened remembering her family's stories about Grandmother Moreland going blind at a young age.

"Hush, now. You're gonna be all right. I'll bet you got all tensed up being in that play. You were Viola, weren't you? You were good. I saw you."

"Thank you. Do you think I'm going blind, Dr. Norwood?"

"No, no, my dear, nothing as bad as that. Lie down now and let me get my ophthalmoscope." She eased Maggie into a reclining position and peered into her eye. "Are you sure you didn't get something in it? Ophthalmalgia is usually the result of an injury." Dr. Norwood looked puzzled. "Yes, you've got some optic neuritis, but I don't know what brought it on unless it was all that running around half-naked up there on that stage."

Tears streamed down Maggie's cheeks. "My head is killing me."

"Now, now, calm down. I'll put some drops in your eye and give you a little laudanum for the headache. I want you to wear a patch for a week or so, and then I'll have a look at you again." She held Maggie's hands. "You're going to be all right, my dear. I promise."

———

It was all Maggie could do to finish her schoolwork for the semester. Wash had written to her, insisting that she come to the Wake Forest Christmas Dance despite the black patch that she wore over her eye. But Maggie refused, not only because it looked funny, but because she was so miserable. All day and night, water poured from her eye, running down her cheek like tears, and her head throbbed incessantly.

Dr. Norwood had written a letter of consultation to a specialist in Richmond. She urged Maggie to persevere until she heard from him. When his letter arrived, she sent for Maggie. "Dr. Reginal McKenzie is the foremost authority on opthalmalgia. He assures me that the symptoms will subside in a few weeks, but it's essential that you wear the patch until the pain goes away. After that, he suggests a dark glass."

Maggie was mortified. "A dark glass? But that would look like I was..." Just today she had seen the near-blind beggar, Woodrow, pushing his cart down Fayetteville Street. He wore not one, but two dark lenses in wire frames that were patched together with dirty string.

"Not forever, dear girl. You're not blind. Just until the inflammation goes away. That's what's causing the pain." She sorted through her bag of instruments and removed a measuring device. "It's not the end of the world. Now, let me take some measurements and I'll have those glasses for you before you go home for Christmas."

———

Two weeks later, when classes were over, Maggie was excited about going home on the train with Wash. They had passed letters back and forth, but she had not seen him since the night at the infirmary. She knew he had been disappointed when she refused to attend the Christmas dance at Wake Forest, but he wrote that he would introduce her to his friends and faculty at the spring formal. Aunt Mag had surprised her with a package containing a dark green taffeta dress for the Christmas dance, and she promised Wash she would wear it for him if he would come to meet her parents the day after Christmas.

Her discomfort had subsided several days before she was to leave for home, and once again Maggie felt giddy and in love. She hadn't wanted to be around Wash—or anyone, really—when she was in so much pain. Now she planned her outfit for the train, shopped for small gifts for her friends, and packed for a month's stay at home. Before she left, she closed her trunk and checked the lock. It was difficult to leave it here, but she knew that her things were safe in the cottage with no one coming or going. Mr. Pullen assured the girls that the premises would be checked on a regular basis.

———

Wash was waiting by the steps to the train. He ran to her and scooped her up into his arms as she neared him. "I declare, you're embarrassing me half to death," she said.

He drew her up the steps and further into the vestibule, shushing her with a kiss. "Embarrassing you, Miss Maggie Lorena? Have you no pity on this wretched fellow who hasn't seen his girl for two whole weeks? I do declare!" he mocked her, shaking his head.

"Off with you, Wash Pridgen. Let's get to our seats. I'm freezing cold."

He held her another second or two, long enough to tease. "Are you wearing your long underwear? Here, let me check so I can report to Dr. Norwood."

"Stop that. Mr. Pullen brought me to the station and he's probably standing out there right now waiting for me to wave goodbye to him." She led the way to their seats and leaned over to look for Mr. Pullen. "See, there he is. Wave to him, Wash."

Wash obediently waved to John Pullen, saying under his breath, "She's my girl for the next month, old fellow."

"How's your eye?" he asked when they were seated. "You're not wearing the patch."

"I can see a little better, but I have to wear these glasses."

"Let me see."

"You won't laugh, will you?" She reached into her bag and pulled out a pair of wire-rimmed spectacles with a dark glass on the left side. "Do they look real funny?" she asked, adjusting the glasses on her nose.

Wash put his arm around her and hugged her. "Not at all, my dear. You're too beautiful. Nothing could spoil you."

"Oh, they do look funny, don't they?" She reached up and quickly removed the glasses. "Dr. Norwood said the dark glass might help. I guess I'd do anything to get my sight back like it was."

"Do what she says, Maggie. I'll write to Uncle Clyde. He may know an eye doctor in Wilmington."

The train was crowded with students, but Maggie and Wash huddled together, oblivious to everyone but themselves. Maggie was wearing a thick blue wool shawl, a Christmas gift from Abigail Adams and Mrs. Burchart. Wash wore a long dark brown leather coat. "It belonged to my grandpa, the one that went out West prospecting and struck it rich. Just before he died, he sent it back home to my daddy and told him it was his inheritance."

Maggie laughed and snuggled up against the cold leather, releasing old smells of tobacco and whiskey.

In Fayetteville, five or six students who had been sitting across from

Maggie and Wash got off the train. Wash moved even closer to Maggie, kissing her on the cheek, playing with her hair. When the train started up again, he blurted out, "Maggie, I plan to ask your pa for your hand, if you don't have any objection."

She had known this was coming, but she wasn't sure she was quite ready for it. His letters had been full of his plans for the future—working with his uncle, living with him in Wilmington—but until now, she hadn't realized how soon they included her. "I thought you might wait until after your graduation. It will be a long engagement as it is."

"No, I've thought about it. I want our families to know my intentions." He squeezed her hands. "I want to marry you as soon as we can after graduation."

"What? You don't mean it."

"Yes, I do." He paused to watch her expression. "Uncle Clyde wants me to come into his practice right away. We could rent a little house in Wilmington."

Maggie pictured a small house near the river with rockers on the porch and a clothesline full of crisp white sheets flapping in the wind. "But what about my schooling? You're not forgetting about that, are you?" She knew he wasn't, not after all their talks. "Aunt Mag has her heart set on me finishing college, and I do, too."

"I know, I know, but Maggie, this is so important. You wouldn't have to teach school if we were married. You could do your writing, help out in the law office, and when we have children..."

"But I really want an education. I've waited so long for the chance. I don't think it would set well with Aunt Mag, or Mama and Papa for that matter. Dr. Adams and Mrs. Burchart, what would they think?"

"They're my friends, too. I know they would want us to be happy."

She thought about that. Abigail Adams and Mrs. Burchart had been like surrogate parents to her and Wash—watching over them, counseling them about their futures. Abigail had once said to Maggie that she expected they would marry when Maggie finished her education.

"You'll think about it?" Wash asked.

"I'm thinking about it right now," she said, a little edge in her voice. "I haven't even met your folks yet, and here you are talking about getting married. What would they think?"

"Oh, darling, I've written them all about you. I don't have many folks, you know. Just Jeff and Samuel at home. I was hoping that maybe after Christmas, before we go back to Raleigh, we might take the boat downriver to Wilmington and you could meet Uncle Clyde and Aunt Lillian."

"Let's not decide just yet. I want to marry you more than anything, but I need to talk to Aunt Mag. I don't think I could bear to disappoint her."

Wash slid back into his seat and sighed. "All right, I can wait for your answer, but not for too long. I could never be happy practicing law in Wilmington with you way up in Raleigh."

Maggie couldn't imagine life in Raleigh without Wash either. She thought about a small house by the river in Wilmington again. It was the first time she had ever thought of living anywhere except in Aunt Mag's little blue-and-white house in Colly.

It was almost dark when the train stopped at Atkinson. From the train window, Maggie saw her father sitting in the buggy alone, talking to a man in a wagon beside him. Wash craned his neck to see. "That's Jeff, Maggie. I wrote and asked him if he would come so he could meet you. Looks like he's bending your pa's ear."

"I can't wait to meet him. Do you think he'll like me?"

"He'll love you, Maggie Lorena. Just like I do. Well, maybe not exactly like I do," he chuckled, taking one last long look into her face.

"I love you, too," she said.

The man standing with G.W. looked towards the train and waved. If she had seen Jeff Pridgen in a crowd, Maggie would have thought him the least likely fellow to be Wash's brother. He dwarfed G.W., standing a head taller, with a good hundred pounds or more on him. Jeff had a heavy beard and wore a hat pulled down to the tops of his ears. She couldn't even see his eyes. Dressed in a heavy leather jacket with pockets all around, he looked like a rugged but well-off farmer.

Wash helped Maggie down the train steps and picked up their bags just as Jeff strode across the platform to meet them. "Let me get those, little brother, you ain't big enough to carry all that," he called out. He tipped his hat to Maggie, picked up all the bags, and led the way back to the wagon. After putting the bags in the bed, he swung around and grabbed his little brother in a bear hug. Then he lifted him up and sat him down on the back of the wagon. "I declare, Wash, you ain't growed an inch."

"Cut it out, Jeff," Wash said, laughing and sliding off the wagon. "I want you to meet Maggie Lorena."

"I'm pleased, to be sure, Miss Maggie Lorena." Jeff extended a thick hand to Maggie. "She sure is pretty, Wash, just like you said."

G.W. ambled over, looking weary in the brightness of the late afternoon. "Shug, you're a sight for sore eyes," he said, hugging her.

Maggie embraced him, feeling his bony shoulders through his jacket. "It's good to see you too, Papa."

G.W. looked closely at Maggie. "I see you're wearing that dark glass the doctor ordered. How's your eye?"

Maggie reached up and touched her glasses. "It's better, thank you. But Dr. Norwood said I should wear the dark glass for awhile." She turned to Wash and Jeff. "I guess you've already met my pa, Jeff. You two probably had a lot to talk about, Pa being in the war with your father and all."

"I've known the Pridgens for a long time, Maggie," G.W. interrupted. "Don't you remember meeting some of them at the reunion of the 18th at Point Caswell?"

"I do, Pa, I certainly do. I remember seeing Wash, but I don't recollect meeting Jeff. The paper said there were more than three thousand people at the picnic that year."

"Capt'n Corbinn, I'd be obliged if I might call on Miss Maggie over the holidays," Wash said. "I've asked her to go to Wilmington with me to meet my aunt and uncle."

G.W. drew back a little. "You're welcome to come calling, but it's up to Maggie as to whether she goes off with you or not. She's a grown girl now." He spit tobacco juice over the wheel.

"You come on over like we said, Wash. I want you to meet Mama and Aunt Mag." Maggie climbed into the buggy with G.W. "Jeff, it was nice meeting you. I expect I'll be seeing you again too. Have a good Christmas."

"Thank you, Miss Maggie. It was a pleasure, to be sure." Jeff grinned and reached out for Wash's shoulder. "Get on up here, little brother. We got a ways to go and it's getting dark already."

Maggie missed Wash before he was out of sight. When they had gone a few yards in opposite directions, she felt a pull, like she was attached to him by threads that stretched and tightened with each step of the horses. She turned to look and he was looking back at her. They waved again. A short distance later, she looked and Wash was caught in conversation with Jeff.

"He'll be coming for me the day after Christmas, Pa. His uncle is paying his way to law school and Wash wants me to go with him to Wilmington to meet them." G.W. was silent, his eyes on the road ahead. "Papa, you don't mind, do you? I mean, you like him, don't you?"

"Oh, the Pridgens are good folks. I don't have anything against them."

"What is it? I thought you'd be glad for me to have a fellow. Wash is going to be a lawyer."

"You know what I think about lawyers, don't you, Maggie Lorena? Huh?"

"So that's it."

"Oh, honey, that's not it. I was just joshing you about him being a lawyer. What I'm worried about is your sister, Mary Ellen. You going to Wilmington and all—you reckon you could put it off for a while?"

She had never seen him look so dejected, but she wondered if he might be trying to prevent her from going off with a beau. It might be a little sooner than he expected. She decided to test him out. "No, I couldn't. If you want to know the truth, Wash is planning on asking you for my hand. He wants me to meet his folks." She pulled her shawl about her shoulders and looked straight ahead. Night was moving in fast, and the sandy road ahead reflected the early moon like a long white ribbon threaded through the tall pines and scraggly oaks. The only sounds were the rough breath of the horse and the steady beat of his hooves in the deep sand.

Finally, G.W. broke the silence. "Look here, shug, I don't have any problem with you getting engaged to that Pridgen boy if that's what you want, but right now with your mama so bad off, it's all that your Aunt Mag can do to take care of her. Somebody's got to go to Mary Ellen over in Burgaw. Katie can't do it because she's the only teacher they've got in Shallotte."

"Pa, that's not fair. You know I would do anything for Mary Ellen, but I want to go to Wilmington with Wash first. I have to go back to Raleigh in just three weeks." Maggie stared at a flare set off along the railroad track behind the train, still burning brightly.

"I hate to tell you this, Maggie Lorena, but the doctor says Mary Ellen's mighty bad off. I was over there day before yesterday and she could hardly get her breath. Cyrus says she's been asking about you, wanting to know when she'd be seeing you."

Maggie pictured Cyrus Devane, the gentle widower with a ready-made family who had asked Mary Ellen to marry him soon after she'd gone to teach school in Burgaw. She put her hand on her father's shoulder, holding back her tears. "Oh, Papa, I didn't know. I'll help take care of her. There's still a whole week before Christmas. I can stay with Mary Ellen a few days, get her on her feet, and still be back in time to go with Wash."

"You might as well know, Dr. Bayard don't think Mary Ellen's gonna make it. There's a sanitorium she could have gone to up around Raleigh, but he says it's too late for that now."

"Oh, no, Papa. That can't be."

"Dr. Bayard has seen consumption before."

Maggie leaned against his shoulder and began to cry. "I didn't realize Mary Ellen was so sick, Papa."

———

Mary Ellen sent word that Maggie was not to come. She said she was feeling stronger every day. Maggie was to stay home and help Aunt Mag get ready for Christmas. Mary Ellen said she might even be there herself to see the old place decorated with magnolia leaves and mistletoe. There was a sadness to the note, but Maggie was hopeful enough to put off her visit until after the holiday.

Chapter 6

Two days before Christmas, Maggie was burning trash out behind the shed when she saw a horse and rider amble up the lane to the house. Smoke from the fire drifted in front of her, shrouding the dark figure from full view. She thought it was a man hunched over, his wide-brimmed hat nearly touching his shoulders, but she didn't recognize Jeff Pridgen until he stopped in front of the chinaberry tree and dismounted. He stood beside his horse for a long time looking at her, his hat held against his chest. Maggie thought she was imagining it. She blinked her eyes, but Jeff didn't move. She took a few steps towards him.

"Howdy, Miss Maggie. I come to tell you... I come to tell you Wash..." He broke down and began to sob, wiping his eyes with his fist.

"What is it?" She ran to him and grabbed him by the shoulders. "Jeff, where is Wash?" He was trying to pull himself together, shifting from one foot to the other, looking from her face to the ground, but the distress in his eyes told her what he could not. She shook him, trying to force an answer. "What's happened to my Wash? Tell me, Jeff. Tell me!"

"He got kilt, Miss Maggie. I didn't want to be the one to break the news to you, but since I knowed you, meeting you at the train station so recently and all, I had to come."

Maggie felt as if her heart had stopped. She sank to her knees on the cold ground. Jeff knelt in front of her and pulled her head to his chest with his rough hands. "I know, I know. I can't hardly believe it myself and I was the one that found him," he said, his voice barely a whisper. "I wish it had been me instead of him...my little baby brother."

He helped her to her feet and she stared at him in disbelief. "He's dead? Wash is dead?"

"Yes'm. I can't hardly believe it either," he said again, shaking his head and wiping his tears with the back of his hand.

"But how?"

"He was out hunting. He tripped...the gun...it went off and...and... Oh, it was awful." Maggie slipped from his grasp and fell on the ground, wailing and weeping. "Hush now, Miss Maggie." He picked her up in his thick arms and walked towards the house. "Let me get you inside. Where's everybody—your pa and your brothers?" He smelled like Wash. This big, burly man, so unlike the fine-featured Wash, smelled like him.

G.W. opened the door. "Jeff Pridgen? What'n the hell? What're you doing here? What's wrong with Maggie? Maggie, shug, what's wrong?"

Jeff sat Maggie down in a chair. "It's Wash, Capt'n Corbinn. He stepped in a bear trap and his gun went off. It blew his whole head off."

"Good God, man!" G.W. said. Maggie swooned again and he caught her before she fell off the chair. "Go get her Aunt Mag, Jeff. You'll see her. She's out there around the barn somewhere."

———

When Maggie roused from the fainting spell, she thought she had been dreaming. Katie was standing over her, a cold cloth in her hand. Wash couldn't be dead. Katie was here for Christmas. Zeb had gone downriver to get her this morning. Wash was coming...

"Did you bring mistletoe, Katie?" The sound of her own voice jarred her back to reality and she put her head in her hands. "He's dead, Katie. Wash is dead."

"I know, sister. Just rest now. We can talk later."

"No, Katie. I wanted you to know Wash. He was the dearest thing in life to me. We were going to get married."

"I know," Katie said. "Zeb told me." She dabbed at Maggie's forehead with the cold cloth.

Maggie sat up on the bed. "He was to graduate in June. We had so many plans." She closed her eyes and squeezed out tears. "How can I go on, Katie?"

"Poor darling Maggie. I am so sorry." Tears streamed down Katie's face and she wiped them with her apron.

Maggie fell back on the pillow, her arm across her eyes. "Where's Aunt Mag? I want to see Aunt Mag."

"She's gone to the kitchen for a glass of water. Here she comes now."

Aunt Mag came into the room, drying her hands. "I declare, I don't know what G.W. would do if I wasn't around here to cook. Here you are laid up with this terrible news and he's wanting to know what's for supper." She sat down on the bed and her voice softened. "Now, Maggie Lorena, I know you think this is the end of the world, but it isn't."

"It may as well be. Wash was my whole life."

"My stars, you still have a life. It's Wash Pridgen that lost his. You'll go on. You'll find your reasons, just like the rest of us. Why, when Archie died..."

"No, this is different. You had him for so long. Wash and I were just..." Maggie stared at the ceiling. "I can't believe he's..."

"Well, you'll learn to accept it," Aunt Mag said emphatically. "You have your schooling, and that Mrs. Burchart and Dr. Adams will help you. Wash was their friend, too." She stood and straightened her apron. "His brother said he'd be back day after tomorrow, said he had something to give you."

Jeff Pridgen arrived a little after suppertime. He sat with Maggie in the parlor, wearing his heavy leather jacket. The heady smell of the old stained leather reminded her of Wash on the train, wearing his uncle's coat. "We buried him yesterday, over behind the house in the family plot. I still can't believe it. He never knew what hit him, Miss Maggie. I swear it was the most unlikely thing to happen to Wash. I don't know what made him go off by himself like that. He never did like to hunt and he sure as hell didn't know much about guns."

Maggie sat in her mother's old rocker beside the stove. She didn't look up when he laid a small green velvet jewelry bag on her lap. "My brother and I want you to have this. It was Ma's. Wash was going to give it to you at Christmas, for your engagement."

Maggie hesitated, then picked up the little velvet bag and held it in her hands, smoothing it as she might a tiny kitten. It was Christmas Eve, and she had dressed in the dark green taffeta dress Aunt Mag had sent to her for the Wake Forest Christmas dance. She had pinned her long red hair up on the sides, and tied the rest at the nape of her neck with a matching bow. "I can't take something of your mother's."

"Samuel and me want you to have it. You see, Wash was different from us. When Papa didn't come home from the War, Mama lost interest in everything. Me and Samuel were mad 'cause Papa had to go off and leave us, but Wash, he never made no trouble for Mama. He looked just like her, too. Me and Sam are big old strappin' fellas like Pa was. Wash, he was lean and lanky, more like Mama. Smart as a whip, too. He used to sit by Mama's bed before she died and read his schoolbooks to her. She loved that."

Maggie had expected a ring of some sort, but instead, the bag held a large creamy cameo set in gold filigree. "It's beautiful, but surely someone in your family wants it."

"No. We want you to have it, Miss Maggie. He worshiped the ground you walked on."

She fingered the cameo, thinking of Mrs. Pullen, wondering if the cameo might be a source of strength. "I'd be pleased to have it. I'm thankful to have something Wash intended to give me. All I have are his letters. I'm much obliged to you and your family."

— — —

When Maggie told her pa that she wasn't going back to school for the spring semester, G.W. said it would make things easier for him. He needed her help and he didn't make any bones about it. Aunt Mag was a different story. On New Year's Eve, Maggie got up early to help with breakfast. Aunt Mag was at her best in the morning, fresh after a good night's sleep. Maggie knew this news was going to rile her, and it did.

"No, I won't hear of it. You're upset, but the best thing in the world for you would be to get yourself back up there on the next train. You've already made your way, folks have taken to you—bent over backwards to help you. Staying here can't bring Wash back or make Mary Ellen well again."

"I'll go back, Aunt Mag. I just can't right now. They expect so much of me. Wash kept me going, made me think I could do it. Without him...I don't know. I just don't think I could stand it. I would die every Sunday when he didn't get off that train."

"Maggie, darlin', I know how you must feel, but wouldn't it be better to go on with your life?" Aunt Mag got up from the chair and began preparing a sick tray for Ellen Corbinn. Her back was turned, and Maggie marveled at how trim she was at her age without a corset. "You know, this comes to all of us women at some time or another. We're called upon to look after others. You'd best not waste your youth."

Maggie went to her, put her arms around her. "I love you, Aunt Mag, but I've got to do what feels right for me. I just can't go back now. I want to be here near Wash's grave for a little while. Mary Ellen needs me, too. I'll go to her, it will help me more to do for others. I won't be wasting time."

"Your mama needs you, too, but she's not holding you back, not as long as I'm around." She dabbed at the corners of her eyes with her crisp white apron. Maggie had seldom seen her cry.

"I know, and she's your sister, like Mary Ellen's mine."

After she'd heard the news of Wash's death, Maggie dreaded seeing her mother. Since she'd come home for Christmas, she'd done everything in her power to cheer her mother up, but now she couldn't hold back her tears. Finally, towards the end of the week, she felt composed enough to sit by her mother's bedside.

"Maggie, don't let this ruin you," Ellen said. "A boy I loved once drowned in the Cape Fear River, but I got over it. And if I hadn't, I might not have married your pa." She was propped up in her bed with half a dozen feather pillows. Nine children had put her there, Maggie thought, but Ellen would be the last one to complain.

Growing up, Maggie couldn't remember the big house ever being straight and pretty all at one time. The house had smelled different then, like old books, kerosene, and boys. Once, Maggie had asked her, "Mama, don't you want a pretty house like Aunt Mag's?"

"Not me, Maggie Lorena. If I had a pretty house, I wouldn't have time for my children. I'd be polishing and shining all the time. No, not me! Your Aunt Mag can have all the fine china and silk lamp shades she wants, but me, I'd rather have my children."

Ellen sat up in her bed and swung her feet over the side. Her ankles were black and blue and her feet swollen to twice their normal size. "Look here now, Maggie Lorena, I may be laid up in bed, but I know what I'm talking about. I don't want you pining away the rest of your life and missing out on chances to marry some nice man like...well, like Cyrus Devane."

Maggie thought she was beginning to sound like Aunt Mag. "I know, Mama, but Wash and I had so many plans. I don't know how I can go on without him."

"Oh, pshaw, girl. You'll go on. There're other fish in the sea. You better go on over there to Burgaw now. It'll help you forget."

——

Abigail Adams had written first to send her condolences, then again to beg Maggie to come back to school in the fall. She had joked that Maggie could join the "old widows club" of which she and her mother were the founders.

We want you here with us, Maggie. Mother misses you and Wash so very much. Won't you at least come back even if Wash cannot? You can live here, with us. You know you were more than just one of my students. You became a part of our family. Please come back.

Maggie had wondered at times if they were really fond of her, or if it had just seemed that way to her because she needed them, just as Ella had needed her. Poor little Ella. She had begged Maggie to come back, too, offering to come down on the train to be with her. But Maggie had told Ella that the only thing she could do to help her through this was to get her trunk to the station and put it on the train.

Chapter 7

It was cold but sunny on New Year's Day when G.W. drove Maggie the thirty-three miles to Burgaw. The old wagon road was a narrow sandy strip through Colly Swamp, carved out by use and time. Along the higher ground, live oak trees and vines grew so thickly that a man could get lost if he wasn't careful. In the low places, wide boards made a firmer surface for horses and wagons, placed there over the years by natives and newcomers intent on crossing the swamp come hell or high water. Closer to the river, nubby cypress knees peeked out from the murky water, surrounded overhead by moss-draped trees reaching to the sky for light. As they crossed the bridge over Black River, Maggie leaned over the side of the buggy and stared into the dark water. From the bank, something broke the surface without a sound, sending ripples spreading towards her. She imagined his face there, reflected in the water. Leaning further forward, she fixed her gaze on the glassy surface. But all she saw reflected was the bright blue shawl that had been her Christmas present.

George stopped the buggy at the end of the bridge. "I need to step over there into the woods a minute, Maggie. Are you all right?"

She straightened her shoulders and put her hand on his knee. He had been especially kind since Jeff had brought the news of Wash's death. "I'm all right, Papa. I'll get down and stretch my legs, too." She walked along the rough plank bridge until she came to the place where she thought she had seen his face. The passing river rippled around the cypress knees in wavy rings. She lifted her long skirt, placed the toe of one foot on a crossbrace, and sat on the rail. The pilings trembled ever so slightly against the current. Once again, she envisioned his likeness in the dappled water. *Oh, Wash, I miss you so.*

G.W. strolled out of the woods and called to her. "Get down from there, Maggie Lorena. I'm not about to go after you in that cold water. C'mon now, Mary Ellen is expecting us. It's almost dinnertime."

The Devanes had a fine home in Burgaw, only a block over from Main Street where Cyrus ran a farm supply and dry goods store. G.W. tied his horse to a rail in the side yard and helped Maggie unload her satchels. Cyrus Devane strode out onto the front porch, his three children pushing past him to get to their grandfather. With his white hair and lined face, Cyrus looked almost as old as G.W., but he was taller and more muscular, carrying himself like a young man. "It's about time y'all got here. These young'uns have been worrying the daylights out of us wanting to know when Grandpa's coming." Cyrus picked up Maggie's bags and watched his children tugging at their grandfather's pockets. "You'd think they'd never seen candy before, wouldn't you?"

"I thought that's what grandpas were for, to spoil children," Maggie said, laughing.

"Maggie, honey, I'm so glad you're here," Cyrus said, giving her a big hug. "Y'all come on in. Mary Ellen's sitting up in the kitchen waiting for you."

Maggie had expected the worst. Still, she was unprepared for Mary Ellen's gaunt face. Her sister sat in a kitchen chair near the stove. She reached out for Maggie. "Maggie Lorena, you've come at last," she said. Maggie kneeled beside the chair, hugging her, feeling every bone in her body through her loose gown, but Mary Ellen pushed her away, holding her at arms' length. Her bony fingers were cold and hard as those of an old woman, and her breath came in short gasps. "Let me look at you, little sister," she said. "I declare, you're a sight for sore eyes!"

Maggie was determined to hold back her tears. Her lovely sister had lost her creamy complexion and the sprinkle of freckles across her nose; her eyes, which had once sparkled like cut glass, were phlegmy and sunken in.

"We missed you at Christmas, Mary Ellen. It just didn't seem right without you and the children there." Maggie tried to smile, but the smile would not steady itself and she felt tears coming instead.

Mary Ellen began to cough, trying to speak. "I wanted to come. Lord knows I did, but I am so weak. It was easier on Cyrus for me to stay right here with Nellie."

Maggie turned to the old colored woman who had been with Cyrus's family since the days of slavery. "Hey, Nellie," she said. Nellie lowered her eyes and shook her head behind Mary Ellen's back.

"Nellie's a big help," Mary Ellen said, a cough racking her whole body. When she finally got her breath, she spit bloody mucus into a blue enameled pan, laid her head back against the chair, closed her eyes and whispered, "I heard about Wash and I am so sorry for you."

Maggie wiped her eyes with a handkerchief. "Don't, Mary Ellen. Don't say anything. I still can't bear to talk about it."

Nellie put her hand on Maggie's shoulder. "I's sorry too, Miss Maggie, but we'uns is glad you're here. She been needin' some of her kinfolk 'round. Nuthin' like kinfolk when you is sick and she sho is sick."

There was little that anyone, even kinfolk, could do for Mary Ellen. She grew weaker by the day and the cough brought up more and more of the thick red mucus. Her flesh hung from her bones, and her skin was flour-white except for the patches of red on her cheeks. Dr. Bayard brought a new cough syrup loaded with morphine, made up by a pharmacist in Wilmington. "It will help her sleep if nothing else," he said.

Maggie spent most of her time in Mary Ellen's room, leaving the care of the children and the house to Nellie. Occasionally she would go into the parlor to play the piano, opening the door to Mary Ellen's room so she could hear the hymns she had always loved. "I'm surprised that you aren't studying music, Maggie," she said. "I always thought that's what you would do."

"There wasn't time, Mary Ellen. I had my preparatory classes, and I got into doing the play. I had to give up teaching my piano student."

"Maybe next..." Mary Ellen closed her eyes, the sentence finished in the recesses of her mind. There was no telling what exactly went on in Mary Ellen's head in those morphine-induced days. With Maggie by her side, reading or writing, Mary Ellen's eyes would suddenly pop open and she would come out with something so remote that Maggie had to search for the meaning behind it. "Papa said I had to sit there until every last morsel..."

"What, sister?

"It was corn, always corn."

"You didn't like corn, did you?"

"Ernest did...always ate my corn."

"I thought it was Baby that always ate your corn."

"Ummm."

But there were also days when she was clear as a bell. At those times, Maggie pretended that the consumption was just a sickness that would wear off. When Mary Ellen was up to it, Maggie would read to her. They both loved Shakespeare, so the first thing Maggie read was *Twelfth Night*. "I wish I could have seen you in the play, Maggie," Mary Ellen said. "Tell me, what happened to your eye? Do you think it was brought on by your nerves?"

Maggie touched her hand to her glasses. "Dr. Norwood doesn't know for sure." She slipped the glasses off. "Does it look funny to you? I mean, do I look cock-eyed?"

Mary Ellen pulled herself up on her elbows and studied Maggie's eyes, first one and then the other. "Yes, you do. It looks as if you're looking sideways out of your left eye."

"Oh, what should I do? Wash said I should see an eye doctor in Wilmington."

"It would be better than wearing that dark glass."

"Well, the dark glass will have to do for now. Getting you well is the most important thing. Besides, I can read just fine."

Mary Ellen smiled and closed her eyes. "'*She walks in beauty, like the night, of cloudless climes and starry skies; and all that's best of dark and bright meet in her aspect and her eyes.'"*

"*Hebrew Melodies,*" Maggie said, tearfully.

"You know it, too?"

"Wash read it to me. He loved Byron."

Mary Ellen opened her eyes and sat up in bed again. "Maggie, if I die, you must have my Byron. Get it for me. It's on the bureau. I want to write something to you."

"Mary Ellen, you're not going to die."

"I know, but if I did, would you stay with Cyrus for awhile?" She propped herself up and looked about the room. It was full of ornately carved furniture—an oversized bed, a marble-top wash stand, a bureau, a dresser and two eight-foot wardrobes. Overhead, a gas chandelier burned softly. "He will be so lonely," she said.

In the low light, Maggie looked at her sister with tears in her eyes. "Mary Ellen, I could never take your place. I wouldn't want to."

"But you could, Maggie. You could have this house. You could have our children to love you."

"No, Mary Ellen. I won't make promises I can't keep."

———

With Mary Ellen on her deathbed, there was little time for Maggie to think of anything else. When she did allow herself to think of Wash, her memories seemed dreamlike—far away and so long ago. Her days at BFU—Abigail Adams and Mrs. Burchart, Mr. Pullen and the Fayetteville Street Baptist Church—were part of that time, that life that she had lost when she lost him. What if she went back? What would it be like without Wash? Could she ever meet anyone to take his place?

———

Mary Ellen died in Maggie's arms at the end of May, two months before her twenty-ninth birthday. That night, they knew her time was near, and Cyrus had gone to get some rest in one of the children's rooms. The house was quiet except for Mary Ellen's short regular gasps. She was fevered and had lost consciousness early in the day. Dr. Bayard said her chest was full of fluid, and Maggie had vowed to stay by her bed despite Cyrus's and Nellie's pleas that she ought to get some rest. She had rolled an old feather mattress into a bolster and propped Mary Ellen up to a sitting position to help her breathe, but her efforts were futile; nothing seemed to relieve Mary Ellen's struggle.

Maggie sat by her bed holding her hand, watching Mary Ellen's chest heave up and down—uh-huh, uh-huh, uh-huh, uh-huh—sounding for all the world like the rusty hand pump out by the back step. The sounds went on all night without a break in the rhythm. At daybreak they slowed, becoming further and further apart. At first, Maggie thought Mary Ellen was easing off and she closed her eyes. Then she realized that her sister was quiet and peaceful for the first time in months.

Before she went for Cyrus, Maggie held her dead sister until the heat from Mary Ellen's fevered body left on the cool night air. She thought of Wash, dead these past five months, cold in his grave. No one had held or comforted him in his hour of death, but he had not suffered as Mary Ellen had. Wash never knew what happened.

At dawn, the room filled with light far brighter than the sunrise. Maggie closed her eyes. Wash would be there waiting for Mary Ellen. She could almost see his face.

———

Aunt Mag didn't want to miss Mary Ellen's funeral, but she didn't want to leave Ellen either. Lizzie had volunteered to stay with her, but Ellen was all to pieces and Mag knew that she should be there to comfort her. G.W. wanted to have his oldest daughter buried in Bethany Cemetery, but Cyrus said Burgaw was where she had lived and gone to church and it was only fitting that she be buried in his family plot.

At the gravesite, Preacher Mizelle launched into a rambling prayer that had everyone shifting from foot to foot. Maggie and Katie stood beside each other, their arms locked together. "Why can't the preacher just get it over with," Katie whispered. "I feel sick to my stomach."

Maggie held a handkerchief up to cover her mouth. "Did you notice how the undertaker painted her up? I was embarrassed. Mary

Ellen never wore a touch of makeup."

Katie sniffed and took a deep breath. "She didn't have to, she was so beautiful. I want to remember her as she used to be before she got sick."

Once Mary Ellen's casket was buried, some of the solemnity lifted and people began to mill about while they waited for the ladies of the church to prepare lunch under the trees. Maggie recognized some of them who had come by to see Mary Ellen along the last. She saw G.W. introducing Cyrus to a heavy-set man. "Who is that over there beside Papa?" she asked Katie. "He must not live around here if Cyrus doesn't know him."

"Where? Oh, I don't know, a war buddy, I think. A lot of people are here just because Pa's a county commissioner. I don't know half of them."

G.W. approached Maggie with the stranger in tow. Maggie figured it was some well-wisher she didn't care a thing about. *Oh Pa, just let me be!*

"Maggie, honey, this is Bill Ryan from Onslow County. Remember me telling you about him, how we stayed together right through the War?"

"I'm pleased to meet you, Mr. Ryan. Pa's told us a lot of stories about the War."

Bill Ryan tipped his hat. "To be sure, Miss Maggie Lorena. I was down in Wilmington and heard of Miss Mary Ellen's passing." He tipped his hat again and made a little bow. "I'm powerful sorry about your sister."

"I sure am glad you came, Bill. I can't tell you how much it means to me," G.W. said.

"How long has it been since you two have seen each other?"

"I expect it's been ten or twelve years, wouldn't you say, G.W.? I missed the 18th's reunion."

"Yep, something like that. Say, Bill, Maggie is a schoolteacher. She's been up there in Raleigh this past year learning about it, but she knows more than most teachers already. I don't reckon you'd be looking for a schoolteacher over there in Onslow County?"

Maggie was shocked. "Pa. What in the world?"

G.W. shuffled his feet in the sand. "Well, I was just wondering since Mary Ellen is gone and all."

Maggie studied her father. What was he thinking? He sounded rehearsed, like he had already discussed it with Bill Ryan. The two of them were all smiles. What were they up to?

"Why, as a matter of fact, we do," Bill Ryan said. "You reckon you might be interested in coming over that way and teaching school?"

"I don't think so, Mr. Ryan. I've been contemplating finishing up my college work at BFU." She glanced at G.W. "You see, the State has a new law about schoolteachers. I need to get my certification before I can teach again."

"Law, if you were to say you'd come, I know somebody who would probably fix it so we could make you an exception. We haven't had a schoolteacher in Stump Sound Township in more than two years. We're desperate," he said. When Maggie didn't respond, he added, "You'd be given your room and board, that's for sure."

Maggie was caught off-guard. During the long days nursing Mary Ellen, she hadn't been able to think of what would come next in her life. It was almost summer and she just wanted to rest. "I'll think about it, Mr. Ryan. I've got so much on me right now."

"Yes'm, I understand that," he said, smiling. Something about him reminded her of Jeff Pridgen.

"I reckon you'd want someone right away."

"Why, yes'm, as soon as you could decide. The schoolhouse has been empty for a couple of years and I don't know what all a teacher will be needing. Soon as you're able, my son Tate could come over to fetch you."

"I can't think straight right now, Mr. Bill. I might do something I'd regret later. I'll study over it and let you know."

Part 2

Onslow County
September 1907

Chapter 8

In late July, Maggie sent Bill Ryan a letter saying that she had decided to accept his offer to teach school in Stump Sound Township. In the weeks following Mary Ellen's death, she had pitched in with all the chores at home, tending to her mother and helping Aunt Mag put up butterbeans, corn, and tomatoes. She knew she was wasting time, time that she should be spending in college, but she couldn't bring herself to go back. Mrs. Burchart had written that the housemother had returned when Maggie did not and Ella had moved into the dormitory. There would be no 'paid' tuition now and she couldn't bear the thought of starting over. Nothing would be the same, especially without Wash.

Bill Ryan had been pretty sure that Maggie Lorena Corbinn would come. He could just tell by the way her face had brightened up when he told her that he was chairman of the school committee in Stump Sound Township charged with finding a new teacher to run the one-room schoolhouse. To subsidize the small pay, he offered her the fringe benefit of living with his family.

G.W. said she'd been mighty melancholy since her beau got killed. When her sister died, he was afraid Miss Maggie Lorena was going to go all to pieces. That or become an old maid. And Bill had told G.W. about looking for a new teacher. Well, two old soldiers could put two and two together, couldn't they? Miss Maggie didn't jump on it right away, but G.W. said give her a little time. He thought a job teaching school was just what she needed.

G.W. had looked mighty poorly at the funeral, thin as a rail and yellow as jasmine, but he'd perked right up when he saw the chance to get his daughter straightened out. And just by chance, Bill thought he might have found a wife for his youngest son, Tate.

"Wait'll you see her, son. You'll be wishing you were back in school yourself. Of course, if she comes, you'll see right smart of her because she'll be staying here at the house with us," Bill said. Tate was the only boy left at home. His brother James had been married for more than ten years, and only two of his five sisters, Hannah and Annalee, were still in the nest.

Folks said Tate was the spitting image of his father, with his large nose and thick eyebrows. Both were heavy-set, big-boned men with sloping shoulders and large stomachs that held their pants up without much assistance from their suspenders. But their likeness ran deeper than looks. Tate could put his finger on what his pa was thinking at any given moment because most likely Tate was thinking the same thing. This time, he was pretty sure that Pa thought he had found him a wife.

"How come she's not married already, Pa? Is she hard-favored?"

"No, no. She's pretty as a picture, son. G.W. did say that she had a fellow that got killed hunting over in Lyon Swamp last Christmas. Stepped in a bear trap his brothers had set, dropped his gun and blew his own head clean off."

Tate winced, picturing himself in the dark swampy woods that surrounded his home. He understood the importance of knowing where your bear traps were. "What in the world was he doing out traipsing around in the woods if he didn't know where the traps were?"

"Oh, he'd been off to college and lost touch with things around home. Went out for a little sport and *wham!* Blew his fool head off."

"That don't say much for book learning, does it, Pa?"

"Now, don't go putting education down, son. You've had enough that you can read and write, but if I could've afforded it, I would have sent you up to Raleigh to the agricultural school."

"College is for rich folks like Reece Evans. And it didn't do much more for him than just make him more uppity than he already was," Tate said with contempt.

"I declare, I don't know what you've got against Reece Evans. You used to play together when you were little. Did he ever try and harm you?"

"No sir."

"Well, what is it then?"

"He just thinks he's better than most folks around here because his grandaddy sent him to college."

"You would have gone, too, if your grandpa had had as much money as Silas Evans did."

"What would you have done if I had gone off to school and left you here with just Mama and the girls to help you on the farm?"

Bill rubbed the stubble of his beard. "I don't think I could've made it, son."

Tate reached over and put his hand on his father's shoulder. "It don't make no difference, Pa. I never wanted to go off to college."

At supper the evening before he was to go fetch Maggie, Bill Ryan developed an acute spell of rheumatism. "You'll have to go, Tate," he said. "My knees are all swollen up. Why, I can't hardly walk." He pushed his chair out from under the kitchen table and limped over to the kitchen sink where his wife, Sally Catherine, was washing dishes, slipping his plate into the sudsy water.

"Look at that, Mama. He was out there greasing the buggy wheels a minute ago."

Sally Catherine dried her hands on her apron and watched Bill limp to the back door. "I declare, sweetness, your rheumatism comes on you all of a sudden, don't it?" She smiled, looking at Tate over her spectacles.

"Come on out here to the barn, Tate. I need to talk to you," Bill said.

Tate followed his pa out to the barn, intent on giving him a hard time. "Why do you want me to go? I don't even know her."

"You will before you get back. I've got the buggy greased and Daniel is just itching to get out on the road a little. I want to make a good impression on Miss Maggie—get her over here in style so as she'll stay awhile."

"You know I've never been over to Bladen County. Never even laid eyes on Capt'n Corbinn, even though I feel like I know him from all you've said. Maybe if we wait a few days, you could go?" Tate remembered the last teacher. She had been an old-maid with a pinched-up face and chalky complexion. He hoped his pa was using better judgement this time.

"No, I don't think we should wait, son. You won't have any trouble finding it. It's just over there on the other side of Pender County." Bill pointed west. "You take the old road by the Shaw place, on across Shaken Creek. You'll see old man Ephraim Ezzels's big two-story house. Watch out for his dogs. If he doesn't have them penned up, they'll try and tear Daniel's legs off. Just before you get to Rocky Point, you'll cross the Northeast Cape Fear where ol' Josh Hart runs the ferry. He's drunk about half the time, but he's a good ol' fella." Bill lowered his voice. "We were in the War together, too. You be sure and tell him who you are."

"I will. How much further is it after that?"

"Oh, another few miles or so. I can't quite remember. Just follow the road until you come to Still Bluff—that's at Black River. After you cross over there, you're pretty near the Corbinn place. It's in the Canetuck community right near the county line. Ask somebody for directions. If I know G.W., he'll be on the lookout for you."

The sun was barely up when Tate hitched the black leather buggy to Daniel's harness, adjusting the bit and bridle, tightening down the worn straps to the belly band. He whistled while he rubbed the top vigorously with a cloth and wiped down the side curtains, removing every speck of dust. Tate was over six feet tall and had little trouble reaching the breadth and width of the buggy top with his long arms. He inspected the wheels, getting down on his knees to look for any axle grease that might get on the new teacher's clothes.

Dusting off an old piece of broken mirror that he kept propped up on a ledge in the barn, Tate surveyed his face, feeling for a clean shave. Hannah had trimmed his dark brown hair close to his neck and combed a little Vaseline through it to make it smooth and shiny. She said he was a nice-looking fellow, and he ought to look his best just in case Miss Maggie turned out to be pretty.

Tate left home just before sunrise, taking the old logging road across the vast lowlands of Onslow County. Yes, he intended to make a good impression on the new teacher. If everything Pa said was true, he just might want to marry her. Getting married was something he had come to look forward to in the last year or so. Sometimes he felt like he just couldn't stand it if he didn't. Maybe this was going to be his chance.

They traveled at a good clip along the sandy roads. Daniel was fresh, and the buggy's thin steel-rimmed wheels spun at top speed. At this rate, he could easily do the fifty miles in good light if the ferries didn't hold him up.

"Whoa, Daniel!" Tate pulled on the reins, slowing the horse as they approached a low spot in the road. Heavy rain had washed a deep gully out of the sand. Edging the buggy around the gully, he was thankful that he hadn't had to get out and muddy his boots. There were long stretches of road where planks had been laid to make it easier for loggers to get back and forth to the river, but the roads hadn't been kept up by the county in the last few years.

The ferries were about all that remained of the naval stores industry that had brought Grandpa Ryan to Onslow County. A great fire had swept through the woods a few years back, burning away the livelihoods of many of the turpentine farmers and leaving nothing but the charred skeletons of the giant trees as far as you could see. A new crop of pines struggled to push its way up through a tangle of wild grapes and scrub oaks, but it would be years before turpentine or lumber was harvested again.

About ten miles from home, the road turned south and followed the Northeast Cape Fear River until it came to the crossing near Rocky

Point. Tate looked over the remains of an old turpentine still at the edge of the river. A big two-story shed where the boilers had been and another smaller shed where wood was still stacked looked empty and forlorn. Rusted hoops and broken-up barrels marked the spot where the cooper's shed had stood, gone now except for a hitching rail standing strong as ever. When Tate was a boy, his grandpa had brought him to the still with a wagon load of rosin that had been boxed out of the huge longleaf pines. Back then, it seemed to Tate that the world was covered in pine trees.

He stopped the horse just short of the river and relieved himself. Long branches dipped into the water, providing water moccasins a safe place to sun. Mosquitoes and gnats swarmed around his head, singing in his ears. He scrambled for the clearing and caught sight of a run-down camp on the other side. Looking up, he saw an old rusted bell mounted on a tall wooden pole. A roughly painted sign read *Hart's Ferry*. He pulled the rope to signal the ferry. The loud clang of the bell hurt his ears, and Daniel reared his head, prancing in protest.

Upriver, he saw the ferryman jump onto the ferry and begin steering downstream with a long pole, letting the current bring him across to the other side. Tate walked about looking at the old distillery. There wasn't much left of it now, but the warm morning sun lifted the smell of turpentine out of the boards.

As the ferry moved in close to the pier, a craggy old man with wild gray hair and a long beard threw Tate a rope line. "Morning, Mr. Hart!" Tate shouted.

"Morning, son. Gimme a hand there and I'll pull her on up alongside the dock." Tate grabbed the rope and tied it to a tall piling, watching Josh Hart swing the raft around to join up with the dock. "Where you headed? I ain't seen you around here before." He studied Tate's starched shirt and looked the buggy over. "You look kinda like you might be going courtin' in that buggy and all." Tate blushed and Josh let out a big laugh. When he jumped onto the dock, a wooden stump on his left leg made a hollow sound on the weathered boards.

"I'm going after a new teacher and bringing her back over to Onslow County. Miss Maggie Lorena Corbinn is her name. She's one of Capt'n Corbinn's daughters, over in Colly. Maybe you know the Capt'n."

"I sure do, son. Every one of them Corbinn girls is as purty as pictures. If you're looking for a wife, you couldn't go wrong there! Say, your daddy wouldn't be ole Bill Ryan, would he? I sure see some resemblance."

"Yes sir, I'm Tate Ryan. My pa said you would remember him."

"I sure as hell do, son." Josh backed up to a piling and scratched his back against the rough post. "Me and him joined up together with the Onslow Grays. I'll never forget your daddy. I didn't have no rifle, never even fired one. He says to me, *somebody better do you a favor, Josh Hart, and teach you how to fire a rifle before you get kilt!* And he did it, right then and there, before we ever got our gear and all." The old man studied Tate. "You sure do look like your daddy. I saw him go by a month or so ago on a barge. Looked like he was taking some hogs down to Wilmington. I figured he got on upriver."

"Yessir. Somebody in Wilmington told him about Miss Maggie's sister Mary Ellen dying of consumption. Pa stopped by on the way back to pay his respects."

"Lord, I reckon he did. Him and me and the Capt'n met up there in Virginia. We was all under General Lee. They called it the Northern Army of Virginia, but they oughta called it the Army of North Carolina 'cause there was more of us than anybody else up there. You tell him old Josh Hart sends his regards."

Josh shoved off from the dock and began singing an old marching song that Tate had heard his pa sing all his life. He glanced at Josh's leg. It was missing just below the knee. Pa's brother, Uncle Mike, had lost an arm at Petersburg and Bill Ryan had been wounded twice, once in the shoulder and once in the arm. Both came back able to take up farming again though. To hear Pa tell it, they were lucky to have come back at all. Grandpa Ryan had almost died of the fever while his sons were away fighting in the War, but he had held on to their legacy and lived to be ninety-one. The elder William Ryan had been one of the first settlers in the lowland piney forests. Like many others, he came looking for a piece of land to box turpentine and got a hundred acres at a time through land grants that the government was offering to help bring families into the vacant backwoods of eastern North Carolina.

"Your pa used to run the turpentine still, didn't he, Mr. Josh?"

"Yep. That was when we was in New Hanover County, but when they divided the county up, we ended up in Pender County. I seen the day when Pa would send twenty or thirty floaters a week downriver, all of 'em loaded with oak barrels full of turpentine and tar. The cooper had a shed right over yonder." Josh pointed a trembling finger towards the pile of weathered boards. "Fast as he could build 'em, Pa filled 'em up. He got every bit of his money back on them floater logs when they got to Wilmington. 'Course, that's why we ain't got no pine trees left. What didn't get eat up with bugs or burned got cut down for floaters."

Josh poled the raft steadily against the river current while Tate held Daniel reined in close to his shoulder. He brushed the horse's nose with his hand. Daniel was jittery, flipping his tail at the biting flies that left black drops of blood on his shanks. A hot late August sun sparkled on the water, but the breeze was cool. Tate could smell fish frying.

"The missus caught a whopping catfish this morning. I reckon there's more than enough for you if you could set down a minute, Tate."

"I'm much obliged, Mr. Josh, but Ma packed me some victuals and Capt'n Corbinn will likely be expecting me for supper."

"Don't count on it, son. You know a bird in the hand is worth two in the bush." The old soldier cackled and steered the raft towards the muddy landing beside a wooden shack. "Come on and speak to the missus, anyhow. She'll give you a drink of fresh water."

Tate waited outside the shack for Josh, who soon returned with a toothless old woman with matted gray hair hanging loose about her shoulders. Pa had told him about Josh Hart's missus. She was a half-breed, cast out by her own tribe, and Josh had taken her in after the

War.

She smiled at Tate. "Maybe you'll set a spell on your way back."

"Thank you, ma'am, but I expect we'll be in a pretty big hurry to get on home before nightfall."

The next crossing was at Still Bluff on Black River, a bustling little river town with a saloon and several stores. Of the two rivers, the Northeast Cape Fear was wider, but the Black was a little deeper and had always seen the most riverboat travel.

Tate found a public ferry down near the boat yard. An old man who looked as if he could have been Josh Hart's brother was propped up against a coil of rope, his legs stretched out on the deck. He wore a faded blue coverall, fringed from wear at the bottoms of the sleeves and legs. Tate could barely see his eyes beneath the wide-brimmed straw hat that shaded his face and neck.

"Can you direct me to Capt'n G.W. Corbinn's place?" Tate asked.

The man stood up, removed his hat and squinted at the sun. "I reckon I could, but first you're gonna have to cross the river," he said without a trace of humor.

"I was planning on that, but I figure there's not much use getting to the other side if I don't know where I'm going." Tate was trying his best to be pleasant, but the man was glaring at him, not budging an inch.

The ferryman crossed his arms and cocked his head. "Where you from? Does the Capt'n know you?"

Tate bristled. "I reckon he knows my pa. He's the one sent me to fetch Miss Maggie Lorena Corbinn to teach school in Onslow County."

The old man wiped sweat from his head and neck with a soiled bandanna. He pointed across the river. "See that creek? That's Moreland's Creek. Follow the road alongside it until you come to an old deserted cabin. Cross over the creek there and that road will take you straight to the Capt'n's house over yonder in Canetuck."

"I'm much obliged," Tate said, watching him sit down on the deck as if he wasn't planning on going anywhere soon. "How long before we leave?"

"Well, I reckon as soon as you give me ten cents," the ferryman said, holding out his hand. Tate dug into his pocket for the coins Bill Ryan had given him that morning, thinking it would be a bargain to be on his way again.

————

Relieved to be on dry land, Daniel picked up a trot on the well-worn road, following the creek through dense thickets of sweet gum and bay myrtle. Overhead, a canopy of cypress and oaks kept the road cool and dark. In his sweat-dampened clothes, Tate was chilled and felt the eyes of a thousand critters on him. He checked his rifle when a large rattlesnake slithered across the trail, but Daniel slowed and pranced sideways, giving the serpent time to cross ahead of them.

The scent of a polecat nearly stifled him, and he worried that he'd carry the musty odor on his clothes. He had bathed at the pump before light that morning, and Mama had lathered up his face with sweet soap and shaved him by the stove in the kitchen. She had starched and ironed a white muslin shirt and laid out a clean pair of rough-dried trousers. They weren't Sunday-go-to-meeting clothes, but they were clean and he sure didn't want to go into Capt'n Corbinn's house smelling like a polecat.

As he passed the deserted cabin and crossed the creek, he wondered what had happened to the people who had lived there. The cabin wasn't burned out or anything, just empty. Across the creek, the ground rose a little and he came out of the woods between two fields of drying corn. Just as he was beginning to wonder how much further he had to go, he saw a rider coming down the dirt road, hell-bent-for-leather, kicking up a cloud of dust behind him. The rider was a long-bearded old man wearing a black suit and a gray calvary hat. Tate was sure it was Capt'n Corbinn.

"Whoa! Whoa, Geronimo! Is that you, Tate Ryan?" he shouted.

"Yes, sir. Capt'n Corbinn?"

"Where in the hell you been? I was afraid you were lost. Your pa has the worst sense of direction of any man I know. I'm surprised he found his way home after the War," G.W. laughed. He got down off his horse. "I'm pleased to meet you, son."

Tate gripped the old artillery man's bony fingers. Pa had said G.W. didn't look well and Tate agreed. His clothes hung loosely on him, and his complexion was sallow against his long white hair and beard. "I'm pleased to meet you, Capt'n Corbinn. I thought I made pretty good time, crossing the rivers and all."

"I'm sure you did, son. Maggie Lorena, she was just getting anxious and worrying the daylights out of me, so I decided to ride down the road a piece to see where you were. Let's get on home before she comes after us." He reined the horse around. "You in the mood for a race?"

"No, sir, Capt'n, my horse is about tuckered out."

"Well, this here is Geronimo, named after my old calvary horse that they took from me when I was captured. Ol' Geronimo had the most sense of any horse you've ever seen," he said, slapping his knee. "Hated the sight of blue, he did. Chances are he threw every damn Yankee that tried to get on his back after they hauled me off to Fort Delaware." He pulled out a plug of tobacco from his pocket and tore off a chew. "You chaw tobacco?"

"No, sir. I mean, I never have."

"Well, here you go," he said, tossing the plug to Tate. "This here is tobacco country. You ain't a man around here unless you chaw tobacco."

Tate bit off a chunk of the pressed tobacco and held it in his jaw. Hot saliva welled up in his mouth and ran through his teeth. "I appreciate you meeting me like this, Capt'n," he said, feeling the brown juice oozing out of the corners of his mouth.

"No trouble, son, no trouble a'tall. I'm anxious to get Maggie Lorena on over there to Onslow County where she can get back to teaching. That girl is a born teacher. I tell you, Tate, she sure needs something to lift her spirits. If your pa hadn't come along with this offer, there's no telling what state her mind would be in."

"Pa was doing us all a favor. We sure do need a schoolteacher."

"Come on, then, let's get on down the road. You sure you don't want to race?"

Tate remembered the tales his pa had told about the wild young lieutenant, about how he liked to whoop and holler. "No, sir, Capt'n. Daniel ain't used to traveling all day like this. I reckon I'd better not put him through a race. You go on though. I'll catch up with you at the house."

"You're sure now?"

"Yes sir. I'll be right behind you."

"Geronimo here is right wound up. It'll be good to give him another run," he said, making a long loop with the rein. Tate wondered if G.W. might really be referring to himself. The old soldier tipped his hat to Tate, dug in his heels and lashed the horse on his left flank. "Gid'up, Geronimo. Get your ass home!"

Tate waited for the first dust to settle before giving Daniel the signal to follow. He set him on a steady trot and watched for the lane where G.W. had turned. When he arrived at the gate, G.W. was sitting on the fence waiting. "What took you so long, son? I thought I was gonna have to go back and look for you." Tate smiled and G.W. let out a loud guffaw that set him to coughing violently. When he recovered, he wiped his eyes with a handkerchief and led Tate along the lane towards the house.

Chapter 9

Maggie and Aunt Mag were on the porch, shelling crowder peas, when they saw Tate and G.W. ambling towards the house. "It looks like G.W. found your Tate Ryan, Maggie Lorena." Aunt Mag grinned devilishly. She had been teasing Maggie all day about going off with Bill Ryan's son.

"Begging your pardon, Aunt Mag, he's not *my* Tate Ryan. Besides, I'm right on the verge of changing my mind about going," Maggie retorted.

"What in the world are you saying, missy? He didn't have to come all the way over here to get you. You'd better be nice to him now, or your pa'll take you out behind the shed with a hickory stick."

The thought amused Maggie, as she knew her aunt had intended. "Well, let's just see what he's like. If I don't like him, I probably won't want to live with his folks for a whole school year." She stood and smoothed her dress as the two men approached the porch. Wash had been on her mind all morning. It was Wash she should be going off with now. No one could ever replace Wash.

"I found him," G.W. called out. He mounted the steps two at a time with Tate following closely behind. "This here's Mr. Tate Ryan. Tate, this is my wife's sister, Mag, and my daughter, Maggie Lorena."

"Evenin', Miss Mag. Evenin', Miss Maggie Lorena," Tate said, tipping his hat. Maggie reached to take Tate's hand, smoothing back a stray curl with her other hand. She was wearing a blue muslin skirt and a loose gingham blouse that she had made from an old dress of Mary Ellen's. It had been a long time since she had taken any pains at dressing, but pride had made her put on the corset that trimmed her figure. As a child she had been skinny as a rail, but at twenty-five, her full figure was greatly enhanced by corsetting.

"I'm pleased to meet you, Tate. I'm much obliged to you for coming to fetch me," she said, letting her hand slide out of his and fall back to her side. He was taller than she had expected, with large brown eyes that crinkled at the corners when he smiled. She could see G.W. watching her.

"Well, sir," Aunt Mag said, "you are the spitting image of your daddy. I met him at G.W.'s wedding. He's a fine gentleman. Maggie Lorena is real lucky to have this opportunity to teach school over there in Onslow and stay with your family. How many brothers and sisters have you got living at home?"

"Hold on, Mag, give the man a chance to get off his feet before you start asking him questions," G.W. said. "Here, Tate, pull up a chair."

"Just me and two of my sisters are all that's left at home, Miss Mag." He struggled to keep the wad of tobacco in his jaw and spat over the porch rail.

Maggie excused herself and returned with glasses of water for Tate and G.W. "How long did it take you to get here?" She was dreading the long drive in the buggy the next day.

"I left at sun-up. Made pretty good time until I got to Still Bluff."

"I suppose you met that ornery cuss Jep Squires at the ferry," G.W. said.

"Yes sir, I reckon that's who he was. What ails him anyway?"

"Oh, he's just an old river rat. He don't mean no harm. His ma and pa drowned in the river when he was ten years old and he's been mad at the world ever since."

Aunt Mag stood, smoothed her apron, and combined the peas that she and Maggie had been shelling when the men arrived. "I reckon someone better get these peas on and start supper."

"I'll take the shells to the hog lot," Maggie said.

"No, your pa can do that when he goes to feed the horses. You show Tate around to the pump and let him wash up. See if he can help you catch that old hen and I'll make some salad for your trip tomorrow. G.W., bring me that mess of roastin' ears you left on the wagon."

"There she goes, giving orders. I thought I was through taking orders when I got out of the army." He threw up his hands in mock disgust and stomped off to the barn.

———

Maggie stood nearby while Tate washed under the pump. He held the handle and pumped with one hand and splashed the water over his face and head with the other. When he had finished, she held a towel out to him.

"Thank you, Miss Maggie. I'm much obliged." He looked at her so intently that she blushed before she had a chance to gather her wits. She'd thought about the long ride over to Onslow County, wondering if she'd feel uncomfortable with a young man who might have courting on his mind. Pa had said Tate wasn't married that he knew of. But courting didn't interest her in the least bit right now. Not so soon after losing Wash.

"I need to get that hen for Aunt Mag. You can help if you like," Maggie said. She had put a long apron on over her dress and slipped into a pair of dusty shoes, wondering why in the world Aunt Mag had waited so late to think about stewing a hen for salad the next day. But knowing her aunt, she supposed it had to do with her liking Tate. Aunt Mag believed in the old saying that the way to a man's heart was through his stomach.

Tate hesitated a moment. "I can help."

Maggie started towards the unsuspecting hen. "Get over there and close her in." The agitated chicken dodged and darted, trying to find an outlet in the circle they danced around her. "Grab her, Tate." He lunged to grab the frightened bird and missed, but Maggie quickly cornered the hen, snatching her up and anchoring the bundle of sharp claws and flapping wings under one arm. She grabbed the hen by the neck with the other hand and twirled her round and round until her neck broke. Stuffing the hen under her arm, Maggie walked quickly across the yard to the dark-stained chopping block. She lifted the axe a few inches above it and whacked off the hen's head with one blow.

Tate looked as if he was going to be sick to his stomach, and Maggie was incredulous. "My stars, haven't you ever killed a chicken before?"

The headless chicken seemed to come to life again, flopping from side to side, end over headless end, slinging long stripes of blood across the sand. It came to rest a few feet from Tate. "No'm, and I don't intend to." He turned away.

"It's just an old chicken, Tate."

"I know, but I don't think I'll ever get used to it. I'd rather shoot a sow in the head at hog killing. There's just something about a chicken that runs around in the yard."

Aunt Mag called out from the kitchen door, "Have you got that chicken ready, Maggie Lorena?"

Tate avoided looking at the headless chicken, its bright yellow legs and feet still clawing at the air. "I 'spect I'd better go find your pa and see about my horse," he said.

Maggie carried the chicken into the kitchen, where she poured boiling water over it in the sink and began to pluck out the feathers by the handful. "If that don't beat all. He's peculiar about killing chickens!"

"Now, don't be criticizing him for that. Your Uncle Archie never killed a chicken in his life and I doubt that Wash Pridgen did either."

Maggie frowned, turning to look at her aunt, who was kneading dough for biscuits. "Please don't talk about Wash. I still can't bear it."

Aunt Mag cleaned the sticky dough from her hands and wrapped her arms about Maggie. "I'm sorry, honey. It's time you put Wash Pridgen aside. He's gone and there's nothing we can do about it. Tate Ryan is here and now. You might start thinking about that."

"Tate didn't come here to court me. His pa just sent him to bring me back to Onslow County."

"Rightly so, but something else might come of it if you're willing to give it a chance."

Maggie pulled away and resumed plucking the chicken. "Humph! I'd rather marry a man who could afford to buy me chickens from a butcher shop, if he didn't have the stomach to kill one." She lit a rag torch and singed the remaining hairy feathers. "I hate to smell burnt chicken feathers," she said, holding her nose with one hand and fanning the bird with the other. "I'll bet Mrs. Pullen never did this." She made a face and tossed the chicken into the sink.

Aunt Mag rinsed the chicken with water and ripped it open with a large knife. "Is that what you're thinking, Maggie? If so, you should have gone on back up to Raleigh like I told you."

"I can't go back yet, Aunt Mag. It's just too soon." She wiped her eyes on the hem of her apron and touched her aunt's arm. "But I will go back. I promise."

"Don't mind me, Maggie. I don't care if you marry a doctor, lawyer or Indian chief, I just want you to be happy. You're the only one who knows what that is." She reached inside the chicken, pulled out the warm slick intestines, and set them aside in a small enameled pan. "After you take these outside to those perish-gutted cats, you better go set a spell with your mama. She's going to miss you when you're gone."

———

Maggie eased into her mother's room, hesitant to disturb her. Ellen Corbinn was propped up against the headboard of the large bed where she had conceived her nine children. Maggie never looked at the bed without thinking about that. "Mama, I was afraid you were asleep."

"No, honey, come on in. I've been waiting for you. Aunt Marybelle sent me some magazines up from Wilmington and I was just going through them one more time so you could take them with you." Ellen's gray hair was pulled back from her face and tied with a white satin ribbon. Her hair had been red once, the color of Maggie's. A scattering of freckles still dotted her sallow complexion. She was only fifty-eight years old, but having so many children had taken its toll on her, and she had been practically bedridden since she started with the change.

"I'm going to miss you, Mama." Maggie sat on the bed across from her mother. "Aunt Mag thinks you're some better. Are you?"

"I don't know, honey. I never knew I could grieve so. Mary Ellen's death has set me back." Tears filled her eyes and she removed her glasses to wipe them. "But I want you to go on over there to Onslow and show them what a good teacher you are. Mag will take care of me."

"I will, but I couldn't go if she wasn't here. I wouldn't leave you." She felt a sudden twinge of guilt—she really did want to go, wanted to be someone else, somewhere else, other than the only daughter still living at home. Leaning across the pillows, she kissed her mother.

"What's he like?" Ellen asked.

"Who? Oh, Tate. He's all right, but don't you go getting any ideas. I'm not ready to think about anyone else just yet."

With tears in her eyes, Ellen reached for her daughter's hand. "Don't let the sight of me in this bed ruin you, Maggie Lorena. I'd much rather be here than be a lonely old woman like Mag."

"Aunt Mag's not lonely."

"Mag's the loneliest woman in the world, honey. No children, no family much except mine. She could have married any one of the boys who came back from the War, but she met up with that carpetbagger Archie MacFayden, and him not man enough to give her children to keep her company in her old age."

"Mama, don't say that. Aunt Mag loved Archie. They wanted children. It...it just didn't happen."

Aunt Mag appeared at the door, followed by Tate. "Tate Ryan wants to meet you, Ellen. Look at him, isn't he the spitting image of his pa?"

Ellen pulled herself up in bed and straightened her shawl. "Well, I declare, he sure is. Come on over here and let an old woman enjoy the sight of you."

"Evenin', Miss Ellen. Pa sent his respects to you. Said he hoped you'd be up to visiting him and Ma one of these days."

"Well, I just might do that, son. The Captain and I have talked about it. Maybe now that Maggie's going to be over there in Onslow County, we'll come for that visit. Umhmmm," she nodded, glancing briefly at Maggie with approval.

"That's why Dr. Bayard wants you to wear that truss, so you can do things again," Aunt Mag said. "Why, I just might go myself."

After supper that night, Maggie lit a kerosene lamp and showed Tate the way to the spare room off the kitchen. It had been intended for a cook to live in, but Ellen hadn't liked the idea of someone else being in charge of her kitchen and had done most of the cooking herself. Instead, it had been used as a birthing room for all of her children. Maggie had been allowed in the room when Baby was born. She had watched Mama push and scream, push and scream, vowing then to Mary Ellen that she'd never have any children. Mary Ellen said Maggie'd change her mind when she found out about boys. Well, she reckoned she'd found out about boys to a certain extent, but she still wondered how one could justify the other.

Maggie set the lamp on the table beside the bed and the reflection off the ceiling lit the room. She walked around the foot of the bed and rested her hand on the iron frame. "I was born in this bed. So were all my brothers and sisters."

Tate tested the mattress with his hand. "Looks like it's no worse for wear."

"It ought to give you a good night's sleep. I expect you're worn out after that long ride in the buggy today."

"Just a little bit." He looked over at the two rocking chairs that sat on either side of a small table. "But if you'd like to set a spell, we could talk some more."

Maggie sat down in one of the chairs and Tate joined her. "You ought to thank me for rescuing you before Pa started in on his war stories. You'd never get to bed."

"My pa never told us much about the War," Tate said.

Maggie laughed. "We can't stop mine. I'm afraid he still holds some hard feelings about it."

"A lot of our people are still fighting the War, Maggie, but I don't see no need of fighting over something that wasn't right in the first place. My folks never owned slaves anyhow."

Maggie leaned against the dresser. "My grandpa had twenty-five Negro slaves. He paid good money for them and he treated them fair. When it came time to give them their freedom, he was glad to be rid of the burden. It didn't make much difference one way or the other, he still had to look after them." She sighed.

Tate was quiet, watching her. She paused as if expecting him to say something, but he felt struck dumb by the lamplight on her face. "We'd best stop this jawing, Tate. I expect you'd like to get started pretty early in the morning."

"Yes'm, Pa'll be expecting us before dark. He sure is excited about having a new schoolteacher. To tell you the truth, I am, too."

"Why are you excited, Tate? Are you planning on coming to school?" she teased.

He looked her straight in the eye. "No'm. I just meant it would be mighty pleasant having you in Onslow County."

Chapter 10

Tate lay awake long into the night. Sleeping in the big feather bed in the room where Maggie said she'd been born made him feel close to her. Damn, she was pretty! Mr. Josh had been right about that. She was good-hearted, too, seeing to it that everybody at the table had more than their share to eat before she sat down herself. Wringing that hen's neck as if it was no matter at all got to him, but he supposed she was just used to it. His ma and sisters took care of that chore, and he never intended to have to do it himself.

The next morning, Tate washed his face in the basin of water that Maggie had placed on the dresser. Brushing his hair with his fingers, he wished he had brought a toilet kit and a fresh shirt. When he stepped into the kitchen, Maggie was standing at the stove frying meat, wearing a muslin apron over a dark blue dress. She had left her hair loose to fall across her shoulders.

"Good morning, Tate," she said. "Did you sleep well?"

He wanted to act as if having breakfast with her was an ordinary thing, but his feet felt glued to the floor. He stood in the doorway a minute longer than he intended. "G'morning, Miss Maggie," he said, walking to the sink. He looked out the kitchen window, trying to settle down. "I slept like a log, thank you."

She stopped what she was doing. "Did you, now? Well, I reckon that old feather mattress does have some good in it. You want some coffee?"

"Don't mind if I do," Tate said. "I'll get it." He brushed by her on his way to the stove. She was taking fat pieces of dough, shaping them into balls, then squashing them down with the tops of her fingers. When he had poured his coffee, he stood beside the table, watching her work.

"I'll have a pan of biscuits ready shortly," she said. "Pa and my brother Jasper have already eaten. Jasper has his own place down the road, but he helps Pa out almost every day."

Tate took a large gulp of the hot coffee. "Good coffee," he said, watching her hands pat out the biscuits.

Maggie looked up. "Didn't you ever see anyone make biscuits before?"

"Yes'm, I've seen Mama make biscuits lots of times. I've just never seen you make biscuits." He grinned at her before putting on his hat. "I'd best go out and pay my respects to your pa. T'wouldn't do to go taking his daughter off without saying goodbye."

——

When Tate got back from the barn, Maggie put a large plate of fried eggs, fatback, hominy and tomatoes before him on the table. "While you eat your breakfast, I'll finish getting my things together," she said, hanging her apron behind the door.

His breakfast finished, Tate rinsed his plate in the sink and looked out the window to see Maggie washing out the slop jars and hanging them against the smokehouse. She stopped now and then to speak to the cats or shoo the chickens. When she reached up to tighten a pin in her hair, he saw the round full shape of her breasts under the dress and felt a thrill of longing run through him.

She saw him at the window and called out, "I'll be right there, Tate, soon as I change my shoes and tell Mama goodbye."

Tate hadn't counted on feeling this way about Maggie so soon. Sure, he had figured he might court her if she wasn't hard-favored or anything, but already he was aching to touch her, to have her. He adjusted his suspenders and tucked in his shirt. Yes, he would court her right and proper, back home in Onslow after she got settled in.

When Maggie appeared on the porch with her hat and her satchel, it was all he could do not to sweep her off her feet and tell her his intentions. He was saved by Aunt Mag, who followed close behind Maggie. "Miss Ellen said to tell you goodbye, Tate. She's sending a basket of pears to your folks. Maggie and I picked them yesterday over at the old Croom place. Your ma can make a mess of pear preserves, if she likes."

"Mama'll be mighty obliged," Tate said. "Capt'n Corbinn's already put a bushel of his late corn in the back."

Maggie hugged Aunt Mag and G.W. "I'll write to you soon as I can. You'll take good care of Mama, won't you, Aunt Mag?"

"Don't you worry a minute about that, Maggie Lorena. My dear sister will never want for a thing as long as I'm here." She leaned close to give Maggie a hug and whispered in her ear, "You behave yourself, missy."

Maggie laughed and climbed into the buggy seat beside Tate. She looked over her shoulder. "Where's my trunk?"

"Oh, your pa put that in first thing," Tate said. "It's right there, behind the seat. He said you wouldn't go nowhere without your trunk."

He was right about that, Maggie thought.

With the added weight of Maggie's paraphernalia, Daniel's hooves dug deeply into the wet sandy soil. Overnight, rain had washed down the dust and turned the brush bright green. Like scattered pieces of a mirror, puddles in the road reflected different views of the mottled green forest and blue sky. Tate felt new, dressed up, starting out on a journey with unknown adventures waiting ahead. He began to whistle. Overhead the live oaks dripped on the buggy top, making little tapping sounds as if to accompany him.

"I'm not good company, am I?" Maggie asked.

Tate looked at her, startled. "Sure you are. What makes you say that?"

"Pa says a man whistles to keep himself company."

"That's all right. I know you've got some thoughts in your head. It's not every day you leave your folks and go off with a man." He looked at the road ahead and grinned.

"Along here is where we come to gather holly at Christmas," she said, gazing out into the thick forest on either side of the road. "In the spring, I come here just to see the yellow jasmine."

Tate looked at the large bunches of green vines wrapped around every dead tree and stump. "It's hard to tell the difference between jasmine and honeysuckle when the flowers are gone, but honeysuckle will sure take over if you let it." He steered Daniel around a deep mudhole and flicked the reins, urging the horse to pick up a little trot. His arm touched Maggie's as the buggy shifted and bounced along on the sandy road. Loosening his collar button, he thought that being alone this long with a woman was almost like courting. He could smell a sweet fragrance drifting from her. It was lilac, like the toilet water that Hannah and Annalee loved to splash on themselves after a bath. He wondered if Maggie bathed by the stove as they did.

The road wound out of the woods and into an open area with fields of drying cornstalks on either side. "That's Uncle Johnny's cornfield," Maggie said. "He's Pa's oldest brother."

Tate leaned forward and peered around the buggy top. "Looks like he had a good crop."

"Uncle Johnny always has a good crop. Of course, Pa says he ought to, Grandpa Corbinn gave him the best bottom land."

"Looks like he's made the most of it too," Tate said.

"All of Grandpa's land was good," Maggie said. "Pa's had a hard time since the War, but he was always a little envious of Uncle Johnny."

"How come?"

"Oh, I don't know. Everyone calls Uncle Johnny a 'sport.' You know, he likes to ride the riverboat and he has lady friends. But he's dead serious about farming."

"The Capt'n seems pretty serious too. He said he was growing tobacco now."

"Yes he is. He's been able to make a little profit on tobacco."

"I don't know much about tobacco. They've been giving out seed at the Farmers' Alliance meetings the last two or three years. I hear they've been growing it up around Richlands and over yonder at some of those big plantations along the New River, but my pa hasn't tried it yet."

As they neared Black River, the woods grew thicker and the sound of the rain-swollen river grew louder. "I love the river," Maggie said. "Listen to it. The river's what brought my Corbinn ancestors here. They came up the Cape Fear and settled around Canetuck. Mama's people, the Morelands, came up the Black River and settled over around Colly Swamp. Back then it was mostly swamp between the rivers, but the settlers cleared it and dug canals to drain off the rich bottom land. Grandpa used to tell me stories about all the wild animals and snakes they killed."

"Well, I can't say my folks have been in Onslow County that long," Tate said, "but my great-great-grandpa came over from Ireland way back. He settled near Kenansville. Grandpa went over to Stump Sound Township and staked out a claim on some vacant land that the government was giving away. He boxed turpentine, but you can't make a living off turpentine anymore."

At the river, Tate jumped down from the buggy, rang the bell for the ferry, and stepped around to the other side to help Maggie. Catching her under her arms, he lifted her to the ground, holding her a moment longer than he should have. When she looked up at him, he pulled away, taken aback by his own boldness. He shuffled his feet, put his hands in his pockets and began to whistle again as he walked towards the water. *I almost kissed her,* he thought, taking a deep breath and wishing in a way that he had.

Maggie followed him along a narrow path that ran along the river's edge. He pretended to look for arrowheads, but he was so keenly aware of her presence behind him that he was afraid that he wouldn't see one if it jumped out at him. In the small cove where they walked, the water was still. Something splashed into the water and moved among the bald cypress knees. Tate held out his hand for Maggie to wait. "Look, it's a beaver," he whispered. They watched the tiny head and eyes dart along the surface of the water for a few minutes, then dive underneath a pile of sticks.

"You don't see too many of those," Maggie said. "Trappers used to come up here right regularly. Papa says you can hardly even find a coon anymore." She had removed her glasses and sunlight danced in her red hair as she looked up at him with a hand held up to shade her eyes. Tate realized he was staring, and started to walk along the bank. He had only gone a little ways when he saw what he'd been looking for and stopped to pick it up.

"What is it?" Maggie asked.

"An arrowhead. Look, it has a cross scratched into it." Tate held it out in his palm for her to see. She came and stood by him, examining the arrowhead closely. "Here, you can have it," he said.

"Why, thank you very much. It'll be a fine keepsake." She put her arms around him and hugged him as she might have one of her brothers. But Tate put his arms around her too, and held her snugly against his large chest. Maggie struggled free, looking upset. "Listen Tate, I need to tell you something," she said with tears in her eyes. "Maybe you already know. I loved someone very much. He was all the world to me. He got killed last Christmas, and I will never get over it. Never, not ever. I just want you to know that."

Tears were running down her cheeks and Tate reached for her again. She didn't resist. "It's all right," he said. "Don't cry." His cheek was against her hair, and he smelled the lilac again. "C'mon now, I hear the ferry."

Chapter II

Across the Northeast Cape Fear, the road turned north, skirting the edge of what looked like miles and miles of marshland. G.W. had told Maggie that southeastern Onslow County was dismal country, full of swamps and pocosins. Every now and then a crane lifted up out of the dense brush, wings flapping and long legs trailing behind, seeking a tall pine for a sentry post. Some day it would probably all be ditched and drained like the Corbinn land in Bladen County. Maggie wondered where the birds would go then.

As the hot afternoon sun beat down on the black buggy top, the earthy smell of the oiled leather made Tate think of his grandfather. Every Sunday, the old man dressed up in his meeting clothes and hitched up the buggy for church. After services, he offered one of his grandchildren a chance to go for a ride. It was always a wild, reckless ride over the rough sandy roads, and each child clamored to be the one to go. Grandpa was partial to Tate, making his rides a little longer and sometimes a little wilder. One Sunday the buggy overturned, throwing the old man and the boy onto the soft pine forest floor and the horse into an early grave. After that, Mama wouldn't let him ride with Grandpa anymore.

Maggie dozed, leaning her head against the side of the canopy. Perspiration glistened on her forehead, holding little coils of red hair captive against her face. He could feel the warmth of her leg almost touching his, her elbow nudging him as the buggy jogged along the sandy ridge. She had removed her glasses and now held them loosely in her hands. One glass was shaded. Pa hadn't mentioned it, but Tate thought she might be blind in one eye. *I could make her forget that fellow that blew his fool head off,* he thought. *I've sure got more sense than that!*

Maggie's eyes flew open. "What?" Straightening up, she stared at Tate. "Oh, I'm sorry. I was dreaming about...oh, never mind." Adjusting her skirts, she slipped her heel underneath the seat, feeling for the trunk. "Where's my trunk?"

"It slid back into the boot when we got off the ferry. It's there, I promise."

"Are you sure? Did you fasten it with a rope?"

"I sure did. It's not going anywhere except to Onslow County. Matter of fact, we're almost home. I expect Ma'll have some pretty good victuals cooked up. I can almost smell her cooking and we're still a mile away." He grinned and lifted his nose to the air, taking in a long breath.

Maggie wrinkled her nose. "Smells more like horse to me."

Tate laughed, wanting to reach over and hug her. Maggie laughed too, and for the first time, he felt that she was warming to him.

Looking out across the scrubby landscape, Maggie tried to find something interesting to comment on. The ground was higher now, and small pine trees struggled to come up through the blackened soil left by the last fire. "Looks like huckleberries over yonder. They take over first thing after land is burned off."

"There's plenty of them all right. Mama puts some up every year. I sure do love huckleberry pie," he said, smacking his lips.

"I'll help your mama with the cooking. I make a pretty good pie."

"No sirree. You're not going to be doing any cooking. Mama says you'll be just like a regular boarder. If I know Ma, she'll be waiting on you hand and foot."

"I'm used to doing my part."

"You'll have enough to do getting the schoolhouse ready and all. I'll help if you'll let me."

Maggie smiled and laid her hand on his arm. "I'm counting on it."

The Ryan homeplace was set in a grove of tall pines at the end of a lane. It was long and low, built of huge pine logs instead of cypress siding like most of the homes around Colly. A porch ran along the front, and two tall chimneys flanked either end. The late afternoon sun was reflected in windows with bright curtains showing through the glass. Beside the house, someone was taking down clothes from the line.

Bill Ryan ran out to meet them when Tate pulled into the yard. "I was afraid it'd be dark before y'all got here." He offered his hand, helping Maggie down from the buggy. "Evenin', Miss Maggie. I declare, it's so good to see you in Onslow County." Maggie could see the strong resemblance between father and son, the older one no less handsome than the younger.

Bill smiled and put his hand on Tate's shoulder. "I hope my boy here took good care of you crossing the rivers."

"He certainly did, Mr. Bill. I'm much obliged to you both."

"Here, let me help you with that trunk, son."

"I see your rheumatism has eased up, Pa."

Bill laughed. "Oh, pshaw, a man can't let rheumatism decide what he can and can't do when there's work to be done."

Maggie looked out across the yard, taking in the log house and tall pines. "You sure do have a nice place, Mr. Bill."

"Thank you very much. I built it myself, long before Tate here was born. When me and Miss Sally Catherine got married, Pa gave me a hundred acres of land and said to make the most of it. I built the cabin first, cut all the timber myself. Tate will be doing the same thing before long."

They stepped up onto the porch. "Well, it looks to be a lot more than a cabin now," Maggie said.

"Yes'm. When we started having young'uns, it wasn't long before we outgrew it." He reached out and patted the stout walls. "I added the sheds on either side and a kitchen out back—put the roof up high enough for a room for the girls and added this here porch." He reached for her satchel. "But don't let me keep you here jawing. Come on in."

Bill led the way into the sparsely-furnished sitting room. A maroon horsehair couch and several chairs were grouped around the large Acme stove that sat on a tin pallet at one end of the room. A long flue, supported by wire, made its way over to a hole in the outside wall.

"You have a seat right here, Miss Maggie, while Tate gets his mama and I go see about the horse and unhitch the buggy."

Tate left through what appeared to be a long hall leading out to a back porch. Maggie stood in the front doorway, looking out over the yard. There were several apple trees on one side and a fenced patch of sweet potatoes on the other. Bits of color dotted the yard, which had been swept clean with a brush broom. Cosmos and dusty miller grew beside the porch steps, and on either side of the walk, big iron kettles spilled over with purple verbena.

"Mama, this here is Maggie Lorena," Tate said, leading a stout little woman into the room.

Sally Catherine Ryan waddled towards Maggie with her arms outstretched. "Maggie Lorena, come here, child, and let me give you a hug. Bill has done nothing but talk about you since he met you at the funeral."

Tate's mother smelled like Aunt Mag's kitchen on a warm evening when chicken was frying and a grape-hull cake was cooling on the shelf. "I'm pleased to meet you, Miss Sally Catherine. I'm much obliged to you and Mr. Bill for the teaching position."

"Well, now, we're much obliged to you, too. None of my girls have been one bit interested in teaching school," she said, reaching up to tighten the pins in the small knot of gray hair at the back of her head. "They haven't had near enough schooling themselves. But we're going to change all that, aren't we?" She squeezed Maggie's hands.

"I hope I can help, Miss Sally. Do you know how many pupils I'll have?"

"Law me, I have no idea, but Bill will know. Let's see, there's Tate's sisters, Annalee and Hannah, the Bannerman boys—that's five, the Gurganuses—that's seven." She closed her eyes as if trying to picture the faces of all the neighbors' children. Thick wire-rimmed glasses pressed deep into the sides of her temples.

"I was just curious," Maggie said. "Two or twenty, it won't make much difference."

"Well, come along and let me show you your room while Tate gets your belongings. I've got supper on the stove and I know you must be perished."

"I hope I'm not putting anyone out. I don't need much more than a bed. I'll be gone most of the day."

"No need to worry about that, honey." She opened the door to a small bedroom. "This was Mama and Papa Ryan's room before they died. When they got too old to live alone, we added this room on so they could come and stay with us. Papa Ryan passed first," she said, lowering her voice respectfully, "and Mama, she just died this year."

"I'm sorry to hear that, Miss Sally."

"That's Tate's room across the hall. The girls sleep up the stairs. Bill and me, we're on the other side of the house, so you won't be bothering us any." She shuffled over to the dresser, where she poured Maggie a glass of water from a tall pitcher. "I just pumped this a little while ago. It's still cool," she said, filling the glass and handing it to Maggie. "You rest up a little before supper. There's a tin basin for water and a thunder pot under the bed."

Maggie was unable to suppress a smile. "Well, I never heard it called that before, Miss Sally."

"You'll probably hear a lot of things over here in Onslow County that you've never heard before. Let's just hope you don't get your ears burned," Sally Catherine said. Her laughter followed her down the the long hall.

Hanging her dresses on wooden pegs that had been driven into the pine log walls, Maggie was reminded of the tobacco barns at home. She ran her palm along the smooth yellow pine. She had seen Pa and her brothers chink the cracks with wet clay that the colored folk brought from the banks of the canal. These walls were chinked with a white powdery substance that looked like chalk, and the logs had been polished smooth as silk. There was no sign of daylight showing through either as there had been in the tobacco barns.

The house was a far cry from Aunt Mag's, or even the big old board house that she had grown up in, but she liked the close warmth of the yellow logs and the smell of wood in her room. These four walls would be her home now, and she figured on spending a lot of time in here.

There was a light tap on the door. "Miss Maggie, it's Hannah. May I come in?"

Maggie opened the door to Tate's sixteen-year-old sister, a plump young girl with dark brown hair and a pleasing face. "Come in, Hannah. I was just putting away some of my things."

"I came to call you to supper. We sure are glad to have you here."

"Why, thank you. What grade are you in?"

"I'm supposed to be in the tenth grade this year. I've passed everything, but last year we only had school for three months because the teacher dropped out when she had her baby. The superintendent, Mr. Thompson, came all the way over here from Jacksonville to finish out the year with us."

"Well, I reckon I'll be meeting Mr. Thompson sometime soon," Maggie said. "I'm looking forward to you and your sister helping me get off to a good start. Which one of you is the oldest?"

"I am. Annalee will be in directly." Hannah bent forward to look into a small mirror that Maggie had hung on a peg in the wall. "Do you think my hair looks good in braids? Annalee said if she was as old as me she'd wear her hair piled on top, but Mama won't let me."

"It looks nice to me, Hannah. There's plenty of years ahead to wear your hair piled on top."

———

At supper that evening, Bill Ryan told one tale after another. Maggie knew that the family must have heard them all many times, but she was a new audience and the stories were his way of entertaining her. They sat at a long table in the kitchen with benches on either side.

Sally Catherine and Bill sat in straight chairs at either end.

Annalee offered to recite her multiplication tables for Maggie. "I won the spelling bee all but two times last year," she boasted.

"Well, you might not even need a teacher, Annalee."

"Yes'm, I do. I think Mr. Thompson was a preacher more than a teacher, because he made us read the Bible instead of our literature books." Annalee scrunched up her face.

"It didn't hurt you one bit to read the Bible, Annalee," her mother said.

Tate tried to turn the conversation to something he knew about. "Say, Pa, I found an arrowhead along Black River today and gave it to Maggie. Tell her about the time you found some Indians camped over there by the river."

"Law me," Maggie said, "your pa'll be plain out of stories before I've been here one evening. I'll help Miss Sally with the dishes and then I'll turn in."

Sally Catherine pushed her chair back from the table. "You'll do no such thing, Maggie. These girls will do the dishes. You better go on to bed, and I'm going to do the same."

"I'd like to take a look at the schoolhouse tomorrow, if someone could show me the way."

"I'll be needing Tate in the field tomorrow, Miss Maggie, but I intend to take you over to the schoolhouse myself," Bill said. "Hannah and Annalee are going to come help you get straightened out. I put the word out at church the last few Sundays that school would be starting just as soon as you get settled. All but the heathen will come running when they hear that old school bell." He chuckled to himself on the way to the sink with his plate.

Chapter 12

Maggie fell sound asleep within minutes of putting her head on the pillow. She awoke to the sound of a rooster crowing and voices coming from the kitchen. Had they had all risen before her? She wondered what time it was as she quickly dressed for breakfast. There'd been a large hall clock at Aunt Mag's, and at Mama and Papa's house as well. She missed the sound of the chimes.

Maggie found Miss Sally Catherine alone in the kitchen. The smell of woodsmoke and coffee lingered heavily in the air, although the back door was standing open. A reddish-brown chicken pecked at something on the porch, edging closer and closer to the door.

"Goodness, I think I overslept," Maggie said, going to warm herself by the stove.

"Well, good morning, Maggie. I was letting you sleep as long as you liked." Sally Catherine gave Maggie a little hug and offered her a chair at the table. She was wearing a green print dress that came within inches of the floor and the same type of flat sturdy black shoes that Ellen had worn around the house. The sound of Sally Catherine's feet shuffling about on the sandy wooden floor reminded Maggie of a time when her mother had been able to make breakfast. Those were the first sounds she'd heard in the morning from her room above the kitchen.

"I can't remember when I've slept in so late. I'm embarrassed."

"Well, don't be," Sally Catherine said, bringing a plate of biscuits and a cup of coffee to the table. "I'll fry you some eggs."

"I'm not going to have you waiting on me like this. Here, you sit down and I'll get my own breakfast."

"Oh, go on with you, girl. These old bones don't know anything other than cooking and taking care of my family. Now, you—you're the new schoolteacher. That's something I can't do." Sally's eyes twinkled and Maggie saw in her expression the spirit that had likely kept her going even in hard times. It was the same spirit that she'd often seen in her mother.

"Oh, you probably could. I think mothers are the best teachers in the world."

"Nope. Now, if it was quilting, I could teach you my Saw Tooth Star pattern, or maybe Tree of Paradise. That one's on your bed," she said, putting a plate of eggs down in front of Maggie.

"I'd love that, Miss Sally. Mama used to quilt a lot, but Aunt Mag was more into making dresses and things to wear."

"Oh, I've made a dress or two myself, but quilting is my love. You'll have plenty of chances to learn. We have quilting parties right regularly in the winter. I'll put aside some scraps I think you'd like."

When Maggie had finished her plate, Sally washed it, wiped down the stove and counter, wrung the cloth out one last time, and carried the dishpan to the door where she threw it out for the chickens to peck at any small particles of food that remained. Out of breath, she sat down in a straight chair near Maggie.

"Miss Sally, I can't have you waiting on me like this. I insist, from now on I'll get my own breakfast." She stood and pushed her chair under the table.

"Well, we'll just see about that, honey. Can't have too many cooks in a kitchen at one time. You have your job to do and I have mine. We'll see." Sally Catherine had a way of finishing all her sentences with a little titter. Maggie couldn't imagine her ever being cross with anyone.

"You're mighty kind to me, Miss Sally. I guess I'd better get a move on before Mr. Bill finishes up his chores."

Sally Catherine patted Maggie's hand. "It's nice having you here already."

Maggie smoothed a cream-colored crocheted spread over the pieced quilt, remembering the fun she and her sisters had sorting through the scrap barrel and putting together quilt squares on long winter days. Sally Catherine's Tree of Paradise was done in red, white, and brown. It was one of the prettiest she had ever seen, stitched in green and white thread. Maggie knew the time it had taken to crosshatch the blocks and double chevrons in the border. It was one thing to piece together scraps, but top stitching was where the art came in. Ellen had been real particular about who she invited to come to her quilting parties. A careless stitcher could ruin a perfectly beautiful pattern.

The only furniture in Maggie's room besides the bed was a bedside table made from cypress sticks, a straight chair and a small pine desk. Opening her trunk at the foot of the white iron bedstead, Maggie carefully lifted out the wooden tray that held some of her most precious possessions. She picked up the letters from Wash and held them close to her heart. She had read them over and over, memorized every word. Life was so compelling to Wash, so urgent. He had so many plans, and she was a part of them. She loosened the drawstring on the velvet bag and rubbed her fingers over the cameo.

Abigail Adams's letters were written on blue lined tablet paper, the mark of a teacher; Mrs. Burchart's, on tissue-thin scented stationery. Both had begged her to come back. One day she might. Reaching deeper into the trunk, she pulled out a tan leather pouch with the initials C.S.A. burned into the leather. A slip of paper cautioned: *Private material. Not to be read or examined until after the death of George Washington Corbinn, Capt., CSA.*

G.W. had never even told Ellen about how Stonewall Jackson got killed in the War. It was a story he was ashamed of, but it was a part of history and he had dictated it to Maggie just before she went off to college. "I want to get the story straight, shug, because someday it's going to come out and I may be dead and gone."

"But everybody knows how Stonewall Jackson got killed, Papa."

"They know he got killed by his own men, Maggie Lorena, but

they don't know firsthand what happened. I oughta know. I was the one gave the order."

"*You* gave the order, Papa? You never said that before."

"General Hill told the 18th that we were never to talk about it, even among ourselves. It was an order. To this day, nobody has told me different."

For the next few weeks, they would go out under the trees after supper where G.W. would prop himself up, his hands behind his head. Maggie had her tablet and pencils, and she would write while he told her stories that led up to the battle at Chancellorsville. When he got to the part where General Jackson was killed, his voice trembled and tears flowed down his cheeks. "It was the last day of April, 1863. I'll never forget as long as I live. General Lee had made an advance that cut the Yanks in half, attacking Hooker's troops in a four-day battle that they say killed ten thousand of our boys and eleven thousand Yanks.

"Two days later, when the word came down that Hooker's reserves had arrived, our troops were still scattered all over hell's half-acre and nobody knew where the front line was. General Hill had told us to dig into a ravine and get ready for a fight."

"Where was General Jackson then, Papa?"

"He had taken about thirty men out reconnoitering. All of a sudden, we heard horses coming towards us, hell bent for leather! Someone fired a shot, but they kept on coming. We knew it was calvary, but in the darkness, we couldn't tell Blue from Gray. When they got about seventy-five yards in front of us, I yelled, *Commence firing!* We let go one round after the other until finally one of Stonewall's men broke through and said, *Cease your fire! You're shooting at your own men!* But it was too late; we had already killed or wounded about half of them."

G.W. was breathing heavily, sweat pouring off his forehead. He rubbed his neck and looked off into the distance, his eyes brimming with tears. "We were following General Jackson's own orders. He told us over and over again, *Nothing is in front of you but the enemy. Fire on anyone who approaches you from the front!* And there the General was, right in front of us and it blacker than hell out there."

Maggie had painstakingly typed the manuscript on the Olivetti and G.W. had asked her to read it back to him, over and over. Each time he had added new details. "I saw it was him when old Sorrel bolted and ran him under a low tree branch. It knocked a big gash in Stonewall's head and the blood was streaming down his face when he came towards us and fell to the ground. We all tried to help him. When I took my coat off and covered him up, he looked at me and said, *George, what happened?*"

"Oh, Papa. Did he die then?"

"No, Maggie, he didn't die. In fact, we never thought he would die. He took three shots, one in his right hand and two in his left shoulder. Hell, I recovered from a shot in the chest at Spotsylvania—lots of the men had taken worse bullets! But the General, he got pneumonia and died eight days later. It was the worst day of my life."

When Maggie had re-typed the manuscript for the third time, G.W. was satisfied that he had told the story to the best of his ability. "Maybe others will write it down, but I'm the one to tell it like it really was," he said. "It was me that give the order." Sadly, he slipped the manuscript into a leather pouch marked with his initials and C.S.A. "This pouch was given to me by the General himself when I got my commission. Now, put it in that trunk of yours, Maggie, and I don't want anyone to ever see it until after I'm gone."

She replaced the manuscript and picked up a tattered doll, all that remained of her childhood. She had shown it to Wash once and he had laughed and said she should begin to make dolls for their children. *Make them all in your likeness, and perhaps they will come true and I will have more of you to love.* The memory brought a smile, then the inevitable tears.

She replaced the doll and removed Mary Ellen's Byron, placing it on the bedside table. Unbundling the Olivetti typewriter, she slipped it from its case. She hadn't touched it since she left BFU, but she felt ready to write again. How often her thoughts raced along as if she were composing a story. There would be time for that now, time to figure things out and maybe write them down. She placed the typewriter on the small table and fell across the bed, stretching her arms behind her head. Today, she began a new chapter in her life.

Chapter 13

Bill Ryan hitched his horse and buggy to a rail outside the old schoolhouse and helped Maggie to the ground. A narrow path led them through rows of cotton that had been planted right up to the steps on either side of the school. Maggie had to lift her skirt and petticoat to keep them from catching on the rough stalks. Unlike the white-washed church building that Aunt Mag had used for a school, this one had never been painted and the dark boards seemed to draw the heat from the sun. Looking out from the top step, she could see a thicket of trees and brush in the distance.

Bill pushed the door open and held it for her. "Hold on a minute now, Miss Maggie, and we'll open up a window or two and get some air in here."

Even in the early morning the air was hot and stale, and Maggie imagined what the afternoons would be like with a room full of sweaty children. She walked ahead of Bill to the nearest window, holding her breath until she'd opened it. The room was in shambles. A potbellied stove was turned over on the floor, and ashes had settled over all the desks. Torn books lay scattered about the tin that covered the floor under the stove, stacks of books were piled haphazardly in a corner, and bird droppings covered a piano and the teacher's desk. Glancing up, Maggie saw where birds had found their way in through a broken window and roosted in the rafters.

"I know it looks like a cyclone hit it. I believe we've had some vagrants in here," Bill said, shaking his head. "I had no idea it looked this bad. The superintendent was coming by tomorrow or the next day to meet you."

"It sure is a mess. You might ask him to give us a few more days to get straightened out."

"I'm going over to Jacksonville to tell him as soon as I leave. He asked me to let him know when you got here because he had a lot of papers and books for you. But don't you worry about Mr. Thompson. He's one of the finest men I know. He's been superintendent since 1903, but this is the first year the county has been able to pay him full-time. Wait till you hear his plans for the new graded school on Harris Creek."

"A new school? You didn't tell me about that, Mr. Bill."

"Well, it's in the planning stages just now. We have to acquire the land and all."

Maggie looked around the room, calculating the work in store. A new school would have been a sight better to come to.

"Let me get on over to Jacksonville," Bill said. "Hannah and Annalee will be over here directly to help you soon as they finish up their chores." He walked around, surveying the room. "I went to school here myself. It was a fine school then, and it's gonna be again."

When he had gone, Maggie sat down in the teacher's chair and stared at the mess. She felt like crying. This was worse than she had thought it could be. She had imagined stacks of books waiting to be handed out and a big chalkboard with colored pictures pasted around the edges. No one had mentioned that there was cotton planted up to the door. Where would the children play? Reprimanding herself for sitting around and moping when there was work to be done, she threw open the remaining shutters. A bird dived out across the top of her head, brushing her hair and making her duck.

Through the window, she saw cotton in every direction. She walked through the cloakroom to the back door and saw a sandy path leading towards the copse of trees in the distance. Right now the thought of a shady stream at the end of a path appealed to her, but she knew it would be a distraction for truant boys who found their satisfaction in crawdads and doodlebugs instead of books.

The cloakroom had a small cot and a deep sink with a rusty pump at one end. Maggie made a mental note to bring a sheet and bedspread to cover the soiled mattress. She would need a pitcher and several glasses for the sink. Windows above a long row of coat hooks gave the room nice light. It was easy to imagine herself spending some quiet time alone here when the children were reading or studying.

Maggie retrieved a broom from the cloakroom and set out to knock down the cobwebs that hung in every corner. By the time she had gone around the room, her loose cotton wrapper was soaked with sweat and her apron smudged with ash. A mouse scampered under her feet and she shrieked and sat down on the piano stool, tucking her knees up under her arms. There was no telling what other varmints were in here. When she was sure that the mouse was nowhere in sight, she carefully raised the cover over the piano keys.

The last time she'd played the piano had been for Mary Ellen. Since then, she'd felt no desire to make music of any kind. It was time to begin again. Children loved to sing songs, and music would be a part of the curriculum. On the ivory keys, her hands looked as if they belonged to someone else. She stretched her fingers, retracted them, anxious to begin, but wondering if her touch would come back to her. Aunt Mag had taught her to play when Maggie was a child, admonishing her to never let a day go by without running through her scales. For years she had made it a habit to practice right after supper every evening, even when she was at BFU. She would have taken advanced piano after her preparatory classes were finished, if she had gone back.

The first notes out were harsh and tinnish. She forced her fingers to run through the scales, wondering how long it would be before a tuner came through. Finally she relaxed and began to hum and play... *Drink to me only with thine eyes and I will drink to thine.* Over and over, she tried the notes until she could add the chords and sing.

Something in the window over her shoulder caught her eye. She looked up, but saw nothing. Starting over, again she caught a glimpse of movement. This time, carefully watching from the corner of her eye, she began to play in earnest, as if she could lure whatever it was out into the open. Hearing footsteps, she hesitated. A man's voice came from behind her. "Don't let me disturb you, Miss Corbinn, I'd like to hear you play."

Maggie thought she should be frightened, but there was something easy and familiar in the voice. She turned slowly on the piano stool. A handsome dark-haired man stared back at her, a smug look on his face. He was sitting at one of the students' desks, dressed in a loose white muslin shirt. His light cotton britches were tucked into polished black calvary boots. "Oh, I'm sorry I startled you," he said, a smile spreading across his tanned face.

"Who are you?"

He crossed his legs, folded his hands and propped his elbows on the desk. "I'm just a neighbor, Miss Corbinn." His eyes were warm and pleasant, and a thick auburn mustache wiggled across his upper lip like a caterpillar when he spoke. "I heard your playing and singing, and I just wanted to sit here and think for one minute that you might be singing to me."

"Do I know you, Mr...?"

"No," he said. "I don't believe so." His cockiness was tinged with humor and she had to hold back a smile.

"Well, how did you know my name?"

"Oh, everybody's heard about the new schoolteacher from Bladen County. Captain Corbinn's daughter, I believe?" His eyes were teasing her, looking her up and down. "And she's every bit as pretty as they said." He rose from the desk and took a few steps towards her. Maggie stood also, thinking maybe she should turn and run. But she didn't budge as he walked towards her, his broad shoulders swaying with each stride. He was taller than he had appeared from behind the desk, and very slender.

"I'm Reece Evans," he said, extending his hand. "I own the land this schoolhouse sits on."

She studied his face, finding it amiable, but his grasp was a little too firm. "I'm pleased, to be sure, Mr. Evans," she said, quickly withdrawing her hand. "But you did startle me."

He stepped back, grinned and made a gesture of innocence with his hands. "The door was open wide to the world, Miss Corbinn. Such a lovely song to waste on the dust and spiders." He took another step towards her. "I slipped in unannounced for fear of stopping you—just as I have."

Maggie backed towards the open window, welcoming a slight breeze. "I'm a bit rusty, Mr. Evans. It's been some time since I sat down to a piano."

He followed her, standing so close that she had to look up to see his face. It was lighter where his hat had been, and his dark brown hair was pressed smoothly against his forehead. "Please call me Reece," he said.

She took a few more steps, and he followed again. Hastily walking to the front of the classroom, she leaned against the teacher's desk, turning to see if he'd followed. But he had stopped his pursuit and stood with his arms crossed over his chest. "It's Maggie, isn't it? I'll call you that if I may?"

She tried to escape his gaze, studying the rafters in the open ceiling. "I suppose you can call me anything you like, Mr. Evans, since I'm just a schoolteacher trespassing on your cotton field." Her voice trembled slightly and she resolved to be calm, looking down at her desk, patting the coil of hair at the back of her head.

"Your good will is the only penalty for that, my dear."

Maggie felt the rush of blood to her cheeks. She wished he would leave, at least long enough for her to calm her nerves. She smoothed her apron and tucked a stray curl behind her ear, unable to come up with a clever reply.

He looked about at the room, which she had only begun to straighten, and started towards the door. "Looks as if you could use some help in here. I'll send someone."

"No, don't. Mr. Bill is sending his girls over here when they finish their chores." She took a deep breath. "But I should thank you for stopping by." The overturned stove caught her eye. "I don't suppose you'd be willing to help me right this stove. I could reward you with a cool glass of buttermilk," she said, picturing the jar of buttermilk that Miss Sally Catherine had sent wrapped in newspaper. She knew the offer of buttermilk sounded silly, but it was all she could think of.

"I've had my reward already, Maggie. Save your buttermilk for the young folks." With some effort, he picked up the old potbellied stove and carried it to the center of the room, placing it on the tin tray. His face was scarlet and his shirt and trousers were smeared with soot.

"Oh my, you've soiled your clothes, Mr. Ev—Reece. I didn't mean for you to do that all by yourself."

Wiping his hands on a large handkerchief, he stood directly in front of her, so close that she could almost feel his breath against her face. "It was my pleasure, Maggie. I'd like to do more than that for you."

"Thank you, Reece. I'm much obliged, but I—I—" She backed up a step. He was making her feel like a schoolgirl—standing so close, staring at her, just waiting for her to make a fool of herself. Without warning, he reached for her glasses and slipped them off.

"Why are you wearing a smoked glass?" He stared at her eyes, holding the glasses down by his side.

"Give me my glasses!"

"Answer my question first."

"You have no right. Please, give me my glasses."

He moved the hand with the glasses behind his back as she reached for them. "Only if you agree to have lunch with me tomorrow. I'll bring a picnic. We'll go down by the creek."

Sidestepping him, she grabbed her glasses from the hand behind his back, folded them and put them in her pocket. "I think not, Mr. Evans. I have a lot of work to do." Her interest in him had turned to irritation now, and she knew it would take everything she had not to fly off the handle.

A look of amusement crossed his face as he reached for his hat. At the door, he turned and tipped it. "There may not be another time,

Maggie. I'll be here tomorrow at noon."

Even after he had closed the door, she half-expected to find him behind her again. He had been like a cat cornering a mouse, batting it around, not wanting to kill it, just wanting to play. Approaching the window, she peered cautiously out, hoping to catch a last glimpse of him, but he had disappeared beyond the cotton.

————

Hannah and Annalee arrived shortly after Reece's departure, bringing their cousin Ben Lanier with them. "Ben's in the eighth grade," Hannah said. "He's our Aunt Sabra's son."

"Hello, Ben. I can sure use your help," Maggie said. "Do you think you could stack all of the desks on one side of the room so we can scrub the floor?"

Ben blushed, ducking his head. "Yes'm, I reckon I could. My mama wanted me to tell you how proud she is for you to be here. Said she'd be over to Uncle Bill's soon to meet you."

"Why, thank you. Tell your mama I'll be looking forward to that."

Between the four of them they cleaned out the dust and bird droppings, shelved the books and polished all the desks with linseed oil. Maggie was exhausted when Tate came for her in the buggy late in the afternoon. "Now all I need is a few children willing to learn," she said.

"You're a hardworking woman, Maggie. Some man is going to be lucky to have you for his wife."

He was flirting with her—buttering her up, as Aunt Mag would say. "Mules work hard, too, but that doesn't make them good wives," she quipped, too tired to care whether or not she sounded sassy.

"Well, I've never seen this schoolhouse looking so good. It'd be a pleasure to be starting school again. There's a lot I need to learn. Maybe someday you'll teach me."

Realizing he was serious, she changed her tone a little. "None of us are too old to learn, Tate. I'd be pleased to help you in the evening if there's something you want to study."

She gathered her things while he closed the windows. When they got into the buggy, she decided to ask him about Reece Evans. "Who owns the land the schoolhouse is on?"

"It belongs to about the orneriest person you'll ever meet," Tate said. "His name is Reece Evans. He knew we were looking for a new teacher this year, and he still planted his cotton right up to the door." Tate's jaw tightened and his face flushed. "Said he wasn't going to be wasting good land with the schoolhouse empty. His granddaddy Mr. Silas Evans built the schoolhouse way back, saying it was always to be used for a school, nothing else. But Reece, he don't respect nothing except money."

"I was wondering why there were no trees around, or a play yard."

"Oh, there used to be trees, but Reece had them cut down because they were sapping the strength from his cotton. He's mean as a striped snake," Tate said, and spit over the buggy wheel. Maggie listened, confused. The attractive face that had pressed so close to hers had seemed anything but mean.

Tate pulled on the reins and turned the buggy down the lane. Sweat ran down his sideburns and dripped off his chin. This was the first time Maggie had heard anything unpleasant in his voice. "His granddaddy raised him, sent him off to school up there in Detroit where he got some kind of agricultural engineering degree, and he came back down here trying to tell us farmers how to do things." He spat over the side of the buggy again. "I don't even like to go to the Farmers' Alliance meetings anymore. I just can't stand him."

"Where are his folks, if his granddaddy raised him?"

"There's no one left but him and his sister, Emily. Mr. Silas and Miss Maude have been dead a long time. They had a couple of boys— one of them was Reece's daddy, Malcolm. The brothers owned a small ship and they went back and forth to France and England out of Philadelphia. Malcolm married a woman up there named Jeanne, and that's where Reece and Miss Emily were born. During the War, Malcolm and his brother Burton both got killed running guns through the blockade at Fort Fisher. After that, Reece and Emily's mama died of typhoid fever. Mr. Silas, he went up there and got them, bringing them down here to raise when they were just young'uns."

"Is Reece Evans a good farmer?"

"Hell no! He's just got a lot of new-fangled ways and tries to show off at the Farmers' Alliance meetings with all his talk about crop rotation and such. Folks around here prefer cotton and corn and they don't need no wine or smoking tobacco to foul up their minds."

"Pa grows tobacco."

"Well, I might feel differently about tobacco if I was growing it."

"Don't you think he might be able to teach his neighbors something new about farming—having gone to college and all? I mean, there's more to education than reading and writing." Tate didn't answer. "Did I say something wrong?"

He turned to her with a look of forced calmness on his face. "There ain't nothing Reece Evans can teach me." After a few moments, he added, "You better stay away from the likes of him."

Maggie bristled. "What in the world do you mean by that?"

"I'm sorry, I didn't mean to be telling you what to do. That man just riles me!" He took a deep breath and the flush drained away from his face.

Tate's remarks reminded Maggie of Uncle Johnny. Maybe Reece Evans was a lot like Uncle Johnny, smarter than the rest. Come to think of it, Uncle Johnny was a real good-looking man. He, too, had gone off to school and come back with new ideas about things like fertilizers and irrigation.

The buggy jostled along on the sandy ruts between the cotton and cornfields. It wasn't far to the Ryans's place, but the road respected the fields and took the long way around. There were no fences, just the road and the fields, and narrow lanes of trees along the creeks to mark boundaries. Tate drove on past his parents' house and turned into the next lane. "I want to show you something," he said. "This is my land. Pa gave it to me to build a house on."

"Well, that's real nice." Maggie looked out at the burned-off land full of pine saplings and briar berries and tried to see a house on it.

"I'm not going to build a log cabin like Pa's. I've always wanted to build a real nice house like you said your Uncle Archie built for your Aunt Mag."

"That sounds pretty ambitious," Maggie said, remembering the comments G.W. had made about the amount of money Uncle Archie had spent just to please Aunt Mag.

Undaunted, Tate looked out across his future homesite. "I can just picture it," he said. "Can't you?"

At supper that evening, Bill Ryan announced that he had put a sign-up sheet for school over at Beardy Mike Padgett's store. "There were five or six signed up before I left. I expect Silas Evans's great-grandchildren will be on the list before the end of the week."

"That's the family who owns the land the school's on?" Maggie asked.

"Sure is. Silas Evans and my daddy applied for land grants at the same time. His grandson Reece owns it now."

Maggie glanced at Tate. "That's what Tate was telling me."

"They were real pioneers. 'Course the difference was, Silas Evans had plenty of money to begin with, coming down here from Philadelphia. He and Miss Maude built a twenty-seven-room mansion they called Evanwood over there on Southwest Creek. They had about two thousand acres out here in the country and a house and the general store in Jacksonville. Their sons both got killed in the War, so Mr. Silas, he left everything to his grandchildren—Evanwood to Reece, and the house and store in Jacksonville to Miss Emily. Funny thing is, Miss Emily and her children don't live in Jacksonville, they live out here at Evanwood with Reece."

"Nobody can quite figure it out," Sally Catherine said. "Miss Emily's husband Duncan McAllister runs the store and lives in the house in Jacksonville. People don't think it looks right, her living out there with Mr. Reece and her husband all alone in Jacksonville, but I can tell you this, that is one fine woman. Why, she sees to it every Christmas that Mr. Duncan stores up enough candy to give every family a sack when they come in to buy their supplies. And she's the one that insisted Mr. Reece reopen the school."

"Is he married?" Maggie asked.

"The devil wouldn't have Reece Evans!" Tate said.

"Now, Tate, don't go showing yourself," Bill said. "Miss Maggie can judge for herself. I doubt she'll be coming across him too often anyhow."

"Well, it's time she met some of the folks around here," Sally Catherine said. "We're going to have a gathering on Sunday after church for you to meet the rest of the family. Betty's coming, and Emma and Sabra said they'd be here. They're our other daughters." She shook her head. "But I don't know about James. He doesn't always make it when we get together. He works all the time. You reckon you'll see James, Bill? I want to make sure he comes."

"I'll tell him. The question is, can we feed all his young'uns?" Bill laughed, almost choking on a mouthful of food.

"He's got a passel, all right," Sally Catherine said, "but me and the girls have never let anyone go hungry. You know that, sweetness."

Chapter 14

The next morning, Maggie walked across the fields to the school-house. She hadn't slept well the night before, her thoughts running over and over her encounter with Reece Evans. In the past, Wash had dominated her thoughts on long sleepless nights. She was distressed that Reece could replace him so easily. When she opened the school-house door, she spied a large bouquet of flowers in the water pitcher on her desk. *Now who in the world...* She walked around the desk, inspecting the flowers. There were deep burgundy and rust colored dahlias, blue asters and black-eyed Susans—nothing you would find along the roadside, but flowers that had been cultivated in a garden. From Reece? She looked for a note. Maybe they were just from some lovely little boy or girl who wanted to welcome the new teacher.

In the cloakroom, Maggie slipped on an apron and tied it over her printed cotton dress. Looking into a mirror that hung behind the door, she smoothed her hair and adjusted her glasses, hesitating only a moment before leaving them on. She had asked Dr. Bayard about her eye on one of his visits to see her mama. He said the eye had healed, but the muscle was weak, making the eye pull slightly to the side. She hated the way it looked.

Reece came at noon carrying a large picnic hamper. Maggie's lesson plans were spread out on her desk, and her lunch pail sat directly in front of her. She looked up when he stepped into the doorway. He seemed younger, clean and fresh in a blousy blue chambray shirt and tight brown riding breeches tucked into his boots.

Placing the picnic hamper on a desk near the door, he crossed his hands over the handle. "Are you ready for lunch?"

Maggie sorted and rearranged her papers, centered the lunch pail.

Undiscouraged, Reece folded his arms and waited for her to look up.

"Reece, I don't have time for a picnic. The superintendent is coming tomorrow and the children in a few days. I have my lunch. Why don't you join me in here?"

"That's not what I had in mind," he said, starting towards her, leaving the basket behind on the desk. "Come now, don't be difficult. You know I've got something in that basket that can beat anything Miss Sally Catherine fixed for you."

Maggie rose to meet him. "No. I'm here to work."

His smile turned into a smirk and he stopped short of her desk. "Are you afraid of me, Maggie Lorena?"

"Afraid of you? Don't be ridiculous. You can see that I have work to do, and you're not helping me by coming over here like we were courting or something." She leaned towards him, the tips of her fingers planted firmly on the desk. Yes, she was a little intimidated, but determined not to show it.

"I am courting you, Miss Corbinn," he said with a touch of sarcasm. "With food and flowers."

Maggie glanced at the flowers. So, it *was* a cat and mouse game. She had figured correctly. And just how far she would be willing to let the intrigue go, she wasn't sure. "All right," she said, shoving her chair under the desk. "I'll go, but I can't stay long." Reece smiled and bowed as she headed for the door.

He led the way along the worn path through the field to the creek, carrying the picnic hamper on his shoulder. Maggie stepped carefully down the slight incline, her eyes on his back. He was trim and muscular and his clothes fit him perfectly. She brushed a flurry of gnats from her face and wished she had taken more time with her hair.

It was a hot September day under a hazy sun, but the air was cool in the shade of the trees along the quiet stream. A long rope-like vine hung from a tall poplar, and she imagined the children swinging across the stream and dropping onto the other side. Up ahead an old moss-covered log stretched from one side to the other, its worn surface a testament to the feet that had chased across it over the years. A clear stream ambled through small piles of brush that had collected here and there, making deep little pools that were reservoirs for tadpoles and small fish. She stooped to pick a stem of pale pink duck potato, slipping it behind her ear. Away from the dusty cotton fields, it was hard to imagine that summer was over and soon the days would grow short and the air cooler.

Leaving the path, Reece trudged along until he reached an open area covered in thick green moss. He seemed to know just the place and Maggie wondered if he had been there before. She stood by and watched him spread a bright rose-colored counterpane over the moss and place the wicker basket on it. He reached for her hand. "My dear?"

She hesitated, glancing up the path towards the school. "Reece, I..."

"Maggie, please sit down."

She took his hand and sat, stretching her feet out in front of her. When he lifted the lid of the hamper, she saw plates and utensils held by leather straps inside. He shook the folds from a white lace-edged linen cloth, spreading it before her. She relaxed against a small tree, lulled by the running stream. Streaks of sunlight filtered down through the tall trees, flitting across the moving water like a school of fish. Something sweet was in the air, honeysuckle or clover. She wanted to take off her shoes, dip her feet into the cool water and run her toes over the moss-covered rocks—until she saw a small green snake slip in on the other side.

"Eeek! A snake." She tucked her feet under her skirt as the snake slithered away.

Reece laughed. "It was only a little snake. They don't eat much."

"That's not funny. I hate snakes."

"Look, Maggie, we're both harmless, the snake and I. I think you will enjoy our company if you allow yourself the pleasure." He did not say it with arrogance, but with conviction.

She untucked her feet and stretched her legs out again. "I'm sorry.

It's been a long time since I've enjoyed a man's company." That was not quite true; she had enjoyed being with Tate to a certain extent, but that was different. She had never felt quite this way before, attracted and intimidated at the same time. "I have so much to do, picnics seem a waste of time."

Reece pulled out a covered platter of cured ham, thinly sliced and arranged neatly around a mound of potato salad. He was preoccupied, giving her a chance to study him. His hands were thick from work, but scrubbed clean with trimmed nails. He was older than she was, maybe by ten years or so. Opening a jar of pickled okra, he speared a pod with a fork and offered it to her. "Nothing is a waste of time if you enjoy it."

"And the beautiful flowers, they're from you?"

"I don't think you'll find many like them around here," he said. "My gardener takes great pride in his dahlias."

"Reece, I haven't meant to sound unappreciative. With the children coming in the first of next week, and the superintendent tomorrow..."

"No need for apologies," he interrupted, handing her the plate. "I don't give up easily."

He is courting me, she thought, watching his deft movements. She had never seen her father or any of the men in her family prepare a plate of food for anyone but themselves.

"You must have a good cook. The food looks delicious."

"I do, and somewhere in the bottom of this hamper is her supreme effort, chocolate walnut cake."

"Do you always eat this way at lunchtime?" She couldn't hold back a smile.

"Only with a pretty girl," he said, reaching into the creek, pulling out a tall, slim-necked green bottle. "And now, a little wine."

Wine! He brought wine and slipped it in the creek before fetching me—so sure of himself. It was like a story in the *Ladies Home Journal.*

Reece poured wine into two pale pink crystals, handed one to

Maggie and raised his glass. "A toast. To us, Maggie."

Maggie nervously raised her glass and sipped. He was watching her, expecting her to say something. "It tastes like honey...or sweetened butter."

Reece took a sip and washed it around in his mouth. "Yes, this is a nice one. We grow the grapes and send them up to Philadelphia, where our vintners make the wine." He held the glass up to the light, admiring it. In the nearby stream, two birds darted in and out of the water, playing a game of tag.

"I'm not in the habit of drinking wine. Pa never allowed us to have wine except at Christmas."

"I imagine there are lots of things your pa never allowed, Maggie, but you're a grown woman. Enjoy it." He poured more wine in both their glasses, then touched his to hers. "Take them off."

"What?"

"Your glasses, take them off."

"Reece, please, I have to wear them."

"Why? You aren't blind, are you? I saw your eye. I think you're just covering up. Your eyes are beautiful."

She turned away. "A crooked eye is not beautiful."

"Some of us might not agree." He moved closer. "May I?" he said, reaching up and removing the glasses. "There, that's much better. A smoked glass only calls attention to it. You don't need these." He slung the wire-rimmed glasses over his shoulder and into the creek.

"What are you doing? You have no right!" She stood up, towering over him, pointing in the direction he had thrown her glasses. "Go and get them!" she demanded.

"Maggie, it's just a cover-up. You know that. Come here." He reached for her, but she pulled away from him. "Sit down, please." He was so calm, she became even more furious.

"No, I will not. You had no right to do that."

He stood up, looking even taller, threatening. "I have a right to do whatever I like. This is my land, remember." There was no humor in his voice this time. Reaching out for her, he grabbed her by the waist and held her tight against him, his lips almost touching hers, saying in a whisper, "Don't waste time, Maggie. I know what I want. I think you do, too."

Suddenly she was not only angry, she was frightened. "Get away from me," she said, pushing hard against his chest. He tried to catch himself, but the grass along the creek was damp and he fell, taking two steps backwards before he landed in the creek.

"Damn you, Maggie!" he shouted. But she was already up the path, running towards the schoolhouse.

Tate was waiting for her on the steps. "Where've you been? I was looking everywhere for you," he said. She pushed him aside, rushing to her desk, gathering her things, shoving Sally Catherine's lunch box into a drawer. "Maggie, what's wrong?" He followed close on her heels.

"Just never you mind. What are you doing here anyhow?" she snapped, her hands on her hips.

"I came to walk you home. I was working in the field across the creek and my mule lost a shoe, so Pa took him on back to the barn."

"You came across the creek?"

"Yes, I did, down at the lower end of the field. Pa thought of it. He said we were working you mighty hard and you might like a little company. What's wrong?"

"It's nothing. I'm just tired and ready to go home."

"Where were you? I looked around and didn't see you."

She picked up her books and papers, avoiding his eyes. "I was just down at the creek. I walked down there to cool off a little—after my lunch. It's a wonder you didn't see me," she said, trying her best to appear nonchalant.

He was trying to make sense of it. She wished he would just go on outside while she gathered her wits. "Where are your glasses? I don't believe I've ever seen you without them."

She had hoped he wouldn't notice, but of course he had. Tate noticed everything like that. "Oh, I dropped them in the creek. I couldn't find them. It's all right. They're probably broken and washed away by now. I have another pair at the house."

"I'll go look. You wait here."

"Tate, I don't want..." But he was out the door and down the path.

My stars, what if Reece is still there? Tate had been obvious, to say the least, about his dislike of Reece. There would be a confrontation. How could she explain?

When she heard Tate's heavy boots clumping back up the steps, she held her breath and waited for the barrage of questions. None came. "Here they are," he said holding out her glasses. "They were hanging on a limb right where anybody could see them."

"Oh, really?" Maggie took the glasses and wiped them off with the hem of her apron. "Some children were playing down there," she said. "They must've found them and hung them in the tree." She closed the door and snapped the padlock into position. "I guess this is my lucky day."

Tate stopped on the bottom step. "You forgot your lunch box."

"I didn't eat my apple. I'll get it tomorrow."

Chapter 15

Superintendent Thompson was a dapper little man with a toupee that didn't quite match the fringe of hair beneath it. He talked excitedly about his plans for the county. "If you can just maintain the status quo here for another year or so, Miss Corbinn, we'll have you a brand new graded school on Harris Creek." She watched him strut around the schoolhouse, examining books and sizing up the room. "We may still use this building, but it all depends on how much money we have to put into the new one. Our commissioners are talking about a special tax. That remains to be seen."

"Might I ask who is giving the land for the new school, Mr. Thompson?"

"Why, of course, my dear. Mr. Reece Evans, an ardent supporter of education—a very generous man."

"I'm pleased to hear that. I met Mr. Evans yesterday."

"Yes, he was in my office later in the day. Said he planned to clear this field next to the school in a few weeks. His cotton is almost ready. Didn't expect us to use this facility this year."

"Oh. Wasn't he aware of Mr. Ryan's search for a new teacher?"

"Well, you see, my dear, everything is political at this stage of the game. Mr. Ryan is on the search committee for teachers, but Mr. Evans is on the school board. Mr. Evans wanted to get the new school started right away, but it certainly wouldn't have been completed until next spring. It seems Mr. Ryan was not willing to have the community's children put off when there was a perfectly good schoolhouse here."

"Well, that certainly explains some things," Maggie said.

———

Only ten students showed up on the first day of school. Maggie was disappointed, but she knew that over the next month as crops were finished and gathered, more and more children would come. That was the way of life for most families in rural counties like Onslow. Children were the workforce. They were needed at home when the weather was good and there were chores to be done before cold weather set in. But some families, like the Ryans, set great store by education and were eager to take advantage of what little the State provided, even if the chores went undone. Others, like the Evanses, wanted their children to have a chance to socialize with their neighbors.

Hannah was a big help in organizing the schoolroom. She knew the children who would be coming, their ages and their approximate grade levels. "Jeanne and Darcy Evans are the smartest ones because Miss Emily works with them at home. They'll help out a lot with the middle grades because they're sort of know-it-alls anyway," she said.

"What about your cousin Ben?" Maggie asked.

"Ben's shy, but he can do his figures the best in the class."

"Good. He can help with the younger children."

"The Bannermans have three little boys in the first, second and third grade levels. Mrs. Bannerman comes every day at lunch and brings them hot dinners."

"Maybe she can help some."

"I don't think she can," Hannah said. "Mr. Bannerman is pretty bad off. A tree he was cutting fell on him a couple of years ago and crushed both his legs. They had to cut them off. Mama says he would have been better off if it had gone on and killed him."

"Oh," Maggie said, flinching. "Are there any other mothers that you think might help out?"

"Miss Oma Ferguson might. She's kind of an old maid. She came and read to us for an hour every afternoon last year."

"Well, anyone would be a help," Maggie said.

When they were all seated, Maggie looked about the room at the children. The test of a one-room schoolhouse teacher was how she divided the grade levels. The first division came between those who could read and those who could not. Two of the Gurganus boys, Joe and Zeke, sat among the children who could not read. She had seen their type before—they were older, yet behind others in their age group. No doubt they would require a lot of attention, Maggie thought, and most of it would be disciplinary. The first thing she did was to separate them and give them responsibility for keeping the blackboard clean and passing out books at the beginning of the day. Keep the problem children busy, Aunt Mag always said.

Towards the end of the first day, Zeke Gurganus raised his hand. "Miss Corbinn, how long are we going to have to go to school this year? Ma said she was going to need me and Joe at planting time next spring."

"Don't be thinking about when school is going to be over already, Zeke," Maggie reprimanded. "We have to have school at least four months. I'm sure that your ma knows that. A lot depends on the weather. We'll take off two weeks in December for a holiday, and a couple in January. January and February aren't too good for working outside, so you may as well be in school. Mr. Thompson, the superintendent, said we had to keep school open at least through April."

Whenever Maggie asked for volunteers to read or write on the blackboard, Jeanne McAllister was the first to raise her hand. Maggie pulled her aside after school. "I really appreciate your volunteering, Jeanne."

"You're welcome, Miss Maggie. I'm glad you're here."

Maggie thought she faintly resembled Reece, but with a head full of blond curls. "Hadn't you planned to go to the Academy this year?"

"Yes ma'am, until Uncle Reece told my mother that you were going to be the new teacher and he thought you would be a good one."

"Oh, he did? Well, I hope I don't disappoint your mother."

"Uncle Reece said Mother should let us go to school with the other children in the neighborhood, so we would have lots of friends."

"Oh, I see."

"Mother didn't have many friends growing up because she was always away at school."

"What about your Uncle Reece?"

"Oh, Grandpa kept him here on the farm until he was in high school. Grandpa wanted him to learn firsthand all that he could about farming. I think he went to school with Mr. Tate."

———

The Ryans's Sunday gathering made Maggie homesick for the times the Corbinn clan had gathered out under the trees at the old homeplace when Mama was in her prime. With Tate's five sisters showing off their culinary skills, Miss Sally Catherine didn't have to cook a thing. "We don't let Mama do all the cooking anymore," Betty, Tate's oldest sister, said. "With us girls so near by, there's no need. Coming home is what we love, so she just gets the house ready and makes the tea."

"Well, she gets to make the potato salad once in a while," Emma said. "Tate won't eat anybody's potato salad but Mama's."

"I won't either," Betty said.

As Maggie met Tate's sisters, she made a point of trying to remember something significant about each one. Betty was stout like Sally Catherine and wore her hair in the same tight little bun. Emma, the next eldest, was taller but just as stout. She was the one who took charge of things, arranging the food, putting the finishing touches on the table. Sabra was the different one. Tall and thin, her dark hair tied back with a ribbon, she took a seat and watched the others do the work.

"I declare, all of you girls sure do favor," Maggie said.

"All except Sabra. Mama didn't know what to think when she came along. Look at her over there, skinny as a rail and lanky as a bean pole," Emma said. "She's married to Charlie Shepherd, and he's a regular roly-poly."

"Is she a good cook like the rest of you?"

"Not hardly. Charlie does the cooking at their house."

It was a beautiful fall day and the men assembled long boards on sawhorses to make the tables. Everyone pulled up a cane chair or a nail keg under two giant live oak trees. "I remember when these trees were no bigger than I am," Tate said. He sat down beside Maggie with a plateful of various desserts centered around a large slice of chocolate cake.

"Are you going to pass that plate around for the rest of us, Tate?"

He rocked back in his chair and laughed. "No'm, but I'll go get you one just like it."

"I'd be as big as the broad side of a barn if I ate all that," Maggie said.

"Well, you may as well look like the rest of us Ryans. Look, here come James and Louise. He's bigger'n Papa ever was. James! Come on over here and meet Miss Maggie Lorena," Tate shouted.

James and Louise sauntered over to Maggie while the children scattered in all directions. James was like a younger Bill, a giant of a man, much larger than Tate. "How'do, Miss Maggie. I heard you were here. I'm sorry me and Louise haven't gotten over here. You can see with those young'uns, we've got our hands full." He stepped over to kiss his mother on the cheek. "Mama knows how it is," he said, and Maggie detected the same little titter in his voice as his mother's.

"I sure do, son," Sally Catherine said. She took his wife's hand. "Louise, meet Maggie Lorena. She's the new schoolteacher, you know."

Louise had a worn-down look, but she smiled sweetly and put out her hand. "Pleased to meet you, Maggie. I've been hoping to have you over to our place, but I just haven't gotten around to it."

"Don't you worry about that, Louise. I've got my work cut out too, and it doesn't leave much time for visiting."

After they finished eating, the menfolk sat around the barn, a few of them chewing and smoking. The women gathered on the back porch. Emma and Betty made a special effort to point out all of Tate's good qualities, chief among them his success at hunting. "You won't ever have to worry about food on the table with Tate around," Betty said.

Emma looked about to make sure that Tate wasn't within earshot. "Maybe Maggie Lorena doesn't enjoy meat from the woods."

"My stars, of course I do. I've cooked my share of squirrel, but venison is what we favor over in Bladen."

"We just wanted to make sure you hadn't gotten above your raisin' going up there to college in Raleigh," Sabra teased. It was said in jest, but there was always a little truth in such a comment.

———

That evening, Maggie wrote to Aunt Mag telling her about the gathering. *They're really nice folks. I feel just like I'm home. Don't go getting any ideas about that, it's just that I'm glad I decided to do this. The schoolhouse was a terrible mess, but once we got it cleaned up, it's as good as any. The superintendent came by and said we'd have a new school at Harris Creek next year, but I doubt that I'll be here.*

Aunt Mag would get a kick out of her descriptions of the children. *The little McAllister children look to be straight out of a storybook. Remember those Jack and Jill pictures? That's what they look like. I love them to death—they're so sweet and polite. But the Gurganus boys—I'm really worried about them. I think one of them has hookworm disease. He's older than his brother, but smaller. I heard they have a clinic in Jacksonville next month. Whether or not their mother will take them remains to be seen.*

By the way, I've met a very interesting man. His name is Reece Evans— owns a big plantation, I hear—also the land the schoolhouse is on. He brought a picnic one day—really fancy. More about that later.

Maggie wrote to Katie too, adding a few more details about the encounter with Reece. *You won't believe what he did, Kate, ripped my glasses off my face and threw them into the creek. Well, you can imagine how I reacted to that! I pushed him, and he fell into the water. He yelled something, but I just hightailed it back to the schoolhouse. I was afraid that he was coming after me, but when I got to the schoolhouse, there was Tate waiting for me. I could have died! I didn't want Tate to know I was having a picnic with someone, especially Reece Evans.*

Chapter 16

After three weeks had passed, Maggie decided that she had probably discouraged Reece. He wasn't likely to come courting again. She tried telling herself that she didn't care, but she could think of little else.

Each day the weather seemed a little cooler in the morning, but by noon, when the breeze had died, the room underneath the tin roof felt like an inferno. After several days, knowing full well that the children would absorb very little book learning in such heat, she decided that the only sensible thing to do was to excuse them early. They were out the door within minutes, and she was not far behind.

Just as she was locking up, she saw Reece at the end of a cotton row astride a beautiful black gelding, his back to her. He was inspecting his cotton, checking the hard green shells, some of which had already exploded into fluffy white balls. His horse pranced impatiently along the edge of the field. She checked the locked door and started down the steps. "Is that you, Reece?" she called out. Silly question. Who else would it be?

He turned and stared. She continued down the steps, feeling uneasy.

"Hello, Maggie," he said without the least hint of warmth.

His back was to the sun and she held her hand up to shade her eyes. "You should have come in. I didn't know you were here."

"I didn't need to. You have your work to do and I have mine," he said, glancing at the cotton field.

A little breeze rustled against her skirt. She didn't know what to say. At first she had looked for him every day, expecting him to be angry, chastising her for pushing him into the creek. But his anger, as well as his earlier persistence, had now turned to indifference. *So that was how he played the game, waiting for the mouse to come to him.* She placed her finger on the wire bridge of her glasses and pushed them back on her nose.

"I see you found your glasses," he said.

"Reece, I'm sorry, but you had no business throwing them in the creek." Turning her back to him, she started to walk away.

He slipped off his horse, but she had reached the lane before he called to her. "Maggie, wait. I've come to apologize." Leaving the black gelding to drink from the trough, he walked towards her. He seemed friendly now, but she wasn't sure she could trust him, not since she had riled him. He stopped a short distance from her, tossing a ball of cotton in his hands. "The cotton is almost ready. When it's picked, we'll plow up the fields nearest the school to make room for a playground again."

"That would be nice," she said. *Careful, Maggie Lorena. He could pounce at any moment.*

"Look, it's been so long since I've been around a decent woman. I'm afraid I lost my—let's just say that I was ungentlemanly." He shifted his weight from one foot to the other. "I'd like to make it up to you. My sister Emily and I are having a soirée on the fifteenth of October. I'd like you to come."

"A soirée? I don't know."

"There'll be music and dancing," he said, tempting her with a smile.

Maggie's face lit up. "It sounds like a fancy party," she said, returning the smile.

"It should be."

"What's the occasion?"

"My cousin and her niece and nephew are coming down from Philadelphia."

"Why, I think that sounds real nice." A soirée—it was the last thing she had imagined in Onslow County. Living with the Ryans, a social life beyond family gatherings seemed highly unlikely.

"It's done then. There'll be lots of people, some refined folks, more like you," he said.

"More like me?"

He reached into the inside pocket of his jacket and pulled out a slim black cigar. Striking a match on his britches and lighting it, he blew out a long stream of smoke that seemed to linger over her. "I don't think I need to explain. You have refinement, some education. A beautiful young woman like you should be associating with her own kind."

Maggie stared at him. "I'm boarding with the Ryans. They're friends of my father's...of mine. I don't see where..."

"Really, Maggie," he interrupted. "You came here for a teaching position, not to take up residence with the Ryans for the rest of your life. Why should they care what you do?"

Maggie looked down at her feet. "I'm sorry, Reece. I can't come unless the Ryans are invited. It wouldn't be right."

A small scar she had not noticed before stood out on his upper lip. He tossed his head back. "Suit yourself, Miss Corbinn. You're a hard-headed woman!" Mounting his horse, he rode off in the opposite direction.

———

That evening, Maggie lay awake long into the night. The smell of the straw mattress made her head stuffy, and she longed for the downy feather mattress on her bed at home. When she finally slept, she dreamed of twirling round and round to music, wearing her green taffeta dress, a man's arm around her waist. She tried to see his face, but it was blotted out, a blank spot in the lovely scene. The room was beautiful, with chandeliers hanging from the ceiling. People sat along the walls, watching them dance.

She awoke with a start, realizing she was cold, and got up and closed the window. A full moon lit the room as bright as day. Wrapping herself in the quilt, she sat down at her desk. The house was far too quiet for the typewriter, so she folded back the cover of a school notebook. *Strange dream...dancing the night away with...someone.* It was the beginning of a story. She called the main character Evangeline, a beautiful lonely girl who rejected all her suitors because they did not measure up to the dream of the man she would marry.

———

The next day after school, the aroma of apples and rich spices cooking on the stove met Maggie coming up the back steps. Sally Catherine was in the kitchen putting up jars of apple butter. "That smells so good. May I have some on a biscuit?" Maggie asked. "I've never made apple butter."

"Pshaw, there's nothing to it, honey. You just make applesauce and let it cook down all day with a little more sugar and a heap of spices thrown in. Most of the time, the apples are so sweet that I don't even add sugar."

Maggie pulled on an apron. "I declare, I hate to see you on your feet all day like this. Couldn't this be done on Saturday so the girls and I could help?"

Sally Catherine wiped her hands on her apron. "Now, listen here, Maggie Lorena, I told you that you're not to be worrying about the chores. You go on to your room—you've been on your feet all day, too."

Maggie hung her apron back on the nail and gave Sally Catherine a hug around the shoulders from behind. "You're mighty good to me, Miss Sally."

"I hear that old typewriter going every now and then. Are you working on a story?"

"Oh, I hope I haven't disturbed you."

"No, not at all, honey. I want you to do your writing." She ladled the apple butter into glass jars. "We'll be reading that story in the *Ladies Home Journal* before you know it. I bet it'll be a good one," she said.

Maggie was already down the hall when Sally Catherine called out, "Did you see your mail? There's a letter from your Aunt Mag, and Mr.

Evans's boy brought an invitation over for you and the girls. I'll bet he's going to have a party."

Maggie steadied herself, one hand on the log wall. "No, I haven't been to my room yet. I've been looking to hear from Aunt Mag. I'll go see what she has to say about Mama."

The cream-colored vellum envelope was on her desk, along with Aunt Mag's letter. She scanned the letter first, but was unable to concentrate on it. The other envelope bore her name and those of Tate's two younger sisters. One of the girls had already opened it. *The pleasure of your company is requested...for an evening of music and dance...a party honoring a cousin from Philadelphia.*

There was a knock at the door and Annalee poked her head in. "Did you see the invitation?"

"Yes, Annalee, I have it right here."

"Oh, Maggie, a dance! Isn't that wonderful?" Annalee spun around the room in exaggerated sweeps and landed on the bed. "What will we wear?"

"I don't know. We'll think of something," she said, knowing full well that she would wear the green taffeta dress, just as she had in her dream.

"Hannah says she's not going because Tate wasn't invited."

"Oh? I didn't notice." Maggie said. She looked at the envelope again. Tate's name was not included. "Well, why would Tate want to go? It's just a dress-up party and he wouldn't like it a bit. You've heard how he feels about Reece Evans."

Annalee danced about the room again. "Oh, he would—just to dance with you!" she teased. "That's what Hannah said."

"Go on with you. You've been reading too many romance stories. Tate doesn't care one thing about dancing with me." But she knew it was true. Tate coveted her attention. He would probably love to dance with her. "If he does, he can come to the Halloween dance at school."

Tate missed supper with the family that night. Bill said he was stacking hay in the barn before cold weather and wanted to finish up before dark. Maggie dreaded seeing him. She had told Reece that she wouldn't go if he didn't include the Ryans, so he had only included the girls. There was no doubt in her mind that Tate would be offended, but there wasn't a thing she could do about it.

———

The last rays of sunlight had slipped behind the horizon when she heard a knock on her door. She opened it to find Tate. "I was wondering if you might like to set out on the porch a spell? It's right nice outside and I'd like to talk if you have the time," he said.

"Of course, Tate. Let me turn down the lamp. I'll finish grading these papers later."

He led the way to a bench between two of the support posts on the wide porch. Even in the twilight, Maggie could see the brush marks of the straw broom where Sally Catherine had swept the sandy yard. Her petunias and geraniums had put out new blossoms and their perfume permeated the night air.

Tate was quiet at first, gazing out across the yard. She hadn't seen much of him lately, except at supper and on Sundays. She thought he might be avoiding her. "Mr. Bill says you've been cutting wood for your house, Tate. How's it coming along?"

"Pretty good. I hauled a load of logs to the sawmill this afternoon." They were sitting close on the bench, their arms touching, the sour smell of cypress and his hard work between them.

"How long do you think it'll be before we have a houseraising?" Maggie asked, trying to lighten the mood.

"Oh, I expect it will be after Christmas."

"That will sure be fun. I love houseraisings. If it's a pretty day, all the ladies can come and we can have a picnic," Maggie said, trying to perk him up.

He didn't smile or show the slightest bit of enthusiasm. "That would be nice, Maggie."

"What's on your mind, Tate? You said you wanted to talk to me about something."

He took a deep breath, raring back a little, his hands on his knees. "Hannah told me about the invitation to Reece Evans's house. She said she didn't think you should go if I wasn't invited. I want you to know I think that's plumb foolishness." His pleasant expression had changed to a stern frown. "I don't have no truck with Reece Evans and he don't have any with me, and that's just fine."

Maggie was relieved. Tate was insulted, just as she'd suspected he would be, but he was making it easier for her. "It wasn't polite of him to ask some of the single folks and not the rest in a family. Maybe we shouldn't..."

She had her hand on his arm and he reached over and put his hand on hers. "Thank you, Maggie, but I wouldn't let you and the girls do that. I'm not going to be a horse's ass just because he is." His gaze was set on the distant horizon. "I wouldn't of gone if he'd asked me, but there's no reason for you not to get acquainted with a few other folks besides us Ryans."

"Tate, you've been so good to me. If you're insulted..."

"Insulted? By that ornery low-down snake? He can't insult me. I don't give a damn what he does."

"What is it, Tate? What's between you and Reece Evans?"

Tate was silent a long time before he answered her. "Nothing you'd understand. We used to play together all the time when we were little. When he went off to high school and college, he came back different, acted like he was better than me. He lived up there in Philadelphia four or five years. 'Bout broke Mr. Silas's heart when he didn't come back down here to run the farm. Right after Mr. Silas died, he brought a girl down here from Philadelphia. I came across her one evening walking down the middle of the road, crying. She begged me not to take her back to Evanwood, but I did because I didn't know what else to do. Reece was drunk when we got there and he raised a shotgun up at me and said he was gonna kill us. Henry, the old colored man that helped raise him, talked him down and I took the girl in the wagon over to Miss Emily's in Jacksonville. I never knew what happened, but

Reece and me never spoke after that."

"I'm sorry, Tate. I didn't know."

Maggie walked back to her room in a state of dismay. How could Reece be so genteel one minute, a complete brute the next? But as fond as she was of Tate, she was more intrigued by Reece Evans. With his education and wealth, Reece had left Tate behind, and Maggie had no intention of being left behind by anybody. If Tate had any designs on courting her, he had a right to be jealous of Reece. She felt an excitement over him that she had never known, even with Wash. Pa and Mr. Bill could do all the matchmaking they wanted, but she had no intention of letting anyone choose whom she would marry.

Chapter 17

Maggie poured a small bottle of glycerine and rosewater into a tub of steaming hot water. Miss Sally Catherine had kept the kettles going all afternoon so that Maggie and the girls could have their baths early in the day. Annalee had brought her the tub first and Maggie lit the kerosene heater to warm the room while she went back and forth to the kitchen with the kettles.

Slipping into the tub, Maggie wondered if she had ever been this excited before. She lathered her feet and legs with a cake of sweet soap that Aunt Mag had put in her satchel. The fragrance of the soap and rosewater made her giddy. Humming softly, she lathered her neck, gliding her hands across her breasts and feeling the hardness of her nipples. There was so much she wanted to know about love, about the elation she felt when she thought about Reece Evans.

Drying herself off, she danced around the room naked. Never had she felt such radiance, such gaiety. Tonight was a dream come true. Reece Evans was a dream come true. She parted her hair in the middle and twisted each long tress into thick rolls that tapered into a V at the back of her neck, securing them tightly with long wire pins. Soft curls escaped around her face, but it was useless to try and tame them. She studied her freckles, wishing she had covered her face more as a child. Aunt Mag had warned her many times to wear her bonnet, but more often than not, Maggie had refused to listen.

She pulled on a pair of Aunt Mag's silk stockings, stretching them carefully over her long legs and attaching them to her garterbelt. Next came her camisole.

There was a soft knock at the door. "Maggie, it's me."

"Come on in, Hannah."

Hannah opened the door, wearing her petticoat and camisole. "Oh, Maggie, you look beautiful," she said. "How did you do your hair? Let me see."

"Aunt Mag showed me how. She used to wear hers this way for special occasions."

"I never saw you look so pretty. I want Tate to see. Let me go get him." Hannah started for the door.

"Hannah. Come back. It's time to put on our dresses. I need you to help me with my corset."

Hannah came back into the room reluctantly. "Well, I hope he's here when we leave because I really want him to see you."

"Don't you think I should put my dress on first?" They both laughed and Maggie hugged Hannah. "Isn't this fun, getting all dressed up to go to a dance?"

"Well, I guess so," Hannah said, "but unless the boys see you, it doesn't make much difference whether or not you look pretty."

———

Reece had sent word that his driver would pick up Maggie and the two girls for the party. Bill and Sally Catherine were out on the porch when the carriage arrived. The driver was a Negro man dressed in a blousy white shirt, gold-colored velvet vest and maroon breeches that came to the knee. He also wore white stockings and shiny patent leather shoes with gold buckles at the toe, and was driving a large two-seated black buggy with flowers painted on the doors.

Maggie waited in the living room with the girls, who were trying not to muss their dresses. "Would you look at that outfit," she said, stifling a giggle.

The girls looked out the door. "Oh. That's just Homer," Hannah said. "I'll bet he feels silly." Maggie suspected that Tate was thinking the same thing if he was watching from somewhere. She'd hoped to run into him, but he'd disappeared right after supper.

Homer jumped down from the driver's seat and came around the carriage to speak to the Ryans. "Evenin' Capt'n Bill, Miss Sally. Mr.

Reece sent me over to fetch the ladies. Is they ready?"

"Well, I tell you, Homer, that is some get-up," Bill said.

"Yassuh, Mr. Bill, dis is what Mr. Reece call firs' class service."

Maggie and the girls came out the door. "Here they are," Bill said. "Maggie, this here is Homer. His daddy Henry helped all the women and children around here during the War. If it wasn't for him, Mr. Silas and Miss Maude wouldn't of had much left at Evanwood. His daddy helped our family out, too."

"You remember all that, Mr. Bill? I won't even born yet." Homer doffed his hat, bobbing his head. "Evenin', Miss Maggie, Miss Hannah, Miss Annalee."

"I'm counting on you to take good care of my girls and Miss Maggie here. Don't you go out hunting any possums on the way home, you hear?" Bill Ryan laughed and slapped his knee.

Homer snickered. "No suh, Capt'n Bill. I won't be treein' no possums tonight, not in this get-up. Mr. Reece, he done give me my orders. I'd best be gettin' on, or he gone be comin' after me." He held out his hand to assist Maggie and the giggling girls into the buggy.

Two stout horses pulled the carriage at a brisk pace along the road past the schoolhouse. After they had gone several miles, Hannah pointed to the open fields on either side of the road where long rows of vines grew on wire strung between posts. "Those are Mr. Reece's wine grapes," she said. "Papa said he had to go to France to learn how to grow them like that." Maggie thought of the delicious wine Reece had poured for her. She looked out across row upon row of grapes. What would it be like to be married to a man who went to France just to learn how to grow grapes?

The driver turned into a narrow lane that wound through what seemed like an endless forest of tall pines. The only evidence of the white sand beneath the brown needle carpet lay in the deep rutted lanes. In the distance, Maggie could see lights flickering through the pines. It wasn't dark yet, but the canopy above them shielded what little light remained in the day.

Maggie pulled the girls closer to her for warmth. "You girls must be on your best behavior tonight. Mr. Reece was most kind to invite us to meet his cousin, so be sure and pay your respects to him."

Annalee was having a hard time sitting still. "Do you think someone will ask us to dance, Maggie? I love dancing."

"I don't rightly know what to expect, Annalee. We'll just have to wait and see."

Maggie was proud of how the girls looked. Sally Catherine had collected hand-me-downs from her neighbors over the years for special occasions like this. Annalee wore a pink calf-length taffeta dress with a ruffled yoke and a wide sash and Hannah wore a pale blue faille dress that hugged her generous curves, making her look older and more sophisticated than sixteen.

"Listen, I hear music," Maggie said. "Straighten up now, we're almost there."

Homer drove the carriage around the driveway that circled the Evans's mansion. Maggie had never seen anything like it out in the country. It was set up on brick pillars that were at least five feet tall, closed in underneath with latticework. The house itself was three stories high, with wide porches ringing the first two floors and windows that went from floor to ceiling. Homer drove the carriage underneath a tall portico supported by thick square posts. Every window was lit and people were milling about in what looked to be the parlor. The house was as beautiful as any of the mansions that Maggie had seen in Raleigh.

Homer brought the carriage to a stop under the portico where Reece was standing. Maggie felt like Cinderella. "Good evening, ladies. I see my coach has brought you safely home." Reece bowed deeply and smiled at Maggie and the girls. "Thank you, Homer, you've done well to bring these beautiful women through the great dismal swamp of Onslow County," he said with exaggerated pomp. Homer chuckled and held the horses steady.

"Alight! Alight, and welcome to Evanwood," Reece said, helping the girls out of the carriage first. He turned to Maggie, sweeping his eyes over her with pleasure. "Maggie Lorena, you are even more lovely than I remembered."

Maggie had worn the green taffeta dress just as she had planned, taking great care to keep it smooth in the carriage. Aunt Mag had inserted matching Alencon lace in panels in the bodice, revealing Maggie's décolletage beneath the sheer lace. Before she left for Onslow, Aunt Mag had insisted that Maggie try on the dress with her corset so that it would fit like a glove. Judging by Reece's lingering gaze, that effort had not been in vain.

"Thank you. Your house is beautiful," she said, stepping down from the carriage.

"Thank *you*, Maggie. My grandfather would have loved to hear you say that." Reece took her arm and led her up the steps. Lanterns were hung all along the facade, their reflections dancing in the tall windows. Inside, he paused in the foyer, watching her take in the architecture and furnishings.

"Oh, I'm sure he was very proud of such a fine home out here in the country. There must be none like it for miles and miles." Hundreds of miles, she thought, observing the thick Persian carpet laid on heart-of-pine flooring. Overhead an electric chandelier burned brightly, illuminating the hall and a grand stairway going up either side.

Reece rocked back and forth on his heels, his hands clasped behind his back. "I hoped you would like it," he said. The girls giggled, and Maggie gave them a sharp look. Reece paid no attention. "Maggie, you will come with me. The younger ladies will join my cousin's children in the back parlor."

Hannah and Annalee looked at each other, then at Maggie. She shrugged and shushed them with her finger while Reece called to a young Negro woman who appeared from a closet under one side of the stairs. "Felicity, take Miss Hannah and Miss Annalee in with the other children and introduce them. I'll send Miss Emily in shortly."

Felicity reached for Annalee's hand, but Hannah turned to Reece. "Pardon, Mr. Reece, but I turned sixteen almost a year ago and I would prefer to stay with Miss Maggie."

"Oh my. Forgive me, my dear," Reece said with mock sincerity. He looked her up and down and bowed slightly. "You certainly are not a child any longer. But I have misled you, Hannah, you will not be in the company of young'uns. You know Miss Emily's children, Jeanne and Darcy, from school, and there are also some cousins from Philadelphia who are much closer to your age than the old folks in the parlor. Now go along with Felicity, and I think you will have a much better time."

Hannah curtsied, a look of disdain on her face. "Thank you, Mr. Reece." She followed Felicity and Annalee. Looking back, she called to Maggie, "Remember, we can't stay too long. I promised Papa."

Maggie was left alone in the hallway with Reece. In the adjoining room she could hear people laughing and talking over the strains of violin music. He stepped closer to her, and she smelled the whiskey on his breath. "Maggie, you have no idea how I've looked forward to this." He slipped his arm about her waist and drew her to him.

"Reece, please," she said, trying to pull away.

"No. It's too late. I've fallen in love with you."

"That's absurd. Please stop. You've been drinking."

"Oh, it's not the whiskey talking, my dear. I've thought of nothing but you for weeks." His arms were about her shoulders, and her struggle was futile. Her hands slipped inside his coat and around his waist as his lips touched hers. Neither of them heard Emily enter the foyer.

"Reece! What's going on here?" his sister demanded. Reece released his hold and Maggie stepped away from him, blushing.

Emily McAllister tapped her foot, wearing a disgusted expression which soon melted into a smile. "I see that Miss Corbinn has arrived. Won't you introduce us?"

"Really, Emily," Reece said, "since we were children, you've had a knack for showing up at the most inopportune times." He turned to Maggie. "She enjoys this sort of thing."

"I'm Emily McAllister, Maggie. Please don't be embarrassed. My brother's impertinence is nothing new to me. It's a pleasure to meet you."

Maggie managed a smile and offered her hand to the stylish, petite woman who stood before her. "Thank you, Miss Emily. It's a pleasure to be in your home."

"Whose home?" Reece asked impishly. "I believe Miss Emily will agree that Grandpa left this house to me and she lives here at my pleasure."

"Reece, your rudeness is intolerable. Come with me, Maggie, I'll introduce you to our other guests," she said, leading Maggie into the parlor. "You'll have to forgive Reece. Grandpa spoiled him terribly." Maggie followed, trying to look pleasant, but she was still trembling from the encounter with Reece. She had wanted that kiss more than anything.

Emily steered Maggie through the room past several groups of people who sat in upholstered chairs between the windows. On the opposite side, velvet settees flanked a large fireplace whose mantel held clocks of every description. The floor was bare for dancing, except for the area in front of the fireplace.

"Cousin Mary Madeline asked to have you brought to her as soon as you arrived," Emily said. She took two cups from a tray offered by one of the servants, handing one to Maggie. "Reece has told her that he is going to marry you someday, but I don't suppose he has told you that," she said, tapping Maggie's cup in a brief toast.

"Please forgive my behavior, Miss Emily. Reece is so beguiling, I don't know what to think."

Emily reached for Maggie's hand. "My dear, I know you're embarrassed, but Reece is like that—so devilish and demanding. Just be yourself and don't let him have his way with you."

"Thank you. I must say he's had my head spinning. I'm never sure if he's serious or not."

"Well, I think it's obvious that he is very fond of you, just as Darcy and Jeanne are." A look of amusement came over her face. "That may be an understatement."

"They're the best in the class. Smart as whips. I wish I had a room full of students like them."

"Thank you, dear. I had considered sending them to the Academy at Richlands this year until I heard that Bill Ryan had found us a new teacher." She looked Maggie over. "Frankly, I'm surprised that someone with your looks would be content to teach school in these backwoods."

"It just seemed the right thing to do at the time, Miss Emily."

"Oh, just call me Emily. I'm not that much older than you. I hope that we can be friends. I'm always in Jacksonville over the weekend. If you're in the store any Saturday, you'll usually find me there. Come to see me and we'll talk some more."

"I'd like that, too. Maybe you can help me figure your brother out."

"That might take awhile. There are far too many other people here who would like to know more about him. Come, let me introduce you to Cousin Mary Madeline. She thinks Reece and I belong to her. We lived with her in Philadelphia while Mother was so ill with typhoid fever. She would have kept us on if my grandfather hadn't come for us." Emily bent to kiss a stout woman whose rose-colored taffeta skirts were spread out over a low round ottoman, reminding Maggie of the cone flowers that grew along the roadside in Bladen County.

"Cousin Mary, this is Maggie Lorena Corbinn, our new schoolteacher."

Maggie curtsied and the woman held out a pudgy hand. "My dear, you are as beautiful as I was told," she said in a small high-pitched voice. "That Reece is a scoundrel, isn't he?" Her eyes sparkled mischievously above fat cheeks smeared with rouge. "Come, sit here by me and let's get acquainted."

Mary Madeline said that she had arrived from Philadelphia the week before, traveling with two nephews. Like a child's, her hair was parted in the middle and braided in pigtails that were tied together at the back of her head with a satin ribbon. She was quite deaf and carried a speaking tube which she offered to Maggie. Each time Maggie shouted into it, someone else in the room would turn to the sound of her raised voice.

"So, you've come to Onslow County to teach school. Now why in the world would anyone want to come to this godforsaken country?" Mary Madeline asked.

Maggie had to laugh. "Living here isn't that bad, Miss Mary Madeline."

"These dratted mosquitoes, gnats and flies seem to pervade the entire South. How do you people tolerate them? I will never understand why Grandpa settled here." She dabbed at her face with a dainty handkerchief.

"Oh, you're quite right, the bugs are a nuisance," Maggie said, indulging her. "But you've come at the wrong time of year, Miss Mary. Once you've smelled the magnolia and the cape jessamine in the springtime, you might have a better opinion of us. I'm sure Reece has fortified this house with window screens. It's the poorer folks in the county who might complain. Why, I understand they have no screens at all," she shouted into the tube. There were screens on the outside doors at the Ryans's house, but not on the windows, which were closed in the daytime to keep out the heat. If the windows were opened at night, mosquito netting had to be draped about the high-posted beds to thwart any mosquitoes who came in on the night air.

"Yes, and I understand they still have outdoor toilets, too," Miss Mary said. "So primitive. A hole in the ground!" She leaned back and rolled her eyes.

"I'm afraid that's true. Not many folks have indoor plumbing." It had taken her awhile to get back into the habit of emptying slop jars and filling kerosene lamps after living in Raleigh.

"So we're primitive, are we?" Reece had made his way across the room to stand behind Maggie's chair. "Cousin Mary, behave yourself.

You'll offend Miss Corbinn. Haven't we provided you with a toilet and running water?"

"Eh? What did you say, Reece? Maggie, give him the tube."

Reece took the tube Maggie offered him.   "I said, you've bent Maggie's ear long enough, Cousin Mary. I'll take her to the table for refreshments and send a plate over for you."

"You'll do no such thing, you wicked boy." She struggled to rise from the ottoman, reaching for Reece's hand. "I've seen the table and I'll not have you bringing me a skimpy little plate. Remember, my girl in Philadelphia trained your cook!" Mary waddled off in the direction of the dining room table, her skirts jiggling with each step.

"She doesn't like the South much, does she?" Maggie asked.

"Oh, she likes it well enough. She just likes to complain. Cousin Mary wouldn't miss coming down here to see Emily and me for anything."

"Why do you like it here, Reece? You could probably live anywhere."

"Yes, I could, but Grandpa left me Evanwood. I think I have a responsibility to him, for one thing, since he raised Emily and me."

"And your parents? What happened to them?"

"Oh, come on. I'm sure the Ryans have told you that my father was a gun runner. He played the odds on both sides and he got killed doing it."

"Really, Reece. You make him out to be such a blackguard."

Reece steered her through an open door out onto the porch. "It's true, it runs in the blood. Ask Cousin Madeline."

Maggie leaned against the porch railing. "What about your mother? Tell me about her."

"There's not much to tell. She died when I was three years old. My grandmother said it was of typhoid, but I suspect it was mostly of a broken heart."

"And your sister? I don't mean to pry, but I was wondering why she lives here with you."

"Emily and Duncan have a home in Jacksonville, but she prefers to be here in the country most of the time. She thinks she needs to take care of me."

Maggie laughed. "I think someone does."

Reece smiled. He was leaning over the rail, toying with a twig that he had picked up off the porch floor. "How about you?" he asked, his eyes focused on something in the distance.

"How about me what?"

"If you think someone needs to take care of me, how about you?"

"Really, Reece, do be serious! You sound as if you're asking me to..."

"To marry me? Perhaps I am. Would you accept?"

"I can't believe this. You're making my head swim with all this talk, and I know you're not serious."

He looked directly into her eyes. "I'm dead serious, Maggie. But have it your way for now. However, I warn you I'll ask that question again." He pointed to the parlor just inside the French doors. "You see those clocks on the mantel? I collected those all over Europe. They mean something to me. A constant reminder that time is of the essence. We can waste it, or we can make the most of it. I intend to make the most of it."

Music was playing and several couples began to dance on the terrace. Reece slipped his arm around Maggie's waist and waltzed her through the door. "*Tempus fugit*, my dear. The evening will be gone and I won't have danced with you." She was giddy with laughter as he swirled and twirled her about until her head grew light. She had dreamed of this—the green taffeta dress, his arm around her waist.

When the music ended, he led her to the punch bowl and introduced her to some of his friends, several of whom were parents of her students. She recognized Elsie Bannerman, mother of the three Bannerman boys. There were dark circles under her eyes, but her face was well-made with cream and powder, a sign that she was not without means. Around her neck she wore a gold chain with several baubles attached to it.

"Mrs. Bannerman, how nice to see you," Maggie said.

"Well, Miss Corbinn, I didn't expect to see you here." Her tone was slightly condescending, and Maggie wondered why. Every day at lunch Elsie had come to bring hot meals to her boys, just as Hannah had predicted. Maggie had tried to engage her in conversation several times, but Elsie left in haste soon after her children were fed.

"And you, Mrs. Bannerman, I had not expected to see you here."

"Well, the Evans and the Bannermans have known each other for ages." She tapped Reece on the arm with a folded silk fan that matched her ochre-colored crepe gown. "Haven't we, Reece?" Her mouth had a twist to it that Maggie did not understand.

He gestured with upraised hands. "For centuries, at least, Elsie," he said with a touch of sarcasm, and walked away.

The little tit for tat made Maggie uncomfortable and she was glad to see him leave. She changed the subject. "You certainly have nice boys. It's a pleasure to have them in my class. Won't you come in sometime?"

"Miss Corbinn, in case you don't know, my husband is an invalid."

"Please call me Maggie. Yes, I know about your husband, but I thought maybe if someone was there at home with him, you might..."

"No, no, I couldn't, Miss Corbinn," she said, fanning herself. "Hank might need me."

"Well, if you ever change your mind and want to stay after lunch, I really could use your help."

"You want me to help with school?"

"Well, yes. There are lots of things you could do. We need to set up a lending library, for one thing," Maggie said.

Elsie Bannerman brightened. "Do you think I could do that?"

"I don't see why not."

"I might be able to leave my husband a few hours a week. Would that work?"

"Why, yes," Maggie said, pleased that she might have won Elsie over.

"You are planning on staying, aren't you?" Elsie asked. "We haven't had a teacher for such a long time. The boys are very fond of you."

Reece returned with two cups of punch and offered them to the women. "I'm not sure how long I'll be here," Maggie said, glancing at him. "I haven't finished my education at BFU. I may return to Raleigh next fall."

"That is, if someone doesn't sweep her off her feet first," Reece said, slipping his arm around Maggie's waist.

"Well, it will not likely be you, will it, Reece?" Elsie said in a biting tone.

Reece looked at her with disdain and bowed. "Excuse us, Elsie, I see some of my guests are heading towards the door."

When they had gone a few steps, Maggie stopped him. "What did she mean?"

"Really, Maggie, she's just one of those women who stir trouble. It's nothing to be concerned about, I assure you. There is no telling what you may hear about me."

"I should see about the girls—I think we should be going," Maggie said, feeling slightly uneasy. There was something she should know about; she was sure of it.

"No, the evening is still quite young and the girls are probably having the time of their lives. I've told everyone that you play the piano."

"Reece, this is preposterous. I can't. I'm so rusty. The piano at school is out of tune, I can't do much more than..."

"I'll have it tuned as soon as I can get a tuner here from Wilmington. Mine was tuned last week—just for you," he said. Maggie had seen the mahogany Steinway from across the room and was dying to run her hands over it, but the thought of playing it for Reece's guests terrified her.

Reece led her by the hand to the piano and seated her so that she faced the room. His guests began to gather around the piano and Reece started a soft clapping. She protested again. "Really, Reece, I'd rather not. Not tonight."

He whispered in her ear. "Come now, Maggie, just a little sing-along while the musicians are out for a smoke."

Before her on the piano was a book of Stephen Foster songs. She opened it, thumbing through the familiar melodies, gaining confidence, seeing the tunes that she had played over and over on Aunt Mag's piano. After the first few chords of *I Dream of Jeannie*, Emily appeared beside Reece and the two began to sing. Maggie was so taken aback that she lost a little of the composure she had mustered. But they sang so beautifully together, his tenor and her soprano in perfect harmony, that Maggie relaxed and began to enjoy the music. One song followed another, and some of the guests joined in the singing. Maggie glanced up to see Hannah and Annalee in the audience. Ending the last song, she slid off the piano bench and curtsied to the applause.

"Really, my dear, that was quite delightful," Reece said.

"Thank you, but I'd say you and Emily were the stars of the show."

"Not hardly. You underestimate your talent. Now, come have some punch before the musicians return and some of this young crowd takes over the dance floor."

"Maggie, you were wonderful," Hannah said, squeezing her around the shoulders. "I wish we had a piano at home so you could play for us."

"We have one at school. I think a tuner is coming next week." She flashed a smile at Reece.

Hannah reached for Maggie's hand. "Maggie, we really should go. I promised Papa."

"Aren't you having fun, Hannah?"

She blushed. "Yes, ma'am. It's just that I promised." But Maggie knew that it was more like loyalty to Tate that brought on her sudden urge to leave.

"Do you think Homer could take us now, Mr. Reece?" Hannah asked.

"Go and get your sister. I'll drive you myself," he said, like an exasperated father. "Maggie, I'd like a word with you in my study before we leave."

The smell of liquor was heavy on his breath and Maggie wasn't sure that she wanted to be alone with him. "Of course, but please call for Homer to take us. You have guests. I'd like to pay my respects to Miss Emily and Miss Mary Madeline."

"Very well. I will be last, but never least. I'll see you in my study." He moved towards the bar.

Cousin Mary had also had more than she needed to drink. Her eyelids drooped and she was breathing heavily. "Maggie Lorena, come here and sit by me. I met Stephen Foster once and let me tell you..."

"Miss Mary, I'm afraid we must leave. It's has been a pleasure to make your acquaintance. I hope you'll return in the spring when the cape jasmines are blooming."

"Dear child, I'm afraid that I was a bit cranky earlier," she said in a slurred voice. "I have always loved it here. It is just that I don't want Reece to know it. He is so terribly arrogant. My word, he thinks this place is a bit of heaven." She shifted in her chair and took a swallow of wine, gulping it greedily. Her face glistened with perspiration and her lip rouge was smeared. "Be careful, darling. He will break your heart, too."

Maggie wasn't sure she'd heard her correctly. "How's that, Miss Mary?"

"Oh, never mind. You look as if you can stand your own. Now be a sweet child and bring Miss Mary another glass of wine. I have to pee and I want to go on up to bed with a little nightcap."

Emily McAllister made her way to them across the dance floor. "Cousin Mary, I'm afraid we've worn you out this evening. Say goodbye to Maggie and I'll see you to your room. Maggie, Felicity will show you the way to Reece's study."

"Thank you, Miss Emily. I've had a lovely time. Thank you for including me and the girls."

"It's been our pleasure, Maggie. You're a far cry from the old-maid schoolteachers we've had in the last few years. I'd like to see you stay on for awhile. Who knows what the future might bring," Emily said.

There it is again—that slight warning, but this time with a touch of hope. Well, one of these days someone is going to let the cat out of the bag.

—

Reece closed the door quickly behind the maid. Pulling Maggie into an embrace, he kissed her. "It's been an evening I've dreamed of," he said. Maggie was at a loss for words. He held her face, kissed her eyelids, the tip of her nose, then her mouth again, exploring, reaching. "Now I'll never let you go," he whispered.

She tried to think of a response, but he wouldn't allow her to get her breath. He smelled of whiskey, and his face was wet with perspiration, but she didn't care. She didn't care that the girls were waiting, or that everyone had warned her that Reece was...*what?*

He smoothed her hair back from her face and looked into her eyes. "Maggie, there are some things about me I need to..." He stopped short and brushed her cheek with a kiss. "No, the time's not right. Let's not spoil it. Just believe me when I say..." But before he could finish, Emily tapped lightly on the door.

"Reece, Homer is waiting."

—

Tate was furious with himself. He had taken for granted that Maggie's living with his folks gave him an edge over the likes of Reece Evans. The son-of-a-bitch was probably wooing her right now! He walked round and round the corn crib. It was cold out, the night air frosty. He was in his nightshirt, unable to sleep with the lamps still lit and Maggie and the girls out so late. What could be keeping them? Hannah had said she'd make an excuse to leave early—she'd make sure Reece didn't get to be alone with Maggie.

Relieved to hear the jingle of the horse's livery as the buggy turned into the lane, he slipped back inside the house and went to his room. From his darkened window he saw Homer help Maggie and the girls out of the buggy.

He moved away from the window and sat on his bed. Where was Hannah? She'd promised to come into his room and tell him about the party. He waited another ten minutes before he started down the hall to her room, but she met him at her door. "Shhh. Annalee's already asleep."

Tate tiptoed back to his room and Hannah followed him in and closed the door. "Where were you?" he whispered. "You said you were going to come..."

"I was talking to Maggie." Hannah hopped up on his bed and sat with her legs crossed under her. "Oh, Tate, I wish you'd been there. We met his cousins from Philadelphia. One was a fat old lady, but there were two boys about my age. They were so nice to me, asked me to dance and everything."

"And 'everything' what?"

She cut her eyes towards him and smiled. "You know what I mean."

"So, you had fun?" He knew she had without asking. Her eyes were all lit up.

"It was the most special time of my life. Wouldn't it be wonderful to live like that—having parties—visiting cousins up and down the coast?"

"To some it might. What about Maggie? Did she have fun?"

"Yes, she did, Tate. She couldn't help it. Everyone was making over her. She was playing the piano and dancing."

"Who was she dancing with?"

"Oh, you know who it was. Mr. Reece, who else? He'd been drinking, as usual, but I think he swept her off her feet."

"Son-of-a-bitch!"

"Hush, Tate. Papa will hear you." Hannah kissed him on the cheek. "I'm sorry. I know if you'd been there, it would've been you she was dancing with."

She slipped out and closed the door. Tate crawled under the covers, resolving to really get going on his house the very next day. If he was going to win Maggie's heart, he would need something to offer her, and he couldn't think of anything better than the house he had been planning for over a year now.

Chapter 18

At breakfast the next morning Maggie listened while Hannah and Annalee talked about the fun they'd had at the soirée. "I was afraid we'd be bored to death," Hannah said. "But Mama, Mr. Reece's cousins were so nice." She sighed and her cheeks turned pink.

"Well now, I know my girls were perfect little ladies, weren't they, Maggie?"

"They sure were, Miss Sally."

Tate was watching Maggie as if he expected her to say more. When he and Bill left to go to the barn, Sally Catherine asked, "What about you, Maggie? Did you have a good time? You aren't saying much."

"Oh, it was a lovely party," Maggie said. "I enjoyed meeting Miss Mary Madeline. She's a character right out of Charles Dickens."

"Maggie played the piano, Mama," Annalee said. "She knows all the Stephen Foster songs."

"I declare, I'd sure love to have been there and heard that."

"Miss Emily and Mr. Reece sang together while Maggie played," Hannah said.

"Do tell. How is Miss Emily? It's been a while since I've seen her."

"She's so lovely. I really enjoyed meeting her," Maggie said.

"And Mr. Reece, I'll bet he was nice to y'all."

"He was to Maggie," Hannah said with a frown. "I don't like him one bit. He was drinking whiskey. I smelled it on him."

"Now Hannah Jane Ryan, I don't like to hear you talking like that," Sally Catherine said.

Maggie got up and went to the sink to rinse out her plate. "Did you tell your mama about Miss Mary Madeline's nephew dancing with you, Hannah? He was a handsome young man. I'll bet he'll be sending you letters."

Hannah blushed. "He might."

"Well, Miss Sally, I'll let the girls tell you some more about the soirée. I need to rinse out a few things and write some letters, it being Saturday and all. Can I help with the dishes?"

"No ma'am. You go on and do your chores. I've got all the help I need right here."

For days, Maggie's head churned with thoughts of the evening at Evanwood—the things Reece had said, things she wished she had asked. Reece had indicated that he might be going away, but when? She hadn't thought to ask. It had all happened so fast, so naturally. Now she had a thousand questions, and they increased as the days went by.

The following week she arrived at the schoolhouse one morning to find the playground stripped of cotton stalks, leveled and raked clean. Another morning, a vase of gold and deep burgundy chrysanthemums was on her desk. She figured these gestures were his way of touching her until he could come. But why? What was holding him back?

Maggie wrote to Aunt Mag and told her that the gentleman farmer who had brought the picnic lunch seemed intent on courting her. Aunt Mag wrote back that the road to hell was paved with good intentions and Maggie would do well not to let anyone turn her head too fast. Maggie decided that she'd keep her thoughts about Reece Evans from Aunt Mag for the time being, at least until she could determine if she was being played the fool.

Aunt Mag's other news was distressing. Ellen had fallen and broken her hip.

Katie's response to the news of the party at Evanwood was exactly as Maggie had expected. *Congratulations, big sis—the belle of the ball! In that green taffeta dress, I'll bet you had his head swimming. But I'm dying to know what the mystery is about him. Ask around. Someone will be willing to tell you the gossip.*

Plans for the square dance on Halloween occupied most of Maggie's spare time for the next two weeks as word spread throughout Stump Sound Township. "Everyone wants to come," Sally Catherine said. "It's been so long since we had any fiddling and dancing. I reckon they also want to come see what the new teacher has done to the schoolhouse."

"Well, you just tell them all to come on," Maggie said.

She had nineteen students now, and each one spent a part of the school day coloring and cutting out paper leaves to stick on the tall windows. The boys gathered cornstalks from the fields, tied them in bundles and stood them in the corners and along the walls around the edges of the room. Emily McAllister sent a small cartload of pumpkins to make jack-o'-lanterns and promised to bring candles to light them. Before the evening of the dance, the desks would be stacked outside to open up the floor for dancing.

Tate was at the schoolhouse almost every day. His excuses for stopping by varied. Sometimes he'd only stay an hour or so, but occasionally he'd stay half the day. "I think I better split some more wood, get that woodpile stacked a little higher before we have some hard cold weather."

"That would be nice, Tate. I wasn't expecting you today, but what I really need is for someone to shovel some lime into the toilet back there. It smells to high heaven."

"Sure. Just let me finish getting this brush off the play yard. I reckon Reece'll plant peanuts right up to the door next year."

"I hope we'll have that new school over at Harris Creek by then, but if we don't, Reece told your pa that he'd leave it uncultivated until the new school is built. I suppose he will."

"Just don't you count on it, Maggie Lorena. It wouldn't be the first time he went back on his word."

"What do you mean by that?"

"I'm sorry. I shouldn't of said that. I don't suppose he'd ever have cause to go back on his word to Pa, but some might see it a little different."

On the day of the dance, Maggie put the finishing touches on the decorations with Hannah and Annalee's help. Just as they were leaving to go home and change their dresses, Bill Ryan came in with two other fiddlers that he'd lined up to play with for the dance. "Just look at this old schoolhouse," he said, raising his hands. "I declare, Maggie Lorena, you are the best thing that ever happened to Onslow County. Don't you ever leave us, you hear?"

"I can't rightly say I won't ever leave, but I can promise you I'll stay through tonight because I love fiddling and I love to square dance."

"Tate loves to dance too, Maggie. He's awful shy, but you get him wound up and he'll dance his fool head off. I guess he comes by it proud."

"Why, I didn't know you liked to dance. You've got enough fiddlers that you could take a break and spin Miss Sally Catherine around a little."

"Sally Catherine doesn't dance anymore. It's her rheumatism and she has sugar in her blood, you know."

"Gracious, Mr. Bill, I'll dance with you. You just let me know when you're ready."

Putting away her scissors and paste in the storeroom, Maggie thought of Sally Catherine and her own mother. They had both worn themselves out before their time, having one baby right after the other. Maggie didn't intend to do that. She'd have one or two, that's all. Her husband would have to hire his field hands.

A row of jack-o'-lanterns smiled at everyone as they came up the steps and in the schoolhouse door. Bales of hay and bundles of cornstalks formed a backdrop for the fiddlers, whose music seemed to be piping in all of Onslow County.

Maggie was ecstatic. It was a bigger crowd than she had expected; everyone in the community seemed to be there, and she was eager to make a good impression. From blue calico print material bought at

McAllister's in Jacksonville, she'd made a new skirt with a wide ruffle on the bottom, pinched up just enough at the hem in back to show her white eyelet petticoat. She had ordered a white lawn blouse with insets of lace from the Sears Roebuck catalogue, and the mailman had brought it just a day before the dance.

Out of the corner of her eye, Maggie saw Tate keeping time to the music, clapping his hands and shuffling his feet. She walked over and stood beside him. "Would you like to dance, Tate? I'm ready if you are."

"Well, yes ma'am! I'll give you a run for your money." He laughed and swung her out onto the dance floor, but the music slowed to a waltz, and he looked confused. "I'm not much at this kind of dancing. When I said I'd give you a run for your money, I was talking about square dancing," he said, holding her awkwardly in his arms.

"Oh, come on," Maggie said. "I'll show you how." He was stiff as a starched collar, concentrating on his feet instead of the rhythm of the music. "Relax, Tate, it's just me."

He stopped and looked at her. "Just you? You're about the most important person in my life."

"Tate, don't. Let's just dance."

"Maggie, I love you," he said, almost to himself.

"What'd you say?"

"I bet you heard me. I said I love you. I mean it. I really do."

Maggie didn't know what to say. She had tried so hard not to encourage Tate, going out of her way to avoid him at times, joking with him in a sisterly way. But this was no joke. Tate was serious. "I told you that day over by Black River..."

"I know, but things are different now, aren't they?"

"Yes...and no, Tate. Some things are different, but..." She wished the music would end, but the fiddlers seemed to go on and on. If she didn't know better, she'd think he had bribed his pa to keep playing so he could get his say in.

"But what? What's different, if you don't mind telling me?"

"I can't talk now. I have to go help with the refreshments," she said, giving him a little hug.

He took her hands in his before she could get away. "I really mean it, Maggie. You hear?"

———

Elsie Bannerman had made all of the refreshment arrangements, baking cookies and enlisting the help of several mothers to make fruit punch. Finding enough punch cups had been her biggest problem. When Maggie came to relieve her, she had stacked up a dishpan full to wash. "I'm going to the cloakroom to wash these, if you can stand here for awhile, Maggie."

"Let me do it, Elsie. I'd like to catch my breath."

"No, you need to be out here."

There was a rustle among the men standing in the corner opposite the refreshment table and Elsie turned to look. "Well, I declare, look who's here," she said. Maggie looked up just in time to catch Reece's eye. He nodded and she smiled.

"Everyone was invited. I guess he didn't want to miss out on the fun," Maggie said.

"He's probably liquored up. Mind you, he doesn't mind making trouble."

"What is it, Elsie? Everyone seems so down on him. I like him. Shouldn't I?"

"He has a lot of history. I wouldn't get tangled up with him, if I were you."

"You sound as if you're talking from personal experience."

"You guessed that right," Elsie said. "We grew up together and folks, including me, thought something might come of it. But not Reece."

Maggie wanted to know more. Everyone in the room seemed to be watching him. She hadn't really expected him to come, although his sister's children said they'd begged him to. Miss Sally Catherine had told her once that he was a brooding kind of man—one who had no happiness coming from inside. With his long face, he certainly looked the part tonight.

She could almost feel his gaze on her as she wandered around the room speaking to her students' parents. At any moment she expected his hand on her shoulder, but the fiddlers began again with a lively square dance and Tate grabbed Maggie's hand. They joined in the large circle forming in the center of the room. The fiddler who was making the calls seemed intent on wearing the dancers out. "Now swing your partner and do-si-do," he called out. Round and round they went for least ten minutes.

When the dance was over, Maggie collapsed on the nearest bench to catch her breath. She glanced around the room. Reece was nowhere to be seen.

Chapter 19

A cold wind blew across the countryside for the next several days, stripping the trees of their dry leaves and bringing in dark clouds. Rain followed, darkening Maggie's spirits as much as her classroom. She found it difficult to concentrate, her mind cluttered with questions. Reece had been so bold at the party. Why hadn't she had some word from him since? Had it only been the liquor talking? And why had he ignored her at the Halloween dance—left without a word? Try as hard as she might, she couldn't understand.

Maggie was standing near the window, giving an arithmetic test to the older students, when she saw someone dressed in a black slicker and a wide-brimmed hat hitching his horse to the rail. The ninth and tenth graders had been reading *The Headless Horseman*, and she was amused at the thought that the dark figure from the story had been reincarnated with his head intact.

When she heard his footsteps on the porch, she whispered to Hannah, "Please take a seat at my desk. I need to step outside for a breath of air." Hannah and the rest of the students turned in unison to watch Maggie wrap a shawl around her shoulders and close the door behind her.

Reece came up the steps and shook the rain off his hat. They stood very close under the small roof above the door, but he made no attempt to touch her. His face was pale and drawn, his shoulders slumped. "Hello, Maggie," he said.

"Reece, why haven't I heard from you? At your house, you said... I thought maybe you had gone away."

"Something's come up. I'm going to Philadelphia. I'm not sure when I'll be back."

"Can't you tell me? I feel I should have some explanation. You said..."

"I meant what I said. Don't ever doubt that, no matter what you might hear."

"I don't understand. What's wrong? What might I hear?"

"Never mind, Maggie. I'll explain it all to you some day. You get back inside now. I have to go." He raised his hand slightly, as if to touch her arm. His eyes were on her face. "You've complicated my life beyond measure. Before you, I didn't really care how long it took, but now every minute is precious. Time shouldn't be wasted. It goes by too fast."

"Reece, you're not making any sense. You must tell me."

"I can't. Not now," he said, and started down the steps. Rain was coming down harder, sheets of it, and she could hardly see him by the time he got to his horse. She threw up her hand to wave, and in an instant, he was gone.

Maggie yearned for someone to talk to. Like everyone else, Elsie Bannerman seemed to have some sort of preconceived notion about Reece. She certainly couldn't discuss her feelings for him with Sally Catherine, who harbored the same hope as everyone else in the Ryan family—that she would marry Tate someday. It was almost time for Christmas holidays and she couldn't bear going home without knowing something. Emily McAllister was the only person who might help her, but she'd have to figure out a way to get to Jacksonville on Saturday. Emily had said they could talk.

Like an old mother hen, Sally Catherine saw that one of her chicks was brooding. "You're pale as a ghost, child, does something ail you?"

"I'm all right, Miss Sally. I need a little tonic, I guess. My spirits are low, mostly."

"Will you be going home for Christmas? The school is usually closed about a month. You're welcome to share ours, but I 'spect your folks would be mighty disappointed."

"Oh, I'll be going home. Aunt Mag said Pa would be here about the fifteenth of December. He has a commissioners' meeting in Burgaw." Her smile was forced.

There was no fooling Sally Catherine. "What ails you? You haven't been the same since the Halloween dance. Has somebody upset you?"

"No, ma'am. I'll snap out of it. I was thinking about asking Mr. Bill if I could take the buggy into Jacksonville on Saturday and buy some linen and lace to make handkerchiefs for Christmas presents. The girls can come too, if they like."

"Sure thing, honey. Tate can drive you. You don't want to go getting aggravated with that horse. Pa says Daniel is ornery with everyone but Tate."

Maggie dreaded the thought of being alone with Tate. So far he hadn't had another opportunity to declare his love, and Maggie wanted to leave it that way. "He'd be welcome to come, but I don't see any need for him to go to that trouble just for me."

"It's no trouble at all. I think Pa needs some chicken feed and I'm out of some of my staples. I'll start making a list for Tate. He might want to take the wagon, if that doesn't matter to you."

Maggie went to bed early that evening, too tired to work on her story and too downhearted to make conversation with the Ryans. Maybe Tate was right, maybe Reece was a scoundrel. How could she be sure of anything when all she had were promises? She tried in vain to put him out of her mind. He had captured her heart the day he walked into the schoolhouse and slipped her glasses off her nose. Wash had offered her love, but he had been so young, just a boy in comparison to Reece. Reece desired her with every glance. She felt his ardor when he neared her.

Hannah and Annalee opted not to go to Jacksonville, making excuses that Maggie suspected Tate had devised. Although Maggie had done nothing to encourage him, he had an air of satisfaction, as if his declaration of love had settled things. In the wagon a few miles from home, she wasn't surprised when he brought up the subject. "Maggie Lorena, you haven't been the same to me since I said what I did at the dance. Is something wrong?"

"Let's not get into that. I'm not in the mood to talk about anything today with this headache."

"I'm sorry. There're some things I've been wanting to ask you."

"Tate, I told you that it would be a long time before I could put Wash Pridgen out of my mind. I'm just not ready yet." She knew it was a lie. Reece had already replaced Wash in her thoughts and dreams.

Tate shifted on the seat and flicked the reins across the backs of the two horses. "Well, how long do you think it's gonna be?"

"Please. Can't we just be friends for now? You're like a brother to me."

"All right, I can wait. You just let me know when you're ready and I'll come courting." He smiled and punched her lightly with his elbow.

She tried to keep from smiling, but he had said it so warmly that she couldn't hold back. "Thank you. I will," she said, reaching over and squeezing his hand.

The road followed along the eastern side of the Evans's fields, and Tate pointed to the lane that led through the thick tall pines to Evanwood. "Old man Silas Evans used to send Homer's pa, Henry, over to fetch me to play with Reece. There weren't too many boys around here then. We had some good times before he got mean as the devil."

"How was he mean?" Maggie asked. "Was he really bad or just a rounder?"

"He was mean, Maggie. He'd catch bullfrogs over in the pond, tie their legs together with a piece of string and watch them drown when they couldn't swim to the top."

"That's awful, but he's a grown man now. Those were just childish pranks," she said, recalling some of her brothers' devilishness.

"You've got some golderned awful high opinion of him. It don't matter what I say, you're not going to believe it."

"No, I'm not. Besides, I don't think you can drown an old bull-frog!" She laughed and his mood seemed to change.

"Let's forget about Reece Evans, Maggie. It's a pretty day and I'm just darn glad to be enjoying it with you."

But Maggie couldn't forget about Reece. He was all she could think about and she intended to make some inquiries in town, if at all possible. There must be some way she could do it without seeming too forward.

With Christmas not too far off, Jacksonville was busier than usual for a Saturday morning. Maggie had been wanting to go to Miss Tucie Ott's millinery shop, but there wouldn't be enough time to do both if she could get up with Emily. She decided to go straight to McAllister's General Store.

"There's no need for you to come in, Tate. I'll get your mother's supplies and you can sign for them when you pick me up."

"That's real nice of you. I could use a little extra time in the feed store. I've got a friend down there who's always trying to beat me at checkers."

"Well, I might not be that long," Maggie said. "But if I finish before you do, I'll go to Miss Tucie's."

He dropped Maggie off in front of McAllister's and she took in a deep breath before pushing open the door. At the front counter she asked the clerk to fill Sally Catherine's order while she went to look at fabric. Duncan McAllister was helping a lady in the shoe department, and another clerk was re-stocking shelves. Emily was nowhere in sight. Maggie went to the dry goods department and walked from table to table running her hand over the fabrics. She was lost in thought when Duncan addressed her.

"Miss Corbinn?"

Maggie jumped when he called her name. "Oh. Mr. Duncan."

"I didn't mean to startle you. It's good to see you. What can I do for you today?"

"I'm doing a little Christmas shopping," Maggie said. "I'd like a yard of this handkerchief linen."

"Oh, that's a beautiful piece of Irish linen. Don't you need some for a blouse for yourself? It would make a nice one."

"Not today, thank you. I'm not much in the mood for sewing. It will be all I can do to get some handkerchiefs made before Christmas." She watched him snip the fabric, carefully cutting along a lengthwise thread. It occurred to her then that she had seen him at the Halloween dance, but not at the soirée. She wondered if that had something to do with his brother-in-law.

"Is Emily in today?" Maggie asked as Duncan re-folded the bolt of linen and put it back in place.

"Not at the moment, but I'm expecting her any time. We're taking my new automobile to Wilmington to do some shopping. I know she'd love to see you. Spends most of her time out there at Evanwood. Never did like it much here in town." He straightened some of the other bolts on the table. "Will you need some thread today?"

"No, I have plenty of thread, thank you."

The doorbell jingled and Duncan looked over Maggie's shoulder. "Here's Emmy now," he said, starting towards the front of the store. "I'll get her. Emmy, look who's here."

Emily McAllister wore a long navy wool coat and a matching wide brimmed hat piled high with burgundy roses set in a bed of gray tulle. Her husband kissed her on the cheek. "Hello, darling," she said. "Maggie, how good to see you, dear. The children loved the Halloween dance. You outdid yourself with the decorations. I'm afraid I'm not much on square dancing, but the young people seemed to really enjoy it." She looked in a mirror on the counter and adjusted the tilt of her hat.

"Emmy, I have a few things to do before I can leave, if you girls will excuse me," Duncan said. "I'll hold this up front for you, Miss Corbinn. Let me know when you're ready."

"Thank you, Mr. Duncan, it was good to see you."

Emily took off her gloves and hat and laid them on the table. "I'm so glad you're here, Maggie. I wanted to talk to you, but... Have you heard from Reece?"

"No, not since he left. Funny, I had planned to ask you the same thing."

Emily's pleasant smile faded into a frown. She took a deep breath. "He hasn't told you, has he?"

Color rose to Maggie's cheeks. Her voice trembled. "Hasn't told me what?"

"Dear, Reece has some problems, but he should tell you himself."

"Tell me what?"

"Oh, I may kill him when he gets back for doing this to you." She held Maggie by the shoulders. "He's married, Maggie. He's got two children up there in Philadelphia. His wife has been in an insane asylum for the last two years and her family wants custody of his children. I thought he would've told you."

Maggie backed away and adjusted her hat. "No, he didn't." She struggled to hold back her tears. She had been deceived, played the fool, and everyone must know. "Thank you. I knew there was more to it. I couldn't imagine..."

Distress showed in every line of Emily's face. "I'm so sorry. He should've been the one who told you."

Maggie steadied herself against the fabric table. "Yes, he should've, but please don't feel badly. You were right to tell me."

"My brother's accustomed to getting what he wants. I think he wants you. Don't be surprised at the lengths to which he'll go to achieve that goal."

"But I don't understand, if he's married?"

"Duncan's waiting. I'll have to go in a minute. I'm sure you'll hear from Reece before long. He always does the right thing, eventually." Emily put on her hat and gloves. "Men like Reece will break your heart. Don't overlook what is closest at hand."

Maggie hugged her. "Thank you. I'll try not to. You and your family have a happy Christmas."

Tate came towards them, a big smile on his face. "You found her, Miss Emily. Come on out, Maggie, and see Mr. Duncan's new automobile." He reached for Maggie's hand.

"Go on," Emily said. "And Merry Christmas to you both."

Part 3

Onslow County
December 1907

Chapter 20

Maggie went home that Christmas filled with remorse at falling for Reece Evans with so little to go on. Like some silly schoolgirl, she had let him work his way into her heart. If only she had listened to Tate. Maybe he was right about Reece being mean. For certain, Reece had tormented her.

G.W. came for Maggie on the fifteenth of December. Although her spirits were low, she tried her best to put on a good front. She would have died before she let on to anyone that Reece had made a fool of her. For the last week or so she'd kept to her room, stitching the narrow hems of the dainty lawn handkerchiefs she was making for Miss Sally Catherine and the girls. She'd ordered red bandannas from the Sears and Roebuck catalogue for Bill and Tate.

"There's a little something for each of you under the tree," Maggie said. "It's not much, but it's wrapped in a lot of love." They were all gathered on the porch, waiting for G.W. to clear his head of catarrh that had accumulated during the night. He stood out in the yard and harked, spit, blew and snorted until Hannah and Annalee began to giggle.

"Hush up!" Sally Catherine whispered loudly.

Maggie thought back to the times she and her sisters had laughed at the same thing. This snorting, harking and spitting was a morning ritual carried on by almost all the men in her family. She stifled a laugh and pulled the girls into her embrace. She felt close to them—to all the Ryans now. They had become her family, too.

Hannah looked up at her with tears in her eyes. "I was hoping you'd spend Christmas with us. Mama lets us make divinity with black walnuts."

"Oh, that sounds wonderful, but don't you know my mama would be disappointed if one of her girls didn't come home for Christmas?"

Immediately, Maggie regretted her choice of words. G.W. had cleared his head and had come up on the porch. "There's some that won't come nohow, Maggie Lorena," he said. "Now let's get a move on. It's almost daybreak."

"I could have taken her home, Capt'n, but she said you had a commissioner's meeting in Burgaw," Tate said.

"I did son, I sure did. It wasn't that much further over here, but I'm about wore out now. These old bones are wanting to get back in my own bed."

Bill hugged Maggie. "Tate'll be over there after you about the tenth of January if that's all right."

"That'll be just fine, Mr. Bill. School opens again on the fifteenth."

"I oughta be there about suppertime," Tate said.

Maggie smiled at Tate. "I reckon you'll be expecting a big pot of chicken and pastry again."

"Now, don't you go to any trouble," Bill said. His eyes twinkled. "He can bag a couple of squirrels along the river and roast them over a campfire."

"He'll do no such thing, as good as you folks have been to me. We'll have his supper ready," she said, reaching out to give Tate a goodbye hug. He wrapped his large arms around her and nuzzled his face in her hair. She closed her eyes. It felt good to be held so tightly. His jacket smelled of wood smoke and animal fur. When she opened her eyes, everyone was smiling and looking at them. She took a step back, her hand still on his arm. "Well, we'd better get moving," she said. "I'll see you in January."

"I'll be there with bells on," Tate said.

When the sun came up over the broad savannah of the Holly Shelter lowlands, the air was almost balmy. Maggie thought back to the time a few months ago when Tate had brought her along this same road. It had seemed more desolate then—hardly a sign of people. Now she was aware of farms every mile or so.

"It's going to be a right fair day," G.W. said. He sniffed the air. "We're almost to the river and somebody's frying fish."

Maggie knew what he was thinking. "Please, Papa, let's not stop anywhere. I can take the reins. I really want to get on home."

"Just hold on now, shug. I wasn't thinking about stopping and eating any of that fish, but I can enjoy smelling it, can't I?"

Maggie laughed. "Sure, but I know you've got that Corbinn stomach and it has to be fed." The Corbinn men's horrendous appetites were another family joke.

G.W. snorted. "Don't tell me the Ryans don't like to eat, Maggie Lorena. I seen those big bay windows."

"They like their victuals as well as the rest of us. Miss Sally Catherine is a mighty good cook."

"Well, how was it living there with them? Did you and Tate get along pretty good?"

"Tate would get along with anyone." *Here it comes, he's going to pick me the rest of the trip.*

"To hear Bill talk, there's not a lazy bone in Tate's body," G.W. said.

"He works hard, I'll hand him that."

"Bill said Tate's building a cabin of his own. You don't reckon he's thinking about getting married, do you?"

"If he is, I don't know anything about it." She was determined not to give her pa any fodder for wishful thinking. "I think he wants a place of his own. Can't blame him for that."

"I'd be surprised if it wasn't you he had in mind, Maggie Lorena. 'Course, he probably knows by now that you have a mind of your own."

My stars, she thought, *he saw Tate hug me and he's already got us marrying!* "Papa, please leave me be about that."

"What ails you, girl? You're not still mourning over that Pridgen boy, are you?"

"I've got a right to my privacy, that's all."

"Well, I hope your disposition improves before we get home. Your poor old ma is really bad off. Mag's waiting on her hand and foot."

"I know. Aunt Mag wrote to me."

"She's just ruined, that's all. It's bad enough that her innards are falling out, now she's got that broken hip," he said, tears filling his eyes. He pulled out a soiled handkerchief and blew his nose. "She's missed you and Katie, shug. I know it'll do her good to have her girls home for Christmas. Oh, I almost forgot, you've got three or four letters at the house. There's one from Philadelphia. Who'd that be from?"

Maggie was startled. It could only be from one person, but she didn't want to discuss it with her pa. "One of my friends from BFU got married. Maybe she moved to Philadelphia."

"Is her last name Evans?"

Maggie kept her eyes on the lane ahead. "It might be. I don't remember, Pa."

The letter was on the table in her room, the writing sharp and slanted, addressed to her in care of Captain G.W. Corbinn. She slipped it into her pocket when Aunt Mag came in.

"I declare, Maggie Lorena, you're a sight for sore eyes. I was out in the henhouse when y'all came up." She held her at arm's length. "Let me look at you."

"I've missed you too," Maggie said, giving her aunt a big hug.

"How's your eye? You still having those headaches?"

"It's not bothering me anymore, but I still have headaches. I think the glasses help. But I want to know about Mama. How's she?"

"Wait a minute," Aunt Mag said. "I want to talk about you. You're looking a mite peaked. Is something wrong?" Maggie had never been able to hide her feelings from Aunt Mag.

"No, nothing's wrong. Now what about Mama?"

"She's perked up a bit, knowing you were coming home. If we can get her into that truss, maybe she can be up a little for Christmas." Aunt Mag looked around the room. "Where's that letter?"

"What letter?"

"The one from that Evans fellow. That's who it's from, isn't it?"

"Aunt Mag, I declare, you are the nosy one!"

"I can smell a letter like that a mile off. That man is trouble."

"You don't know anything about Reece Evans except what I've told you," Maggie said.

"I know enough to tell you he's not your kind. I planned to give you a good talking-to when you came home and this is as good a time as any."

"I'm not a young'un anymore, Aunt Mag."

"Well, I don't cotton to a man who lurks around the schoolhouse with picnic baskets."

Maggie blushed. "It wasn't like that."

"You listen to me, he'll get you in trouble. I know what I'm talking about."

Maggie opened her satchel and began to unpack the few things she had brought home. "Is Jasper around? I feel like it's been years since I've seen any of my brothers."

"Don't go changing the subject on me again. Have you been encouraging that Evans fellow?"

"We're acquainted. I went to a dance at his home. That's all."

"Oh, really. Well, what in the devil is he writing to you for?"

"I don't know, but I reckon he might tell me in this letter."

Aunt Mag swished her skirt around and started out the door, but Maggie stopped her. "Please don't say anything about this to Mama or Papa, you hear?"

"Maggie Lorena, you've had a lot of hurt in the last couple of years." She took in a deep breath. "I just hate to see you getting tangled up with someone who's not your kind."

Maggie glared at her aunt. "So, who *is* my kind? Tate Ryan? You of all people—you taught me to want more out of life than what my mama has. I love Tate. He's good, kind and gentle, but I want refinement and education like you had. And I want my children to have a pot to pee in."

Aunt Mag stared at her. It wasn't like Maggie to talk back to her. "I'm sorry, honey. I guess I shouldn't have said anything." *There's more to it*, she thought, closing the door behind her.

———

Ellen Corbinn was propped on several pillows, bundled in a thick pink shawl, her nightcap pulled down over her ears. A small kerosene heater filled the room with oily vapors. The carved walnut headboard of her marriage bed towered behind her, making her look even more frail than Maggie had expected. She knelt beside her mother and embraced her. "Mama, I've been so worried about you."

"Law me, child. Don't you be worrying yourself over me," Ellen said. "Let me look at you. My, if you aren't the prettiest of my girls." She patted the bed beside her. "Sit here and tell me all about Tate. Are y'all courting yet?"

"Why in the world is everybody so interested in Tate Ryan?" Maggie tried to sound nonchalant, but after the conversation with Aunt Mag, her nerves were frayed. She smoothed her mother's covers and sat down on the edge of the bed, the unread letter from Reece crackling in her pocket. "His folks asked to be remembered to you. They're fine people."

"I know they are, honey, but what's Tate like?"

"I declare, he's nice as he can be! You'll see him again when he comes to fetch me after New Year's."

Ellen's face brightened. "Well, now, I'd say there might be some real courting going on the way back to Onslow County since y'all have gotten to know each other." She laughed loudly, holding her distended belly, then stopped still and looked at Maggie through tears. "Oh, Maggie Lorena, you can't imagine how bad off I've been."

"But you're better now, Mama. Aunt Mag said so."

"Oh, honey, I don't mean to be unkind, but what could Mag know about the pains of an old woman like me who's had nine children? My whole insides are dropped. Sometimes I think I'm going to turn wrong side out. God only knows what's going to become of me."

"You're going to be all right. Papa said Dr. Bayard had ordered a truss for you."

"I'll wear it if I have to, but with this hip, I know I won't ever be able to work in my garden again."

Maggie reached over and hugged her. "Don't say that, Mama. Miss Sally Catherine sent you some pear preserves, and I'll make biscuits for breakfast. You'll be better tomorrow just because I'm here. Now get some rest." She started towards the door.

"Maggie, I want to live to see you married. Why, I had four or five children when I was your age. You mustn't wait too long."

"I can't get married until someone asks me, can I?"

"You didn't answer my question a while ago. Has Tate been courting you?"

"Mama, what in the world! Tate Ryan is just about one of the nicest people I know, but courting is another thing." Maggie sat down on the bed again and took her mother's hand. "I'm not real sure I want to marry a farmer and have eight or nine children. Look at you. Your health is ruined."

"But I have you children, and that's worth everything," Ellen said, dabbing her eyes with a dainty handkerchief.

"I know. Don't be getting upset now, it's not good for you." She kissed her mother on the forehead. "Get some sleep now, and I promise you'll be the first one to know if Tate Ryan or anybody else proposes to me."

Maggie crawled into bed with Reece's letter and pulled the quilts around her. She felt a little heat from the kerosene lamp, but not enough to take away her chill. She held the envelope for a long time, looking at his hand, wondering when he had written it. The envelope was sealed with wax, the imprint of a large *E* pressed into it. She broke the seal and unfolded three sheets of paper.

Sunday, the 12th of December
Philadelphia
My Dearest Maggie,

    Emily has chastised me and said I owe you an explanation. She's right, as usual. Please forgive me. As to my hasty departure, I was called to Philadelphia by my attorney to appear in civil court to answer a charge of abandonment of my children. Yes, my children. I know this is a shock to you, but I beg your understanding.

    I have been married for five and a half years to Christine; but, if the truth be known, it was never a marriage. Consummated yes, but never a true marriage in light of the fact that my wife is mentally ill. I had no idea until we had been married less than a year. She was with child and she tried to take her life. After the baby was born, all seemed well for a year or so. Then another child was on the way and she tried to take her life again. What finally convinced the doctors that she was insane was her attempt to drown our precious baby girls, Mandy and Agatha. I had no choice—I had to have Christine committed to an asylum. At that time, my wife's parents took my little girls to care for them until I could settle my affairs in Philadelphia and bring the children to Onslow County.

    Unfortunately, my plans for an annulment have not been successful since the State of Pennsylvania does not allow divorce by reason of insanity. To further thwart my plans, my wife's parents have decided that the girls would have a better life in Philadelphia than I could ever devise for them in the backwoods of Onslow County. That may be true, but I will not have them grow up without a father as well as a mother. No one could love them more than I do!

    That first day in the schoolhouse, I fell in love with you. I intended to tell you my situation over lunch by the creek the next day, but I behaved badly and you were angry with me. I planned the soirée at Evanwood, confident that I could win your affection in a proper setting. It was an unforgettable evening and I knew that I had found what I had been looking for all my life. If leaving without explaining my circumstances seemed ungallant, please try and understand that I'd hoped to spare you.

Unfortunately, as things stand now, it may be years before I can ask for your hand in marriage. Christine's parents have charged me with abandonment in a ruse to impress the courts, further complicating my petition for a divorce. My attorney says we have a good chance of defeating the charge only if I remain here with my children until this is settled.

I ask for your patience. There are difficult times ahead, but I may have a solution. I will return briefly to Evanwood at the end of January, hopefully with some answers. Until then, you have my undying affection and best wishes for a happy Christmas.

Yours, Reece

Maggie closed her eyes. He had trifled with her affections for good reason. But how could he think that the truth wouldn't matter to her once his affairs were settled? There were children involved! Couldn't he have told her that? Now he was asking her to wait. She re-read the letter...*it may be years*. Ellen had waited years for G.W.

Aunt Mag was already in the kitchen with a hot fire going in the cookstove when Maggie came down the next morning. "I've got your buttermilk and flour all ready. I suppose you've been practicing over there at the Ryans's."

"On the contrary, I haven't made a biscuit in so long, I may have forgotten how," Maggie said, putting on her apron.

"You look like something the cat drug in, Maggie. What did that letter say?"

"Please leave me be about the letter."

"Humph! You usually tell me what's on your mind without my asking." Aunt Mag turned back to the stove, putting every muscle in her body into stirring a big pot of grits.

Maggie concentrated on rubbing lard into the mountain of sifted flour. She poured buttermilk over it and stirred and lifted the moistened flour until it formed a large ball of soft dough. "He's married," she said, roughly pinching off balls of dough and rolling them around in the palm of her hand before placing them in the pan.

Aunt Mag looked up. "Who's married?"

"Reece Evans," Maggie said, flattening the tops of the biscuits so hard with the backs of her fingers that the pan slapped against the table. "He's married and he has two little girls!"

Aunt Mag's jaw dropped and she wiped her hands on her apron. "See, I told you. I knew he was no-account. He ought to be tarred and feathered for trifling with you."

"No, it's not like that. He had his reasons. His wife's insane and her parents have the children and he wants them with him, but her parents think they would be better off in Philadelphia."

"What?" Aunt Mag wiped her hands and sat down in a chair she had pulled up to the work table. "Well, I'd say they might be." She studied her niece for a moment. "You're not thinking about waiting around for him to get free, are you?"

"I don't know what I'm thinking. I was hoping you might help me figure out what to do."

Aunt Mag busied herself again, working at a frantic pace. "I'll think about it," she said. "Better get those biscuits in the oven. The menfolks'll be in here any minute wanting their breakfast."

Chapter 21

On Christmas Day, all of the Corbinn children except George Jr. were there for the family gathering. They brought gifts and food, making a special effort since Ellen was ailing. Zeb and his wife Sattie came with their two boys and three girls. The youngest one, only a few months old, was named after Mary Ellen. When Jasper arrived, he invited all of them out to see his new Model-T Ford. George Jr. had sent it down from Detroit and arranged for Jasper to pick it up from the dealer in Wilmington.

In the kitchen, Sattie joined Aunt Mag and Maggie, who had worked all week making up big pans of onion-laced cornbread for stuffing and baking sweet potato and apple pies. G.W. had saved one of his leanest smoked hams for the occasion, and they'd scraped the heavy salt and mold off of it and boiled it in apple cider until it was fork-tender. There was enough fried chicken to feed an army, by G.W.'s own admission.

When they were all gathered at the table, Aunt Mag rolled Ellen into the room in a chair that Jasper had rigged up. Ellen was beaming. "Dear Lord, I never thought I'd see the day when all of my children would put their feet under my table again."

"You're not forgetting about George Jr., are you, Mama?" Jasper asked. "Junior wouldn't like that."

"No, son, I'm not forgetting about my precious Georgie. He was my eyeballs and I thought I'd die a natural death right then when he was lost in the woods for four days." Maggie knew what would come next; it was always the same. "I was carrying Maggie Lorena at the time. It's a wonder I didn't lose her."

"We know, Mama, that's why she's so high-strung," Raymond said. "What's your excuse for Katie? She's pretty high-strung, too."

Their laughter filled the room and Katie threw a biscuit at her brother. "Watch your mouth, Ray. Pa, get the strop after him!"

"All right, you young'uns hush up. Your mama can't sit here too long. Let us give thanks," G.W. said, bowing his head. "Lord, bless this food to the nourishment of our bodies, in Jesus' name we pray, amen."

Ellen cleared her throat. "G.W.?"

He quickly bowed his head again. "And let us not forget our dearly departed sister, Mary Ellen. May she rest in thy bosom through eternity." A chorus of amens followed before they all began to pass the heavy bowls and platters that sat before them.

Weariness came over Maggie at the mention of Mary Ellen's name. She longed for the day to pass so that she might be alone in her room with her thoughts. Looking around the table at her brothers and sisters, she tried to recall a time when life had been simpler. A time when all she had to think about when she got up in the morning was what to put on, or how many children would be absent from Aunt Mag's little schoolhouse across the road—a time when Mama would have been on her feet and Mary Ellen there helping out in the kitchen. Only a few years had passed; now everything was changed. She looked at Zeb beside Sattie, their baby girl sleeping in a basket between them. If Wash had lived, she might be expecting a child herself.

Katie was watching her from across the table. "Maggie, are you all right?"

Everyone turned to look at Maggie, and she pushed her chair back from the table. "Yes, I'm fine. I'll get some more biscuits." In the kitchen, she stopped at the sink and splashed water on her face, determined not to cry. Wash Pridgen was gone, and now Reece had asked her to wait for him. It wasn't fair. What was she supposed to do in the meantime? People had to have things to plan on. If Reece was not a part of her plans, then she might decide to go back to BFU, or marry Tate Ryan. What would she do if Tate asked her?

After the meal, Zeb sent his youngsters out to play and the men gathered around the stove in the parlor to smoke and catch up on the latest farm news. Katie and Maggie finished up in the kitchen while Aunt Mag and Sattie took the baby in to set a spell with Ellen.

"Tell me about Tate," Katie said. "Do you like him?"

"I like him all right, but I don't think I want to marry him, if that's what you mean."

"I didn't mean anything, but Mama sure is hepped up about it. I reckon she's afraid you're going to be an old-maid schoolteacher."

Maggie flung a dishtowel across the back of a chair so hard that it snapped. "I wish everybody would stop harping on me about marrying Tate Ryan!"

"Whoa, girl. I didn't realize it was such a touchy subject. Has Tate even asked you to marry him?"

"No, not yet, but he's working up to it. He told me he loved me and he keeps talking about this house he's building, like it's for me."

"You don't sound like the feelings are mutual."

"Kate, I couldn't say this to everyone, but I don't want to be married to a man like Tate. I love him to death, but he's satisfied with so little and I want so many things."

Katie pulled Maggie into her arms. "I know. You always did. Maybe if you went back to school, you might meet someone else."

"Things are different now, Katie. At first, I felt like I could never ride that train again to Raleigh. Now I'm not sure I would if I could. They've asked me to stay on in Stump Sound Township and teach at the new school at Harris Creek next year. It seems they're making some special arrangements for county teachers. I'll have to take some tests. I really love what I'm doing. My superintendent has sort of taken me under his wing. Besides all that, there's Reece Evans."

"Oh, I wondered if anything had come of that."

"Shhh, here comes someone up the back steps. I don't want anyone to know about this," Maggie said. "I'd never hear the end of it."

Jasper stormed into the kitchen through the back door, his face streaked with perspiration. "I can't get that damn automobile to crank.

I've tried everything I know how and it still won't crank. I'm going to haul that piece of shit back to Wilmington and tell the son-of-a-bitch that sold it to me to shove it up his ass!"

"You better not let Pa hear you talking nasty like that," Katie said.

"Hush up, little sister," he said, taking a long swig of water. "I was going courting tonight."

"Well, I guess you can't depend on these newfangled machines when it comes to courting. You'd be better off with Pa's buggy and Geronimo hitched up to it."

"I heard he preferred the old delivery wagon with the bed in back," Zeb said, coming in from the parlor with the baby on his shoulder.

They all laughed and Jasper drained the last drop of water from the glass and set it down hard on the dish drain. "Sure as hell'd be more fun than getting married and having young'uns."

"Don't be too sure," Zeb said. "A married man can get it anytime he likes."

"That ain't the way I heard it."

Maggie handed the last dish to Katie to dry. "So that's the way men talk about marriage. Now we know, Katie."

"Some men, not all men," Zeb said. "Katie, c'mon if you're going with us. I've got to get home in time to feed the livestock."

"I'll be along in a minute," Katie said. "Maggie, honey, Sattie wants me to come up there and spend a night or two with them, get to know the baby. When I get back, we need to talk some more."

When Katie returned home the next day, she was bubbling over with excitement. "Zeb and Sattie are so happy. Cecil and Emmett are the cutest little boys, and the girls are precious. Poor Sattie hardly has a minute to herself with the baby, but she and Zeb still hug and kiss like they just fell in love."

Maggie was giving the parlor a good cleaning, closing the doors to the rest of the house and opening the windows to air out the room. "They seem happy all right," she said. "I can't remember when they weren't sweethearts. Sattie was only sixteen when they got married."

"It's just so sweet the way they look at each other, even after five children," Katie said.

Maggie had rolled the rug back and swept up the sand that had sifted through. "If you'll help me, we can drag this rug out." she said. "I'm sure it hasn't been done in years." They pulled the old Persian carpet out into the yard and hung it across the clothesline, using two long tobacco sticks to beat it.

"Mama always did this in the spring, Maggie. What's got into you? I can think of lots of other things to do on a pretty day," Katie said, whacking great puffs of dust and sand out of the rug.

"Aunt Mag can't do everything, and I don't know when we'll all be back here. Besides, one day is as good as another when it comes to cleaning."

"Finish telling me about Reece. You said you had a letter from him."

Maggie pulled the letter out of her apron pocket. "Here, you can read it for yourself."

Katie sat down on a bench and read the letter. "Well, I'd say this man has a problem," she said when she finished. "Sounds as if he's really in love with you, Maggie. What are you going to do?"

"I don't know, sister. I don't even know what he's asking of me. He said my patience, but it sounds like a lot more than that."

"Are you in love with him?"

"You mean, am I attracted to him? Katie, this is a man like you've never dreamed of around these parts. He's educated, refined and handsome as the devil."

"But are you in love with him? I mean do you like *everything* about him? Do you feel like you can't stand it when you're not with him?"

"Is that what love is?"

"Yeah, that and wanting to get all over him like a dirty shirt."

Maggie laughed. "I declare, where do you get these things from?"

"You didn't answer me."

Maggie smiled. Katie had a way of getting directly to the point.

"Well, yes, I guess I am. And what's so frustrating is that I've hardly been with him except for the evening at his house, but I can't think of anything—of anyone—else."

"Doesn't sound as if there's much hope for the future though, does it? Maybe you'd better give him up before you get in any deeper."

"I don't know if I can. He said he might have a solution. I need to know what he's thinking. I can't imagine..."

"What if it's something you couldn't agree to?"

"Well, we'll just have to see, won't we?"

Chapter 22

The sun shone brightly all through the holidays, but the evening Tate arrived the wind picked up, bringing frigid air down from the North. By morning, gray clouds threatened snow, and ice covered all the watering troughs. Maggie had gotten up a little earlier than usual to finish her packing and was in the kitchen folding her laundry when Aunt Mag stomped in the back door shivering and cursing the cold. "I hate cold weather—makes every bone in my body hurt. Those dratted chickens may have to starve before I go back out there with any more corn."

"Looks like the weather could have waited another day or two to change. I dread that long ride back to Onslow County," Maggie said.

Aunt Mag hung her heavy coat on a hook beside the door and backed up to the stove to warm her behind. She had never admitted her age, but Maggie knew that she was a year older than Ellen, which would make her sixty-five. Still, not a hair on her head was gray. Like most women her age, she wore her black hair parted in the middle and pulled into a tight bun at the back of her neck. Since Archie died, she'd only worn black dresses, even around the house, but she was never without a brightly-colored starched apron.

"You're looking a little thin, Aunt Mag. I wish you would let Lizzie come in and stay with Mama and Papa a few days. You could go visit Aunt Lib in Wilmington."

"My stars, I don't need to go to Wilmington. And I'm not thinning down. Don't you be worrying about your old Aunt Mag. I can take care of myself."

"I know, I just hate for you to work so hard all the time."

"Well, let me tell you, it's a whole lot better to wear out than to rust out. But listen, I need to talk to you a little bit. Over here in the pantry in case your pa comes in."

The pantry was a small room between the birthing room and the kitchen where shelves ran from floor to ceiling, each one full of jars of canned vegetables and fruits. There was a tall window at one end and Maggie remembered how as a child, she'd sat there on a stool and counted the jars. "I figured you'd forgotten what we talked about," Maggie said.

"No sirree, I've thought about it. Don't let that Evans man trifle with you. You need to look at what's closest at hand. Maybe it's Tate Ryan, and maybe it's not, but..."

"I thought you wanted me to go back to school!"

"I did, Maggie Lorena, but it may be too late for that now. You might've missed your chance with that Pridgen boy getting killed and all." She reached down, tightened the lid on the lard stand, and slapped it with her hand. "I'm thinking with my little house here and all that you just might..."

"Well, I'll be. I never would have thought I'd hear you say that."

"Things change, Missy, and I change my mind to adjust to the circumstances."

"Aunt Mag, I've been thinking, too. I don't want to end up like Mama."

"Who says you'll end up like your mama? Every marriage is different. I reckon my mama thought I'd have as many children as Ellen, but I didn't, did I? There are ways a woman can keep from having so many children."

Maggie was a little embarrassed. Aunt Mag had never before discussed anything so intimate with her. "What do you mean? I always thought you wanted a lot of children."

"Oh, I reckon I would have taken what the good Lord gave me, but Archie, he was content without any, and I liked being able to go and do things with him. We tried at first, but we got used to things the way they were. We had you to keep us company."

Maggie thought about the nights at Aunt Mag's house when she'd heard the springs squawking in the room next to hers. "But how did you—how did you stop it from happening?"

"Uncle Archie just spilled his seed on the floor. I don't mind telling you."

Maggie felt a blush creeping over her. "But I thought Uncle Archie couldn't...that you couldn't..."

"Pshaw!" Aunt Mag said. "It suited me for everyone to think what they would. Me and Archie knew what to do." She turned to the row of canned vegetables beside her and rearranged them on the edge of the shelf.

Maggie started towards the closed door of the cramped pantry, her hand on the doorknob. "Is it all right to do that...I mean, can a man stop like that?"

"Why, sure he can if he's a mind to."

"I didn't know it was like that, Aunt Mag."

"Of course you didn't, you've never been a married woman." She reached out and took her by the shoulders. "Listen, Maggie. You can have things any way you want them with a gentle man like Tate, but a man like Reece! Law, he'd have his way with you day and night and you'd be as big as your pa's old sow out there once a year. Mark my words, young lady, you're better off with somebody like Tate Ryan." She took Maggie's hands in hers and held them tightly. "He spoke to your pa last night, you know."

"What? No, I didn't. He had no right! He hasn't talked to me about it." The thought riled Maggie. She was ready to give Tate a piece of her mind right then and there.

"He said he declared his affections to you at the Halloween dance. He said you didn't seem to object. He wanted to know if G.W. approved before he approached you again."

"What did Pa say?"

"G.W. said he told Tate that it didn't make a damn what he thought—that you had a mind of your own and he could take his chances asking you."

Maggie smiled. Maybe she had underestimated her father. She opened the pantry door. "There's a letter on my dresser. Will you put it in the mailbox for me tomorrow? I left a penny for the postage."

Aunt Mag was perturbed. "And suppose I decided to take a look inside, would I find it to my liking?"

"You wouldn't do that. I've never known you to go opening someone's mail, so don't start now." She grabbed her aunt by the shoulders and hugged her. "Trust me, Aunt Mag. I'm no fool."

As they loaded the buggy, Maggie was on edge, figuring that Tate would be brave enough to broach the subject of marriage before the day was over. How she'd get around him she didn't know. He had brought two quilts to wrap around their legs and he wore his heavy hunting jacket and a wool scarf. While they tucked themselves in, Aunt Mag came out onto the porch with a hat box. "Take this hat, Maggie Lorena. Your Uncle Archie bought it for me in New York. It was the latest fashion up North twenty years ago. He said all the women wore long Mackintoshes and fur hats and he thought I oughta have one. Archie sure was good to me."

"Yes he was," Maggie said, smiling. After the tale her aunt had told in the pantry, whenever Uncle Archie's name was mentioned, Maggie knew she'd always think about him spilling his seed on the floor.

As they made their way through the woods to Black River, Maggie thought she'd never been so cold in her life. On the ferry, she got down from the buggy and stamped her feet to warm them.

"Stand over here behind the buggy with me," Tate said. "The wind's not so bad." He put his arms around her and she snuggled against him. Standing this close, Maggie was afraid he'd seize the opportunity to ask her to marry him, but she was warmer and decided to take her chances. Tate was quiet, just gazing out across the river.

Maggie couldn't get Reece off her mind. His letter had touched her heart, but there were so many questions left unanswered, questions that would have to wait until he returned in late January. In the letter she'd asked Aunt Mag to mail to him, she'd told him that she'd be willing to listen to his plan. She couldn't imagine what it would be.

———

By the time they reached the Northeast Cape Fear, Maggie welcomed Josh Hart's invitation to come inside and set a spell. "It's cold enough out here to freeze a witch's tit," Josh cackled. His beard was scruffy, filled with lint and bits of food, and he was wearing an old wool coat that looked as if it might have been through the War with him. "With that wind whippin' down the river the way i'tis, we might have a time git'n across," he said. "C'mon inside, the missus will make us some scalding hot coffee to warm up our insides afore we take off."

"I'd like to use your toilet first, if I may, Mr. Hart," Maggie said.

"Shore, t'be shore, Missy. Hep yourself. Hit's right over yonder in that l'il grove."

Maggie entered the old two-seater outhouse and closed the door, the stench forcing her to hold her breath. Most decent folks threw in a shovel or two of lime every now and then to quell the odor. She lifted her skirts and sat down on the wooden seat, a draft of cold air swirling against her bare bottom. Closing her eyes, she strained to force her water to come, thinking she might freeze to death if she didn't hurry.

Maggie held her gloved hand over her nose, looking about for something to wipe herself. On the dirt floor in a corner was a bucket half-full of rough red corn cobs and on the wall beside her, hanging on a piece of wire, was an old Sears and Roebuck catalogue. She removed her glove, reached up and tore out a page. Before rubbing it soft in her hands, she read an advertisement for *The Ladies' New Medical Guide,* touting the author, Dr. R. Pander, as *instructor, counselor, and friend in all delicate and wonderful matters peculiar to women.*

Maggie studied the page and Aunt Mag's words came back to her. *A man like Reece Evans, law, he'd have his way with you day and night!* This wasn't the first time today she'd thought of that. On the same page, a larger, more expensive volume called *Dr. Hooker's Plain Talks and Common Sense Medical Advisor* promised a list of topics on marriage and sexual relations: *Male and female elements in all nature; the effects of sexual isolation; the sexual characteristics of different persons; the prevention of conception;* and *the duties of married life.*

Tate and Josh Hart stamped around on the porch of the nearby camphouse. Her curiosity would have to wait. She stuffed the page deep into her pocket and tore another off.

"We was about to come and see if you fell in, Miss Maggie," Josh said, slapping his knee and heehawing like a donkey. Tate looked down at his feet and started the little shuffling routine she'd seen him do when he was embarrassed. "Y'all c'mon inside now, before the missus throws that fish she's cooking out the winder to the cats."

After they crossed the river, the road was deserted and the wind raced through the pine trees, whining and howling like a frightened hound. Maggie pressed the quilts against her legs and hunkered down in her heavy coat. "How much further? I declare, it seems like it's taken two days to get back."

"You can snuggle up a little closer, Maggie. I'll warm you." He looked straight ahead. "You didn't seem to mind on the ferry."

"Yes, but there were other people around then. You might take advantage of me way out here in the woods," she joked. Tate looked down at her and smiled. He shifted the reins to his left hand and held her with his right arm. Maggie leaned closer. If Reece had not come into her life, she might say that this was right where she belonged.

Chapter 23

After talking with Capt'n Corbinn, Tate had made up his mind that he wasn't going to say anything else to Maggie about getting married until he could offer her something more than a promise. He intended to have his house practically finished before he popped the question. He could see her now, making little curtains for the kitchen windows and scratching in her flower garden. Another month or two wouldn't make a bit of difference. Besides, Maggie had been melancholy since returning from Christmas, almost as bad as when he brought her to Onslow County the first time. Then she was still mourning the boy who had shot his head off. When would she ever get over it?

Many nights Tate heard her in her room pecking away at the type-writer, sometimes even after he had gone to bed. When he'd filled the kerosene heater, he'd seen a stack of papers turned face-down on her desk. He asked Sally Catherine about it one day when she was scrubbing the kitchen floor.

"All I know is she's writing stories, Tate. She got a letter the other day from the *Progressive Farmer*. I think she sent something off to them, but she keeps everything to herself."

"I know she does, Mama. I don't ever hear her in the kitchen talking to you like she used to."

"Maggie Lorena has a lot on her mind, son. They've asked her to stay on here at the new school next year, but I don't imagine she will. You know she still sets a lot of store in getting her college education."

Tate helped his mother up off her knees and pushed a chair under her. "You oughtn't be down on your knees like that. Where're Hannah and Annalee?"

"Oh, go on with you. I'm a little short of breath, that's all."

Tate pulled a chair up close to her. "Mama, what if I was to ask Maggie to marry me? Do you think that would keep her here?"

Sally Catherine smiled at him. "I reckon it's worth a try, son. I thought you might have that in mind the way you've been working on your house."

———

January turned into February and Maggie couldn't remember a more miserable time in her life. She tried to blame it on the weather, the cold daily trek across the soggy fields, or the long sleepy afternoons cooped up in the one-room schoolhouse, but she knew better. Not hearing from Reece had disheartened her. Putting him out of her mind was a losing battle. He'd said the end of January. Now it was well into February and despite her daily resolution not to think about him, by nightfall she found herself enthralled again.

When the postman delivered Dr. Hooker's *Medical Advisor*, there was postage due, raising a few questions from Sally Catherine about "that book" she got in the mail. Maggie had told her that it was a schoolbook, one she'd read when she was at BFU, one she wanted to read some more—that much was true. After that, she'd kept it hidden away in her trunk until bedtime when she'd eagerly read what Dr. Hooker had to say about *better and higher love*.

———

Anticipating that Emily would have some word from Reece, Maggie sent a note home by Jeanne McAllister, asking if she might call on her the following afternoon after school. Emily sent word back that she would come to the schoolhouse herself with Homer that afternoon to pick up the children.

Except for Jeanne and Darcy, the schoolroom was empty when Emily arrived the next day. "Wait for me in the carriage," she said to her children. "I'd like to talk to Miss Corbinn for a few minutes." She watched them go out the door. "I've been wanting to see you too, Maggie. Reece told me he had written to you. How much did he tell you?"

"He told me that he's been married for five years, that he has two daughters and a wife who's insane. But he says he wants to marry me." Maggie laughed at the ridiculous way it sounded.

Emily laughed too. "Oh, he does have a habit of oversimplifying things, but this is too much."

"I just don't know what to do or what to think. Reece asked me to be patient. He says he has a plan."

"Well, my dear, I think it's very simple. Reece has asked for—promised—too much. It doesn't look as if the court will grant the annulment, and I don't expect Christine's parents to back off. You will just have to refuse him, put him out of your mind."

"I see," Maggie said. "Yes, it sounds very simple—not easy, but simple."

Emily was pensive, walking around the schoolroom, stopping at Darcy's desk, running her gloved hand over it. "It would have been such a pleasure to have you in our lives," she said.

Maggie didn't know what to say. Her mind was a jumble of questions. She asked Emily to sit down. "Will you tell me why no one besides you and me seems to know that Reece is married?"

"Elsie Bannerman knows," Emily said.

"Oh. And why is that?"

"They were romantically involved once. Elsie and Christine—Aubusson, her last name was then—were roommates at Vassar College. Elsie invited Reece to the Spring Frolic and he only had eyes for Christine. Needless to say, Elsie felt betrayed by them both. That summer, Christine's parents took her to Europe and Reece followed. They were married on shipboard on the return voyage."

Maggie felt that she had been kicked in the head by a horse. "I can't believe it. Poor Elsie. I knew there was something, but she didn't say what."

"Oh, I doubt that Elsie would discuss it with you. She was extremely bitter. Married her husband very quickly—his accident almost finished her. She seems to have come out of it now. You were kind to get her involved in the school. She is qualified to teach, you know."

"No, I didn't. But please tell me what happened after Reece and Christine were married."

"Well, things went downhill very quickly. Reece hadn't wanted to marry Christine, but her father caught them in a compromising situation and insisted that the ship's captain marry them. Of course, Mr. Aubusson knew that Reece was educated and wealthy, that my grandfather was worth a fortune. At the time, his business was failing and he saw an opportunity to have his daughter married without having to put up a dowry."

"I can't imagine that Reece went along with that."

"Reece didn't have much choice, Maggie. He planned to have the marriage annulled once they reached Philadelphia, where he would have the help of Uncle Malcolm's family. But word had come while he was away that Grandpa was very ill, so Reece caught the train and arrived just as he was dying. Grandpa never knew, thank God! When Reece returned to Philadelphia to proceed with an annulment, Christine told him that she was pregnant."

"But if he loved her, I don't see why..."

"Reece never loved Christine. He was infatuated at first, but he married her because he had to. I think that's what drove her out of her mind. She was crazy about him. When I went up for the baby's christening I saw what was happening. He was indifferent towards her—towards the baby—and he detested her family. I didn't know until this past year that she had tried to commit suicide."

"But he said they had another child," Maggie said.

"Yes. I think he felt sorry for Christine, for their beautiful little daughter. He went to work in Mr. Aubusson's firm, tried to make the marriage work. He thought he might learn to love her. A second child was born and one day the maid found Christine in the tub with both of them." Emily collapsed into a chair and put her head in her hands. "Oh, it's too dreadful..."

Maggie was aghast. "It's all right. I don't need to know any more."

Emily pulled a handkerchief from her sleeve and wiped her eyes.

"There's one thing that I hesitate to tell you, Maggie, but I think it's only fair. Reece never cared for anyone the way he seems to care for you. He told me that he was going to ask you to wait for him, that you were what he had always dreamed of in a wife. I believe he means it."

"Now I'm even more confused. What should I do?"

"Like I said in the beginning, refuse. Think of yourself. Leave your position here if you must. Reece will have what he wants one way or the other and you may not like some of his methods."

Maggie sat at her desk after Emily left, going over the story time and time again, each time more astounded than the last. The sky began to darken and she knew she would have to hurry to get back to the Ryans's before nightfall.

Chapter 24

Winter may have been bleak and bare to Maggie, but to Tate and other farmers, the cold winter months provided blessed relief from the demands of the soil. Cold weather was a time for mending fences and sharpening tools, a time for catching up, taking stock, and in Tate's mind, building a house. On the second Saturday in February, fifteen men showed up to raise the walls. Several of their wives and children came, filling Sally Catherine's small living room to capacity. Maggie and Hannah stayed in the kitchen, cutting out quilt squares at the table.

"Tate's house will go up real fast now," Hannah said.

"Mmmhmm, I expect so," Maggie said, concentrating on the pattern she was cutting out.

"I guess he's going to be an old bachelor, living there by himself."

"I reckon so."

"He's going to ask you to marry him, Maggie."

"Don't be talking like that. Marriage is something two people talk about in private. It's not something to be discussed by everyone else in the world first."

"Don't you want to marry Tate?"

"My stars, Hannah! It's not something I want to talk about, especially with you. You'll be running to Tate and telling him everything I said."

"What's the matter with you? Don't you like Tate?"

"Of course I like your brother. Who wouldn't like Tate?"

"Reece Evans doesn't like him."

"Oh, for heaven's sake. That's just child's talk."

"I heard Mrs. Bannerman say she saw him in Jacksonville yesterday."

Maggie put down her scissors and stared at Hannah. "Are you sure?"

"I just heard her say it a few minutes ago. Why don't you go and ask her yourself if you're so interested." Hannah got up from the table and stirred a pot of stew on the stove.

"Maybe I will," Maggie said, hating herself for letting on that she cared. "What do you have against Mr. Reece, Hannah?"

"I don't have anything against him. I just don't like him, that's all. Mama says he can't be trusted. She says he's got something to hide 'cause nobody knows where he is or what he's doing most of the time."

Maggie sorted all the little pieces she had cut into stacks and pinned them together. "Well, did it ever occur to anyone that he's a very private person, that he doesn't want everyone knowing his business?"

"I declare, Maggie, like Tate says, you sure do take up for him. I'm going to go see how the house is coming along. Do you want to go?"

"No, not now. You go on. I told Tate I'd make some biscuits. Tell him we'll ring the dinner bell when they're ready."

Hannah put on her coat and wrapped a scarf around her head. She stood by Maggie at the table. "I'm sorry if I sounded nosy. I just want you and Tate to get married more than anything."

Maggie took her hand and squeezed it. "It's all right, honey. But even if he asked me, I couldn't say what I would do right now."

The weather suddenly turned spring-like. The cold raw wind that had pinched and bit every inch of exposed flesh turned northward, and a soft summer-like balm blew over the farms in lower Onslow County. Maggie knew better than to think it was spring. Ellen Corbinn had called it *pneumonia weather*, saying that unseasonably warm weather opened up the pores and brought on the worst kind of sicknesses. But the change had helped to lift Maggie's spirits.

They had several days of the balmy weather, the old potbellied stove losing its heat for the first time since November. The schoolchildren were wild as squirrels running and chasing on the playground, coming inside hot and sweaty. The boys took off their shirts, and the girls pulled off extra petticoats and stuffed them in their booksacks.

Maggie had sent the children home an hour early to get them out of the stuffy schoolroom when the rain began. Closing the windows in the cloakroom, she looked out and saw Reece pumping water for his horse. At first, she couldn't move, mesmerized by the sight of him, afraid he might vanish—like in one of her dreams. He looked up and she stepped quickly away from the window.

Glancing in the small mirror, she removed her glasses and slipped them into her pocket. At the sink, she drank a sip of water, then dabbed at her face with a small towel. The door opened and closed. His steps across the sandy floor seemed familiar. How many times had she thought she heard him, only to turn and not find him there?

She looked over her shoulder, saw him throw his hat on the bench, stop just short of her. "Hello, Maggie," he said, his eyes sweeping her face, her hair, the bodice of her blue print dress.

"I heard you were back."

His brown leather breeches were dusty from riding and his face glistened with perspiration. "News travels fast in Stump Sound, doesn't it?"

"Some news," she said. "Elsie Bannerman saw you in Jacksonville last Friday."

"And you think I should have come here before now?"

"I said no such thing."

"Come here," he said. But she turned away, her back to him, watching a water bug struggle to climb the side of the sink.

He took a step, slipped his arm around her waist. "I said come here." His grip was firm. He turned and crushed her against his rough linen shirt. Unshaven, he still carried the clean scent of lavender on his skin. He bent his face to hers, kissed her. She closed her eyes, her arms wound tightly about his neck as he laid her down on the small cot. "I was afraid you'd never come back," she whispered.

His hands explored her, his lips greedy, devouring. "I told you I would."

Nothing in her life—not Dr. Hooker nor Ella Bradley—had prepared her for this. Entwined, they rode the crest of a rain-swollen river. No words stemmed the tide. No hand diverted the course. Outside, drops pounded the tin roof, splattered the window. Lightning, sharp, bright, flashed overhead.

Washed and spent, he seemed to sleep, eyes closed, his arm across her chest. It was as if they had always been like this, quiet, content. "I've missed you," she said. He snuggled closer, kissed her ear. The clock on the schoolroom wall chimed four o'clock. She felt his muscles tense slightly. "Did you settle things?" she asked. He opened his eyes, not answering, just looking. Her perspective was so close that his face became a blur. His eyes closed again. Minutes went by. She tried to move, feeling uneasy. But he tightened his hold, and she was caught in his grasp. "Reece, please."

He released her, sat up, and covered her with her blouse, reaching for his britches. "Nothing is resolved."

Maggie pulled the coverlet over her. "You should have told me sooner," she said, looking at the wall.

He sat down on the cot and lifted her into his arms. "I told you, I have a plan. This is my life, not the Aubussons's." His face was stern, but she touched his cheek and he softened, attempting a smile. "I intend to live out my life with you, one way or the other." He looked away, as if running something over in his mind. "Come, it's getting late. Someone may look for you. I'll help you dress."

"No, please, I can do it myself."

He stood and straightened his clothes. The rain had stopped and the sun was out again. At the small sink, he pumped a glass of water, took a sip, and handed it to her, sighing. "Nice rain. It feels like spring, doesn't it?"

It seemed perfectly natural that he would stand there, relaxed, and comment upon the weather, but Maggie was not so easily disarmed. "Reece, we need to talk."

"No, not now. I told you, I have a plan."

"But you said it might be years before…"

His jaw tightened and he reached for her arm and pulled her to him, his face contorted. "I said I have a plan. You must trust me."

"You're hurting me," she cried.

Releasing his grip, he rocked her in his arms, her face against his damp shirt. "I never intend to do that. Please try and be patient with me. I'll be here after school tomorrow."

When he had gone, Maggie retrieved her pantaloons from the floor, knowing her life was changed. She had no feelings of guilt or remorse. She had been as willing as he. Latching the door, she retrieved a cloth from beneath the sink and wiped her face, studying her reflection in the small mirror. She looked different, new. Her hair, a tangle of red curls, glowed in the sunlight. She pulled it into a pile on top of her head and danced about the room in her bare feet. Never before had she felt so radiant, so full of pleasure. He said he had found a way, but needed more time. She could give him that—a little time—if it meant a lifetime of this.

That evening she bathed carefully before crawling into bed with Dr. Hooker's book, reading again with even deeper interest his *plain talk,* his *valuable lessons.* What really interested her was his admonition that *great care must be given as to the time of the month.* Maggie was apprehensive, unable to remember the date of her last period. Dr. Hooker had suggested that she keep a calendar, but the only calendar hung on the schoolroom wall. She closed her eyes. Tomorrow, she would study it.

Chapter 25

The weather turned cloudy and cold again as quickly as it had warmed and the old stove in the schoolroom had a hard time catching up. Maggie shivered beneath the blue shawl when she greeted her children the next morning. She felt that they were watching her, wondering why she was different. Well, she felt different—like a door to another world had been opened and she was standing on the threshold. But as the day wore on, she felt the first pangs of guilt. What must he think—she hadn't resisted at all.

She had straightened the cot before she left, so this morning there was no sign of what had gone on in the cloakroom. Blushing, she imagined her embarrassment had one of her students or a parent chanced to come by.

The rain continued all day, making a steady beat on the tin roof. After lunch, Maggie called a study hour to settle the children down. She looked out across the classroom and Zeke Gurganus smiled at her. His tousled hair was the color of straw and his face covered in freckles. She'd taken a real liking to him even if he was mischievous as the devil. She smiled back. *He's up to something.* Looking down at the book on her desk, she pretended to read, but out of the corner of her eye she saw Zeke's arm go up to send a spitball flying across the room, zapping his brother just above the ear. Joe retaliated, making a direct hit between Zeke's eyes. "Owww!" Zeke cried, and everyone in the class looked at him and began to snicker.

Maggie was on her feet with a ruler in her hand before the boys saw her. "You'll stay an hour after school," she said, whacking each boy in turn on the shoulder.

Maggie regretted the punishment immediately. Reece had said he would come after school. But she had to maintain discipline in her classroom, especially with the Gurganus boys. Zeke was thirteen, but his twelve-year-old brother was already a head taller. They were both starved for attention. Lord knows, they didn't seem to get much at home. Zeke was nothing but skin and bones. The doctor at the hookworm clinic in Jacksonville said hookworm was taking all of his nourishment. Mr. Bill had taken the boys to the clinic in November and seen to it that both of them had a new pair of shoes. The doctor had said that most hookworm entered your body through a break in the skin, so going barefoot was no longer allowed at school.

The cold rain beat against the window panes, causing them to fog over inside and drip condensation on the wooden sills. Periodically Maggie glanced at the clock, hoping each time she looked that the hour had passed. But only thirty minutes had gone by when the door opened and Reece stepped inside. Zeke and Joe turned around to gawk at the tall figure dressed in black oilskin. Joe snickered and Reece went and stood over him. Rain from the wide brim of his hat dripped on Joe's schoolwork. "Something funny, boy?"

"No sir, Mr. Reece. I-I didn't see you come in, that's all," Joe said, cowering.

"Well, take a good look now, 'cause I want you boys to go on home. I need to discuss some business with Miss Corbinn." Joe looked at Maggie and then at his brother. Reece raised his voice. "I said go on. Now, you hear?"

"Go on, Joe—you, too, Zeke," Maggie said. "But I expect you to behave yourselves tomorrow. Go on," she urged.

The Gurganus boys scampered out, looking uneasy as they passed Reece. Maggie rose and walked to the window, trembling as she tried to raise the sash enough to let in some air.

Reece stood beside her. "Here, let me." When he raised his arms to open the window, she smelled the clean scent of lavender again. They stood very close, his gaze warm. He drew her into his arms and kissed the top of her head. "Oh, my, my, you are lovely," he said.

"Reece, yesterday—you must think me..."

"Nothing could have stopped me, Maggie Lorena. You are all that I have thought about for months." He tried to kiss her, but she turned her head. "I don't have much time," he said.

"In your letter at Christmas you said..."

He stared out the window, his jaw rigid. "Things have changed. My wife's father pulled some strings—arranged for Christine's release from the asylum—claims her children need to be with her." He let Maggie go and stared out at the rain, the lines in his face growing deeper. "I still can't believe it. In fact, I'm furious," he said, slamming his fist on the sill. "Aubusson had no right to do that. Christine is mad."

"I'm so sorry, but there must be something you can do."

"Unless I can prove her insane, I will never see my children again." His face was grim. "Don't you see? I can't live with her insanity, and she will never consent to a divorce."

"That's not right," Maggie said. "What about us? Surely a judge will intervene."

"Humph! Her father is very influential. No judge in Philly would defy him. If only my grandfather were alive..." He pounded his fist on the windowsill again.

"Reece, I'm so sorry. I know how much your children must mean to you."

He embraced her. "Everything. They mean everything to me," he said, his voice soft and sad. "But this doesn't change how I feel about marrying you. I have a proposition. It may sound bizarre, but I don't think you will be able to refuse."

She pulled away, studying his face. He was so confident. "But what can you do if she..?"

A smile curled beneath his mustache. "It's very simple. I'm going to build a house for you. It will be our home eventually, but until then it will be yours." Now he was excited, waiting for her reaction, but she could only stare at him. "You will have servants and running water," he continued, holding her by the shoulders. "An engineer in Philadelphia is building a generator—there will be electric lights."

"You're building a house for me? You must be joking."

"No, I'm not."

"Really?" She put her hand to her mouth to stifle a giggle.

He swept her off her feet, twirling her across the schoolhouse floor. "That's right, my dear, a house of your very own," he said, coming to a stop near her desk. He tried to kiss her, but she pushed him away.

"Reece, I—I don't know what to say. People will talk. It wouldn't be right."

"Right for whom, Maggie? Only you and I have to agree." He reached for her hand, but she pushed him away again and walked to her desk, leaving him by the window.

"What about Emily? What in the world would your sister think of me?" She shook her head, almost in tears.

"Emily only wants what I want. She knows how much I love you. She knows the problems involved. Why would she think less of you?"

"Reece, please. I can't just go along with this. I need some time to think. It's not so simple for a woman to..."

"Nothing in life is simple, Maggie." He picked up his hat, brushing away the raindrops and placing it on his head. "I have to go now. Make an excuse to work here at the school on Saturday. I'll come for you at ten o'clock." He turned to leave.

"Wait. Your proposal, it sounds so preposterous. I just don't know if I could."

Reece stared at her. "How could you not?"

She wanted to protest again, but the words wouldn't come out. He took a step towards her and put his finger on her lips. "Please, don't say anything else until you see what I have planned for you—for us." When he picked her up to kiss her, his hat fell to the floor and he kicked it aside. The stubble of his beard scraped her lips and cheeks. Instinctively, she pulled away. He glared at her for a moment, then stooped to pick up his hat. "I'll see you on Saturday."

Chapter 26

Escaping the Ryans's Saturday routine was easier than she had thought it would be. Sally Catherine and Bill were helping Bill's sister's family with a hog killing, and the girls were meeting their friends at a neighbor's house for a sewing bee.

Tate had gone hunting early that morning, and she was glad that she didn't have to contend with his questions. But just as she started out the kitchen door, he came up the wooden steps to the porch carrying a half-dozen limp squirrels by their tails. "Morning, Maggie."

"Good morning, Tate. Looks like you got some nice fat squirrels."

"Sure did. I promised Mama I'd bring something home for supper, and I don't think she'll be disappointed." He threw the bloody squirrels onto a wooden table by the pump and wiped his hands on his jacket.

"She'll be real proud of those. If you'll dress them, I'll help cook when I get back this afternoon."

"Where are you going?"

"I've got some chores to do over at the schoolhouse. I won't be long."

He followed her down the steps. "I was hoping to take you over to see my house. It's coming right along. The brickmason from Jacksonville will be here to build the chimneys on Monday." Maggie continued down the path toward the road, smiling and listening. "We put tin on the roof last week before it rained. It's dry as a bone inside. Don't you want to come and see?"

She stopped suddenly and he almost ran into her. "I'm real anxious to see your house, Tate, but I have some work to do at the schoolhouse today. How about first thing tomorrow after church?"

"That'd be just fine," he said, a big grin spreading across his face.

"Mama gave me some yellowbell bushes she rooted, and a crape myrtle that came up here in the yard. Maybe you could show me where to put them." His ruddy cheeks glowed from being outside in the cold air. In his heavy hunting jacket he reminded her of how Wash might have looked the day he was killed. Tate did that real often—brought back memories of Wash.

She smiled and reached out to touch his arm. "I promise I will. We'll get a pussy willow I saw over by the ditch bank, too. It would be real pretty up near the house." She buttoned her coat and tied a long scarf across the top of her small felt hat. Since Christmas, she'd kept her distance, but she knew he still had his hopes up. "Look, I need to go now."

"What you got to do? Maybe I could take you over in the wagon, help you out."

"No, I want to walk. And you need to dress those squirrels."

"Well, all right. You want me to come get you later?" he called to her.

"I said *no*," she yelled back.

Tate walked back towards the house wishing he could figure Maggie out. She seemed to like him right much, but every time he had a chance to be alone with her, she was going off in another direction.

By the sink up on the porch, he slit open the fat squirrels' bellies and skinned off the fur, thinking about a conversation Hannah had had with Maggie. Hannah said Maggie's ears had perked up when she'd heard that Reece Evans was back in Stump Sound. Why in the world was she so interested in the comings and goings of that sorry jackass? Maybe he should tell Maggie what Elsie Bannerman had told him.

Elsie and Tate were the same age and had known each other since they were little children. Her family owned a big tract of land over near Evanwood and they'd figured she might marry Reece someday. But Elsie had told him what had happened with her best friend, Christine, when they were off at college, and she made Tate swear he would never tell because it would make her look bad. Tate had seen Elsie outside the schoolhouse a day or two ago and she'd chided him about hanging around there so much.

"You wouldn't be sweet on the new schoolteacher, would you?" she asked.

Tate put down his tools and walked over to Elsie's carriage. "Now that you mention it, I want to ask you something. Does Maggie ever say anything about me?"

Elsie laughed. "Mmmhmm, I thought so."

"Wait a minute. Look here now, I'm serious. I really like her. I'm thinking about asking her to marry me. What do you think?"

"Wouldn't hurt to ask her, Tate. If I know Maggie Corbinn, she'll let you know right off how she feels."

"Well, I got the idea that she might be interested in Reece Evans. Does she know what you told me?"

"No, and you swore you wouldn't ever tell anyone. Besides, Reece isn't likely to be courting her. He won't ever be free to get married again, the way I hear it from my friends in Philly."

"Don't you think Maggie ought to know that?"

"Look, Tate, you're worrying yourself over nothing. Maggie's not going to get tangled up with him. He's not around much anyway."

"Well, I think you ought to tell her..."

"I told you I didn't want anyone around here to know about that. Now don't you go breaking your word."

Elsie's probably right, Tate thought. In another month or so, he'd have the house in such shape that Maggie could see how fine it was going to be. He'd wait a little bit longer before he asked her to marry him. Maybe by that time she'd realize that Reece Evans wasn't her kind at all. Maybe by then he would've made a complete ass of himself in her company. She'd know then that her place was with him, Tate Ryan.

A bright winter sun shone over the fields of dry cornstalks and plucked cotton as Maggie walked the mile and a half to the school-house at a steady pace. Except in the worst weather, she walked every day, convinced that the exercise would keep her from getting as stout as Miss Sally Catherine. Most days she spent the time planning the school day for the children, thinking up games to help them learn math or songs to keep them awake. But today her pupils were the farthest thing from her mind. All she could think about was Reece's proposal to build her a house. It was ridiculous, but the idea aroused her curiosity.

The rain had taken the pneumonia weather right along with it on an easterly course, leaving a brisk wind to whip her skirts around her legs. Approaching the schoolyard, she saw a buggy at the hitching post and recognized Reece's horse. She took several deep breaths, wrapped her arms about herself and tried to slow her pace to a stroll. At the buggy, she stopped to rub his horse's nose, letting him nuzzle her hand. She needed the extra time to build up her resolve, remembering Emily's precaution—*Reece will have what he wants one way or the other and you may not like some of his methods.*

Maggie entered the schoolhouse through the cloakroom door, half-expecting him to meet her there, but she didn't hear a sound except for the steady ticking of the schoolroom clock. She peeked inside. He was sitting at her desk, absorbed in something he was sketching. "Reece?" she said, taking a step towards him.

Startled, he whirled around. "Maggie, don't ever do that." He was on his feet now and coming towards her. For a moment, she thought he meant to strike her.

"I'm sorry, I didn't mean to scare you."

"Well you did. I don't take kindly to people sneaking up behind me—not even you."

"I wasn't trying to sneak up on you," she retorted, removing her coat and hat and tossing them on a student's desk.

He took a deep breath and held out his arms. "Forgive me, darling, I was lost in thought." He kissed her, the urgency gone but his ardor undiminished. She thought how perfectly they fit together, how natural it seemed to be this close to him. "I have something to show you," he whispered, his face against her cheek.

She saw that her books and papers had been moved to the floor. On her desk were several large sheets of paper. "Sit here," he said, sliding her chair out from the desk. "You see that?" He pointed to a large block of print in the right-hand corner of the first sheet. *The Residence of Maggie Lorena Corbinn on Catherine Lake, Onslow County, North Carolina. Designed for Reece Langley Evans by John Garris, Philadelphia.*

Maggie laughed out loud. "You're serious. You've already had the plans drawn." *Before you talked to me,* she thought. Overwhelmed, she studied the plans, going from the layout to the block of print with her name emblazoned within it. "I can't believe it, a house for me."

Reece stood back, his arms folded across his chest, enjoying her reaction. "That's right, a house for you, Miss Corbinn."

"But I don't understand. What about you? When will you...?"

"In time, Maggie, in time." He turned his attention back to the plan and flipped the pages until he came to the last one. "Look here, on the third floor, there's a solarium, completely glassed in. The windows open out over the lake."

"The lake?"

"Oh, yes, my dear, Catherine Lake, just north of Evanwood. It's part of my grandfather's original tract. You'll see, I'm taking you there today."

Reece flipped the pages back to the front elevation. The house was elegant, large and square, with two stories and a porch that wrapped all the way around. Tall windows went from floor to ceiling. Cornices above the porch rail were intricately drawn, with brackets and curlicues that formed oval frames across the front. Maggie had never seen anything like it, even in Raleigh.

Reece turned to the rear elevation, pointing to the solarium again. "There should be steps here, down to the lower porch. I'll give this to the architect next week." Handwritten notes in the margin indicated the change.

Maggie looked up at him. "You're leaving again?"

"I have to go back to Philadelphia. It's the only way I can get custody of my children."

"But we have so many things to talk about, Reece. What you're asking of me...I don't know. I have to think."

"You'll have plenty of time to think, Maggie. Come, get your coat. I want to show you."

Maggie was relieved that Catherine Lake was due north of the schoolhouse. Meeting up with any of the Ryans would be unlikely. As they neared the lake, she could see yellow jasmine vines twisting their long tendrils through all the shrubs and trees. It would be spring soon and the woods would be a mass of yellow, just like at home. Interspersed among the scrubby oaks and tall pines were dark green hollies and thick cedars. She thought of Christmas, imagined gathering greens for the mantel, picking out a tree for the parlor.

Occasionally, she caught a glimpse of the water. A lake would be more tranquil than the river. There could be a dock and a small boat, a place for the children to bathe. Smiling at the thought, she looked at Reece and he turned towards her. "Happy?" he asked.

The question disarmed her, brought her back to reality. What would people say? Accepting such an offer would be blatantly disregarding all that she believed marriage should be. She'd be hidden away like...like a mistress. She shuddered at the thought. "I guess so."

He put his arm around her and drew her closer. "You make me happy. Please don't spoil it."

Reece turned the buggy down a long lane that led to an open space where soil was piled around a large hole in the ground. The underbrush had been cleared all the way down to the water and the lake shimmered in the morning sun. "There it is, Catherine Lake. Beautiful, isn't it?"

"Oh, yes. Look! I've never seen so many cranes at one time. They're everywhere."

"There are hundreds of them at this time of year," he said, helping her down from the buggy. "They're courting. They come here to mate."

Like us, she thought. "This place is beautiful, Reece. I can see why you chose it."

He took her arm and walked towards the site, stopping at the center of the large excavation. "Madam, your new home," he said, bowing and gesturing towards what she imagined would be the front steps. "If you'll come inside I will lead you up the grand walnut staircase to the second floor, where I will swiftly deposit you on the carved rice planter bed that I recently purchased in Charleston, and there, my dear, I will ravish you to your heart's content." The merriment in his eyes belied his sinister tone.

She laughed and took his hand. "You're embarrassing me."

"So? I love to see you blush, Maggie Lorena. It becomes you." He caught her in his arms, forcing the breath out of her. "You would like that, wouldn't you, Maggie?" he whispered. "To be ravished to your heart's content?"

"Please, I can't breathe."

Reece released his hold, cupping her face in his hands. He ran his fingers through her hair, removing the pins, allowing it to tumble about her shoulders. "It will work, Maggie, I know it will."

Could it? she thought. A lovely home, more lovely than any she had ever seen; a nursery, rooms for their children. He would be a wonderful father—stern, but loving, just as he was with her. A large crane flew directly over them, wings flapping loudly, and a long white feather floated to the ground. Maggie picked it up. "A sign from above?" she said, laughing.

"They'll get used to us soon enough. The children will love them. Come, let me show you where the bedrooms will be." He unrolled the plans again, spreading them on a pile of logs. "This will be our room, and this will be Agatha's, and this Mandy's. Their governess will stay here."

Maggie followed his finger, looking out across the excavation. "And the nursery for our children?"

Reece straightened up, hesitating before he spoke. "I don't want more children, Maggie. Wouldn't you be content with Mandy and Agatha? They will need a mother—a sane one."

"That's a lot to ask. I've always wanted children. Not a houseful like my folks, but one or two."

"I don't think that's asking too much. Not for all of this," he said, indicating the house site, the lake, with its crystal waters blinking in the sunlight. "Mandy and Agatha are beautiful girls. You'll love them. Think about it, Maggie. I have and I really don't want any more."

On the way back, Reece talked of the chandeliers he had ordered from England, velvet draperies for all the windows, fine mahogany furniture for every room. There would be steam heat and a large kitchen with hot and cold running water. When they neared the schoolhouse, he offered to take Maggie back to the Ryans's.

"No. I'll walk."

He glared at her. "They have to know sooner or later, Maggie. Why not now?"

"No, I don't think so," she said, her temper flaring. "They wouldn't understand—not at all. They may even know you're married. Everyone except me seems to know something about you."

"I warned you, you might hear things."

"You might have told me sooner, yourself."

"There are some things better left unsaid...until the right time."

"I'm sorry, Reece. I don't think you have any idea exactly what you're asking of me. My head's swimming with your proposal. Just let me off at the schoolhouse. I need to think."

He looked straight ahead. "Don't think about it too long, Maggie," he said, his voice cold. "I might change my mind." He was silent until they reached the schoolyard, but when he lifted her down from the buggy, he held her against him for a long time. She tried to speak, but he stopped her. "No. That's enough," he said, climbing back into the buggy and lifting the reins. "I can see that I've asked too much of you right now." He reached into a satchel, pulling out a thick parcel. "Here, I had a set of plans made for you. They might help you think about things in a more positive light. You can write to me at that same address in Philadelphia."

As soon as he was out of sight, she went inside the school, her heart racing. *He must be mad!* She threw the parcel across the room. Pacing up and down the rows of desks, bumping against them in her haste, she upset one desk completely. *That's it! He is an arrogant madman! What kind of woman does he think I am?* Wouldn't people see that he'd compromised her morals with a fine house? And how could he disregard her longing for children of her own? No, she wasn't ready to strike that bargain just because he was content with a couple of prissy little girls— who would probably hate her.

Chapter 27

The next morning, Maggie was relieved to find that it was raining again. Since the buggy was a two-seater, Bill and Tate would likely be the only ones going to church. Best of all, Tate wouldn't be counting on her to go see his house. After yesterday, she knew she'd find it difficult to praise his efforts.

She had slept miserably. As outrageous as it sounded, she was intrigued by the thought of living in the house on Catherine Lake. She could see herself gathering roses in the flower garden, carrying them to a sink with running water, filling vases and placing them all over the house. She'd have her writing table in the solarium, where she could look out across the lake and watch the cranes dip their long beaks into the tranquil water. In the parlor, they'd play card games or checkers with the little girls. At night, he'd come to her in the rice planter bed and... Here the pleasant thoughts ended. Reece didn't want more children, and she wanted a baby of her own.

For days after that, she tossed the proposal about in her head, vacillating between the dream and reality. She would be his mistress, a kept woman. How could she explain such an unethical proposal to the Ryans, to her own family? She would be disowned, of that she was sure. A scarlet *A* emblazoned upon her chest would be a mild rejection compared to what she would receive from her church. Aunt Mag would be the most difficult to face; then again, Aunt Mag had often chosen a different path from what had been expected of her. Come to think of it, this was just the sort of thing Aunt Mag might have done.

Impulsively, she wrote to her. You could never tell about Aunt Mag. She had a sense of adventure. Maybe when she heard that Reece wanted to build a house for Maggie—that he already had the plans drawn up...

What would you do? Without your guidance, I would never have made it this far. I know you would like Reece if you got to know him. I love him and he loves me. If it were not for his problems, he would be an answer to all of my prayers—a wonderful intelligent husband, a fine home, children, travel abroad. There would be no need for me to finish college. I would have servants, time to read and study. Oh, don't you see, Aunt Mag? It would be a dream come true. If I refuse him now, I may lose him completely.

Deep down inside, Maggie knew better, but she needed to hear Aunt Mag say it. And she did. *I can't believe I helped raise such a fool! Don't you see what he is doing, Maggie Lorena? He won't ever get rid of that crazy wife in Philadelphia once he has you set up in that pretty house. Why should he buy the cow when the milk is free? I told you when I last saw you what you ought to do. Marry Tate Ryan, if he'll still have you— if you haven't already ruined yourself. You better watch your step, Missy. Like I told you, a man like that Evans fellow will have his way with you and then where will you be?*

Maggie cringed to think that Aunt Mag might be right. Reece had had his way with her all right, but she had wanted it, too. No one need ever know that but her. What if she were to accept Reece's proposal, with the stipulation that their relationship remain chaste until such time as they could marry? She decided to ask Katie. Katie had a romantic streak a mile wide.

Katie replied: *Really, Maggie, this is just about the wildest thing I've heard in a long time. Sounds to me as if he's head over heels in love with you. Ooo-la-la, what I wouldn't give for a man like that! I'll probably get stuck down here in Shallotte with a fisherman who stays gone for days at a time. I can't tell you what to do, dear sister, but that is a proposition I'd find hard to turn down. Of course it would kill Mama and Papa. Maybe you better think about that.*

But it was Emily McAllister who'd persuaded Maggie to write to Reece and decline his offer. Maggie had sent word by Darcy and Jeanne that she would like to call on Emily. The next afternoon, she rode home with the children and Homer. Pulling into the circular drive, listening to the wind in the pine trees, Maggie thought that without the lights and laughter of the party, Evanwood was a lonely-looking place.

Homer hopped out of the buggy and reached for Maggie's hand while the children scampered out and up the steps. "Miss Emily said I should take you home when you's ready, Miss Maggie. Jus' lemme know when."

"Thank you, Homer. I shouldn't be too long."

Emily was waiting for her at the door, wearing an elegant dress of apricot-colored wool. "Maggie, I'm so glad that you've come. We need to talk." She showed Maggie in and they sat in the parlor, where an enameled porcelain stove put out a wonderful soft heat. Maggie glanced around at the plush furnishings, most of which had been removed from the room the night of the soirée. A richly oiled mahogany table beside her held a collection of daguerreotypes, framed photographs of children and soldiers in uniform.

Felicity, the young colored woman who had taken their wraps on the night of the soirée, brought in a tray with a pot of tea and some small cakes. Emily sat primly with her hands in her lap and watched the young maid until she had closed the door. Pouring the tea, her hand trembled slightly, rattling the delicate cup in its saucer. "I hardly know where to begin," she said.

Maggie sat on the edge of her chair. "You've heard from Reece?"

"Yes, two days ago. He sent me a bill of goods for some things he's having shipped to Mr. Ott's warehouse in Swan Quarter. I am to sign for them and have them delivered to Catherine Lake."

"That's what I wanted to talk to you about," Maggie said. "He told me about the house and showed me the plans when he was here last."

"He says that he intends to put the deed in your name. Whatever is he thinking?"

Maggie felt as if she were being accused. "He asked me to live there while he resolves the business with his wife and tries to get custody of his children."

"And, you, Maggie, do you believe that he will be successful?"

"I don't know what to believe or what to feel about it. I know that I love Reece, that if he were free and were to ask me to marry him, wild horses couldn't stop me. But that doesn't mean that I would be willing to be a kept woman, to be his mistress."

Emily's face flooded with relief. "Oh, thank goodness. I was so afraid that you had succumbed to his charm, to his drive to do things his way despite whom or what he tramples upon." She rose from her chair and paced back and forth in front of Maggie. "Listen, there is nothing more I would love than to have you as my sister-in-law. I feel a deep affection for you, so much so that I would not have you compromised for any reason. Reece cares very little for convention. I suppose it's because he did the right thing by marrying Christine and it has done nothing but bring him heartache. But this is too much, he is asking you to give up your honor." She stopped in front of Maggie's chair. "Mandy and Agatha are precious children, but I believe I am right when I say that you would want children of your own."

"Yes, we discussed that, but he doesn't want more children."

"And he was adamant about that?"

Maggie nodded her head. Emily began to pace again. "Reece told me that he intends to have an operation. He knows a German surgeon in Philadelphia who performs an operation that prevents fertilization. He promised Reece that he would not lose his manhood, only his ability to father a child. I don't think he would want me to tell you this, but I think it only fair that you know."

Maggie was stunned. She had never heard of such a thing. "I don't know what to say. It seems that you're always telling me things that I should know when Reece can't or won't tell me."

"I'm sorry, dear, I just don't want Reece to take advantage of you. He's my brother and I adore him, but he has not been entirely ethical in the romance department."

Emily asked Homer to bring the carriage around to take Maggie home. "I'm afraid that Reece will be terribly annoyed with me. In his letter, he asked me to try and convince you to accept his proposal. I may have done just the opposite."

"No, Emily. What you've told me makes a difference in my thinking. I'm afraid that I was mighty attracted to the idea of a beautiful home on Catherine Lake, but there's more to consider than a house. I'm much obliged to you."

Maggie thought that writing her letter to Reece was one of the most difficult things she had ever done. She imagined him reading it and tearing it to bits. But she knew it had to be done and Emily had promised to mail it for her so as to avoid talk. She wrote several drafts before she was content, keeping one copy in her trunk and burning the others in the kitchen stove.

My dearest Reece,

I must decline your generous proposal to build a house for me on Catherine Lake. Your offer has tempted me almost beyond my ability to resist, but I know that I could never hold my head high again in my family or in the community. Please know that I will anxiously await the news of your divorce. Only then can we determine our future. With undying affection, I am,

Your Maggie Lorena

"I'm very proud of you," Emily said when she read it. "Who knows, a miracle may happen and Reece will have his divorce in a year or so, but I will be honest with you, Christine's father is very influential and he detests Reece. He may never be free of her."

"I reckon I know that. You'll let me know when you hear from him again?"

"Of course, dear, but you can expect him to be angry. As you know, he doesn't like to be denied."

Chapter 28

Several weeks went by with no word at all from Reece. Had he accepted her rejection so easily, or was he upset? Perhaps he'd had second thoughts, realized that he was asking too much. No, Reece would never be contrite; but if he truly loved her, he would understand. She thought of the long years her mother had waited for G.W. She could wait, too. But, as Emily had suggested, perhaps she should leave Onslow County, return to BFU. The time would pass more quickly if she were immersed in school.

⎯⎯

Maggie's thoughts changed rather suddenly when she realized that the sickness she felt every morning was not due to her heartache. She had not missed a menstrual period since she was thirteen years old. Checking the calendar at school, she saw that about six weeks had passed since her last period. Dr. Hooker's *Plain Talk* said anxiety could bring on the delay, cautioning the reader to wait until she had missed two periods in a row before assuming she was with child. Maggie refused to believe it; yet the days went by and her second period did not come.

Fortunately, Miss Sally Catherine was having spells of her own and didn't seem to notice Maggie's morning sickness. "I just don't know what's come over me," Sally Catherine said. "It's like I'm plumb worn out and the day hasn't even started yet." It was Sunday, and Maggie had dragged herself into the kitchen a little late in hopes of avoiding as many of the Ryans as possible.

She peeked under the cover of a platter at the back of the stove and saw that Sally Catherine had gotten up early and fried chicken. "You just worry about getting dressed for church, Miss Sally. The girls and I'll finish dinner up when we get back." She led the older woman to her bedroom and helped her get into her Sunday clothes.

"Tate's been wanting to show you his house," Sally Catherine said. "He can't understand why you haven't been over there to see all that he's done. Won't you go see it with him today?"

Maggie knew she couldn't put off seeing the house any longer. What could it hurt? She would tell him that she might be leaving soon, that Aunt Mag couldn't take care of her mother any longer—anything to save face. She really had no choice but to go home to Canetuck, have the baby in disgrace and hope that someday Reece would be free. The thought had entered her mind that perhaps Emily would take her in until she could have the baby, but she couldn't bear the thought of everyone in Stump Sound Township knowing, especially the Ryans.

"Why, yes ma'am. I know I've been putting him off, but I've been having a little spell of not feeling so good myself."

"I know you have, honey. What is it? You're awful pale. There's a tonic in there on my shelf. It might be your liver."

Maggie eased Sally Catherine's dress over her head and smoothed it across the front and back. "Don't be worrying about me, Miss Sally. I'll be my old self in a few days." She brushed the older woman's long hair and twisted it into a knot at the back of her head.

"You've worn yourself out teaching and taking care of me, that's what you've done. Don't think I haven't noticed all the little things you do to help me out. But I don't want you neglecting other things."

"Do you think Tate feels hard towards me?"

"I think he might—a little. Go on over there with him today after dinner just to satisfy him. The girls will help out in the kitchen."

Tate sat between his mother and Maggie in church that morning. Maggie did not feel like singing and she wished that Tate would share his hymnbook with his mother instead of her. He sang out heartily, looking at her, emphasizing the words with smiles. His joy and rhythm were contagious, bidding her to let go of her unpleasant thoughts and join him in the singing. It worked. By the time worship services were over, she had cleared her mind and come up with the perfect solution. The Lord had shown her the way, sure as the world.

At the dinner table after church, Tate couldn't keep his eyes off Maggie. He knew what he was going to do and it gave him satisfaction. "If y'all will excuse us, I'd like to take Maggie over to see the house. Maggie, how about it?"

"Miss Sally, would you and the girls mind if..."

"You go right ahead, honey. I know how anxious Tate is for you to see it."

"I thought we'd walk, Maggie. It's a nice day."

"Fine. Just let me change my shoes. I saw some daffodils along the road. We'll pick some for Miss Sally on the way back."

Maggie changed her shoes and met Tate out on the back porch. Walking along the edge of the field, she felt as free as the dappled sunshine that filtered though the tall pines overhead. Tate reached for her hand and she took his willingly. They walked along in silence, Maggie thinking about how right it felt to be going to see Tate's house at that very moment. Preacher Mizelle over in Canetuck said that there came a time in everyone's life when the Lord allowed them to get lost in some deep dark cave, just so they'd be more grateful when they found that little speck of light that led them out.

Approaching the house, she had to shield her eyes from the glare off the shiny new tin roof, high-pitched to allow for a room upstairs. It was a simple square house with a porch across the front, a far cry from the picture on the plans that Reece Evans had given her. She'd hidden them in the folds of her blue serge jumper, putting the parcel in the bottom of her trunk alongside G.W.'s manuscript.

Only one side of the house had cypress siding at this point, but a new brick chimney stood proudly on either end. Most likely, he would have the house finished before it was time to put the crops in. Spring was a wonderful time of year for moving into a new house—*and for a wedding*, she thought.

"My goodness, Tate. You've done a fine job. I think you missed your calling."

"I can build a house if I need to, Maggie, but I wouldn't want to make a living at it. Come on inside and I'll show you the rest." They climbed the wide steps and crossed the porch, entering what Tate said would be the parlor. There were other rooms on either side and a hall that led to the kitchen.

Maggie walked straight back to the place where she knew she would spend the most time. "Look at this! You put windows all across the kitchen. Wouldn't the table be nice right here where you could look out?"

"Yes'm, and I figured I'd build a dish cabinet in that corner over there. There's an enameled sink over at McAllister's store in Jacksonville that I'm going to put into a wooden cabinet." He demonstrated the height and width with his hands. "A hand pump'll be at one end."

Maggie struggled to blot out Reece's words...*running water and electricity, too...a man in Philadelphia building a generator.* As if reading her mind, Tate said, "Maybe someday there'll be electricity out here in the country, but I expect it will be a long time before that happens."

She felt a pang of misgiving. Tate's house was no different from most any old farmhouse, but she'd already decided that she could get used to anything under the circumstances. "The house is real nice, Tate. Let's see the rest of it."

"Well, come on," he said, grabbing her hand.

They stood in the center of one of the bedrooms that looked out over the adjacent woods. "This will be my room and the other is a spare room...in case I get married one day and have me some children," Tate said. She was looking out the window and his eyes were on her back. "What would you think about getting married, Maggie?"

She sat down on an empty nail keg, her head swimming. "I've thought about it, Tate, but no one's asked me yet," she said, her tone devoid of emotion.

"What if I was to ask you, would you marry me?"

"Marry you, Tate?"

"I'm sorry, Maggie. I guess that wasn't proper and all, but I thought you knew I was gonna ask you."

She tried to think of something witty to say, but nothing would come. "I'm sorry, I reckon I did. Maybe I should think about it before I give you my answer though." She forced a smile and stood to kiss him on the cheek. "I'm much obliged that you would ask me, I really am."

Sitting around the table at supper that evening, it was all Tate could do not to tell his family that he had finally asked Maggie to marry him, but until she accepted, he knew it wouldn't be proper. Maggie had left the table early, saying she was a little under the weather. "She's probably just sick of school like I am," Annalee said. "We need some new books. I'm so tired of those same old books."

Bill cleared his throat and took a long swallow of buttermilk. "All them books are going to be replaced next year, Annalee. Mr. Thompson announced that at the last meeting. He said we'd pass the old ones on to the new colored school at Richlands."

"When did they get a school at Richlands?" Tate asked.

"They're building it right now, son. Miss Emily said she asked Reece about it last time he was home and he told her to go on and give a little piece of land on the back side of Evanwood. I think he's due back from up North sometime this month."

Just the mention of Reece's name was enough to spoil Tate's dinner. He finished his plate and put it in the sink. "If y'all will excuse me, I think I'm gonna go work on some cabinets in the barn."

"All right, son, but remember it's Sunday," Bill said. "By the way, what did Maggie think of the house?"

Tate grinned. "She liked it, Pa, she really did."

Everyone at the table stopped what they were doing and looked at him. Sally Catherine nodded her head, smiling. "Mmmhmm, I told you so," she said.

Maggie folded the quilt back and stretched facedown across her bed, sobbing into the pillow. This was not the way she wanted her life to turn out. Tate was not the man she had wanted to marry. *Too bad Reece didn't have that operation before now,* she thought, turning and flinging her arms over her head. She stared at the ceiling, thinking that at least everyone else would be happy that she was marrying Tate. She got up and washed her face. *Might as well go tell him before I change my mind.*

———

Maggie wrote a joint letter to her parents and Aunt Mag, telling them that Tate had finally proposed and they wanted to get married right away. *Easter Sunday, in fact, if it suits you. We just want a small wedding. Aunt Mag, I know Mama is ailing and we should make it as easy on her as possible. I'd like to get married right there in the house if it's all right. Will you ask Reverend Mizelle if he'll perform the service? I thought I'd wear that dress you were making for my graduation, if you've finished it. I know it's short notice, but Tate's house is almost done, and we want to be together as soon as possible. Miss Sally Catherine and Mr. Bill have given us their blessing, but they can't come to the wedding. Miss Sally is not doing so well right now with her heart trouble and blood sugar on top of that. She and Tate's sisters want to have a little reception and a housewarming when we get back.*

Please don't be upset with me, Aunt Mag—I know how much you counted on me living in your little house. Maybe I will someday.

Chapter 29

News that Tate Ryan was marrying the schoolteacher spread like wildfire in the community. Emma, Betty and Sabra came to visit, making plans for the housewarming. As usual, Emma took the lead. "Mama, we don't want you to do a thing," she said.

"I guess we won't have potato salad," Betty said, laughing. "I'd just as soon not have any if I can't have Mama's."

Sabra was making out a list of neighbors and friends. "We're not going to have dinner anyway, so don't get your underwear all in a twist."

"That's right," Emma said. "We're just going to have cookies and punch."

"What about pound cake?" Sally Catherine asked. "That's easy. I know I could do that much."

"Please, don't y'all go to so much trouble," Maggie said. "Especially you, Miss Sally."

"Now honey, we're all so happy you and Tate are getting married. In fact, I can't think of a soul who isn't thrilled about it. The housewarming will be like having a second ceremony here in Onslow County. Just let us enjoy doing this for you."

With all the to-do going on, Maggie was sure Reece would get word of the marriage. He should have been the first to know, but there hadn't been time to make a calculated decision. If he'd been at Evanwood, she might've explained to him beforehand, but with him in Philadelphia, she simply had to do what she had to do. What if he wanted this child? What difference would it make? She would be the one who was scorned. To have a child out of wedlock was even worse than being his mistress.

But he did deserve some sort of explanation, whether he accepted it or not. Maggie thought of fabricating a story. She could tell him that she did not love him after all. She could say that Tate had won her heart. Finally, she decided to simply tell him the truth. Sealing the letter in a vellum envelope, she slipped it into her booksack to take to Emily McAllister the next day. There was no need for Emily to know her reasoning—she was only doing what the older woman had advised.

Weary from all her deliberation, Maggie washed her face and slipped on her nightgown. Some of the Ryans were still up. She could hear them talking in the parlor. Just then, there was a loud knock on the front door. Maggie cracked her door open and heard Miss Sally say, "Who in the world is that at this time of night?" Maggie couldn't see the parlor, but she could hear Miss Sally shuffle across the floor and open the door. She was talking to someone.

Suddenly, Hannah came around through the hall, a frightened look on her face. "Mr. Reece is on the porch. He's talking to Mama."

Maggie's heart nearly stopped. "What does he want?"

"He asked to talk to you. Mama told him you'd gone to bed."

They heard Reece shout, "Tell her I want to see her. Now!"

"What in the world, Reece! Is something wrong?" Sally Catherine asked.

"You're goddamned right there's something wrong! Where is she?"

"Oh, no," Maggie whispered. "Hannah, you'd better go get Tate."

"Why?"

"Go get Tate!"

Hannah scurried out through the kitchen to the barn and Maggie heard Reece barge into the living room. "Where is she?" he demanded again.

"Annalee, go get Miss Maggie," Sally Catherine said.

Annalee started down the back hall, but Reece followed, pushing past her. "Get the hell out of my way. I'll find her myself."

Maggie stood in her doorway, afraid to move. Reece was charging towards her like a mad bull. "Reece, wait, please. I need to talk to you," she pleaded.

He forced her back into the room, slamming the door behind him. Shoving her onto the bed, he pinned her arms against the mattress. "Is this what you want, you ungrateful bitch?" he demanded, glancing about the room, his hands tight around her wrists.

"You're hurting me," she cried, turning her face from side to side, avoiding his eyes. "You don't understand. I wrote you a letter. It's in my booksack."

He leaned over her, pounding her with his words, saliva spraying from his mouth. "You can keep your goddamned letters. I understand completely. You weren't willing to wait. I offered you everything. Everything!"

She struggled against him. "Reece, stop it. Please let me up. Things have changed."

"*You've* changed, Maggie Lorena. Emily wrote to me. She said you were going to marry Tate in a few weeks. What's the rush? You couldn't wait a little longer? You'd throw away everything we had between us just to get married now?"

"It's not like that," she sobbed.

Tate threw the door open and glared at Reece. "What in the hell are you doing in my house?" he shouted.

Reece spun around, his eyes full of hate. "You son-of-a-bitch. You low-down sorry son-of-a-bitch. I'm gonna kill you."

"No you ain't. You ain't gonna kill nobody. You get the hell away from my girl and outta this house!" Tate reached for Reece's collar, but Reece drew back his arm and hit him solidly on the jaw with his balled fist, sending Tate sprawling across the room, upsetting the unlit kerosene heater and Maggie's writing table. He tried to sit up, but Reece pounced on him and started bashing his head against the floor.

Grabbing his arm, Maggie tried to stop Reece, but he flung her aside and sent her tumbling into the bedstead.

A deafening blast reverberated throughout the room, causing bits of the wooden ceiling to rain down. Bill Ryan stood in the doorway, a shotgun aimed at Reece's head. "Get off my son, Reece Evans, 'fore I kill you."

Reece held his grip on Tate for a moment longer, his eyes testing Bill and the smoking gun. He pushed away against Tate's shoulders, standing to face the older man, his nostrils flaring with each breath. He looked at Maggie sitting on the floor against the bed sobbing, her head in her hands. Then he looked at Tate and took a deep breath. "You should let your son fight his own battles, Mr. Bill. This is between me and him."

Bill lowered the rifle until it was level with Reece's abdomen. "Any trouble with my son is trouble with me. Now get out of my house, and don't you ever come back."

"It will be a pleasure if I never see any of you again," Reece said, glaring at Maggie.

Sally Catherine stood in the doorway. "You oughta be ashamed, barging in here like this. Miss Maude, she..."

At the sound of his grandmother's name, Reece turned pasty. He stopped in front of Sally Catherine, waiting for her to step aside. "Yes, Grandmother would be disappointed in me, wouldn't she, Miss Sally? Excuse me, please."

As soon as Reece was out the door, Tate went straight to Maggie, helping her onto her feet. "Did he hurt you, Maggie? Are you all right?"

She pushed him away and lay down on the bed. "Just leave me. All of you, just leave me be."

"Go on out, Tate," Sally Catherine said. "You, too," she said to Bill. "Hannah, get some rags and clean up that kerosene, then you and Annalee go on to bed. Just let me sit here with Maggie 'till she gets hold of herself. That's right, honey, just get it all out." She pulled the chair closer to the bed and patted Maggie on her back.

When Hannah had gone out, Maggie turned over, pulled a handkerchief from her pocket and blew her nose. "I'm so sorry, Miss Sally. I'm just so sorry to put you and Mr. Bill through this."

"You want to tell me what it was about? I can guess, but maybe you oughta tell me so I get it right."

"Oh, he just had some notion that I was interested in him. I guess he heard that Tate and I were going to get married and it made him jealous. I don't know why he should think that I..."

"Shhh, it's all right. I heard a little talk after that dance at Evanwood last fall. You know how womenfolk talk. But I didn't think much about it after I heard that he had a wife up there in Philadelphia that he was ashamed to bring down here because she was insane."

Maggie sat up. "Where'd you hear that?"

"Oh, there's not much that gets past the colored folk working over there," Sally Catherine said. "I believe Homer told it."

Maggie began to feel very sick, her stomach cramping unmercifully. "I'm all right now. Please go on to bed and I will, too."

"Why sure, honey. And I'll talk to Tate, if you want me to. I'm sure he's worried about you."

Maggie had completely forgotten about Tate—that he might be expecting some sort of explanation. "Thank you, Miss Sally. Tell him I'll talk to him in the morning. I just need to get some rest now."

When Sally Catherine had gone out, Maggie closed her eyes and saw the fury in Reece's face as he hovered over her—*couldn't wait—just had to get married!* If only she had gotten her letter to him, he might have understood. She curled herself into a tight ball and sobbed into her pillow. Her back and stomach ached and she felt sick. Suddenly she felt a warm rush of fluid between her legs and she jumped up and sat on the pot beside the bed, feeling for all the world as if she were turning wrong side out.

The cramping went on all night, and so did her tears. She slipped out of bed long enough to remove the letter from her booksack and put it in the trunk. *If only I had gotten the letter to him!* No, he wouldn't have understood even then. She was trapped in a circle of events beyond her control, trapped into marrying Tate. She had no one to blame but herself.

Chapter 30

Easter Sunday was a beautiful day for a wedding. The weather had warmed and there was bright green new growth on all the trees and shrubs. The yellowbells and quince were long finished, but the mock orange bushes around the back of the house were filled with long branches of sweet-smelling white blossoms. Aunt Mag had sent Jasper and Zeb out into the woods to gather ferns and bamboo which she'd arranged with sprigs of the mock orange in tall vases on the mantelpiece.

Aunt Mag was in her element. She hadn't done a home wedding since Ellen got married. In the parlor, she had her nephews remove the stove and push all the furniture back to make room for the folding chairs Preacher Mizelle would bring after Easter Sunday church services. Katie was directing the food preparation, leaving Aunt Mag free to help Maggie. She wanted to be the first one to see Maggie in the wedding dress she'd made for her.

She'd started the dress to while away the lonely days when Maggie was in Raleigh, figuring it would be her graduation dress. Years ago, Archie had bought the fabric—a whole bolt of white embroidered batiste—on one of his trips to New York. She'd saved it, knowing there would come a time when she would want to make it up for Maggie. Now that she thought about it, all the seniors at BFU on graduation day looked like brides in their long white gowns. Their pictures had been in *The Biblical Recorder*.

Aunt Mag held up a long pair of lace-trimmed drawers for Maggie to step into. She had laid out a trousseau of underpinnings on the bed. There was a nightgown of batiste and point de Paris lace from Ellen, a silk full-length underskirt and pink cambric drawers with a matching corset cover from Aunt Mag, and a pair of silk stockings from Katie.

"Where's Katie?" Maggie asked. "I thought she would be here by now."

"Oh, she'll be here directly. It takes Zeb and Sattie a while to load up all those young'uns. Katie gets a big kick out of helping the little ones get dressed. I sure wish she'd find herself a husband."

Maggie laughed. "I know. We used to talk about a double wedding—marrying brothers."

"Let me ask you something before she gets here. How'd you get rid of that Evans fellow, anyhow?" Aunt Mag asked, fastening Maggie's corset.

"Now, don't go spoiling my wedding day with your questions, Aunt Mag. I don't even want to think about him."

"Well, I was just wondering. I thought he had turned your head for sure." She lowered the wedding dress carefully over Maggie's head, fastening the sixteen tiny pearl buttons up the back.

Maggie twirled in front of an oval floor-length mirror that had belonged to Mary Ellen. Aunt Mag watched her, pleased to see Maggie in the dress after all this time. "It's a beautiful wedding dress, Aunt Mag— much too pretty for a graduation, don't you think?" Seeing the tears in her aunt's eyes, she turned and threw her arms around her. "Oh, Aunt Mag, don't be sad. I love you. If it wasn't for you, I would never have gone to college at all."

"I just hate to see you stuck over there teaching school in Onslow County when you should have finished your education first."

"Well, you're the one that told me to marry Tate if he asked me."

"I was just afraid you were going to do something foolish with that man. He had you awestruck, filling your head with big houses and servants. You've got all the house you'll ever need, right here between the rivers. Don't you think you could talk Tate into coming over here to live?"

"I know you were counting on that, and I was, too, but Tate is so excited about his house. Just give me some time and I'll talk him into it.

Right now, I don't think I could."

The door opened slowly and Katie peeked in. "May I kiss the bride and wish her luck?"

Maggie held out her arms to her sister. "Oh, Katie, please do."

"Let me look at you, Maggie Lorena," she said, walking around her. "Aunt Mag, the dress is absolutely beautiful. I'd be jealous if I didn't have Mary Ellen's wedding dress to wear."

Aunt Mag hugged Katie and kissed her on the cheek. "I'd have done the same for you, but everybody knows you dreamed of wearing Mary Ellen's dress ever since she married Mr. Cyrus."

"Well, I dare say I need to find a husband first."

Aunt Mag smoothed the folds in the long dress. "Now, don't you go sitting down or anything, Maggie Lorena. Here, put these pearl pins in your hair. Your Uncle Archie would've wanted you to wear them."

"Did you wear them on your wedding day?"

"I did. He gave them to me that very morning in the ivory box over there on your dresser. You see to it that you keep them in there, you hear?" Aunt Mag looked at Katie. "I want you to wear them, too."

Katie kissed her aunt on the cheek and they watched Maggie put on the earrings. "Now that's a pretty sight," Katie said.

"I never saw a prettier bride." Aunt Mag was on the verge of choking up. "All right, I'll slip on out and let you talk a minute more. It's almost time to get started."

Katie looked at Maggie through the mirror, waiting for Aunt Mag to close the door. "So, tell me what happened. I'm dying to know."

"I couldn't do it," Maggie said. "It wouldn't have been right."

"You might have toyed with the idea of being Reece Evans's mistress for just a little longer," she said, a twinkle in her eye. "What's the rush?"

"Shhh, Kate—they'll hear!"

Katie took Maggie by the shoulders and turned her around. "You're not expecting, are you?"

"Of course not."

"I'm sorry. I guess I shouldn't have asked that. It's just that you didn't seem too enamored with marrying Tate. I always thought we'd have a double wedding."

"Wash's death changed things, Katie."

"How's that?"

"Oh, by me going to Onslow County and all, meeting...Tate."

"I've met someone, too. I haven't even had a chance to tell you."

"You're teasing. Who? When?"

"Oh, he's a well driller over in Pender County. I've known him for over a year, but we just started courting," Katie said, smoothing Maggie's dress. "See, if you'd waited a little longer..."

Maggie spanked her playfully. "Go on with you, Katie Corbinn. It will be more fun this way. You can have your own wedding." Maggie pushed the hairpins into the knot in her hair, attaching a small sheer veil and bringing it down over her face. "How do I look?"

"Never prettier," Katie said, touching her cheek to Maggie's. "I'll go get Mama. She wants to see you before you go in."

G.W. pushed Ellen into the room in the chair that Jasper had made to get her around at Christmas. Ellen's face was pale except for the two spots of rouge that Aunt Mag had rubbed on her cheeks. She was dressed in a pink floral voile dress that Maggie remembered from Mary Ellen's wedding. "Mama, you look gorgeous," Maggie said.

"Mary Ellen would've wanted me to wear this dress," she said, her eyes filling with tears.

"Oh, Mama. I hope this isn't too much for you."

"Honey, I wouldn't miss this day for anything in the world. I know it means you'll be leaving us."

Maggie knelt beside her, the white eyelet dress spreading out like a tent. "It's not like I'm leaving for good. I'll be back to see you every chance I get. You said yourself that you wanted me to marry Tate, didn't you?"

"Oh, I do, honey. I really do," Ellen said. She took a deep breath and sighed. "Whew! G.W., get me a glass of water. I'm about to thirst to death."

"You're just trying to get rid of me, Ellen," he said. "Don't think I don't know it. Well, get on with it. You're keeping a lot of folks waiting out there in the parlor."

He left the room and Ellen turned to her daughter. "He'll hurt you at first, Maggie. He's a big man. But don't be afraid. After a time, you'll get to liking it."

If she only knew! Maggie thought. "It's all right. I'm not a bit worried."

"You be good to him and he'll be good to you," Ellen said. Maggie had the feeling that she had been practicing this litany of do's and don'ts. "He's a gentle man. You can't go flying off the handle at him."

"I know. I need someone like Tate. He calms my nerves instead of making me mad. Did you see the ring he's giving me? It was his great-grandmother's. She wore it when she got married in Ireland."

"I saw it. Now you remember, it takes more than a ring and saying the words to make a marriage. It's hard raising children and trying to make ends meet, but if you pull together, you can do most anything."

Maggie was still on her knees with the dress spread out around her when Aunt Mag reappeared at the door. "Get up off that floor, Maggie Lorena. I declare, it took me all evening to press that dress and here you go mussing it and Tate hasn't even seen you."

Maggie stood quickly and kissed her mother while Aunt Mag straightened the dress. "Somebody needs to tell Pa to come get Mama. It's time," she said.

Coming into the parlor on Tate's arm, Maggie was radiant in the long white gown. G.W., in his full Confederate regalia, waited with the preacher in front of the mantel. As large as he was, Tate looked light on his feet, waltzing Maggie down the aisle between two rows of folding chairs. Reverend Mizelle called out in his deep revival-meeting voice, "If there's anybody in this here room that knows any reason why this man and woman should not be united in holy matrimony, let him speak now or forever hold his peace."

In the silence that followed, Aunt Mag's eyes were on the bride. What was she thinking behind that make-believe smile? Maggie had been as close as any child she might have had as her own. She wasn't fooling her old Aunt Mag one bit. Maggie wasn't in love with Tate Ryan. Aunt Mag sighed. *Well, love wasn't the only reason to get married—sometimes a woman just had to do the right thing.*

When Tate slipped his great-grandmother's ring on Maggie's finger and the preacher pronounced them man and wife, everyone stood and clapped. Jasper pushed Ellen up beside Maggie and G.W. and Aunt Mag stood beside Tate to form a receiving line. One by one her brothers came up and hugged and congratulated them. After the small group of neighbors and friends had wished them well, G.W. pulled Tate aside. "I want y'all to know that there will always be a place for you here," he said.

"We're much obliged, Capt'n Corbinn, but I expect we can make it on my little farm with Maggie teaching and all. I'm anxious to get on back home as early as we can tomorrow morning. Pa always plants his corn on Easter Monday and I'd like to get mine in, too."

"Did you ever consider growing tobacco?"

"No, sir. I'm not opposed to it. I just don't know anything about it."

"Well, you keep it in mind, son. Tobacco is the coming thing. Let me just say this, if you and Maggie Lorena ever want to come back over this way, she's got some land. I could get you started in tobacco. There's plenty of folks over here, including me, who'll teach you how to grow it."

"Thank you, Capt'n. I'll keep that in mind."

Chapter 31

Tate couldn't remember a better summer in all of his thirty-one years in Onslow County. Married for four months, he had a place of his own, a wife that made him smile just thinking about her, and a good stand of corn and sweet potatoes. Sally Catherine had seen to it that Bill plowed up a little garden for Maggie, fencing it off to keep out the coons and rabbits. Sharing seeds from her own garden, she had prepared little packets, labeled them with pictures from an old seed catalogue, and written the time they were to be planted on each one.

Maggie had delighted in her kitchen garden. She'd scattered the turnip seeds herself and planted cabbage, two rows of butterbeans and several hills of squash. Miss Sally had started the tomato plants in little paper cups. Every afternoon Maggie climbed over the low chicken-wire fence with her hoe and spent an hour or so chopping weeds and dipping water over her vegetables.

Tate followed his lengthening shadow home across the fields, the smell of frying fatback luring his tired legs along the foot path. He hoped Maggie had picked a mess of the rough-leafed turnip salad. He loved the way she washed it a half-dozen times to remove the sand and stirred it around in the hot grease until it was a wilted mass of bitter greens. Every evening she piled his plate high with vegetables, thick slices of salty fatback and lacy cakes of fried cornbread.

He was careful to see to it that there was always plenty of firewood cut to fit the cookstove and stacked on the back porch. He had let it run out a few times right after they were married, until one evening when Maggie put raw meat and vegetables on the table. "Done or raw, it fills the craw!" she'd said. Maggie had a side to her like that, but he was determined to get used to it.

Some days he would bring home a squirrel if he had his gun along, but today he had only the long-handled hoe and a towsack full of tools for mending fences. Plodding across the field, the bottoms of his trousers heavy with wet black sand, he kept his eyes fixed on the house. From the distance, he could see her going in and out the door, throwing out water or talking to the three cats that had taken up there.

Maggie called the house her little 'cabin in the wildwood.' She had swept it out and cleaned it good the very first day they moved in and soon had feedsack curtains at every window just like he'd imagined. It would be a fine house when he got finished with it, but with the growing season at hand, it was all he could do to keep up with the plowing and planting. Maggie complained about the unfinished house to the point of aggravation, but she would learn that a man had to do things in his own time.

As he lifted the gate and swung it open, she waved to him, picked up a towel and came down the back steps. She was girlish in a long loose print housedress, her feet bare and her hair caught back in a ribbon behind her head. He'd have to hand it to Pa, he sure knew what he was doing when he brought her over to teach school. There hadn't been a day since that he didn't praise the Lord for his Pa's foresight.

"Evening, Tate. I saw you coming. Come over here to the pump and I'll help you wash up." He thought she sounded playful and he liked that. Giving her a peck on the cheek, he had to hold himself back to keep from grabbing her by the waist. Maggie had let him know early in their marriage that she didn't appreciate the smell of his hard work or the dirt that came with it. If he had any intention of getting close to her this evening, he'd have to get washed up before supper. All that rubbing and scrubbing was hard on a man with tender skin, but he reckoned Maggie's favor was worth it.

"Are you of a mind to be soaped down?" she asked, looking him over with a wrinkled nose. It was sort of a game she played, acting like she wasn't interested in what might happen if she did.

"That depends on you, Maggie Lorena." He grinned as he removed his hat and unbuttoned his shirt.

"Quit your foolishness. Supper's on the stove." She stood firmly in place, one hand on the pump handle and the other holding the towel.

He liked her like that—not wearing a corset, her large breasts straining against her cotton dress. It felt good to have a wife, knowing what to count on. "Since you asked, I believe I am of a mind to be soaped down good. Would you mind getting the tub?"

"Tate Ryan, you've got the devil in your eye and I've got things to do, but I'll get the kettle." She tried to turn away from him before she smiled, but Tate saw the edge of a grin in her profile. Maggie had some needs of her own, something he would never have suspected in a woman.

She fetched the kettle of boiling water from the stove and a large galvanized tub from the nail where it hung on the porch. Slipping a bar of soap into her pocket, she returned to the pump to find him naked, his fair torso a striking contrast to his ruddy face and arms.

Paying no mind to his nakedness, she pumped two buckets full of water, adding half of the contents of the hot kettle to each. He stood in the tub and shuddered when she poured the first bucket of warm water over him. When she began to rub the bar of soap over his back and shoulders, her hands gliding smoothly over his tired muscles, he closed his eyes and savored her touch.

"Sit down," she said.

He closed his eyes while she lathered up his hair and massaged his scalp. "Oh, honey, that feels so good."

"Now, stand up and turn around. I can't reach all over you from here."

He stood and turned slowly in the tub, facing her, catching her eye. "I'm powerful dirty," he whispered, breathless with anticipation. "You better..."

Smiling sweetly, she picked up a large tin cup and doused him. Tate doubled over. "That oughta cool you off," she said, standing back, her hands on her hips.

He covered himself with his hands. "Dern, Maggie, why'd you do that?"

"I said quit your foolishness, Tate Ryan. Now, rinse yourself off and come on inside."

"Aw, you always rinse me off."

"All right, but your supper's getting cold." He sat down in the tub and she picked up the other bucket and poured it over his head. Waiting until he cleared his eyes, she handed him the towel.

Tate grinned at her, water dripping down his face. He began to sling his head from side to side like a wet dog. "Don't!" she yelled, her hands in front of her face, but before she could move away, he had soaked her face and shoulders.

Tate held out the towel. "Here, honey, let me dry you off. I'm sorry. I don't know what come over me," he said, looking impish.

"I know what came over you, the pure devil! Now finish washing up and come have your supper before it gets cold." She stomped off in the direction of the porch.

He could never tell about Maggie Lorena. One time she was silly and playful and the next, serious as all daylights. Gathering his dirty clothes, he strode to the clothesline, pulled off a pair of clean overalls, and stepped into them. He felt refreshed, but his loins ached and it would have suited him to go without any dinner at all with the banquet Maggie had waiting for him beneath her skirts.

After supper Tate took his usual place on the porch, stretched out along the edge of the floorboards, his head propped against the thick pine support post. Maggie sat in an old rocking chair shelling peas in her lap. It was his favorite time of day—his tired body was at rest and he loved the smell of the earth just before the sun set. Maggie was always anxious to tell him about her day. It didn't matter what she said, he just loved to hear her talk. Tonight she was worried about Lauren Padgett, Ben's little girl, who came a month early when her mama died of fever. "Ben wants to start her in first grade this year and I think it's too soon," she said.

"Did you tell him that?"

"Yes, he stopped by today. He was over here to see your pa."

"What did he say?"

"Well, you know the Padgetts, they don't want anyone to get ahead of them. He said she was going on seven and he thought she was ready. I don't want to tell him she's slow. What do you think I should do?"

"Oh, I don't know, honey. Just do the best you can. That's all folks expect of you. Schoolteachers are scarce as hen's teeth out here in the country and most folks are just glad you're going to be here when the new Harris Creek school opens. I don't know where they're going to get the rest of the teachers."

"Well, they'd better start sending some of the girls around here up to BFU if..." She stopped in the middle of her sentence and stared out into the yard. He waited for her to finish, but she picked up the bowl of peas she was shelling and carried it inside. Maggie was like that. She'd just stop in the middle of what she was saying and go off in another direction. There was no need to ask what was wrong. He knew she still thought about what she had missed by not going back to school.

She stood in the doorway. "Tate, I'd like you to get those screens on the windows before too long. We need screen doors, too. I just can't stand all these flies in my kitchen."

"I told you I'd get to it. I've got about all I can do right now, honey. Can't you put up with it a little longer?" he asked, trying not to sound irritated. He had heard some talk about a house Reece Evans was building on Catherine Lake—it would likely be a fine house, with more screened windows and doors than you could shake a stick at. "It's the money, too. We may have to wait until the corn comes in."

"There's money in the coffee can. I got paid five dollars for that article I sent in to the *Progressive Farmer*."

"All right, I'll try to get started the end of the week."

"Promise?"

"I promise, but why when I've got so much on me?"

"Because if you don't, I'm going to leave you and go home and stay with my folks until you do."

Tate sat up. "Now, you know you wouldn't go off and leave me—us just getting married and all?"

"I might," she said, smiling. "I don't intend to live in a half-finished house the rest of my life."

"You won't have to," he said, getting up and going over to her. "I'm going to give you everything you ever wanted, wait and see." He kissed her, closing his eyes and thinking about all the things he could do to make her happy that didn't have anything to do with screen windows and doors.

She looked up at him, her expression innocent. "Tate, I want a baby. I really want a baby."

"Well, yes ma'am. I think I better start working on that right now." He picked her up and carried her into the bedroom, sitting down on the iron bed. "If you're wanting a baby real bad, Miss Maggie, maybe we should start practicing."

She slid off his lap and stood before him, swaying her hips this way and that, slowly unbuttoning her loose housedress. Her hair had fallen across her face and she looked through the long curls, her eyes teasing him.

"God a'mighty, Maggie Lorena," he said, "I'll never get used to how beautiful you are." He buried his face in her stomach, kissing her navel and groping above for her breasts as she fell across him on the bed. He came quick, almost as soon as he entered her, wishing like always that he could make it last longer. Later that night, he woke to find her in the other room, tapping out something on her typewriter.

———

For awhile, Maggie was obsessed with having a baby. She was twenty-six years old. It was time they started a family, and a baby could make things right. Having babies together brought a man and woman closer. Maybe carrying Tate's child would erase Reece completely from her mind, something that she'd been unable to do.

For the most part, she felt she'd made the right decision. Waiting for Reece would have driven her mad, even after the miscarriage. And she would have been miserable living with the Ryans with Tate wanting to marry her. No excuse would have satisfied him. Knowing how Reece felt about having more children, how could she ever have been happy with him? Yes, she had done the right thing.

Tate had never questioned her about the night that Reece barged in. If he saw marriage to her as a victory of some sort, that was fine with Maggie. Right now she wanted his baby more than anything, but what had happened so easily in the heat of passion was not so simply accomplished by design. After they had been married six months, all she had to show for their "practicing" was a case of the whites, that maddening itch that Dr. Hooker said was caused by excessive marital indulgence. And she was tired of Tate wallowing all over her, tired of the let-down feeling she had when it was over.

Just before school was to start, she put him on notice. "I want to hold off on trying to have a baby. I need some rest. I'll sleep in the other room until I can get some relief."

"Maggie, honey, don't go off to another room. I won't bother you."

"Yes, you will. The doctor says rest is essential and I can't get any rest with you pushing up against me all night."

"You've been to see the doctor?"

"No, but I've got a doctor book that tells all about it. Married women get this way all the time. Now, you'll just have to leave me be until I can get straightened out."

Tate was real proud of Maggie's writing when it came out in a magazine or the newspaper. *The Progressive Farmer* had paid her five dollars for her story about canning fruit in jars, and for another one about scuppernong grapes. She was always sending news of the community to *The Jacksonville Times,* and they put every bit of it in the paper. But it didn't make sense to him when she would stay up half the night, working by the light of a lamp.

Maggie was a slow riser due to her late hours, and until school started Tate made his own breakfast in the morning. Like most farmers, he liked a full plate of bacon and eggs in the morning before going out to work in the field. Sometimes he left her sleeping and came back to find her still in bed at noon. All of that changed when Maggie started getting ready to open the school. She also resumed her nagging about the house.

"You promised to finish up the house before cold weather. I'm getting sick and tired of stepping over buckets of nails, and the parlor is piled high with junk."

"Maggie, I've got all I can do just to keep up with the crops." Why couldn't she stay off his back about the house? *Hellfire, I'm just one person!*

"Couldn't you at least finish up the kitchen? You said we would have a pantry and some shelves. I've got nowhere to put my canning jars or the dishes and things Aunt Mag gave us."

"I'll do it, I promise. As soon as the weather turns cold, there'll be plenty of time."

She'd been serious when she told Tate that she would leave him if he didn't finish the house. Some of it she would have done herself, but she'd never been any good with a hammer and nails, and Tate said it would double his work if she made a mess of things. He seemed to put everything else first—the hog pen needed to be enlarged, he wanted a smokehouse of his own. Before they got married, the house was all he could think about, but since then he'd been dragging it out.

Tate didn't like it when Maggie accused him of putting things off, but he liked it even less when his mother criticized him. "You'd better get on it, Tate. It won't do to let a house go unfinished too long—not with a new bride," she said.

"Now, Mama, don't you go fussing at me too. I can't stand but one woman at a time complaining. You know how it is, I've got to get the crops in and go to market."

"You should have had it completely finished before you got married."

"If I was rich I'd have a bunch of carpenters there night and day, but I'm not, and Maggie knew that when she married me."

Chapter 32

Maggie spent several days straightening the school, marking new books and planning the curricula for twelve grades. She finished up on the Friday before school began, but her enthusiasm for teaching had vanished. She dreaded the long days cooped up in the hot little one room schoolhouse. In another six or eight months the new school at Harris Creek would be completed, but Mr. Thompson said she'd have to take some correspondence courses in order to stay on.

Maggie wasn't in the mood to take courses, much less teach school. The more dissatisfied she became with her life in Stump Sound Township, the more she thought about the mansion that Reece had built on Catherine Lake. She had taken the plans out only once, pictured his hand tracing the rooms and imagined living there.

When the last of the paperwork was done, she sat at her desk, her head resting on her hands. Memories engulfed her. Only a year ago she'd met Reece...*that first day in the schoolhouse...I knew I had found my true love.* She smiled at the thought of him landing in the creek...*Damn you, Maggie!* Well, she felt damned, like a curse was upon her. She began to cry. Everything she had wished for—hoped for— was gone. Reece had warned her...*there may never be another time.*

Walking into the cloakroom, she sat down on the bench and closed her eyes. *I don't intend to lose you...*but she'd forfeited his love in favor of convention. If she could just explain to him! What had her impatience gained her but a sentence as the humdrum life of a farmer's wife, when everything could have been hers? She watched a spider scurry across the floor. *Going to waste on the dust and spiders.* Those were Reece's words. Going to waste—just like her life! She stepped on the creature, grinding it into the floor.

She decided then and there that she had to go and see him—see the house. No one would know if she was careful. Daniel was hitched to the buggy outside. Mr. Bill had insisted that she take it this morning. Catherine Lake was only a fifteen-minute ride. If she could remember the turn-off, she'd be there in no time, then back home before supper. Her stomach quivered with excitement. It was the thing to do—why had she not thought of it before?

A well-worn lane off the main road was the signpost she needed to direct her to the lake house. Reece had commented that the narrow cart path would gradually widen as lumber and building supplies were brought onto the property. Two sentry-like brick pillars stood several feet off the road, their huge iron rings waiting for chains to bar curious passersby. Maggie maneuvered the horse and buggy over the crushed oyster shells packed in deep ruts at the entrance. Making her way down the lane and through the forest, she listened for sounds that would indicate the presence of workmen, but she heard none. There were no barking dogs or cackling hens either, only the twitter of birds and the rustle of dry leaves as squirrels scampered about in the leopard spots of sunlight on the forest floor.

Around a bend the road brightened, indicating the clearing. Maggie reined Daniel in and the horse reared his head in protest. "Hold on, fellow, I need to gather my wits." She gripped the reins, closed her eyes and took a deep breath. What would she say? *I wanted to see you—see our house.* No, she would come to the point. *Reece, there are some things I need to tell you.* What would he say? Surely his anger had abated by now. He would be reasonable, listen to her. Daniel stamped and snorted, his long tail swatting the bloodthirsty flies.

The house stood in a circle of sunlight, the lake's silvery reflection blinking in its windows. She had seen it a thousand times in her mind's eye. Now it stood before her, a red brick mansion, more beautiful than any she'd imagined.

She stopped the carriage under the trees near a large truck smelling of oil and gasoline. It seemed out of place so far from the city. There was a carriage house a short distance away, its eaves trimmed in the same white spindles and curlicues as the house. Reece had promised an automobile—he would bring it down from Philadelphia, then up the New River by boat. The doors to the carriage house were closed, but she could imagine the shiny new car behind them. It would be just like Reece to have a fancy car.

Climbing the steps to the house, she was amazed that Reece had been able to accomplish such a lived-in look so soon. Big pots of Wandering Jew hung between each of the curlicued arches, reminding Maggie of Aunt Mag's porch, thick with overflowing pots of the same vine. A swing hung at one end and there were four rocking chairs at the other. Turning the bell, she waited for a response, trying her best to appear composed in case someone was peeking from behind the lacy curtains. There would be servants; Reece was not one to manage without them. She turned the bell again and called through the screen door, "Hello!" Strolling the length of the porch, running her hand along the painted rail, she smiled at the empty flower boxes that flanked the steps. Petunias would be beautiful there next summer.

Trying the screen door and finding it open, she stepped into a large foyer. "Reece," she called out. No doubt, he was here—his coat and hat were thrown across an ornate chair, one of a pair that stood on either side of a carved marble-topped table. In the large gilt-framed mirror that hung above it, she imagined herself finely dressed, her hair well-coiffed in the latest fashion. There would be jewels about her throat. She touched his coat, rubbed her fingers across the fine linen.

On either side of the foyer were two beautifully-furnished sitting rooms, one containing a piano. Maggie walked across the richly-patterned carpet, sat down at the piano and played several chords. It was finely tuned. He knew how much she loved a piano.

Something was cooking. Making her way through the dining room and the pantry, she found the kitchen at the back of the house. Her heels made little tapping sounds on the green linoleum floor as she crossed to lift the lid on chicken stewing in a deep pot. The stove was a sight to see, its black iron sides polished and gleaming, nickel-plated trim edging out its doors. Beside the stove was a long wooden cabinet with a built-in white enameled sink and two faucets above with 'hot' and 'cold' marked on the silver handles. A steady stream of water splashed into the sink when she turned them.

The house was completely still, but she expected to come face to face with Reece or a housekeeper at any minute as she made her way back through the hall into the foyer. Climbing the stairs, she smiled to herself. Keeping such a fine house would be her pleasure. In a hall mirror, she inspected her reflection. Her cheeks were flushed and the twist of hair that she had piled on her head early this morning had slipped. She removed the pins and shook her hair loose about her shoulders. Reece liked her like that.

The door to his room was open and she walked in and stood before the elaborately carved high-poster bed. A small stepstool was pushed against one side. Mounting the steps, she was careful to keep her balance on the tiny risers. There must be the down of a hundred geese in this mattress, she thought, falling backwards onto it, throwing her arms up over her head. She closed her eyes, imagined him finding her there sleeping, like Goldilocks. A breeze came through the open window and brushed her cheeks.

In the stillness she heard something. There it was again, a child's gleeful, squealing laughter. Maggie sprang from the bed and bounded up the steps to the solarium, stopping at the windows opening out to the porch. More cautiously, she peeped out the window until she could see the lake. Two young girls were romping and playing in the water. Two older women wearing little caps on their heads and long white aprons watched them from the shore. *He has custody of the children!*

On the glassy lake, a man was rowing a boat with long hard pulls, propelling it rapidly towards the shore. A woman sat very still in the bow, a parasol in one hand, the other dragging through the water. There was no mistaking Reece's profile—his broad shoulders, the strength in his arms. Maggie held her breath, taking in the scene. Suddenly reality emerged and she felt faint. Clinging to the doorway, she gulped for air, forcing herself to remain upright. If only she could make it to the carriage. She descended the stairs, grasping the banister with both hands. At the landing, her knees buckled and she felt as if she would have to crawl the rest of the way. But she took deep breaths again, avoiding the sight of his coat on the chair, and made her way out the door and down the steps to the waiting carriage.

Daniel lurched forward without instruction, heading out through the forest. Coming to the end of the lane, he picked up a trot and kept it up until they reached the schoolhouse, where he pulled the carriage and its lone occupant under the shade of the trees. In the stillness, Maggie could hear the wild beating of her heart. *He had brought his wife and children to live in her house.*

Chapter 33

Tate filled a tin cup with water from the bucket under the pump and placed flowers in it. There were buttercups and bluebells, red clover and a long stem of cow vetch. Maggie loved flowers. She had planted some in her garden, but he had picked these on his way home from work because yesterday, after school, she'd had a spell—Mama called it hysterics. When he found her, she was all to pieces sitting by the barn crying her eyes out. Mama said some women got hysterics when they had too many things on them. Tate didn't think Maggie had so much on her, but he was willing to listen to his ma about such things.

He slipped off his shoes on the back steps and walked quietly through the hall, peeping into their bedroom. She was still in her bedclothes, propped up with papers piled all around. "Maggie, are you all right?"

She looked up at him and tears came into her eyes. "I can't stand it here any longer, Tate. I'm not going to teach school this year."

He sat down beside her on the bed. "What do you mean?"

"I said I can't teach school anymore."

"Oh, you have to, honey. Everybody's counting on it."

Her hair was in wild disarray, her eyes puffy. "No. Don't you see, I can't go back to teaching school. I just can't right now."

He couldn't believe she would say such a thing. "You're not yourself, Maggie Lorena. School starts Monday. There's no one else to do it this late. Pa would have a fit!"

She threw herself into his arms and sobbed against his chest. "I can't, I just can't."

"Hush, now, just hush your crying. I'm going to go get Mama. Maybe she has some tonic you can take." He set the cup of flowers down on the table beside the bed.

"I don't want your mama, Tate. Stay here with me, please. I'm not well, I tell you. I can't teach school. They'll have to find somebody else."

"Now, don't say that. We'll talk to Pa. He'll know what to do. I've got to go get Mama."

———

Sally Catherine said she'd seen it coming. "I noticed it right from the start, Tate. It's nothing you can't put up with, I reckon, but Maggie's high strung. She just can't hold up with a whole lot of things not going her way. You know, she didn't come here to Onslow County to get married. That was your and your pa's idea, and I dare say she's regretting it already."

"Mama! What are you saying?"

"I'm saying Maggie Lorena is about to go crazy living over there in that half-finished little house of yours. Why, she's lived in Raleigh, and I dare say she's taken a step or two down, marrying into a poor family like ours."

"Ma, we're not poor. We've got a house and clothes on our back and enough food on the table. I don't see how you can say that Maggie Lorena was stepping down marrying me."

"Sometimes I think you're a pure fool. Women like Maggie want education. They want fine houses and fine furniture."

Tate had never seen her so hepped up. "I see you've been thinking about this, Mama. What're you trying to say?"

"I'm saying that women like Maggie Lorena don't want so many children, and they want a wet nurse to take care of them." Sally Catherine sat down in her rocker and started it in motion. "I thought this was how she was from the beginning, but when she said y'all were getting married, I figured she knew what she was doing."

Tate snorted. "Then she should of married someone else."

———

Maggie was in the kitchen. She had slipped on a dress and stood barefooted at the kitchen sink, the cup of flowers in her hand. "Thank you, Tate. I didn't notice the flowers when you brought them in."

"Mama sent you some of her tonic and some headache powders. She said for us to come over there for supper. Said it would do you good to get out. You need to talk to Papa anyway. I'll take you in the wagon if you like."

"Oh, all right, but don't say anything about what I said."

"You mean about not teaching school and all?"

"I'm sorry, Tate. I don't know what's come over me the last few days."

"Well, I'm glad you've changed your mind. Pa wouldn't take kindly to your quitting like that. The superintendent wouldn't either."

Maggie placed the cup of flowers on the windowsill. "I spilled some water. Would you take this towel and get it up while I straighten the kitchen and feed the chickens?"

Tate sauntered off in the direction of the bedroom, a towel in his hand. If this was what hysterics were like, he wondered how much of them he could stand. What Mama had said was the worst thing—how she thought Maggie might be sorry that she'd married him. Well, Maggie didn't have to marry him, but she had, and he reckoned she'd just have to make the best of it.

Tate wiped up the water on the bedside table, noticing that Maggie's trunk was open against the side wall. His curiosity got the best of him and he walked over and stood before it. She was so secretive about her trunk that he'd often wondered what she kept in it besides her clothes. There were papers and letters and little boxes of things in the wooden tray across the top. He figured a stack of letters tied with purple ribbon were from the Pridgen boy.

Tate stared at a single letter lying halfway under a stack of handkerchiefs. He pulled it out gently by the corner of the envelope, careful not to disturb anything. Bending over the trunk, he studied the large, evenly slanted lettering, nothing at all like the hen scratch he managed to make when he had to write his name. He touched it. It had the feel of fine linen. It would be Reece's writing—Reece would have a perfect steady hand like that. Listening for Maggie, he nervously picked up the letter and lifted the seal, the bright red wax like a burning coal on his fingers. He scanned the words. *That first day in the schoolhouse...at the soirée in my home... I knew I had found my true love...my children...my wife...never a marriage...backwoods of Onslow County...lunch by the creek...ask only for your patience...may have a solution...undying affection.*

"Tate, where are you?" Maggie called from the kitchen. "I'm ready to go."

He replaced the letter in the envelope and slipped it under the handkerchiefs, his hands trembling, his heart drumming in his ears. "All right, I'll be there in a minute."

It was a good thing that Bill Ryan dominated the conversation at supper that evening, because Tate and Maggie had very little to say. "I'll take those old books out to the colored school one day next week, Maggie," Bill said. "They'll be real proud to have them."

Maggie forced a smile. "I cleaned them up as best I could, Mr. Bill. There's not a thing wrong with them except the covers are about worn out."

"Do you reckon we'll ever see the day when blacks and whites will go to the same school?" Sally Catherine asked.

"It'll be a cold day in hell as far as I'm concerned," Bill declared.

Maggie came to life. "They do it all the time up North. My professor friend at BFU, Abigail Adams, says the blacks up there talk just like white folks and some are a lot smarter."

"I think if the Lord had intended for blacks and whites to mix, he wouldn't have made such a big difference in their coloring. Black is black and white is white," Bill said.

"Not all white folks are the same either," Tate said.

Bill turned to his son and laughed. "You're right there, son. There are some sorry mean white folks in this world, but I'm happy to say that I don't know many of them."

Tate stood up and leaned on the back of his chair. "Maggie needs to talk to you about something, Pa."

Maggie stared at him incredulously. "Tate, I told you..."

"Wait a minute," Bill said, turning to Tate. "You're not forgetting about the Farmer's Alliance meeting tonight, are you? One or both of us should go."

"No sir, I was planning on going. Are you?"

"No, you go on without me. I'll stay and keep the womenfolks company."

"Maggie, I'll see you back at the house," Tate said, giving her a peck on the cheek.

"He looks peaked, Sally Catherine," Bill said after Tate had left. "What do you reckon ails him?"

"I reckon he's just got a lot on his mind." She struggled out of her chair and started towards the kitchen. "Come with me, Maggie, and I'll wrap up some of this pork and sweet potatoes for you to take home. Tate said you weren't feeling much like cooking."

Maggie cleared the table and had turned towards the kitchen when Bill stopped her. "What was it you wanted to talk to me about?" he asked.

"Oh, it was nothing, Mr. Bill. I figured it out myself."

What she had reasoned out was that Mr. Walter Thompson would just have to find another teacher.

She stood for a long time looking at the house that Tate had built for her. The cypress siding had weathered to a dull gray, but the shiny tin roof still caught the glint of the late evening sun. There wasn't a tree in sight to shade the house, and the bushes Maggie had planted were dry stubs from lack of rain. Reece's words came back to her. *Is this what you call a better offer?*

She wished she had never gone to the house on Catherine Lake, climbed the stairs, run her hand over the fine linen, but that didn't matter now. She knew what she would have to do to get as far away from Onslow County as possible. In the distance, across the fields of drying corn, thunder rumbled.

Climbing to the top step of their porch, she sat down and cogitated. Reece had thought she was being spiteful, marrying Tate. Now he was being spiteful in return, bringing his wife and children here to flaunt them in her face. The next thing would be his two little girls in her class. Chances were they would be there Monday morning on the first day of school.

In the bedroom, she gathered her clothes and stuffed them into the trunk. There would be little need for their meager collection of household things where she was going. Looking around the room, she stopped at the flowers in the tin cup. *I'm sorry, Tate.* Then she closed the trunk lid, locked it. She slipped the key into her pocket and dragged the trunk to the front hall near the door, where it could be easily retrieved. She could get it out herself, if need be.

The thundercloud was closer now, throwing jagged bolts of lightning at the parched earth. Maggie worked fast, filling a lamp with kerosene. She carried it to the parlor, lit it, turned the wick up high, and placed it on a rickety table in front of the window. As the storm drew nearer the wind began to howl and blow, tossing the distant pine trees to and fro, sucking the feedsack curtains in and out. She removed the glass chimney from the lamp and watched the curtains flutter. Closing the door behind her, she went out on the porch to wait. No one could blame her for what happened next.

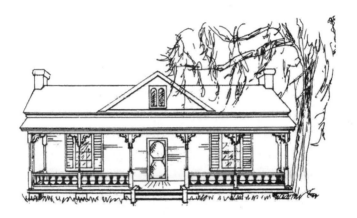

Part 4

Bladen County
October 1908

Chapter 34

Seeing his house burnt to the ground when he came home from the Farmers' Alliance meeting had hurt Tate in the worst way. His folks were all to pieces too. Pa said lightning struck the house and it went up like fat kindling. Maggie was so stunned when he got there that she couldn't say a word. She just sat on her trunk, staring out into the empty field where the house had stood. Pa had told him how Maggie came to get him, screaming that the house was on fire and begging him to come get her trunk out. Was that all she cared about?

G. W. didn't waste any time getting over to Onslow after he heard about the fire. "Tate, you know I wouldn't have had this happen for the world, but there's some good can come of it," he said. "Won't you and Maggie come on over to Bladen and make a new start? You know, it's time you tried tobacco farming, and I'm desperate for some help. Jasper's gone off to Wilmington to work in the shipyards. Says he's tired of farming." They were standing in the Ryans's yard and the old soldier turned his head and spat a long stream of dark tobacco juice out between his teeth. "You know what I think about that!" he said.

Tate looked out across the pasture and fixed his gaze on the corn drying in the field. "It's up to Maggie. She can have her say. She might rather stay here in Onslow County."

Maggie stood beside her father. "There's nothing keeping me here except you, Tate. Your pa has already talked to Mr. Thompson and gotten a teacher lined up. He told him my nerves were too frayed to teach school, after the fire and all."

She was wearing one of her church dresses and had a pretty bauble pinned to the neck of it. Rubbing her fingers over it, she waited for him to say something, but he was thinking about how she'd been acting since the fire. Everything they had except for that trunk had gone up in smoke, but she hadn't cried or gone all to pieces. And she refused to even talk about starting over. All she said was that it was a sign that the good Lord wanted them to make a new beginning—somewhere else.

It had seemed strange, moving back home temporarily with Maggie, them sleeping in his old bed and all. Mama had said they could have Maggie's room, but he told her right off that the memory of Reece Evans storming into that room had tainted it for him. He guessed it had for Maggie, too, because she didn't complain one bit. In fact, just when his heart felt the heaviest she wanted him in the night, kissing him and getting on top of him like she couldn't stop if she wanted to. Something about it didn't seem right, not after all they'd just been through. But with so much on his mind, it sure helped to get him to sleep.

He'd always wondered what it would be like to live over there in Bladen County. Now might be the time. A man needed his own place, a place where he didn't have to answer to anyone but himself. G. W. and Maggie were waiting for his answer. "We'll need a place to live until I can build us a house," he said.

G. W. studied him for a moment. "You're not forgetting about Mag's old place, are you, son?"

"No, sir. I reckon we could live there for awhile, until we caught up a little. If Maggie wants to, that is."

Maggie jumped up and put her arms around his neck. "Oh, Tate! It's what I want more than anything. You know how much I love Aunt Mag's house." He hadn't seen her happy like that in a long time. He reckoned he could put up with anything for awhile to make her happy again. And he did know how she felt about Aunt Mag's house. He thought she'd come to feel the same way about the house he'd built for her. Now he had his doubts as to whether even Reece Evans's mansion could have measured up to how strong she felt about moving back to Aunt Mag's place. It was all she'd talked about since the fire.

"Well, I guess that's it, Capt'n. We'll be on in a week or two. I've got to wrap things up around here, get the corn and sweet potatoes in," Tate said. "We're going to need what little money we can scrape together to make a new start."

G. W. climbed into his delivery wagon rig and pulled an old gray army blanket over his legs. "Just take your time, son. Get your business taken care of and we'll be waiting for you. I'll get Mag to see about opening up that old house. I imagine the dust and spiders have just about taken over."

Dust and spiders. The words hit Maggie hard, but she kept her composure. "Papa, please tell her I'll do the cleaning when I get there. I'll be needing something to do."

Tate thought she looked awful washed out. It was more likely that she would be laying up in the bed with Aunt Mag waiting on her. "Pa wants Maggie to meet the new teacher and show her the ropes before we leave. That's the least we can do."

Maggie wouldn't look at him. She just kept smoothing her apron and pacing back and forth. She sure was anxious to leave Onslow County and he guessed that was what he saw as a good sign. She wanted to get as far away as she could from the likes of Reece Evans. He thought about the letter. *That's what should've burned!*

"I reckon some of your folks can help you load up over here," G. W. said. "We'll get you in at Mag's house."

"There's not much here to load up. About all that's left is Maggie's trunk."

"We saved all we could, Tate," she said, her eyes filling with tears.

G. W. slammed his hand down on the wagon's dashboard. "Goddammit, don't you two start blaming each other for what did or didn't happen. It's too late to do anything about the past. Just come on home like I told you." He spat and softened his tone. "Maggie, your poor old mama isn't doing too good. I'll tell her you're coming. It'll please her no end."

When Tate got used to the fact that his house was gone, the thought of building a new one that Maggie would be proud of began to appeal to him. G. W. had told him about an old man over in Colly who could draw up anything you wanted. If he made as good on his crops as G. W. had said he would, there was no reason why he couldn't build a house to suit most anybody.

Sally Catherine cried when they left. "You were like a sister to me, Maggie Lorena. I'm going to miss you something terrible."

Maggie tightened her arms around the old woman's shoulders and tried to stifle her own tears. "I know, Miss Sally. You were mighty good to me. I'm going to miss you and the girls too."

"Those poor children, they liked to bawled their eyes out this morning getting ready for school. I know it's not far, but they feel like somebody's died."

"Oh, please, don't cry. We'll be back, won't we, Tate?"

Tate bent over to kiss his mother. "You know we will, Mama."

There were tears in Bill's eyes when he hugged Maggie. "I know it wasn't always to your liking here in Onslow," he said, "but if you get back over yonder to Bladen County and they don't treat you right, you come on back, you hear?" His arms were around Maggie, but he caught Tate's eye, made sure he was listening.

"I expect the next thing we'll hear is that you're in a family way," Sally Catherine said. "I want me a whole passel of grandchildren before I get too old to enjoy them." She wiped her tears on her apron. "You're going to need some help on the farm. You better get started."

Tate was busy checking the load and tightening the livery on the two horses he had borrowed from Bill. When he'd sold the corn and sweet potatoes, he'd made enough money to buy the wagon, but horses would have to come later. "I'll be back over here in a week or two with the horses. Maybe you could take me back to Bladen County, Pa?"

"Why sure, son. It'll give me a chance to see y'all in your new home. I heard it's a mighty pretty place."

Tate gave Maggie a boost up onto the wagon seat. "It'll do until I can build another one."

"I guess all that practicing paid off, Tate," Maggie said after they had crossed the rivers.

"What?"

Maggie blushed and smiled. "I said I guess all that practicing paid off. It's too soon to say for sure, but I thought you'd like to know that a baby might be on the way." She had saved the news until they were alone, hoping that it would lift his spirits.

Tate straightened up and looked at her. "You don't say!"

"I was going to wait and tell you after we got settled, but I'm feeling so nauseous." She wiped perspiration from her upper lip and fanned herself with her handkerchief.

"You want me to stop awhile, get you some water?"

"No, let's just get on home. The sooner the better."

"I'm glad you told me, sweetness." He had never called her that before. "It'll make things a little easier, having a young'un to look forward to."

Maggie was pleased to see Tate grinning all the way to Colly. He had been so distracted since the fire. Losing his house, leaving his family was heartbreaking for him, but she refused to think about it. What was done was done, and in the long run they'd be better off. Already she was thinking about setting up housekeeping at Aunt Mag's house. It would be wonderful to have Lizzie so near. Seeing Miss Sally Catherine down on her knees scrubbing the floor or standing over the washpot for hours had made her realize how fortunate her family had been to have colored help.

Tate stopped the wagon at G. W.'s long enough for Maggie to try and speak to her mother, but Ellen Corbinn was in a deep sleep and couldn't be roused. "She's been like that for a few days," G. W. said. "We didn't want to tell you until you got here, but Dr. Bayard says she's got breast cancer on top of everything else. I don't think it will be much longer." He blew his nose in a large handkerchief and wiped his eyes.

Maggie cried too, as much for him as for herself. They'd been together for so long—Mama had been his sweetheart all during the

War. "I wish you had told me, Papa. Did she know I was coming home?"

"I told her, but I don't know if it registered. Dr. Bayard has her on right much morphine. When she's awake, she just stares through me. Y'all just go on. Mag's down there. You need to get settled before dark."

————

Aunt Mag was waiting for them, sitting in a rocker on the front porch of her old home, bird-like in her black dress against the pale blue boards of the house. The yard had been swept clean and brush was piled high in the oak grove. At the sight of the yard and house, Maggie was overcome with emotion. It was so good to be there and to know she was home again, but it was bittersweet, knowing how it had come about. She needed to tell somebody what had happened—get it off her chest. *But not about the fire.*

Aunt Mag stepped off the porch stiff-legged, coming to greet them. For the first time, Maggie noticed how old she was getting. "I'd about given you out," Aunt Mag said. "I came over here early this morning to open up the house. Lizzie and her young'uns piled up the brush and swept the yard." She reached her bony fingers up to help Maggie from the wagon. "I know you're worn to a frazzle."

When Maggie fell into her arms sobbing, Aunt Mag was taken aback. She'd imagined Maggie laughing and happy, even after losing her home in a fire, just because she was coming home. "Maggie, darling, what on earth!" Aunt Mag's bad hip was killing her, but she hugged her niece and let her have her cry.

Tate jumped off the wagon and came around to help, but Aunt Mag signaled him to let her handle it. "It's all right now. You're home," she said, walking Maggie to the porch. "Tate, I think there's a cloud coming up. Maybe you'd better pull the wagon on around under the shed while I take Maggie inside."

"Yes, go on around back, Tate. I'm all right. I'm just so glad to see Aunt Mag."

"All right, but you call me if you need me."

"Now, isn't he sweet," Aunt Mag said. "That's just like something

Archie would've said."

Maggie waited until Tate had gone around the house. She stopped on the porch and drew Aunt Mag aside. "So much has happened since I last wrote to you," she said, peeking around the corner post to make sure that Tate was out of earshot.

"Well, I reckon I can imagine how you feel," Aunt Mag said, "but you're not the first couple who has been burned out and had to start over."

Maggie stared out into the oak grove, her eyes fixed on a clump of dead grass. "That's not what I meant, Aunt Mag. I almost left Tate."

"What are you saying, girl?"

"I was fed up with living in that half-finished cabin, so I went there, and I saw him with *her*."

"What? Saw who? What are you talking about, Maggie Lorena?" Then it dawned on her. "You went to that Evans fellow's house?" Maggie nodded. "And you saw him with who?"

"He was with his wife and their two little girls. The housekeeper and a nursemaid, I guess, were there too."

"Good Lord. What did you go there for? You didn't think that he would want..."

"I didn't think anything, I just wanted to try and explain."

"Try and explain what?"

"That I married Tate because...because..." But she couldn't say it.

"Maggie Lorena, what am I going to do with you? You are a plumb fool! And I warned you. I warned you not to get mixed up with him and you did it anyway." She grabbed Maggie by the arm. "Come on in the house right this minute," she said, hustling Maggie inside.

"She was there with him, Aunt Mag, that crazy woman—in the house he built for me!"

"I've never heard such talk. You should be ashamed of yourself. Don't you ever, ever let me hear you tell this again. Do you hear me, Missy?"

Maggie had never seen Aunt Mag in such a swivet. Never before had she denied her hugs and comfort. "You don't understand."

"I don't know what's to understand," Aunt Mag said coldly. "Seems to me you've just had the devil in you." She herded Maggie into the bedroom. "Here, put this dressing gown on and lie down in here and think about what you said." She hesitated at the door. "You better straighten up and fly right before supper."

Aunt Mag stood in the hall thinking about what Maggie had told her. She had it figured right—the hasty wedding, the fake smiles. *Maggie Lorena married Tate because she had to!*

Chapter 35

Tate hated Aunt Mag's house from the day he set foot in it. The musty smell of the wine-colored horsehair furniture crammed against the walls of the sitting room near stifled him. He wondered how on earth a man could live in such a room. It didn't say much for Uncle Archie.

In the dining room, two corner cupboards were filled with tiny teacups and rose-colored glasses so thin they'd nearly break in your hand. Six squatty little chairs that creaked and groaned under a man's weight sat around an oval table. Whatnot shelves and pictures of fairytale people hung on every wall, and there were half-round tables and bookcases with enough knickknacks to fill Woolworth's five-and-dime store in Wilmington.

In the bedroom, Maggie had shown him how Uncle Archie had stood before the long mirror every morning, doing his deep breathing exercises to rid his body of the impurities built up during the night. The high bureau where he had kept his toiletries remained just as he had left it.

"You can use his things, Tate. Aunt Mag said so."

"I'll set my things up on the porch, if you don't mind. I feel all cooped up in here. It's like your Aunt Mag and Uncle Archie still live here."

"Don't be foolish. It's time you learned some refinement. This is the only home we've got for the time being, and you may as well make the best of it."

"This is not our home. It's a house, that's all. A house full of somebody else's whatnots and do-dads. There's nowhere for me to sit down and put my feet up after a hard day in the field. I can't even get my knees under the dinner table!"

"Tate Ryan, you're the most ungrateful man I've ever seen in my life. Why, if it wasn't for this house, we'd still be living over there in Onslow in that half-finished cabin of yours."

"I don't rightly think so. It burned, remember?"

"Yes, it did, and I can't say I'm sorry. Some things happen for the best."

Early the next morning, Tate went out to explore the farm with one of Lizzie's boys and Maggie took the wagon down to Canetuck, anxious to see her mother. If Aunt Mag was still vexed with her, she soon got over it when Maggie told her that she was expecting a baby. "Law me, I never thought I'd see the day. Let's go in and tell your mama."

"Don't you think we should wait? Something might happen."

"Pshaw! Maggie, nothing's going to happen, and your mama is feeling so poorly. Maybe it will give her a lift."

The shades were drawn against the late afternoon sun, and there was an odor of sickness in Ellen's room. "Poor thing, she's suffered so much," Aunt Mag whispered. "I knew her insides were worn out from having all you children, but cancer..." Maggie had heard stories many times about how her grandmother and Aunt Mary had both died of breast cancer. Her mother had said then that it was a horrible thing, the breasts rotting away.

Maggie tiptoed over to her mother's bed and knelt down beside her. Ellen's eyelids fluttered a little. "Mama, I'm home."

Ellen opened her eyes and stared at the ceiling, a slight smile creeping across her pale face. "I declare, you are," she said feebly. She lifted her hand as if to touch Maggie's face, and Maggie took it in hers and pressed the gnarled fingers against her cheek. "Yes, and I'm going to stay and help take care of you."

"Oh, no, you can't do that," Ellen said, taking her hand back and waving it in front of Maggie's face. "Tate'll be needing you to fix for him over there in Onslow. And what about your teaching?" She sounded clear as a bell. Maggie glanced at her aunt. *Didn't you tell her?*

Aunt Mag shook her head, and Ellen closed her eyes again, off in another world. "It's the morphine," Aunt Mag whispered.

Maggie leaned very close to her face. "Can you hear me, Mama? I've got some good news." Beneath her closed lids, Ellen's eyes darted about, making silent acknowledgment. "I'm going to have a baby." Maggie waited, but Ellen breathed deeply, sound asleep.

"Ellen! Wake up!" Aunt Mag boomed. "Maggie Lorena has something to tell you."

"What?" Ellen said, her eyes wide open now. "Oh, Maggie, when did you get here?"

Maggie choked back the tears and tried to smile. "Mama, I came to tell you that I'm going to have a baby."

"You are? A baby? Well, I'll be. Does Tate know yet?" Maggie started to answer, but the deep breathing resumed and she knew that Ellen was already asleep.

———

Along the last, Maggie sat beside her mother's bed every day, begging her to hold on so she could see her grandchild. Maggie still had six months to go. She thought about the other child she had carried only a few weeks. It would have been about two months old. But the circumstances surrounding it would have likely killed her mama before the cancer did.

Ellen Corbinn died on December 30, 1908. When she passed in the night, Aunt Mag waited until morning to tell G. W. She made his breakfast first, then called him to the table and let him eat while she put on a large kettle of water to wash the sheets. When he had finished, Aunt Mag sat down beside him with a cup of coffee. "It's over, G. W. You can go in and see her when you like. She's at peace now."

"My Ellen's gone? When?"

"She died in the night. I'm sorry to have to tell you." She sighed, glad it was over for both of them—and for Ellen.

"Why didn't you tell me?" he cried, staring at her with those sharp eyes that had cut many a man down to size. "I might've done something." His chin dropped to his chest and tears fell into his plate.

Aunt Mag stood behind him, her arms around his shoulders. "Now, G. W., you knew it was coming. You oughta been prepared for it. Dr. Bayard told you it could be any time." She couldn't stand to see him cry—an old man like that who had seen so many soldiers die, crying like a baby. Her own tears had dried up long ago. Ellen had suffered enough and she prayed every night that the Lord would go on and take her. "Remember what they say about one having to go out before another comes in? Just set your sights on that new baby of Maggie's. By spring, you'll be bouncing it on your knee."

It was a bitter cold day, the wind blowing, ice standing in the ditches as the procession of wagons and buggies made its way to Bethlehem Church. "Thank God," G. W. muttered into his beard.

"What's that you said, Papa?" Zeb asked.

"I said, thank God it's cold as hell out here! The only blessing we had in the winter up there in Virginia was that the dead were froze when we buried them and we didn't have the stink."

Jasper put his arm around G. W.'s shoulder. "Aw, c'mon, Pa, don't be thinking like that. Just remember how pretty Mama was when you married her."

Maggie and Katie were riding just behind them in the two-seater wagon, and Tate sat in the wagonbed with the casket. Maggie closed her eyes, thinking about how she and Aunt Mag had laid Ellen out in the family parlor, dressed in the pink floral voile dress Ellen had worn in both of her daughters' weddings. It had fallen to Aunt Mag and Maggie to bathe and dress the body, something Maggie had never done before.

"What are you thinking about?" Katie asked.

"Just Mama. In that pretty dress."

"I had hoped she would be wearing it in my wedding. I didn't even get to tell her about Roy."

Maggie perked up. "Has he asked you?"

"He sure did. He's coming to talk to Papa next week. Right now, he's down in Georgia drilling wells. I reckon he'll be gone right smart doing that."

Maggie hugged Katie. "Oh, I'm so happy for you. We'll be right here together having babies."

G. W. turned in his seat to reprimand them with a hard look. "What're you girls giggling about with your mama laid up back there in the casket?"

"I told Maggie that Roy was coming to talk to you next week. I want everyone to know, Papa."

"Oh, that," G. W. said.

"I've already told him," Katie whispered, "but he said to wait until after we buried Mama before we told everyone else."

They were approaching the church and Jasper and Zeb hopped down off the wagon to help Tate with the casket. "Where are y'all gonna live?" Maggie whispered.

"Papa said we could have that little piece of land across the road from Grandpa Corbinn's old place. There used to be a house there, I think. Maybe Tate will help us build a new place. We won't want much at first. Just a couple of rooms."

"Oh, you know he will, Katie. Maybe it will help take his mind off building one for me. Right now, I don't want to live anywhere but in Aunt Mag's little house."

Chapter 36

G. W. made sure that Tate had everything he needed to start tobacco farming. He turned over two of his best fields to him and loaned him a team of mules and a double plow. Since Uncle Archie had never farmed, G. W. had cleared some of Aunt Mag's land and farmed it like his own. Now it would be Tate and Maggie's. G. W. also bought the tobacco seed and paid Tate's dues in the newly formed Farmers' Union. As a county commissioner, he had taken on the Farmers' Union as his pet project. "It's the only way we'll ever get any decent prices," G. W. said. "Besides, you can get your potash and nitrogen for almost nothing through the Union. This way you can mix up your own chemicals. Half of what you get at the feed store is sand."

"I thought the Alliance was pretty active over here," Tate said.

"No, sir! We've got the Farmers' Union going now and that's what'll put us farmers back on our feet. You wait. By the time that young'un Maggie's carrying grows up, farming will be paying what it used to before the War."

"It'll take him and a bunch more like him to make a living farming, Capt'n. I'm counting on Maggie to give me a whole lot of little farmers."

"Well, you sure will need them. Half of the colored boys around here have moved up North to get out of farming. Lizzie said her cousins were living in those big tenement houses up there and can't find work."

"I don't know why anyone would want to go up North."

"Georgie sure made good up there in Michigan working for the Ford Motor Company. He got Jasper a good deal on that new automobile."

"Well, I don't want one," Tate said. "I think it might just be another aggravation."

Tate wasn't at all sure about how Zeb and Jasper would take his moving onto Corbinn land and making his future sons its inheritors. They were the only two Corbinn boys who had stayed around Colly and Canetuck. The rest of them knew their names were on the land and were content to let Zeb and Jasper farm it for them. That might change after G. W. was gone. Still, none of the Corbinn boys had been known to mince words when it came to land.

"How come you didn't build your house back over there in Onslow, Tate? I sure as hell wouldn't want that piece of shit Uncle Archie built for Aunt Mag," Jasper had said when they first came. "Maggie Lorena, she sure pulled one over on you. Hell, I wouldn't be surprised if she burnt down that house herself just so she could get back here."

"Hush up, Jasper," Zeb said. "If she hadn't come back here to live, she was going to inherit the land anyhow. The land's all I care about. Grandpa gave it to Aunt Mag, just like he did to Mama."

But Tate knew they were leery of him having his name on the deed if anything should happen to Maggie. This was Corbinn land and they wanted to keep it that way.

With the shroud of Ellen's sickness and death lifted, winter turned into spring, and Maggie was the happiest Tate had ever known her. All day long while he was out in the fields, she busied herself airing the mattresses, washing curtains, whitewashing the fence, trimming the hedges. Tate was amazed. When G. W. brought her two dozen biddies and a couple of little bantam roosters from the hatchery in Burgaw, she doted over them no end and wanted him to build her a chicken house.

Tate had balked at first. Every day was cut out for him. The tobacco beds were planted and the barn just about done, but in no time the seedlings would need to be set out. G. W. said he would need at least six sleds and he had only built four. Determined to keep Maggie happy if it harelipped the devil, he dropped everything and promised to build her a hen house the very next day.

She drew an outline in the sand of where she wanted the chicken house. When Tate brought the boards up from the barn, he watched her drag the stick through the sand, stand back and eye it, then turn a corner and go again. Her belly was big now and her breasts all swollen. He'd be glad when the baby came and she'd let him get close to her again.

"Don't make it too big, sugar, I don't have all that much sawn lumber."

"I need at least six boxes for the nests and a big roost inside," she said, her hands on her hips. "It has to be at least that big. Don't you want to do it right?"

"Sure, I do, honey, but if I make it too big, you won't be able to get to the grapes next fall without stepping in all that chicken mess."

"You let me worry about what I'll be stepping in, Tate Ryan. I want my little Reds and Rocks to have plenty of room to grow." She walked over and kissed him on the cheek. "It'll mean a little more chicken and pastry in the pot for you, too."

Tate finished up most of the chicken coop in a couple of days. The finishing touches would have to wait. All the time he was working on it he had wondered why Aunt Mag never had one. There was just about every other kind of outbuilding on the place. When she stopped by to see how it was shaping up, he asked her.

"It was Archie," she said. "He couldn't stand the sight of a chicken, much less the taste of one. Archie loved beef, and that's pretty scarce around here."

"I remember Aunt Mag used to come to our house every Sunday to get a piece of Mama's fried chicken," Maggie said. She was brushing out the chicken coop and throwing pieces of board into a small fire.

"You be careful or you'll bring that baby on too soon," Aunt Mag warned.

"Dr. Bayard said I was strong as a horse and I can do whatever I feel like."

"I'll have to say I am amazed at that," Aunt Mag said.

Tate wandered off towards the barn with his tools, and Maggie sat down on the chopping block. "I'm scared, Aunt Mag. Does it hurt much?"

"How would I know, Maggie Lorena?"

"You do know. You helped Mama with all of hers."

"Lizzie is the one you ought to talk to. She's brought more babies into the world than you can shake a stick at. Had a few of her own, too."

Maggie rubbed her hands over her round belly. "I think it's time to put her on notice. I've been having some pains the last few days."

Two days later, Maggie's contractions started about daybreak. Tate went for Lizzie, who said there was no need to hurry; first babies usually took all day and sometimes into the night. But when she got there, Maggie was writhing in pain. Lizzie sent Tate for the doctor, and Freddy for Aunt Mag, who was the first to arrive. "I don't think this chile is gone wait 'til Mr. Tate and Doc gets here," she declared.

"Oh, Lizzie, I'm afraid," Maggie cried.

"Ain't nuthin' be 'fraid of, Missy. You'll forget it once it's over."

Dr. Bayard arrived about noon, just in time to see Maggie strain and bear down. The baby's tiny head popped into view. "That's it," he said, washing his hands in a basin of scalding hot water that Aunt Mag provided. "You've done it, Maggie. Now, just one more little push. There, there, that's it!"

Tate came to the door, anxious and wringing his hands, but G. W. jerked him back. "Get the hell out of there, man. That ain't no place for you."

Lizzie lifted the newborn baby and Dr. Bayard cut the cord. "Well, he looks like a healthy baby boy, Maggie." He slapped the baby on the bottom, eliciting a loud cry. "Good lungs, too."

Maggie tried to look over her knees. "Let me see."

"Jus' you hold on a minute while I gets him cleaned up." Lizzie turned to Dr. Bayard. "Where was you? Dat young'un was comin' outa her feet fust. I was 'fraid I was gonna hafta cut her open myse'f!"

"I'm sure you could have done it as good as me, Lizzie. You've taught me a thing or two," he said.

"Well, she's pretty tore up now, but I ain't gonna be the one stitchin' her up and have her yellin' and screamin' at me."

Dr. Bayard patted Maggie on the arm. "Y'all step out of the room and tell Tate he's got a son. I'll get her stitched up before he comes in. You won't kick me, will you, Maggie?"

Her eyes were closed and she breathed deeply. "I just want to rest, Dr. Bayard. Can't you leave me be for awhile? I want to hold my baby."

"Not on your life, unless you want to bleed to death. You'll be seeing plenty of the baby after Lizzie gets him cleaned up." He set out his medical kit and prepared the sutures.

Lizzie came back in, carrying the new baby swaddled in a blanket. "Here he is, Miss Maggie—a li'l worse for wear, but he'll be all right." She laid the baby in Maggie's arms.

Maggie nuzzled her cheek against the new baby's. "He's a sweet little thing. Mama's just going to love you to death," she said, closing her eyes.

"That laudanum's takin' 'fect now, Dr. Bayard. I think you can stitch her up wid'out her kickin' you."

"What will you name this little fellow?" Dr. Bayard asked.

Maggie eyes were closed. "William Jackson." She smiled, content with the name she and Tate had chosen. "Tate said first sons were always named William in his family. The Jackson is for someone Papa knew in the War."

"Oh, Stonewall Jackson, the General?" Dr. Bayard asked. Maggie didn't answer. "Well, he's a fine baby boy, and I hope the first of many for you and Tate."

Maggie sat up, leaning on her elbow. "Dr. Bayard, I don't want any more children. I don't want to be like Mama. I thought you might help me and talk to Tate."

"Now, Maggie, you know it's natural for a man and woman to desire one another."

"I know, but I read about this operation. Isn't there something..."

"Whoa. Now listen here, young lady, you're trying to put me out of business. You'll feel differently in a few weeks." He finished up the sutures and pulled the cover over Maggie. "But I will have a word with Tate."

Tate was gentle when he broached the subject a week or so later. "Mama had a hard time with James and Hannah, but she said the rest of us were as easy as falling off a log."

"You believe everything you hear, Tate Ryan?" Maggie said. "There's nothing easy about having a baby. Look at me now, my bottom still isn't healed up and I may never be able to fit into my corset again!"

Tate smiled at the thought. He liked her best without her corset. Dr. Bayard had warned him to leave Maggie be until she was ready. "She'll let you know, young fellow," the doctor had said. "Women are strange. Just when you think they'll never open up to you again, they're all over you."

For the next two weeks, Tate slept on a cot under the tobacco shed where he could tend the fire in the barn. Somebody had to keep it going to cure out the golden leaves, and it might as well be him as long as Maggie was healing up. But late into the night, he would wake and think about how good it would feel to be up against Maggie, to be inside her. He was tempted to sneak into the house and crawl into the big iron bed. He'd been known to change her mind on occasion.

His chance came a little sooner than he had expected, when the baby was about three weeks old. The air was cool as Tate bathed on the back porch after supper that night. Shivering, he slipped into a clean nightshirt and rubbed himself all over to try and warm up. In the bedroom Maggie was propped against the pillows, nursing the baby. She was wearing the silk gown she had worn on their wedding night. Tate thought that he had never seen a more beautiful sight than her with her long red hair falling over her breast in the lamplight, but he forced himself to remain calm, climbing into bed beside her. "He's a hungry little fellow, isn't he?"

"Law me, I reckon! I feel like an old sow," Maggie said. She lifted the baby and placed him on her shoulder, leaving her wet nipple exposed. Tate looked hungrily at the suckled breast before rolling over on his side to face the wall. He was determined to wait for the right opportunity.

"If you're feeling up to it, I'd like to take you and the baby over to see Mama and Papa in a week or so," he said.

"I reckon we could," Maggie said. He felt the bed shift as she placed the baby in the cradle beside her. When she had tucked the blankets snugly around the tiny infant, she turned down the wick on the kerosene lamp and snuggled beside Tate under the covers. Her feet were cold against his legs, but he didn't move. She let out a sigh and rolled against his back, sliding her arm around his thick waist. Dr. Bayard was right. She had let him know when she was ready.

Chapter 37

In the next year, the Ryan family prospered as Tate urged one crop after another out of the reluctant soil. His profits were not abundant, but even meager success went a long way towards lifting the weight of the heartache he'd felt when he first came to Bladen County. And he had a son. That was worth all of it.

Maggie was happy, too. After William was born, she painted every room in the house, using her egg money to buy the paint. She also took the money she earned writing up the community news for the *Bladen Journal* to buy some little romper suits and a book of fairytales that she planned to read to William when he was old enough.

Only one thing worried Aunt Mag. Maggie expected too much of Tate. The poor fellow had all he could do trying to farm, but as soon as he stepped into the house in the evening, Maggie put him to work. Aunt Mag stayed with them on occasion in the first few months after the baby was born, and she saw for herself what Archie would have called Tate. Hen-pecked.

"Maggie Lorena, you better let that man have his rest. Most men won't put up with a wife telling them what to do after a hard day's work."

"Well, Tate's different from most men. I have to tell him what to do or he wouldn't ever get anything done."

"Anything *you* want done," Aunt Mag said pointedly.

"Look at the chicken house out there! He never did finish that."

"I don't see the chickens complaining."

"Why do you always take up for him? I thought you wanted me to have nice things. It's a good thing your house was here for us, or we wouldn't have a place to live."

"You better count your blessings, Maggie Lorena. Not everyone would find you easy to live with."

Aunt Mag knew she had hurt Maggie's feelings, but she thought someone should jerk a knot in her. She continued to have her say. "Another thing, Tate said he gets up in the night when the baby is colicky and walks him and rocks him. Don't you know he has to get up in the morning and go to work in the fields? Poor Tate, he looks worn to a frazzle."

"Poor Tate! What about me? I'm worn out, too, and I have to get up and take care of the baby all day long."

"Maggie Lorena, I blame your Pa and your Uncle Archie for spoiling you rotten. But neither one of them would have put up with you as a wife for one minute. Don't you know a man likes to be waited on and catered to? That's the way you get what you want."

Maggie was sitting in a rocking chair, holding the baby. She began to rock a little more vigorously. "I think I know how to get what I want," she said.

———

Katie and Roy had gotten married at Bethany Church in the spring and they were living with G. W. and Aunt Mag until they could build a place of their own. Roy was off in South Carolina drilling wells, and Zeb and Jasper had taken on the project of starting a house for them. Maggie expected Tate to help out. She set great store by what he did for her sister. But Tate was reluctant to get too involved in building a house for Katie because a project like that would really cut into his time. Maggie didn't seem to realize how much she asked of him. He loved it when he could spend a whole day in the field by himself. If he was anywhere near the house, it was Tate do this and Tate do that.

Tate had helped out a couple of Saturdays, but Maggie bragged on him to the point that he was embarrassed not to do more. He had to admit he was a better builder than either one of his brothers-in-law. "Tate can build just about anything." she told Katie. "You should have seen our little cabin over in Onslow." Finally, in order to save face, Tate found himself down there on a regular basis. It was a way of pleasing Maggie and she was a lot more pleasant when she was beholden to him for doing what she asked.

Maggie also took a lot of interest in Katie's house. She was so proud of his work that he began to think about the place he would build for her and their children. He'd overheard Maggie talking to Katie one afternoon. The sisters often met at the house under construction.

"Every room needs to be bigger than Aunt Mag's," Maggie said. "You don't want to feel cooped up."

"I thought you loved Aunt Mag's cozy little house."

"I did and I do, but since William was born, I see things a little differently. You have no idea how much room a baby takes up."

"Roy says we'll just add another room on every year when the babies start coming." She laughed, and Maggie thought how much she sounded like their mother.

"You want to end up like Mama?"

"My stars, Maggie Lorena, how you do go on about ending up like Mama. She was happy. She liked having babies." Katie blushed. "I reckon she liked what she had to do to get them, too."

"Well, that's not always what it's cracked up to be. I intend to be more than an old sow all my life. I suspect I'm carrying another child right now, but this will be this last one, I assure you."

Tate had chuckled at the conversation. Things were starting to go his way for a change. There'd be at least five or six more, he was sure, and the house he'd build for Maggie would make Aunt Mag's look like a cracker box.

Even Maggie marveled at how easily Ralph Lendon Ryan came into the world. She'd hardly complained at all during the nine months, and when her contractions started it was no time before she was holding another little red-faced Ryan in her arms.

When the weather warmed again in the spring, she and Tate borrowed her father's delivery wagon rig and journeyed over to Onslow

County to show off their new baby. They had made the trip when William was about the same age, and again when Hannah got married, but Maggie vowed this would be the last time until they could get an automobile.

"Having a baby just gets easier every time," Sally Catherine said. "Why, who wouldn't mind having a houseful of little boys like this?"

Maggie held her tongue. No one in the family seemed to agree with her decision to have a small family, most especially Tate. "He was an easy one all right," was all she said.

Sally Catherine had lost most of her teeth since Maggie's last visit. At the dinner table, she watched Annalee cut her meat into tiny pieces and mash the potatoes with a fork. "This is what you have to do when babies come into the world with no teeth, and again just before old folks go out," Sally said.

"Oh, Mama, you're not going anywhere for a long time," Tate said.

"Except for my teeth, I guess I'm doing pretty good since I went off sugar. I just can't do much anymore."

"Well, you can sit there and hold this baby for me, Granny Ryan," Maggie said. "I'll help Annalee with the dishes and put the food away."

When Maggie joined her in the kitchen, Annalee had already filled the dishpan and added some soap to the water. "How are things with you, Annalee? This is your last year at the new high school, isn't it?"

"Yes, and I hate it. Nobody likes me."

"What? Nobody likes you?" Maggie thought a minute. "You mean you don't have a boyfriend."

"Well, yes, I guess that's what I mean. Hannah got married right after she finished school and I don't even have a boyfriend."

"I declare, I guess you're going to be an old maid," Maggie said, trying to joke about it.

"Mrs. Bannerman said that lots of women never find their true love, or if they do he's not the one they marry."

"Elsie Bannerman?"

"Yes, ma'am. She's the Dean of Girls at Jacksonville High School."

"My stars, how things have changed since I left. Please tell her that I said hello, Annalee."

With one child barely weaned and another pulling at her breast, Maggie continued to push Tate away nearly every time he approached her in the night.

"I told you I'd let you know when it's safe. Now leave me alone."

"But sweetheart, women are supposed to have children. The good Lord intended it," Tate said. "We can't make it on a farm without some children to help us out."

"I've got all I want."

"Aw, Maggie. You don't mean that. You're just tired. Come on. You know you like it."

"No I don't, not tonight. Now go to sleep."

At first he didn't believe she really meant it. Most of the time he was so worn out by bedtime that nothing mattered much to him once he hit the bed. But in the daytime as he struggled behind the plow, tilling up the coarse grass between the rows of corn and tobacco, he imagined her coming to him in the night, her long red hair floating out behind her, the lamp lighting her face. She could be like that, wanting her way, almost evil-looking. Weeks went by, then months, and all he heard from her at night was her rustling around among her things in the little room and tapping on the old Olivetti typewriter.

"What're you writing about, Maggie?"

"It's just a story, Tate."

"Would you read it to me? I'd like to know what you're writing about."

"You wouldn't enjoy it at all. It's a romantic story—a book I'm writing. It's a woman's story. Now, you wouldn't want to be reading that, would you?" She smiled at him from her desk.

He looked about the room at the books and papers piled around her, the old trunk standing open. Sorrow flooded his heart.

"I miss you," he said. "Won't you come to bed with me?"

"No, it's my time."

"Will you come when it's over?"

"Don't go eliciting promises out of me, Tate. I told you how I feel."

―――

When the baby was a little older, Maggie set aside two or three hours each day just to get down on the floor and play with her boys. Abigail Adams had sent a box of books to each one when they were born, and Maggie knew the books by heart now. In the afternoon, Lizzie came to do the wash and straighten the house, and Maggie spent the time writing while the children napped. As the boys grew older, Tate sometimes surprised her during the day, stopping by the house with a tobacco sled and taking the boys for a ride, sometimes keeping them the rest of the afternoon.

Maggie relished those times when she knew the boys were safe with Tate and she could read her newspapers and magazines. There was so much going on in the world...moving pictures and aeroplanes, a war brewing in Europe.

Besides her column for the *Bladen Journal*, she was a correspondent for the *Wilmington Star*. Sometimes she thought her life had turned out pretty good after all. Then a mood would come over her, and everything she saw or did became dark and dreary.

Katie worried about her. "You spend too much time by yourself in that little room of yours, Maggie. No wonder you're melancholy. You and Tate need to take a trip, go up to Raleigh or something."

Maggie asked Tate what he thought about a trip for just the two of them. "We could go over to see Mama and Papa again, I reckon," he said.

"That's not what I meant."

"Well, what did you mean?"

"I meant we could leave the children with Aunt Mag and Lizzie for a day or two and go up to Raleigh. Maybe visit Abigail Adams and Mrs. Burchart."

"What do I need to go up there for? I've got too much to do right here and I sure don't need nothing up in Raleigh."

"Maybe I need something up in Raleigh," Maggie said. "Did you ever think about that?"

"You just don't have enough to do, sitting around with the children all day—writing half the night. Maybe you ought to come help me out in the field. That'd wear you out."

———

Helping Tate out in the field was the last thing Maggie intended to do. Women who worked in the heat and sun alongside their husbands got old before their time, with stooped shoulders and skin that looked like leather. Look at Emily McAllister and Elsie Bannerman. They weren't doing it. As soon as her children were old enough, Maggie'd take them on the train and go places. If Aunt Mag wanted to, she could come and they'd travel all up and down the seaboard like she and Uncle Archie used to do. Tate would just have to fend for himself.

Chapter 38
1912

Maggie heard from Abigail Adams almost every month. She would send cartons of books and magazines and make suggestions as to where Maggie might seek publication. *Just keep writing and writing! Leave no stone unturned until your work is published by a major house. New York, Boston—that's where you should set your sights.* At the end of the school year in May, she wrote asking if she could come to Colly for a visit. *Mother has gone to England, one last time, she says, but you know Mother— always the dramatist! I'd love to come and see you while she's away. There is nothing I would rather do than meet your family and see those adorable little boys.*

Maggie was pleased no end that Abigail would want to maintain the friendship, when it was obvious that she had more to gain from it than Abigail did. Abigail kept her in touch with a world of books and learning that Maggie still hungered for. She said that she had adopted Maggie, and she intended to prove that it was possible for a young married woman to continue her education at home if necessary. Among the papers that she sent to Maggie was a prototype of a correspondence course in Language Arts. *Dr. Vann has not approved it yet, but you will be my guinea pig. While I am there we will go over it with a fine-toothed comb. As a writer, you'll help me prove that a woman can be just as successful as a man, and still have a family.*

—

Abigail's visit turned out to be a blessing. Tate picked her up at the train station in Atkinson, and by the time they had gotten to Colly, he felt like he knew her as well as Maggie did. "She was wanting to know everything about farming, how we grow tobacco and cure it," he said.

"Didn't I tell you that you would like her?" Maggie asked.

"She said she might put something about it in a book she was writing about the South. How about that?"

Maggie was amused that Tate would be so impressed. He usually didn't pay much attention to anyone outside the farming community.

Aunt Mag couldn't get enough of hearing about all the places Abigail had been. "Me and Archie did a lot of traveling, but we never got to Europe. It was one of those things we talked about."

"Well, you could still do it. That's where Mother is right now—on a ship to Cherbourg, France."

"No, I don't believe I could, Miss Abigail. I'm still needed here—guess I always will be."

Abigail brought suspenders made in England for Tate, a string of black jet beads for Aunt Mag and a silk parasol for Maggie, but the biggest hits were the toys she brought for William and Lenny. "I declare, it's like Christmas," Maggie said.

Tate showed William how to hook up cars to a small wooden train engine Abigail had given him, and Lenny sat on his mother's lap chewing on hand-carved alphabet blocks. "I should have come before now," Abigail said. "These children are precious, Maggie. Have you had their photographs made? I would love to have a picture to show Mother."

"Not yet. It's something I'd like to do, but the photographer hasn't been by this year. My brother Jasper has a camera but he's not around too often."

"Well, when you do have some pictures, please send me one. These children could win the 'most beautiful baby contest' at the Fair next year."

"I wish Papa were here. He's heard so much about you." Maggie had warned Abigail that her pa's health seemed to be going in the same direction her mother's had gone. He hadn't been out of the house for weeks.

"I have something for him, too, Maggie, if you think he might be up to some company."

"Oh yes, I want you to meet him." Maggie turned to her aunt. "You'll tell him we're coming, won't you Aunt Mag?" she said, a hint that she might get him ready. G. W. was spending more and more time in his bed, but he refused to have visitors see him in his nightshirt.

―――

When Maggie and Abigail arrived he was dressed in his calvary uniform and seated in a chair in the parlor, one hand on his lap and the other propped on the hilt of his sword.

"My land, it is an honor and a pleasure to meet you at last, Dr. Adams," he said in his most formal tone. "Please forgive me for not standing, but I am a little indisposed at the moment." His voice was slurred by the morphine Dr. Bayard had prescribed for him and his eyes were full of phlegm. Aunt Mag had brushed his hair to one side and combed his long white beard, but he carried the musty odor of an old man who could no longer wash himself.

Abigail strode across the room in her flat-heeled shoes with the confident masculine gait that betrayed the soft sensitive woman Maggie had come to know. She reached for G. W.'s hand and shook it heartily. G. W. made a gesture as if to rise, but his knees gave way and he fell back in the chair with a groan.

"You'll forgive an old man, won't you, Dr. Adams? I'm about worn out with this world."

Abigail reached for a straight chair and pulled it up right in front of him, sitting so close that their knees touched. "Oh, Captain Corbinn, it is such an honor to meet you at last." She took his palsied hand in hers. "I'm sorry that I've come at a bad time for you, but Maggie has told me so much about you, about your experiences in the War. I couldn't leave without meeting you."

"She told you what?" The old man's eyes darted to Maggie, then back to Abigail.

"She told me that you were a hero, Captain, but it's what you have done since the War that impresses me. It was bad enough that our soldiers had to fight their own countrymen, but then to return home and have the burden of Reconstruction placed so squarely on their shoulders! It's men like you who are the heroes of war." G. W. straightened his back and tucked in his chin. "You came back and started over, rebuilt your farms and families, and got involved in politics to bring about the changes we needed to build a new South."

Maggie had heard Abigail's impassioned speeches before, when she was a student at BFU. Recently, Abigail had taken charge of a commission to form a state literary and historical association whose purpose would be to create a public library and a North Carolina museum of history.

"I did what I could," he said. "What'll come of it, I'll be damned if I know! The world is changing everywhere you look. Flying machines and ships carrying two thousand or more across the ocean at a time— sinking, too, I might add. Automobiles scaring the daylights out of horses, women wanting to vote! It don't seem natural, but then the War was about the most unnatural thing." His voice trailed off and familiar tears welled up in his eyes. "It was the Devil at work."

"The War hurt a good many men like you, didn't it, Captain?"

"Hell, yes! There was nothing but evil come from it. It killed a lot of good men and wrecked our country, all for a bunch of infidels who were better off as slaves than they'll ever be as free men."

"Now, Papa, don't go getting upset. You told me that you didn't think a man should own another man's life."

"I know I did, shug, but they went about it the wrong way, shoving it up our arses." He nodded his head to Abigail. "Pardon me, Dr. Adams, but that's the way I am."

"You won't offend me, Captain Corbinn."

By the end of the week, when it was time to say their goodbyes, Abigail was like a member of the family. They all hated to see her leave. G. W. asked to see her privately one last time. "There's something I want to ask you, Miss Abigail."

"Yes, sir?"

"There's a historical document that Maggie's holding for me, something I think that museum of yours might be interested in."

"Yes, sir. What is it?"

"It's something that happened in the War. Maggie wrote it up for me. When I die, I'm going to ask her to give it to you. I think you'll know what to do with it."

"Thank you, Captain Corbinn. I'm honored that you trust me. I will do my best with whatever it is."

G. W. died the next Tuesday at noon. After Abigail left, Aunt Mag said that he put on his nightshirt and slipped into bed, and he had never gotten up again. Dr. Bayard said that G. W. had probably had colon cancer for awhile, but the worst pain came towards the last, the heavy doses of morphine barely able to keep up with it. When Dr. Bayard ran out, the old soldier's final doses had to be sent up from Wilmington on the steamboat *John Dawson*. Aunt Mag said the morphine was the only thing that helped to ease him out of the world. She had done all she could.

After he passed, Maggie and Aunt Mag washed him all over with sweet soap and dressed him in his best uniform. Aunt Mag found the two gold dollars that G. W. had asked to have placed on his eyes when he died. Maggie thought the effect was scary in the flickering lamplight. His eyes seemed to wink at her. Pa would have gotten a kick out of that.

The next morning, Aunt Mag bent over G. W.'s face. "Who's gonna take your place, old man?" she asked, as if expecting an answer.

Maggie had to stifle a giggle. "Why are you asking him that? You looking for another old man to care for?"

"Good Lord, no. It's just that you know what they say about one going out, another coming in? Well, when Ellen died, your William came to take her place. Seems like that's how it always happens, Maggie. The Lord keeps replacing us. We have to remember that; otherwise, we might just grieve ourselves to death."

"Don't you be counting on me to bring in any replacements for you, Aunt Mag."

"Well, it's a good thing you're not the only one in the family we have to depend on." Aunt Mag arranged a tablecloth over the dining room table. "I don't suppose you feel like going out in the woods and gathering some greenery to brighten up the room."

"No, but I'll send Tate. He won't mind."

Maggie went to the kitchen to make biscuits for the crowd who would come back to the house after the funeral. "Are you going to be all right here in the house by yourself?" she called out.

"Law, yes! I don't want anyone else to wait on. Your pa was the last. Now you young'uns are going to have to wait on me." She laughed, but knew it was true.

Maggie stood in the doorway. "Tate asked me last night if I thought we should move in with you because you were getting on in years."

Aunt Mag laughed. "What'd you say?"

"I told him he wasn't fooling me one bit, he just didn't like your little house. He never did."

"Oh, I knew that, but you did and I thought that was what mattered."

"You know I'll take care of you when the time comes, don't you?"

"Pshaw! That day's a long way off. Besides, you can't even take care of yourself and your own young'uns. It'll all fall on Tate, mark my words."

Maggie knew she hadn't meant to be cruel. Aunt Mag was just like that. She said what she meant and meant what she said.

Chapter 39
1914

In January, Abigail Adams wrote insisting that Maggie come to Raleigh for a visit. *Mother is not well and the doctor says it's her heart. After the holidays, I wanted her to stay at home in Boston and let me finish out the semester here, but she insisted on returning to Raleigh.* Abigail said she was handing in her resignation and was leaving the university at the end of the semester. *You must come to see her, dear. She asks for you constantly! Your letters have meant so much to her. She says it is one of her greatest sorrows that you were unable to finish your education. The Music Department is putting on a festival the week of January 15th...a wonderful occasion for us to all be together. I know Tate will want you to come. You will, won't you? Just so there will be no excuses, I am sending you a train ticket.*

That evening, Maggie slipped into bed beside Tate right after he had blown out the lamp. "I really want to go, Tate. Aunt Mag and Katie think it will do me good." It was a cold night and her long legs were warm against him. She lifted his arm and placed it under her head. "It would be so exciting to see and hear all of that beautiful music."

"How long would you be gone?"

"Only a week. A whole week of nothing but lights and music and good conversation. Why, I might not ever come back!" She giggled and turned her head towards him, the cold light of the moon washing over her through the sheer curtains. Tate was perfectly still. "You don't mind if I go, do you?"

"Go ahead, if that's what you want. Me and Lizzie can take care of the children." *As usual,* he thought.

"Are you sure you don't mind?"

"I don't mind," he said, staring at the shadowy branches dancing across the ceiling. *But I do, and I don't know why.*

———

The train was an hour late arriving in Atkinson, and William and Lenny were tumbling all over the wagon trying to be first to see it. "Here it comes! Here it comes!" William said, seeing the black smoke over the trees before the engine showed itself around the bend.

"Mama, why can't we go with you?" Lenny asked. "I never rode the train before."

"I have. Grandpa Corbinn took me to ride on the train for my birthday one time," William said. "We rode all the way from Currie to Atkinson. Papa picked us up at the station."

"Why didn't I get to go?"

Maggie laughed. "You were just a baby, Lenny, or Grandpa would have taken you, too."

"I want to go now. I want to go with you, Mama," Lenny cried.

"Well, you can't go this time, son, but Mama and Papa will take you on the train for your next birthday. I promise." Lenny climbed up onto her lap and she hugged and kissed him. "You'll be a good little boy for Papa, won't you?"

"Yes'm, but how long are you going to be gone?"

"Not too long, honey." She looked at Tate. "Papa's going to take real good care of you, aren't you, Papa?"

Maggie and Tate exchanged glances. "I always do," Tate said.

William squeezed into the seat beside them. "Here it is! Look, Papa. Look at those pistols!" He started churning his arms. "Choo choo, choo choo."

"Pistons, son," Tate said.

Maggie had seen the new black iron engines on the Wilmington to Weldon Railroad in Burgaw, but the Cape Fear and Yadkin Valley Line that came through Currie and Atkinson had only recently replaced the old funnel-tops like the one she had ridden home on with Wash. That train ride seemed like a hundred years ago.

Tate lifted her and the children up onto the platform, where she hugged and kissed her sons again. "Now remember, Mama's going to bring you both presents, but if you're not good while I'm gone, we'll just save them until Christmas."

"Oh, Mama, we'll be good," William said.

Maggie hugged him again. "I know you will, son."

Tate was stiff as a new shirt when she hugged him. "I'll bring you a present too, if you're good." He smiled half-heartedly and she kissed him on the cheek. "It's not like I'm never coming back," she whispered. "Don't look so glum."

A porter took her hand to help her up the coach steps. "Just a minute," she said, turning to Tate. "Don't let them go near the drainage ditch, you hear."

"Maggie, stop worrying yourself. You know I wouldn't let anything happen to the boys."

"BOARD!" The conductor stood beside Tate, waiting to mount the steps. "Excuse me, sir. We're running late as it is." Tate stepped back, the same little half-smile fixed on his face. How she longed to see him break out into a big grin. For a moment, she regretted the plans she had made without much consideration for him—but only for a moment. If it was up to him, she might never go anywhere except to church and Sunday school. She needed some time to herself.

———

Before she could take her seat, two young girls raced past her, knocking her hat askew and pushing her into the end of one of the high-backed upholstered seats. She was about to go after them to remind them of their manners when she saw a heavy-set woman wearing a long white apron over a dark dress waddling down the aisle towards her.

"Oh, Miss, I'm sorry. I asked them to wait for me to go to the toilet, but they are so wound up, being on the train and all. Are you all right?" She touched Maggie's arm.

"I'm fine. I have children of my own, two boys. Actually, they're a lot younger—they might have knocked me down completely!" They both laughed as Maggie squeezed past the nursemaid and into her seat.

"Law me, I'd better go after them. Mr. Evans would have my head if anything happened to them."

"Mr. Evans?"

"Yes, ma'am. Senator Reece Evans, it is now. He's in the Legislature. Do you know him?"

Shaken, Maggie hesitated a moment before answering. "Evans? It sounds familiar. But I don't believe I know a Senator Evans. Where's he from?"

"He's from Onslow County. His sister put us on the train in Wilmington and we're going up to Raleigh to spend a few days with Mr. Reece. He's a fine fellow, he is. The best father in the world to these poor motherless girls."

"I lived in Onslow County a few years back. I may have heard his name before."

The two young girls came running back through the train, giggling and laughing. "Agatha! Mandy! Stop that running! You almost knocked this poor lady down. Now apologize, or I'll tell your father."

"Oh, we're sorry, ma'am," the older girl said to Maggie. "You won't tell Papa, will you, Melissa?" Holding her skirt with both hands, she curtsied. "Please excuse my manners, Miss..."

"Mrs. Ryan."

"Please excuse my...our manners, Mrs. Ryan." She curtsied again and her sister did the same. The younger one was the spitting image of Reece, her dark hair curling about her face much as his had done the day she met him. The older girl was the opposite, fair and blonde, probably like her mother. But Melissa had said *motherless*. What could that mean?

"Of course I will, but only if you will tell me your names. My, what lovely little girls," Maggie said, trying to steady the quiver in her voice.

"I'm Mandy, and I'm almost eleven. This is my sister, Agatha. She's nine."

"And I'm Melissa Burns, their governess." She made a little bow.

"We're pleased to make your acquaintance."

Maggie nodded. *Has it really been that long?* She was calculating the years, trying to appear nonchalant. "So you're on your way to Raleigh to see your father?" she said. Her mouth felt so pinched up that she could hardly get the words out.

"Yes, ma'am. He's a senator," Mandy answered. "Are you going there too?"

"Why yes, I am. I'm going to visit some friends."

"Daddy works in the Capitol where there's a statue of George Washington dressed up like a Roman." Agatha bobbed her head up and down, her little corkscrew curls jiggling above her shoulders.

"Yes, I've seen it. I went to college in Raleigh."

When the train lurched forward, Melissa told the girls to get into their seats. "Let Mrs. Ryan have a little peace now. If you behave yourselves, we'll visit with her again when we get to Fayetteville. Come, now."

Maggie settled into her seat and looked out of the window. Tate, William, and Lenny were waving frantically, trying to get her attention. A feeling of foreboding came over her and she wanted to get off the train and go to them. Instead, she lifted her hand and smiled. How strange that she would encounter Reece's children—the children that meant everything to him. *Just as mine do to me.*

As the train pulled out of the station, she closed her eyes and told herself that she deserved this time alone to help her get back on track. Of late she had not been able to concentrate on her writing, sitting for hours sometimes in her little room looking at a blank page in the Olivetti. The half-finished manuscript of *Evangeline* that she had begun in Onslow County had lain untouched in her trunk for more than a year. Before Lenny was born she had worked on it night and day, but at some point she'd realized that it was her own story she was writing and she was aghast that she might have revealed too much. She'd decided to take it to Abigail, who'd tell her if she should pick it up again.

That morning, before she'd left, she dug deep into her trunk and pulled out the old leather packet containing the story G. W. had told her. She'd packed it and *Evangeline* in her satchel along with her blue serge jumper. When the houseplans slipped out of the jumper's folds, she'd paid little attention, but now she wondered if it had been an omen of some sort. Meeting Reece's children on the train had opened a closed book.

She felt in her purse for the trunk key, finding it inside a zippered pocket where she had pinned it. If Tate became curious about her trunk, he'd have to break the lock to get inside. Before the fire, the trunk was just something of hers that he moved from place to place without the least interest in it. But since then, when something was misplaced, he'd make remarks like, *Maybe you should've put it in your trunk so it wouldn't get lost.* Or, *Did you look in your trunk?* She hadn't picked up on it at first, but then one day she figured it out. He'd looked in her trunk and seen something he didn't like. After that, she always kept it locked, and most of the time she wore the key on a string around her neck.

When the train reached Fayetteville Maggie waited for the girls to come forward, but there was only silence from the far end of the car. She turned and saw Melissa asleep, her head against the side of the high seat. Agatha peeked around the back of hers and caught Maggie's eye. She slipped out and ran on tiptoe down the aisle. "May I come and see you now, Mrs. Ryan? Mandy is asleep too, and I am so bored."

"Of course you may, Agatha. Please sit down. That's a pretty dress you're wearing."

Agatha smoothed her dress across her knees and crossed her white-stockinged legs at the ankle. "Thank you, ma'am. My grandmother bought it for me in Philadelphia. She lives there."

"Well, it's lovely. If I had a beautiful daughter like you, I would always keep her in pretty frocks," Maggie said, increasingly discomfited by Reece's eyes in the child's face.

"Do you have any children?"

"Yes, I have two little boys, three and five."

"Yuck! I hate boys. They're so mean."

"Not all boys are mean. Some are very nice."

"You sound like my grandmother," Agatha said, a frown on her face. "Where do you live?"

"I live in the country, not far from where I got on the train. Where do you live?"

"I live in the country, too, most of the time. Sometimes I stay with my grandparents in Philadelphia." The child was studying Maggie, her large eyes scanning Maggie's face.

"Oh. I've never been to Philadelphia," Maggie said.

"Don't you want to know about my mother?"

"Of course. Where is your mother?"

"She's dead. She fell out of a boat and drowned in the lake."

Maggie made a small gasp and looked out the window. *She drowned in Catherine Lake?* Agatha stared at her, waiting for a response. "I'm so sorry, Agatha. That's very sad."

Agatha bowed her head and fidgeted with her hands. "Daddy said her mind was sick." She looked up at Maggie. "She went away for awhile to get well, but Daddy said she would never get well, so she's gone to heaven."

"You must find comfort in that. I'll remember her in my prayers."

"Thank you, Mrs. Ryan. May I ask you something?"

"Of course. What is it?"

"Why are you wearing those funny glasses? Does your eye hurt?"

"No. It doesn't hurt. I just can't see very well," Maggie said, adjusting her glasses.

"May I try them on?"

"I guess so, if you'll be careful and not break them." Reluctantly, Maggie removed her glasses and handed them to the child.

Agatha adjusted the wire over her ears and peered at Maggie. "Do I look funny?" she asked.

"No, Agatha. You look as if you might have a problem with your eyes. Now, give them back and we'll talk some more. Tell me about school."

When Agatha returned to her seat, Maggie closed her eyes and tried to put things together. Christine was dead—no longer an obstacle to Reece. Reece was in Raleigh.

Chapter 40

Abigail Adams was waiting on the platform when the train pulled into the station. She was dressed in a long black coat with an attached cape that she held tightly at her throat with one gloved hand. She threw up her other hand to let Maggie know she had seen her through the window. Maggie looked about for Mrs. Burchart, but she was not in sight.

"Maggie, Maggie, I'm so glad you're here," Abigail said, embracing her. "Where has the time gone? It's been over a year since I've seen you!" She held Maggie at a distance, scanning her face. "Still beautiful as ever."

"No, I don't think so," Maggie said. "Children age you. Look at these crow's feet!" She was sure that Mrs. Burchart would notice the extra pounds *and* the crow's feet.

"How are the children? And Tate?"

"Well, the children wanted to come, if that's what you mean. I can't say the same for Tate. He's a homebody." They laughed and Abigail led Maggie towards the stationhouse.

Maggie looked about for Mrs. Burchart, but Abigail frowned and shook her head. "She's not here. She had a spell a week ago—couldn't get her words out. Doctor Norwood thinks she may have had a little stroke. While we were home for Christmas, she wasn't really herself. Her nieces noticed it, too. We were only back in Raleigh a few days when she fell and bumped her head. The doctor told her that she may be having little strokes that could lead to a large one. She's very upset, afraid that she'll die on me. Isn't that absurd?"

"I am so sorry, Abigail. I know how quickly things change with older people."

"I never think of Mother as being old, but she's very frail. I'm really worried about her."

They walked along the covered portico, following a porter who had taken Maggie's bags. "Well, I'm even more glad that I've come now. We'll have a wonderful time going to the concerts."

"I'm afraid not, dear. She had another fright two days ago. Her speech came back, but it scared her so that she insists that she needs to go back to Boston where her doctor is. I can't let her go alone."

Maggie stopped and reached out to touch Abigail's arm. "I'm so sorry. What can I do?"

"She's made up her mind. I can't change it. Neither can you, I'm afraid. I'll have to take her home as soon as she has seen you. We're scheduled to catch the 8:30 train tomorrow morning."

"Oh, dear," Maggie said. "There must be something..."

"Just come and be with her awhile, dear. We'll have the evening together. The Pullens have begged to have you stay with them, but naturally I didn't want to commit you. I thought you might just like to stay at my house as we planned. Joella is there and I have your tickets to the music festival."

"I'd like to stay, but it won't be the same without you, Abigail."

"I know, dear. I know how much you have looked forward to this trip. By the way, were those the Evans children waving to you when you got off the train?"

"Yes. Do you know them?" Maggie tried to look calm. She fiddled with her gloves as the porter loaded her bags into the taxi.

"No, not really. I know their father, Senator Evans. I've seen them with him," Abigail said. "Had a couple of run-ins with him in the legislature. He's determined that women will never vote as long as he lives— of course, that's because of his liquor interests. He and all the others like him are afraid they'll be put out of business by the votes of women, and rightly so. He hasn't been much help with funding for the Historical Association. How do you know them?"

"I met Ree...Senator Evans when we lived in Onslow County. I didn't realize that he had run for the Senate." Maggie climbed into the taxi and slid across the seat, relieved that in the darkness, Abigail couldn't see that she was flustered.

"Oh, yes, after his wife died. I understand that he's very well liked by his constituents—he's been able to get a lot of road work done in Onslow County so the schoolbuses can get around out in the county. But he's a real diehard when it comes to women's rights."

"That doesn't surprise me," Maggie said, reflecting momentarily on Reece's proposition.

As the taxi drove through the city of Raleigh, Maggie was amazed by the electric streetlights on every corner. Even the side streets were paved now.

"Look at all of the automobiles. I think everyone in the city must have one."

Abigail rummaged in her purse for coins to pay the driver. "Mother hates them, says they are so undignified, but I'm thinking I'll get one up North."

"Jasper showed up at Papa's funeral with another new one, a Model-T Ford. I wish you'd met Jasper. He's a lot like Papa."

"Well, then I know I'd like him," Abigail said. "Here, I'll get your bag. We'll have to round up another valise for you to take back. You should see the clothes Mother wants to give you."

"Oh, no. I couldn't," Maggie said.

Abigail laughed. "Well, you try your luck at arguing with her. She always wins, you know." Maggie returned her smile and pictured the frail old woman sitting like a queen on the cottage porch.

—

Joella met them at the door. "Miss Maggie, it's sure is good to see you. I declare, you done growed into a woman! C'mon in here. Miss Burchart, she practically worn out holding herself up 'til you gots here." She struck out ahead of Maggie towards the back of the house, but Maggie paused long enough to look around the parlor where she had spent so much time with Wash at the Sunday teas.

Joella stood in the doorway to Mrs. Burchart's room. "Here she is, Miss Burchart, that chile you been waitin' for." Mrs. Burchart sat slumped in a narrow rocking chair beside a heater, her face lit by an electric floor lamp. She looked smaller than Maggie remembered, dressed in a beige satin dressing robe that draped over the chair and puddled on the floor. When she saw her protégé she seemed to regain her stature, lifting her arms, her long sleeves flowing like wings as she reached out.

"Maggie, my love, I thought you'd never get here." Maggie went down on her knees and hugged her. "It has been such a long time, my child. Here, let me have a look at you." She reached over and tilted the lamp towards Maggie.

"I'm afraid I won't bear much inspection right now, Mrs. Burchart," Maggie said. "I must be a sight after being on the train all day."

"It wouldn't make a bit of difference if you were covered with soot from head to toe, dear," she said, taking Maggie's hands. The actress had come to life, as if she had stepped out onto a well-lit stage. "Sit here beside me and tell me everything."

Abigail excused herself to see about dinner and Maggie sat down on a small chair beside Mrs. Burchart. "There's not much to tell about me, Mrs. Burchart, but what of you? Tell me what happened. Did you have a fainting spell?"

"It was nothing, really, but it frightened me. I told Abigail that I should have stayed in Boston after Christmas. I'm getting too old to go on the road, that's all. And I'm experiencing a little stage fright at the thought of that final curtain." She laughed and took Maggie's hands. "Now that was melodramatic, wasn't it, dear?"

"Can't I change your mind? You ought to stay here with Abigail. There are good doctors in Raleigh, you know. And I do want to be with you."

"Oh, my darling girl, I want to be with you, too! It's not the doctors, Maggie. It's a feeling I have. I need to go home. If Abigail insists on coming with me, she can turn around and come right back. You will stay here and wait for her, won't you?"

"Of course. That's not a problem, but won't you need Abigail up there with you?"

"Now, don't worry about that. She's committed to the university, and we do have a home in Boston, you know. I have family to look after my needs. I just want to go home," she sighed. "Abigail understands."

The conversation at dinner was lighthearted and full of remembrances of the short time Maggie had spent at BFU. When Vanessa Burchart was ready for bed, she asked Maggie to come with her. "I have some clothes for you, some things you'll enjoy for the concerts. They're laid out there on the divan. You can try them on when you have time."

Maggie stared at the elegant dresses draped across the furniture, each with a cape or feather boa as an accessory. "Oh, Mrs. Burchart. These are your beautiful dresses—I couldn't. You'll need them again."

"No, dear, I'm done with concerts and the like. My dressing gowns are all I want to wear. I'll leave the clothes there and you can take what you want. The rest will go to the Ladies' Aid Society." She hugged Maggie and sat down on her bed. "If you can't be an actress, at least you can dress like one."

"How can I ever thank you?"

"By coming here to see me. That was all I wanted, dear. Now, go on and gossip with Abigail. We leave early in the morning."

After Mrs. Burchart retired, Maggie and Abigail sat at the kitchen table, reluctant to end the evening. "I brought the manuscript Papa told you about," Maggie said.

"Oh, yes, he was very secretive about it. I can hardly wait to read it. It must be of great historical value if he wanted to give it to the museum."

"He wanted to set the record straight. It was something he wasn't very proud of, but I think others will see it differently."

"Men are funny about things like that, my dear. He wanted his peace," Abigail said. "I'll read it on the train tomorrow. When I return, I'll deposit it in our Civil War archives. Years from now, research historians will find it extremely valuable. That's what he wanted."

"There's something else I'd like to ask of you," Maggie said. "I've worked on this manuscript off and on for the last few years. I've put a lot of time into it, but before I do anything more with it, I wish you'd tell me if it's worth the effort."

"Well of course, Maggie dear. I'll take it on the train with me too. I'd hoped you were working on something, but with a family I know it takes a little longer." She picked up the manuscript. "Hmmm, *Evangeline*. Sounds romantic. I can hardly wait to read it."

Not until she had said goodnight and gone to the small bedroom next to Abigail's did Maggie allow herself to think of Reece Evans. Since the boys were born, she had tried to shut him completely out of her mind. But seeing his children on the train today had awakened memories. What if she should see him? What would she say? What would *he* say if she told him she had gone there, seen him in the boat with Christine? Maggie was more grateful than Abigail would ever know that she had offered her the opportunity for some solitude. Especially now, with the memory of Reece exposed like an open wound.

The next morning, Maggie insisted on going to the train station with Mrs. Burchart and Abigail. John Pullen had come for them promptly at eight o'clock. "My dear girl, you are more beautiful than ever," he said, his round face rouged from the exertion of climbing the few steps to the porch.

Maggie blushed. "You are too kind, Mr. Pullen."

"No, no, it's true! You are a breath of springtime!" He sat in a large chair, its frame sagging under his weight. "Unfortunate, this business about our friend Mrs. Burchart. But I know how she must feel. There's no place like home when you're not well." He fanned himself with his hat and took a sip from a glass of water Joella brought in. "You needn't worry, Mrs. Pullen and I will be your hosts for the festival. You'll come and stay with us, won't you?"

"Thank you, but Abigail has asked me to stay here and look after things. I wouldn't want to impose on Mrs. Pullen. I understand that she's not in the best of health just now."

"A little under the weather. That's all." He shook his head as if to rid himself of the thought. "We have Mrs. Hagan with us, you know. And Charlotte would love to have you."

"You're both very kind, but Abigail has made all the arrangements for me here. It will be less trouble for everyone." *For me, especially,* she thought. As fond as she was of the Pullens, under the circumstances she took a dim view of staying with them. She was not in the mood to mind her p's and q's day and night.

"But, my dear, you'll be alone! What about your meals?" He stood indignantly. Maggie almost laughed at his courtliness. She had always loved that in Mr. Pullen.

"Joella will be here with me," she said, handing him her coat. "Will I see Mrs. Pullen tonight?"

"Oh, yes, the Mozart concert," he said, his face lighting up. He reached for her hand. "But I insist that you dine with us beforehand."

"I'd be much obliged, if you're sure it would be no trouble."

He kissed her hand with a grand gesture. "It will be my greatest pleasure."

———

At the train station, Mrs. Burchart was hand-carried on board by a pair of strong young men. While Abigail checked the bags, Maggie watched the mail clerk tie up his sacks and hoist them onto a cart. He was the same clerk who had teased her about her frequent letters to Wash. She had started over to speak to him when Abigail returned. "Are you sure you won't be too lonely? Joella could spend the nights— unless you really want some time alone."

Maggie had come to love Abigail's intuition. "I really do, Abigail. It's been so long since I had time to myself. Just some time to think about things other than the day to day."

"Well, the concerts are really why you're here, and the Pullens will be with you tonight. Tomorrow night I've arranged for Professor Morris, a dear friend of mine, to escort you to the Chopin gala. He's quite the gentleman. I'm sure you'll enjoy his company. And the Pullens have insisted that you attend the third and final concert with them. Mendelssohn is my favorite," she sighed. "I do hate to miss this. I really wanted us all to be together." Her eyes filled with tears. "Mother wanted it, too."

"Oh, Abigail. I'm sorry, but I can see how much she wants to go home. She's afraid, isn't she?"

"Yes, she is. And I am, too."

"I'll be here when you get back."

"Promise," Abigail said, hugging Maggie one last time before she climbed the steps to the train. "It might be as much as ten days."

"I promise. Tate said I could stay as long as I liked, and I'd like to see the campus. A lot has happened here since I left. I might even do some work in the library, if I may."

"Yes, you must! I should have thought of that."

"I'll write to Tate. I'm sure he won't mind. Lizzie will take care of the boys."

"How would you like to monitor some of my classes? Just sit in, help the girls with their writing? It would mean so much to me."

"I would love it, Abigail. It's the least I can do, since you sent me a ticket."

When the train pulled out of the station, Maggie buttoned her long coat and turned up Salisbury Street, admiring a row of new houses that had been built close to the campus for the faculty. In the distance was the gleaming dome of the State Capitol. Reece would be there now— Senator Reece Evans, Onslow County. The sound of his name, even in her thoughts, flustered her. She crossed to the far side of the street as she strode past the capitol square. *If I passed him on the street, what would I say?*

She was startled when someone called out her name. "Mrs. Ryan! Mrs. Ryan!" Maggie turned to see Melissa Burns hurrying towards her.

"Mrs. Ryan, I thought that was you."

"Hello, Melissa. How are you?"

"I thought I'd never catch you. I wanted to tell you that I told Senator Reece about meeting you on the train and he said he thought he remembered you."

"Yes—maybe so. We used to live there."

"Well, I declare. It is a small world, isn't it?" Melissa said. She had such an impish look that Maggie was confident Reece had told her more. "Where are the children?" Maggie asked.

"They're with the Senator now, right over there on the other side of the Capitol feeding the pigeons. Come on, I'll take you over to them."

Maggie was tempted. How she'd love to see him, but face to face? He'd been so angry, and he'd have no reason to feel differently now. "I'd love to, Melissa, but I'm on an errand for my hostess and I need to get back to her house as soon as possible. Please say hello for me," she said, her heart pounding.

"All right, I'll tell them I saw you. The girls will be mighty disappointed. They sure took a liking to you, especially Agatha."

"Tell her I'll see her another time," Maggie said, hurrying off.

She pushed open the door to Brigg's Hardware store and headed straight towards the rear, where she knew another door opened out onto Salisbury Street. The store was dimly lit and a musty odor of seed and oily sawdust permeated the air. She looked around for the usual farm implements, but instead of farm machinery she saw a large display of gleaming white appliances, clawfooted tubs and kitchen sinks. Stopping beside a bathtub, she absentmindedly ran her hand up a long pipe that formed a gooseneck at the top.

A young gentleman in a long apron approached her. "May I help you?"

"Oh, I was just looking," she said, quickly removing her hand.

"That's a tub shower. We just got 'em in. It's supposed to have a curtain hanging around that ring at the top so everything in the dadgummed bathroom won't get wet when it goes off."

They both laughed and Maggie wiggled the showerhead, which had not been tightened down. "What will they think of next?"

That evening, Maggie took her seat beside Mrs. Pullen in Jones Auditorium. At dinner she had been amazed to find the once-robust woman pale and thin. Mrs. Pullen had directed all conversation away from herself, eliciting every morsel of information possible about Maggie's life since she had left BFU. After the auditorium lights were lowered and the musicians began to tune up, Maggie felt obliged to inquire about her health. "I'm sorry to hear you haven't been feeling well, Mrs. Pullen."

"It's nothing serious, my dear. Just a little gout in my back. When the weather warms, I'll go to Hot Springs for the cure. You'll go, too, won't you, John?" she said, turning to her husband.

Mr. Pullen reached over and patted her hand. "Of course I will. We'll make a real holiday out of it, just you and I. We'll dance in the evening and soak up the curative powers of the springs in the daytime. My gout is bothering me a little, too." He stood and twisted from side to side. "Charlotte, isn't that Glen Joslin over there? I need to go speak to him if you ladies will excuse me."

"Say hello for me, dear," Mrs. Pullen said as he slipped past them. "Don't be gone long."

When he was out of earshot, she placed her hand on Maggie's arm. "Nothing ever stays the same, does it, Maggie?" She stared straight ahead. "You've survived without Wash. You were still young, you found Tate. What will John do without me?"

"Please don't say that. You'll be fine. You're going to Hot Springs. I've heard the waters are wonderful there."

"It's too late. John knows, but he doesn't want to believe it." She closed her eyes and took a deep breath. "Take care of your husband. He is a valuable ally at a time like this."

John Pullen returned from the other end of the row just as the music began. Maggie closed her eyes, wanting to shut out everything except the haunting beauty of the pianist's rendition of Mozart's Piano Concerto No. 21 in C. The music seemed to surge through her and she was overcome with sorrow, both for Mrs. Pullen and for all the things she had missed in her own life. She vowed to have more music in her home. The piano in Aunt Mag's house was so out of tune that she had not even attempted to play since the children were born. She would get it tuned, begin to play again. Maybe someday she'd be able to buy a Victrola.

Aware of movement behind her, Maggie opened her eyes. She felt a light tap on her right shoulder. Startled, she glanced to the side and saw that someone was holding a rolled-up program against her sleeve. She reached to take it. Simultaneously, Mrs. Pullen nudged her. "Isn't he wonderful, Maggie?" she exclaimed as the piece ended and everyone began to clap. The program dropped into Maggie's lap and she turned to see who was behind her, but the seat was empty and the people on either side had eyes only for the pianist who was taking his bows.

"Yes, he is," Maggie responded, still distracted. There was only one person who might have...

"What is it, dear?" Mrs. Pullen asked. "You look as if you've seen a ghost."

Maggie put on a big smile. "Oh, it's nothing. Someone dropped this program in my lap. I just wondered who. Did you see, was there someone sitting behind me?"

John Pullen craned his neck. "Why no. That seat was empty, I believe."

"I saw someone out of the corner of my eye."

"Really? Well, what on earth?" Mrs. Pullen said, glancing behind Maggie.

John Pullen turned around in his seat. "Shall I ask the others behind you?"

"No. It's all right. Perhaps I was mistaken," Maggie said. She unrolled the program. A large circle had been drawn around the theme for the next section, *Tempus Fugit.*

Chapter 41

Sitting at Abigail Adams's desk, Maggie looked out across the classroom of young women. She wondered if some had been forced to come to college by their parents, or if they were all there looking to improve their futures. Since the turn of the century, women's rights had been in the forefront of the news. Suffragettes like Helen Lewis were preaching a woman's right to have a say in politics. Local suffrage leagues had formed all over the state. In Europe, a war was raging and the United States had been called on to join their allies against German aggression. Men and women alike were volunteering to go, and there was talk of a war to end all wars where men would be drafted, thus vacating jobs in industry that might become available to the 'weaker sex.'

Maggie had left BFU seven years ago. Maybe she was older and wiser now, but she still felt that she belonged there, surrounded by intelligent people, books and music. How had she stood the isolation of living in the country? This was where she wanted to be.

Wearing the blue serge jumper and a new white blouse that Aunt Mag had made for her, Maggie could have passed for a student. But she felt more like a professor when she looked out at the youthful faces in Abigail's class.

A student approached her desk. She was scrawny like Ella Bradley, and had the same mountain twang in her voice. "Mrs. Ryan, will Dr. Adams be gone very long? I need her to read my essay before my presentation. It's only two weeks away."

"I expect she will be gone about ten days. I could look it over, if you like."

"Are you a teacher?"

"Yes, as a matter of fact, I am, or used to be; whatever, I think I could help you with your essay. Do you have it with you?"

"Yes, ma'am, it's in my booksack. I'll get it."

Word spread that Maggie was not just a monitor, she was a teacher, and several other girls approached with papers to read. By the time the class was over she had read them all and made her comments in the margins. As she packed up her things to leave, she thought how different her world might have been if she had finished college.

Walking back to the cottage where Abigail lived, memories of Wash overwhelmed Maggie. It was bitter cold and a misty drizzle painted her hair and coat with silver droplets as she walked along feeling his presence under the trees where they had pledged their love and stolen kisses. So many promises, so many plans for the future—all of them for naught. Where would she be now if he had lived? Certainly not on campus under these circumstances. She would never have known Reece Evans either, never have met and married Tate, never have had her precious boys.

As she passed the cottage where she had spent her only semester at BFU, yellow light spilled from the windows into the gray afternoon, and someone moved about in the dining room setting the table—a cottage girl like she had been. There were lace curtains in the living room windows, but upstairs where she had shared a room with Ella Bradley, a bare bulb hung from the ceiling. Ella had packed up Maggie's things when she didn't return after Wash died. She'd written often at first; then her letters became few and far between. Abigail said she had left BFU and gone to nursing school.

Maggie climbed the steps to the Adams's cottage and rang the bell. Mrs. Burchart's rocker was turned up against the wall and the bare wisteria vine looked like a tangle of ropes twisting this way and that through the porch railing. The vine shaded the porch in warmer weather and had provided a canopy of privacy for she and Wash when they'd sat in the swing.

It seemed to take forever for Joella to get to the door, and Maggie shivered. What if Joella had gone home after all? Finally, she heard the twist of the lock and Joella opened the door, letting out the homey smell of bread baking. "Oh Joella, I'm so glad you're here," Maggie said.

Joella wore a black frock and a white apron over her stout frame. Her hair was tied up in a red cloth. "Well, yes'm, I tol' you I'd be here when you gots home."

"I know you did, but...well, I guess I was just feeling lonely. It's good of you to stay while Miss Abigail is gone."

"Law me, you look plumb worn to a frazzle! C'mon in here in the kitchen and lemme fix you some hot coffee."

Maggie removed her coat and hat and hung them on the hall tree, glancing in the mirror as she did so. She thought she looked tired, older. Being around fresh young faces could do that to you. Thinking of Wash had cast a pall over her too. That and the dark, dreary day. Long ago, she had decided that her moods were affected by the weather. Mary Ellen had loved to curl up by the fire and read on rainy days. Not Maggie. Until the sun shone, her spirits sagged like rain-laden clouds. Here in Raleigh, where she had known such happiness—so much hope for her future—it seemed even worse.

"I'm all right, Joella," she said, following the maid into the kitchen, "but I will have a cup of coffee if you have some on the stove."

"Yes'm, I do." Joella shuffled over to the stove, lifted a blue-speckled enameled coffeepot, and poured the steaming liquid into a cup. She stirred in a heaping spoonful of sugar and placed it in front of Maggie. "A gentleman was here to see you this afternoon, an impawtant-lookin' man—all dressed up in fine clothes I never seen the like of."

"Who was he, Joella?"

"I don't rightly know, Miss Maggie. He just asked when I expected you home." She walked back to the stove and replaced the coffeepot. "I told him I didn't know 'cause you was over there at the college helpin' out Miss Abigail. He jus' said he'd call again."

"It must have been Professor Morris," Maggie said. "He's supposed to take me to the concert tonight. Do you know him, Joella?"

"Yes'm, I think I knows him, and this here gentleman didn't look like no college professor I've ever seen."

——

That evening, when Dr. Morris called for Maggie, Joella helped her slip on her coat and whispered emphatically, "It won't him for sure!" Maggie glanced at the aging history teacher who had volunteered to escort her to the second night of the music festival. He was short and had a large bay window which made him look top-heavy in his black evening suit with its long tails. Maggie extended her hand. "Professor Morris, you are so kind to escort me to the Chopin concert this evening."

The professor raised her hand to his lips, barely touching it with his moustache. "It's my pleasure, Mrs. Ryan," he said, bowing slightly.

"Please call me Maggie, Professor Morris."

"Only if you will call me Clinton, my dear."

"Of course, if you insist, Professor." She laughed. "I'm sorry, it's like I've stepped back in time and I feel like a student again. By the way, Clinton," she said with deliberate emphasis, "did you send someone by earlier today?"

"Why, no. Why do you ask?"

"Joella said I had a caller, but he didn't leave his name."

"Perhaps you have an admirer, Maggie dear. I wouldn't be surprised."

——

Abigail Adams had reserved the same seats for each night of the festival. Maggie glanced at the empty seat behind her before the house lights went down, drawing her attention to the lighted stage. When the orchestra began to play she was captivated, falling into the rhythm of Chopin's *Grande valse brilliante*. In her mind's eye, she danced alone in a long white eyelet gown, swirling and turning, lifting and swaying. When the final notes came, she remained very still until Clinton startled her out of her reverie. "Bravo! Bravo!" he shouted.

He took her arm and they stood and clapped, but her head was swimming and she felt flushed, as if she had really been twirling about on a dance floor. Taking deep breaths, she tried to regain her composure. The audience was enthusiastic, calling for an encore. She leaned towards her escort, speaking above the din. "Clinton, I'm a little too warm. May I meet you in the lobby at intermission?"

"Oh, my dear, of course. Allow me to accompany you."

"No, please don't. I'll be fine. I know my way around. I just need a little air." Before he could protest further, she slipped out of her seat and hurried up the aisle as the audience sat down for the encore.

Several men milled about the lobby, smoking and talking in low voices. A young usher approached her. "Can I help you?" he asked.

"Yes, is there a side door where I could step outside for a moment? I'm a little overheated."

"This way, ma'am," he said, leading her to the side exit door. Maggie pushed the door ajar and breathed in the cool air.

"Maggie," a familiar voice called to her.

Suddenly she was chilled and she let the door come to. It was him, she was sure of it.

"I saw you come out," he said. His voice was deeper, softer. "Maggie, turn around." She felt dazed, unable to move. "Look at me, damn it!" he said, sounding more like the old Reece. She turned, half in fear, half in anticipation.

He was very close and she tried to step back, but she was against the door. "Reece, I didn't know you were here."

"Yes, you did."

Her hands, folded in front of her, were ready to strike, to push him away. But when she looked into his eyes, she saw a glint of his previous ardor and she didn't want to move. "I knew you were in Raleigh."

"Why are you here with that old widower?" he asked, his dark eyes narrowing. He had changed a great deal in six years—lost his rugged outdoor look and become a distinguished gentleman with a smartly-trimmed beard and mustache.

"Dr. Morris is my escort this evening. My friends arranged it."

"Melissa said you were here to visit friends. I don't see any lady friends."

"What on earth! You have no right to question me about my friends—about anything." She was breathing heavily, angry at him, but more irritated at herself for letting him rile her. She tried to push past him.

"I told you once, I have the right to do or say anything I please." He paused and added, "Especially when it concerns you."

"This is not your cotton field, Mr. Evans," she said, glancing about to avoid his eyes.

"You owe it to me."

"What do you mean, I *owe* you? I don't owe you anything!"

He sighed and stepped aside. "Yes, you do. You took something very valuable from me," he said, but this time there was less cynicism, some tenderness in his voice.

"Reece, what happened was beyond my control. There were circumstances. I wrote to you." But she couldn't tell him the truth. Not here, not now. "I didn't think you were free to give anything," she murmured.

"I'd given you my heart and soul, Maggie Lorena. You took that." There was grief in his eyes.

"I don't know what to say. I wanted to tell you...so much time has gone by now."

"All I asked for was time, Maggie. Christine's gone now. You see, if you had only waited just a little while, she would have been gone."

"Little while? It seems so long ago to me." A chill ran up her spine. *Mommy fell out of the boat and drowned.* "Agatha said it was an accident—she fell out of a boat."

He read her thoughts. "No, I had nothing to do with it, if that is what you're implying."

"It doesn't matter now anyway, does it?" Maggie said. The music had stopped and there was loud applause in the auditorium. She stepped around him. "People are coming out for intermission. I must find Professor Morris."

He reached out and touched her arm. "I still love you, Maggie. You will always belong to me whether you like it or not."

She felt faint again. "Stop it. You mustn't talk that way. I'm married now. I have two sons whom I adore more than anything on earth." Her words brought tears to her eyes.

"But you aren't happy with Tate Ryan, are you?"

"Of course I'm happy! Why would you say such a thing? My children mean all the world to me."

"I'm not talking about your children. I'm talking about you. Children can be happy anywhere. I've seen you the last two nights. You love music, people, lights. You were meant for this kind of life. I tried to tell you."

She glanced away. "So it was you who dropped the program in my lap last night. You might have spoken to me. It would have been more civil than this."

He grabbed her arm, opening the door and leading her out into the cold night air. It was dark and he pulled her against his chest in an unrelenting embrace. The scent of him ignited her senses and she wanted nothing more than to give in, but she struggled to free herself.

"Reece, please. You mustn't. This isn't right. Please, let me go."

"I may never let you go," he said, his breath hot upon her cheek.

"It was a long time ago. You must have understood." She exhaled the words, so tight was his hold.

Someone pushed against the door, opening it a crack. He held it firm against his back. "I understood nothing." The door was jarred again. "You simply made a choice, a poor one I might add."

"Reece, someone wants to get out. You must let go the door."

"Will you have dinner with me?"

"No."

Someone rapped loudly on the door from the inside. "Is someone there? This is the usher. We must have this door open!"

Reece opened the door and bowed to Maggie. "I believe your escort is inside, Mrs. Ryan."

"What in the world are you doing, sir?" The usher looked as if he was ready to hit Reece.

"Pardon us, young man. The lady was overheated. Please allow her to return to her seat," he said, showing Maggie inside. "Good evening, Madam. I hope you've sufficiently recovered."

"Yes, thank you," Maggie said, staring at him. "I'm recovered. Good evening."

Chapter 42

The following day, Joella greeted her at the door when she returned from classes. "That gentleman was back here again today, Miss Maggie," she said. "He say he know Miss Abigail. Say he spoke to you last night and forgots to tell you what time him and his chil'ren would be picking you up tonight for the music festival."

"Well, he's mistaken about that, Joella. I'm going with the Pullens again tonight."

"'Scuse me, Miss Maggie, but you ain't. Mr. Pullen, he comes by jus' after dat gentleman left and he say tell you Miss Pullen, she's powerful sick and the doctor he say she shouldn't go nowhere a'tall. He say he 'ranged for you to take two of Dr. Adams's students to the concert 'less you wanted to make some other plans. So, I tells Mr. Pullen 'bout dis other gentleman who comes by and say he's gonna fetch you with his chil'ren, and he say dat's jus' fine 'cause of Miss Pullen and all."

Maggie felt her knees buckle and she held firmly onto the sideboard. "What time did he say, Joella?"

The old colored woman relaxed, a broad smile spreading across her face. "He say you was to have supper with dem and I was to take the evenin' off. 'Go on home now,' he says and he gives me a dollar."

The nerve of him! Maggie thought. "You didn't take it, did you?"

"No'm. I tol' him I works for Miss Abigail and I does what she says and she tol' me to take care of you 'til she gets back, and I didn't know if you'd want to be going off with him or not."

"Thank you, Joella. I appreciate that. It would be lonely here without you," Maggie said. She walked back to Mrs. Burchart's room where the clothes she had been given were laid out across the back of the divan. It can't hurt, she thought. His children will be there. Tate would be furious. She felt a twinge of guilt. But it couldn't hurt him if he didn't know.

—

She bathed in the cold bathroom off the porch, the kerosene heater no match for the draft of winter air coming in under the door. Back in the warm room she tried on several dresses, miming the airs of a great stage actress. She chose a simple black satin-backed crepe dress, with rows and rows of little tucks on the sleeves and down the center front. The flared skirt was shirred up at the hem in back to reveal tiny rows of ruffles on the taffeta underskirt.

Maggie studied her reflection in the long oval mirror, striking different poses, rehearsing what she would say. The dress was stunning and black was becoming on her. Everyone said so. It was by far the most elegant dress that Reece had ever seen her in, or was likely to ever see her in again. Determined that he not see the extra weight she had gained with the boys, she had Joella tighten her corset until she could hardly breathe.

She twisted a long red curl that fell from just above her ear to her shoulder and removed her glasses. A year ago she'd sent off for a stronger lens, again requesting the shade in the left side. She regretted it now that she needed her glasses more for her nearsightedness. He'd been right, the dark glass was only a cover-up. She hadn't worn her glasses in public since she'd been in Raleigh.

When she heard Joella let him in, she grabbed a long black velvet cape and draped it across her arm. Taking one last glance in the mirror, she saw the array of perfume bottles on the dresser. She put the cape down on the dresser stool and reached for a tall amethyst bottle with a clear crystal top, tilted it ever so gently to wet the stopper, and dabbed the stopper behind her ears. The scent was Vanessa Burchart's. *Can I live up to the part?* she asked herself.

—

The dining room at the Andrew Johnson Hotel where the Evanses were staying was noisy and crowded with men. Most of them nodded to Reece and made small gestures to rise as Maggie passed their chairs on the way to a large table in a far corner. Reece seated her with excessive flair and she felt that everyone in the room was watching.

He wasn't oblivious to her discomfort. "They're envious of me, Maggie, that's all," he whispered into her hair as he pushed in her chair. He was wearing a tan suit with wide black pinstripes and black velvet lapels, a striking accent to his dark hair, which was now peppered with gray. As always, he carried a light scent of lavender.

He looked at his pocket watch. "The girls will be down soon. I asked Melissa to have them here promptly at 6:30. That should give us plenty of time to get to the auditorium."

"There seem to be mostly men here," Maggie said.

"Of course. Most of these gentlemen are legislators or lobbyists and their wives are at home, keeping the fires burning." He smiled playfully. "A lot of our work is accomplished here, outside of the House and Senate chambers."

"How long have you been a senator?" Maggie asked.

"Over a year. Bill Ryan didn't tell you?"

"Your name hasn't come up since we left Onslow County, Reece. That doesn't surprise you, does it?"

His only reply was a smirk as he opened the menu. In the silence that followed, Maggie resolved to be gay and enjoy the evening. That's all it was, an evening of dinner and music. She was entitled to that, and as her host Reece was entitled to pleasant company.

"I see you're no longer wearing that damned smoked glass," he said without looking up from the menu.

"I don't have to wear it all the time," she said, annoyed that he would make an issue of it.

He glanced away and saw the children and their governess at the door. "Prepare yourself, the girls are coming."

"You sound as if I'm about to be assaulted."

"There may be some truth in that. They've looked forward to this all day. In fact, it was their idea." Reece rose from his chair.

"Oh, I see. I thought it was yours," Maggie said under her breath.

He motioned to Melissa and the children, smiling. "I'm like putty in their hands."

"Mrs. Ryan, Mrs. Ryan! You're here, you're here!" Mandy and Agatha came running across the dining room with Melissa in pursuit. Maggie thought they looked like little princesses in their silk taffeta dresses, with stockings and patent leather shoes.

"I told them to behave like young ladies and here they come tearing through the dining room. I'm sorry, Senator Evans." Melissa waggled her finger at the girls. "You're going to hear about this from me," she scolded.

Maggie thought of her own children, two rough-and-tumble boys, far from being little gentlemen. Tate was seeing to that. She felt color rise in her face at the thought of him.

"It's all right, Melissa. I'll turn them both over my knee before the night is over," Reece teased. "Go on and have your dinner and I'll return them to you soon after the concert. Have a good evening."

"You're not going with us, Melissa?" Maggie asked.

"Melissa has family here. She'll be with them this evening," Reece said, dismissing the governess with a wave of his hand.

Melissa bent to hug each of the girls and warned them again to behave. She turned to Maggie. "Have a nice evening, Mrs. Ryan. I'm sure the senator and the girls will take good care of you. G'night, now."

"Daddy, I need to go to the toilet," Mandy said immediately after Melissa had gone.

"Really, Mandy! You should have taken care of that upstairs in the room."

"I'll go with her," Maggie said. "Would you like to go with us, Agatha?"

"No, ma'am. Daddy promised me a soda tonight and I can't wait to have it."

It was a nice feeling, walking through the dining room with Reece's daughter—a feeling that she had never imagined she could have when he had told her that these would be the only children she would have with him. She had not wanted them, thinking that only her own children could provoke such a nurturing feeling. But these were dear children, like her own, and they needed a mother.

When they reached the ladies' room, Mandy pulled Maggie aside. "I don't really have to go to the toilet. I just wanted to tell you something, Mrs. Ryan. I knew you would take me."

Maggie smiled. "Now, how could you have known that?"

"Because I knew Daddy would get mad, and he did."

"Well, what is it that you wanted to tell me?" Maggie asked, unable to imagine what the little girl with Reece's eyes could have to say to her in private.

"Daddy says you used to be his sweetheart before you got married to somebody else. Is that true?"

Maggie's stomach somersaulted. "That was a long time ago." She turned the little girl around by the shoulders and directed her towards the toilet. "There are some things grown-ups don't discuss with children, Mandy. Now you go to the toilet anyway, even if you don't have to, just in case."

Mandy lifted her skirts, pulled her pantaloons down and sat on the toilet. She looked up at Maggie innocently. "I wish you could still be his sweetheart, Mrs. Ryan. Then maybe you could be our mother, too."

"Mandy! You mustn't say such things. I already have a husband. And your father shouldn't have told you about something that happened a long time ago." Maggie stood in front of the mirror and powdered her nose in an effort to cover her emotion. Here was a child, frustrated, trying to understand feelings that Maggie did not understand herself. Tears filled her eyes and she dabbed them away with her handkerchief.

Mandy finished and stood beside Maggie at the sink, her head bent sideways trying to see Maggie's face. "Are you crying, Mrs. Ryan?"

"No, dear little one. I was just wiping the shine from my nose. Wash your hands now. Your father and sister are waiting."

Back at the table, Reece assisted her with her chair. "Thank you, Maggie. It's good to have you with us. It feels like a family."

"Yes, it does," she confessed.

They had finished their meal and were leaving, the girls running ahead, when Reece waved to someone across the dining room. "There's Talmadge Yancey. Come, Maggie, I'll introduce you. The girls will be fine for a minute or two."

"Reece, really. I shouldn't be here."

"And why not? If you avoid people, they think you're doing something wrong. Since that isn't the case, I'd like to introduce you to a senator friend of mine." He took her arm and led her around the tables, crossing the large dining room. Senator Yancey rose to meet them and extended his hand to Reece while looking directly at Maggie. "Talmadge, I'd like you to meet Maggie Ryan, one of my former constituents from Onslow County."

Talmadge Yancey smiled broadly, made a slight bow and touched his lips to her hand. "Mrs. Ryan, it is indeed a pleasure." He turned to the woman sitting beside him. Mrs. Ryan, Miss Connie Capps. Connie, you know Reece, of course."

Maggie nodded to the blond-haired woman, who was wearing an elegant red taffeta dress that revealed a full bosom and a touch of black lace. Miss Capps smiled at Maggie, acknowledging the introduction. She glanced at Reece. "Delighted, I'm sure," she said, in a deep Southern drawl.

"Please join us," the senator said, indicating the two vacant chairs that remained at the table.

"Not tonight, Talmadge. We're on our way to a concert at the auditorium and the girls are waiting."

"It was nice meeting you, Senator—Miss Capps," Maggie said, anxious to be out from under their scrutiny.

But Talmadge Yancey wasn't finished with her. "How long will you be in town, Mrs. Ryan?"

Before Maggie could answer, Reece flipped his pocket watch open and checked the time. "Excuse us, Talmadge, the children will be getting anxious. *Tempus Fugit!*" He took Maggie's arm. "Good evening, Connie. Talmadge, I'll see you in committee at noon tomorrow."

———

The concert that evening concluded the music festival with a stunning presentation of Vivaldi's *The Four Seasons*. Although the music was stirring, Maggie felt distracted. All she could think about was the closeness of him, the reality of being there with him. She was aware of every gesture—the slight rise and fall of his chest, his gaze upon her. The touch of his arm against hers was electrifying. She longed to reach for his hand resting on his knee, take it to her cheek, feel the warmth of it against her lips.

By the time the concert was over, both of the girls had fallen asleep. "We'll get a taxi back to the hotel, Maggie. I'd like to take the girls up to our room before I escort you home," Reece said.

A warning bell went off in her head. "I can manage alone, Reece. I saw several students that I know from Abigail Adams's class. I'll walk along with them."

"Do you really think I would let you do that?"

"Look! I must go. I don't think I should have come with you this far. It was a wonderful evening. Please, let me go."

"Wait here with the girls while I find a taxi. I'll only be a minute," he said, completely disregarding her protest.

Maggie and the girls sat on a cushioned velvet seat that formed a circle around one of the fat columns in the lobby. Agatha placed her head in Maggie's lap, but Mandy had perked up and sat quietly watching the audience leave. Maggie thought again of her little boys who would grow up in the country, never knowing anything but farming. She yearned to see them, wished they were here with her for the music festival, just as Mandy and Agatha were.

When she climbed into the taxi Reece had summoned for the ride back to the hotel, Maggie rubbed her hand over the shiny leather seat, laughing to herself. Automobiles were replacing horses everywhere, even in the country.

Reece was occupied with the sleepy girls, bundling them close. "We'll have you there in a minute," he said.

At the hotel, he turned to Maggie. "Would you mind helping me get them upstairs?" Reluctantly, she slid across the seat and stepped out into the cold night air. Reece carried Agatha, and Maggie held Mandy's hand and led her up the stairs.

In her nightclothes, Melissa met them at the door and took her drowsy charges inside. "My goodness, it's too late for these little darlings to be out. Just look at them, practically walking in their sleep."

"Put them to bed, Melissa, and have them ready for breakfast at nine," Reece said.

"That's not going to be easy, Senator, getting them up and moving that early, but I'll do my best." She glanced at Maggie.

"Goodnight, little ones," he said, kissing each of them on the cheek. "Say goodnight to Mrs. Ryan." The girls mumbled a sleepy goodnight to Maggie and Melissa closed the door. In the hallway, Reece unlocked the door directly across from the children's room. "Please come in for a moment, Maggie. Please."

Chapter 43

Cold rain beat against the stationhouse windows the next day as Maggie waited for the morning train to Atkinson. Joella had been contrary when Maggie'd asked her to help pack Mrs. Burchart's clothes. She would have little use for the lovely gowns and dresses in Colly, but it seemed ungrateful to leave them.

"Miss Abigail 'specting you to be here when she gets back," Joella said.

"I know, but my plans have changed."

"She gone be mad at me already, leavin' 'fore you gots home las' night."

The night before, Reece had asked the desk clerk to have a taxi deliver a note to Joella from Maggie saying there was no need for the maid to stay. The driver took Joella home and brought the key back to the desk clerk.

Joella carelessly stuffed the dresses into an old steamer trunk that Mrs. Burchart had given Maggie. "Be careful with those beaded things." Maggie stooped to pick up several beads that had popped off a navy blue chiffon dress. "Listen, I'll explain everything to Miss Abigail. There was no need for you to stay here last night. The party at the hotel went on until the wee hours, and Senator Evans needed my help with his children."

"Hummph! Say de spider to de fly!"

"My stars, Joella, what are you insinuating? Senator Evans is a gentleman. You have no right to imply otherwise."

"Yes'm. But I don' know how I'm gone explain all dis to Miss Abigail," she muttered. "She expectin' you to be here when..."

"Joella, please try and understand. I really need to get home to my family. I shouldn't have said I would stay until she returned. Just give her this note and you needn't explain anything. Now, please, I need your help if I'm to catch the ten o'clock train."

The exchange had unnerved Maggie no end. After she had finished packing, she said goodbye and walked the five blocks to the station, where she sent a taxi to pick up her bags.

Once seated on the train, she closed her eyes and let the rhythm of the churning wheels lull her. There would be talk—Melissa and Joella, for sure. Very little went unnoticed by household help. Lizzie was a good example of that, speaking little, seeing much. Maggie was confident that Abigail would understand and respect her privacy. Someday, if she asked, Maggie might explain. But for the immediate future, she would let written words suffice.

Drowsily, she felt for the gold scarab bracelet Reece had given her, rubbing her fingers over the smooth stones. He had said it was not expensive—something she might have bought for herself. Glancing through half-closed lids as the train flashed across the landscape, she longed to go back to him, leave everything else behind.

Reece had pleaded with her to stay, protesting over and over that she belonged to him, that fate had brought them together again. He cried when she told him about the miscarriage, saying that he would have taken care of her if he had known. He promised that he would take care of her children now, educate them, treat them as his own. Lying in his arms, she thought she had never been so happy.

But just before dawn, she'd awakened with a start. There was no way that she could leave her sons, and Tate would never give them up. Reece had cried. She had cried. In the end, they both had agreed that they would not contact one another. Unless something happened to Tate, Maggie was bound to him for life. They would put the children first. Reece told her how devastated his girls had been by their mother's insanity, by her death. He said he didn't want to cause such pain in her children. Maggie had been surprised that he had softened that much.

———

Returning early was a gamble. There would be questions, espe-cially since she had only mailed a letter three days ago telling Tate that she would stay another week. She would particularly have to avoid Aunt Mag's scrutiny. She'd notice something different about Maggie, even if Tate didn't. Even at her age when most old women seemed to turn inward, aware only of their own aches and pains, Aunt Mag could see through things, figure them out. "You're not the same twenty-four-year-old girl that went up there to Raleigh, so don't go trying to act like it," she'd warned when Maggie left.

The loading platform at Atkinson was empty except for the old stationmaster, Narley Hinson, who had known Maggie most of her life. "Just hold on now," he said. "The Capt'n would come back from the grave and haunt me if I didn't get you back over to Colly safe and sound. I'll get my grandson to take you in the wagon."

Narley's grandson, Ham, was a strapping fifteen-year-old who Maggie remembered as one of Aunt Mag's first-grade students back in the days when she had helped out in the school across the road. He hitched up the wagon while Maggie waited on the platform.

Ham hadn't forgotten Maggie either. "I ain't going to go back to school next year. Pa said I didn't have to, with Grandpa needing me at the train station and all."

Maggie tried to smile, but she wasn't feeling very conversational, especially when it came to talking with a backwoods boy who wasn't the least bit interested in bettering himself. "That's nice," she said.

"I hate school." He spat a long stream of tobacco juice out into the dusty road.

"Well, I don't think I'd be bragging about it," Maggie admonished. "Your ignorance is showing." The boy shot her a surprised look over his shoulder and didn't speak another word on the five-mile trip over to Colly.

Maggie passed the time trying to bring herself back to reality. Tate would be coming in from the fields when she got home, and Lizzie would be in the kitchen fixing supper. There was no telling what the boys had gotten into while she was gone. Lizzie thought little boys should be left to their imagination when it came to playing. A sudden fear swept through her. What if something had happened to one of them? She was relieved when finally they pulled into the oak grove and she saw William and Lenny playing with their little cars on the porch.

The children both looked up, seeing the wagon come down the lane. "Lizzie, somebody's here!" William called out.

Lizzie came to the door and peered out. "I declare, it's your mama, comin' home."

Both of the boys jumped off the porch, running towards the wagon. Lenny stumbled and fell flat on his face. "Wait for me, Willie," he cried.

William had reached the wagon and was running along beside it. His freckled face was streaked with dirt and he was wearing an old shirt that Maggie thought he must have pulled out of the ragbag. "Hey, Mama, I didn't know it was you."

"Yessir, Mama's home. Stand back now and let Ham pull up there by the steps. Lenny, honey, are you hurt?"

"No'm, but Willie pushed me," he whimpered.

"No I didn't. You're just a baby."

"Oh, come on up here, both of you, and give Mama a hug." She reached out for her sons and they clambered up on the wagon, hugging and kissing her.

"Evenin', Miss Maggie," Lizzie said. "We won't expectin' you today. I'd of had these young'uns cleaned up."

"That doesn't matter one bit. I'm just so glad to see my little boys. Help mama down, now." Maggie stepped down off the wagon, Willie taking one hand, Lenny the other. "How're you doing, Lizzie?"

"I'm all right, I reckon. Mr. Tate gone be s'prised to see you."

"I know, but I just decided I wanted to get home, see my boys."

Ham set her bags down on the porch and climbed back up onto the wagon. "I'll be getting on back, Miss Maggie." He was just a kid and she regretted that she had been impatient with him.

"I'm much obliged for the ride, Ham. You go on back to school next year, you hear? Once you stop, it's hard to go back."

"Yes'm. That's what Mama said." He drove away and Maggie knew the warning had come too late. Boys like Ham didn't really want an education.

"Hand me my satchel, William. Mama's got some presents for you. Have they been good, Lizzie?"

Lizzie smiled, her lips pursed to keep the snuff juice inside her mouth. "Yes'm, good as could be 'spected."

"I have," William said, grabbing for the small package Maggie had slipped out of her satchel. For a moment she couldn't take her eyes off her oldest son, thinking about how close she had come to leaving him—all of them.

Lenny sat on the porch step, looking glum. "Papa said I had to tell you something."

"What, son?"

"He said I had to tell you first thing that I broke one of Auntie Mag's teacups."

Maggie pictured the row of tiny teacups in different patterns that Aunt Mag had collected over the years and placed on a small whatnot shelf in the dining room. She knew each one by heart. "Which one?"

The child looked up at her. His freckled face was smudged with dirt and his red curls hadn't seen a comb since she had left, but he was adorable with his little pouting mouth and his sad eyes. "The one with purple flowers."

"Oh, that one. Well, it wasn't even one of Mama's favorites," she lied, picturing the delicate bone china cup. "Come here and give Mama another hug. You can have your present, honey." She hugged him and kissed him on the forehead. "Where's your papa?"

"I'll get him," William volunteered, running towards the barn.

Lenny scampered off in the same direction. "No, me!"

"Well, both of you get him," Maggie said, laughing.

Tate hurried towards the house, a worried look on his face. "What in the world, Maggie Lorena? Did something happen?"

"Nothing happened, Tate," she said, meeting him halfway. "Can't I come on home when I'm ready?" She smiled, holding her arms out for a hug.

"Well, sure, honey, but I would have met you at the train," Tate said. He hugged her and kissed her on the cheek. "Your letter only came yesterday. You said you were going to stay on until Abigail got back."

"I was, but I changed my mind. There was no telling when Abigail would return and I missed you and the children."

"That's mighty nice to know," he said, rocking her in his arms. He smelled of wood smoke and she knew that he had been burning off the new ground. She let him hold her like that for a long time, her face against his chest. "I missed you, honey," he said. "I really missed you."

She closed her eyes and thought how glad she was to be home again. Everything that had happened in the last week seemed merely a dream. And dreams were just that, things that had never happened. She promised herself that she'd only think about the future, not the past.

That night Tate was persistent, rubbing her leg and reaching for her breast. Exhausted, she begged him to let her get some rest. "But honey, you've been gone up to Raleigh. I missed you. I need..." She hadn't resisted further. Instead, she'd rolled onto him with an eagerness that surprised her. Afterwards they lay, out of breath, holding each other in the moonlight. "I might have to let you go to Raleigh again," Tate whispered.

During the first few weeks, her thoughts turned to that evening with Reece in Raleigh time after time. Not just the hours they'd spent in each other's arms, but the dinner, the concert, the life they might have had together. His lovely girls had been so affectionate towards her.

But Reece had nothing to lose. She'd have lost her own children and her respectability. Gradually she became more and more convinced that she'd done the right thing. Her thoughts turned less frequently to him, and more often towards ways to make a better life for her children.

One of the first things she did was to have the piano tuned. She would teach the children to play. They weren't too young to learn the scales and simple songs. To enhance her own skills, she ordered a correspondence course in piano for herself. It had taken all of her egg money, but she intended for music to be a part of their lives. Maggie also planned to spend more time doing simple things with the children. Even in cold weather, she bundled them up and took them on long walks through the woods. On warmer days they carried a picnic lunch to share with Tate, who was clearing land over in Lyon Swamp.

Tate loved it when Maggie brought them to where he was working. He wanted the boys to see what the land was like before it was drained and cleared. Sometimes when Maggie would go back to the house, leaving them with him for the rest of the afternoon, he would pull them around on a tobacco sled, pointing out snake holes and deer tracks. He hoped that William and Lenny would also work this land, tilling up the rich black sand with a steel plow, digging ditches to drain the bottom land. In time, Zeb and Jasper would appreciate the fact that his boys were half-Corbinn.

Aunt Mag noticed the change in Maggie after she came back from Raleigh. "She's a different person," she commented to Lizzie.

"I 'spect she found out she don't b'long up there. She's country folk like us, even if she does have some hifalutin' ways."

"I declare, Lizzie, Maggie's no different from me," Aunt Mag said. "I did my best to teach her to appreciate some of the finer things in life."

"She ain't like you, Miss Mag. She's high-strung as the devil. I seen it since she was a little girl. She'd have a fit and fall in it when she didn't get her way."

"Well, she's grown up now, Lizzie."

"Mister Tate don't think so. He tol' me come gets him if she go into one of her states. He say he worried about the chil'ren when she starts rantin' and ravin'. Other times she jus' don' pay no 'tention to nuthin'. Jus' sits in a chair and stares. I seen her do it in her little room lotsa times."

"Well, maybe she's better now after going to Raleigh," Aunt Mag said. "Something up there must have agreed with her."

"Mos' d'time she is, but I seen her rummagin' in her trunk t'other evenin'. She always be down after dat."

———

No one knew better than Maggie how things could get the best of her from time to time. Sometimes her dark moods were brought on by dreary weather; other times a little memory could grow like a flame burning a hole in her heart. Those were the times that Maggie went through her mementoes, those little things she had salvaged from her losses. Then her resolve would vanish and she wanted nothing more than to slip into another world where there were no memories.

———

When Maggie felt the first wave of nausea, she thought nothing of it. The boys had been sick with upset stomachs and she'd seen the condition go through the whole family many times. But when the sickness continued the next morning and the next, she didn't even have to look at the calendar.

Tate Yancey Ryan was born the next October, a squalling red-faced infant bearing no marked resemblance to either of his brothers, who had come into the world with little ringlets of red hair and the characteristic Ryan noses. "Well, he's a different little runt, I'll say that!" Aunt Mag said after she had bathed him and wrapped him in a soft flannel blanket. "If I didn't know better, I'd say that young foot salve salesman that used to come through here had gotten into your britches."

"Aunt Mag! Lizzie and Dr. Bayard will hear you."

"Oh, they're out in the kitchen. Besides, I was just teasing." Aunt Mag held the baby up for inspection. "I declare, Maggie, he's too pretty to be a boy." She laid the squirming baby in Maggie's arms and he

turned his head towards his mother's breast. "Lookie there, little pump-
kin, you know what you want already."

Maggie winced. "He'll have to get it without my help, Aunt Mag. I
hurt so bad."

"That'll pass, Maggie Lorena, but this baby can't wait."

"I know, I know. Let me have him. Where's Tate?"

"He's gone over to Lizzie's to get the boys. I expect Katie will be
here directly, too." She leaned over and kissed Maggie on the forehead.
"Look at him go to town. He sure is an eager little thing. What're you
going to call him?"

Maggie had spent months deliberating over a name for the unborn
baby. Tate had said it didn't matter one bit to him, so she'd decided on
names that would have significance to her; a girl would have been named
Abigail. "Yancey. Tate Yancey, but we're going to call him Yancey," she
said.

"Where on earth did you get that name from?"

"I heard it in Raleigh. I just like the name."

"Oh, well, we can call him 'Tater' or something like that."

"No, I want him called Yancey," Maggie insisted, raising her voice.

"My stars! Don't go yelling at me. I declare, you are ill as a hornet.
I'm going out to the kitchen and see about supper. Tate and those boys
will be perished." She closed the door firmly behind her and stood
outside a moment, contemplating Maggie's attitude. *There's more to it,*
she thought. Anyone could see that.

Maggie drifted between sleep and wakefulness, the tiny baby nuzzled
against her breast. She dreamed that Reece came into the room and
stood at the foot of the bed, a smile on his face. The bed was clean and
smooth and she was propped up on five or six pillows. Her hair, freshly
combed and curled, was spread about her shoulders. The baby suckled
her breast. Reece walked around to the side of the bed, picked up Yancey
and held him tightly, touching the baby's cheek to his own.

The door opened. "Were you asleep, sweetness?" Tate asked, his
face a blur at the end of the bed. "The boys want to see their little

brother mighty bad." Walking around the bed, he sat down beside Maggie and placed his hand on his new son. "He's a fine boy, Maggie Lorena. You did good. I'm proud to have another son, aren't you?"

She closed her eyes. "I had hoped for a girl."

"You're disappointed?"

Maggie opened her eyes again and tried to smile. "Of course not, Tate. I can always depend on Lizzie or someone to help me in the kitchen, but good farm hands are hard to come by."

"This little one sure has got a lot of growing to do before he'll be a farm hand," Tate said, running his index finger along the tiny arm and fingers. "I'll bet he don't weigh more than four or five pounds."

"Did Dr. Bayard tell you that he heard a little heart murmur...I think that's what he called it," Maggie said, groggy from the laudanum.

"Yes, he did, but don't be worrying about that now. Doc said he'd keep a check on it."

"All right, Tate. I thought this was too easy. I hope nothing's wrong."

He leaned over and kissed Maggie on the forehead. "Having babies gets easier every time, just like Mama says." She wouldn't look at him. "I'll get the boys now," he said.

Chapter 44

Maggie had barely gotten her strength back when news came that Tate's mother had taken a turn for the worse. Annalee had written that her diabetes was really bad. Sally Catherine had an infected toe and the doctor thought he might have to amputate her foot. "I imagine she's got blood poison," Maggie said.

"She was doing so good since Betty's daughter had come to stay and help out with the cooking," Tate said. "If anything happens to Mama, I don't think I could stand it." He paced the floor. "Do you reckon we could go visit soon? I want her to see Yancey. It might do her a lot of good. You know how she dotes on babies."

"Well, yes, we can go just as soon as I'm able," Maggie said. "I don't think I'm up to that long wagon ride over to Onslow yet. Besides, Yancey's not nursing real good."

"We can take your pa's old delivery wagon. Zeb's been working on it in his spare time. The boys would love that."

"Well, you might think it sounds like fun, dragging three young'uns across two counties in an old delivery wagon, but not me. It's an automobile we need."

This was not the first time Maggie had mentioned an automobile to Tate. "I suppose everybody in Raleigh was riding around in one," he said.

She studied him, wondering exactly what he was thinking. "Lots of people were."

"It might be a long time before we have an automobile, Maggie Lorena."

Tate didn't have the least desire for an automobile even if he could afford one. The contraption Jasper drove down from Wilmington for the Capt'n's funeral broke down on him three times before he got there. Jasper himself said he almost drove it off the bridge, it made him so hellacious mad. A horse and buggy were the most dependable things Tate could think of.

———

Bill Ryan sent Homer to tell them that Sally Catherine had died in her sleep. When Tate saw the colored man standing at the door, he thought it had something to do with Reece. He felt his old fury rise. "What you doing over here, Homer?"

Homer hung his head. "I's sorry to hafta tell you dis, Mr. Tate, but it's yo mama. Mr. Bill asked me to come. I reckon y'all been 'specting it."

"We've been expecting it, but it don't make it any easier," Tate said, reaching for a caneback chair on the front porch to steady himself. They'd put off going to see her for too long. He sat down and let the tears come. *I should have gone by myself.* He felt like he had let both of them down, his mama and his papa—leaving Onslow when they had always counted on him.

Maggie had her share of tears, too. Sally Catherine had looked after her like she would have her own daughter. At times, Maggie thought her mother-in-law might have seen more and known more than Maggie had been aware of. But if she had, she'd kept it to herself.

———

News of Vanessa Burchart's death followed close behind Sally Catherine's. They were both women who had counseled and encouraged Maggie, each in their own way, but Maggie reflected that probably neither would have liked the other. Mrs. Burchart had been sophisticated, carrying herself so elegantly, stepping out onto a stage each time she entered a room.

Along with the letter from Abigail telling her of Mrs. Burchart's death came a large box of elegant underpinnings that Abigail insisted her mother wanted Maggie to have. Also in the box was *Evangeline* marked up with a multitude of comments and suggestions for revision.

I'm so sorry I've had this so long, but I devoted myself to Mother's care for the last year and I was unable to finish the editing until just recently. Maggie, this is a winner! Finish it and send it back to me.

After her third child, Maggie's weight gain escalated and she found herself in housedresses most of the time, able to wear only a few of the high-fashion dresses Mrs. Burchart had passed on to her. This was an unexpected pleasure for Aunt Mag, the recipient of Maggie's hand-me-downs. "I'm grateful to Vanessa Burchart, I can say that. I feel like I did when Archie was traveling up and down the coast and keeping me in the latest fashion."

"It's good to see you in pretty colors again. Papa used to say that he reckoned you were going to mourn Uncle Archie the rest of your life."

"Well, that old coot! He never said that to me. Besides, I stopped wearing mourning clothes for Archie a long time ago, but it seemed like with one after the other dying like flies, I might as well keep it up." She looked at Maggie over her glasses. "I noticed you never wore any."

"Oh, come on, Aunt Mag, that fashion went out a long time ago. One good black dress to wear to a funeral is all I can afford. They don't make feedsacks in black."

Aunt Mag preened in front of the long mirror in Maggie's bedroom. "Well, I'll have to say I still have my figure, even if my face looks like a dried-up old apple."

Maggie stood behind her, observing her own image in the mirror. She pulled her shoulders back and tried to hold her stomach in. "How come some women lose their figures and some don't?"

"You're just cut out to be stout, I guess, like your mama was. When you wear your corset you look as good as any of the women around here, but those old loose housedresses don't do much for you."

That was Aunt Mag—just full of straight talk. But Maggie enjoyed the comfort of her housedresses, especially since she was nursing Yancey. Naturally, she had nursed the other two, but only until they would take their milk from a bottle. With Yancey, she was content to suckle him at one breast and then the other for as long as he liked. He was so small and frail, looking up at her with little blue eyes. When he cried, he didn't wail out long and loud. He'd just primp his little mouth up and sob like his heart was broken.

Tate had noticed the different little cry. He was good about holding Yancey while Maggie readied herself for bed. "He cries kind of pitiful-like, don't he?" he said, swaying his large frame to and fro to comfort the baby. Maggie reached for Yancey and snuggled her cheek against his head. "Mama's precious baby just has a tender little heart, that's all."

"You sure do dote over him, Maggie Lorena. He's almost four months old now and you're spending all of your time with him. What about Willie and Lenny? You used to bring them out to see me in the field."

"I can't do but so much, and this baby needs me the most. Besides, I'm not neglecting William and Lenny one bit."

"Well, I think it's time you stopped bringing Yancey into the bed with us. It's not right. I'm scared to death I'm going to roll over on him."

"I guess we'll just have to set up a cot for you in the boys' room until Yancey gets old enough for the crib," Maggie said.

Which is exactly what Tate did. He knew there would be no getting close to Maggie with the baby in the bed. And he suspected that was why she kept it that way.

Even to herself, it was difficult to admit that Yancey might be Reece's child. When he was older, she was sure that she would know. Already, William was a miniature of Tate. If Reese was right, if it was their destiny to be together, maybe this child was a part of that destiny.

Chapter 45
1917

William was eight years old and in the third grade when the United States finally gave in and joined the Allied cause in Europe. Maggie was glad that G. W. wasn't alive to witness all the young men going off to war again. At first they were just being sent to the shipyard in Wilmington; then they were going to Camp Bragg in Fayetteville and Camp Polk in Raleigh for field artillery training. After the principal at Canetuck School joined up, there were only three teachers for eleven grades.

"The superintendent wanted to know if I'd come in and teach," Maggie said.

"The next thing you know, they'll be calling up the old schoolmarms like me," Aunt Mag said.

"He said they might have to close the school if they can't find enough teachers, but I can't do it," Maggie said. "I'm not going to leave the little ones with Lizzie all day long. Yancey's just a baby."

"Somebody needs to do it, Maggie Lorena. If you want, I could help out with Lenny and Yancey."

"No, I'd rather teach William at home. I can teach him just as good as anyone, maybe better."

The school did close and for the next year Maggie and many of the other mothers homeschooled their children. When the war was over, the principal was one of those who came back, bringing a French wife with him. But just as it looked like they had enough teachers to reopen the schools, an especially virulent strain of influenza began to take its toll on Colly as well as the rest of the state and the country. The flu didn't seem to infect healthy children or the older folks as much as it did those around Maggie and Tate's age. Mr. Bell, the postmaster at Currie, lost his wife and her two sisters within a week of each other, leaving ten children for the remaining family to help raise. The whole community was on guard; schools stayed closed and church services were canceled. Even funerals were kept private to keep contagion down.

Maggie was terrified. Dr. Bayard had warned her at Yancey's two-year-old checkup that he would be more susceptible to sickness than the other children. She wanted to isolate him from everything and everyone, even his family. Several times, Tate found them locked in the bedroom. He tried to tell Maggie that fresh air would be better than being locked up in a room, but you couldn't argue with Maggie about things like that. Not when they concerned Yancey.

When the epidemic subsided and things went back to normal, Maggie stopped scalding the dishes and mopping the floor with bleach, but she still kept a close watch on Yancey. He was four now, but growing very slowly in comparison to the other boys. He had started walking late, and not until then did she notice he was out of breath following the slightest exertion.

Maggie decided to take Yancey in to see Dr. Bayard. She had a lot of respect for the doctor who had gotten his training up North and come back down to the country about the time she'd gone away to college. At one time Aunt Mag had set her sights on him to marry Maggie, but Dr. Bayard had met a young nurse in Baltimore whom he soon brought down to Atkinson to help him in his practice.

Dr. Bayard's office was on the first floor of a large old home on Main Street. He and his wife lived on the second floor, and they rented out two rooms on the third floor. Bessie Bayard answered the bell when Maggie arrived with Yancey. She wore a starched white uniform and a small cap on the back of her head.

"Good morning, Miss Bessie," Maggie said. "Is the doctor in today?"

"Well, look who's here. Little Yancey Ryan is bringing his mama in to see the doctor."

Yancey beamed. "Mama's not sick. I am."

Bessie felt his forehead and pinched his earlobe. "You don't look sick to me. I'd say you just want a piece of the horehound candy over there in that jar."

"I 'spect that's all it is, Miss Bessie, but since we're here, maybe we'll see the doctor just for a little checkup," Maggie said, winking at the nurse.

"All right, but the doctor doesn't like to waste time on well people," she teased. "Come on in here, Yancey, and I'll go and get him." She led the way to one of the examination rooms.

Dr. Bayard came in jiggling some coins in his pocket. "I've got a penny in my pocket for whoever can catch it." Yancey held out his hands and the doctor tossed him the coin.

"Look Mama. I caught it."

"I see you did, son." She turned to Dr. Bayard. "I've just been worried about him with so much sickness going around. He's not growing very much and..."

"Hop up here on my table, little fellow, and let old Dr. Bayard listen to your tick-tock." Yancey climbed the small steps to the leather-covered examination table in Dr. Bayard's office and sat down eagerly. "I climbed up all by myselfs," he said.

"You sure did, son. I'll bet you're tired now," he said, watching Yancey's chest heave in and out. The child nodded. "Listen Maggie, you can hear it. It's a whooshing sound." He offered the stethoscope to her and she placed the tubes in her ears, listening intently.

"Yes, I think I can. What is it?"

Miss Bessie lifted Yancey down off the table. "Why don't we go get a piece of that candy while the doctor talks to your mama?" She put her hands on his shoulders. "You do want a piece of that candy, don't you, even if you aren't sick?"

"Yes'm, I sure do!" Yancey scurried out ahead of the nurse and she closed the door behind her.

"Remember, I told you that I heard something when he was born?

Well, I think it's worse. He may have a hole in his heart," Dr. Bayard said.

"Oh, no!" Maggie steadied herself against the examining table.

Dr. Bayard helped her into a chair. "I wish I was wrong, Maggie, but I'm afraid I know what a normal heart sounds like. If you want to, you could bring Lenny or William in to compare."

"No, I don't need to bring the boys in, Dr. Bayard. I believe you. But what does it mean?" Maggie wrung her hands, afraid of what he might say.

"It's hard to know right now, Maggie. He'll probably always be small for his age and not have as much energy as the other boys. But the bad thing is if he gets sick, he'll have a hard time getting over it. There's still some flu going around. Just watch him real close. Try and keep him as well as possible."

Chapter 46

With William and Lenny in school, Maggie and Yancey had the house to themselves most of the day. He loved for her to make up stories to tell him while she worked around the house. One of his favorites was a story her Grandmother Moreland had told her as a child. Maggie thought it would make a wonderful book. She asked Aunt Mag if she remembered some of the details.

"Law me. I remember it just as if Mama was sitting right here beside us telling it herself. Little Pearl Jessup's papa was a Chinaman living in Wilmington. He became a Christian and wanted to move his family back to China to save the infidels, but he died before he could get the money together for the passage. So little Pearl took up the banner, and she set out by herself to cross the United States to get to California. Now, what Mama loved to tell was all the little adventures little Pearl had along the way."

"That's what I remember," Maggie said. "I think she made them up as she went along. Don't you?"

"I expect so. They seemed real to me, but now that I think about it, they might have been Mama's way of teaching us Bible lessons."

For weeks, Aunt Mag came every few days to sit and talk about Pearl's stories. Yancey listened too, and they taught him 'Jesus Loves Me' and other songs that Aunt Mag remembered. "Mama would have loved you, Tate Yancey," she said to the child. "She used to wish and wish for a little boy."

"Tell me about the buffalo," Yancey said, tugging on her sleeve.

"Oh, those buffalo had these big old horns that curved around on the sides of their heads, and their hair was curlier than your mama's. Little Pearl used to get up on one and ride all day. That's how she made such good time getting to California, riding on the buffaloes, holding onto their horns, singing 'Onward Christian Soldiers.'" Aunt Mag broke into song and began marching around the parlor. Yancey followed, stomping his feet in her tracks.

Maggie finished Pearl's story and sent it off to Galleon Press in New York City, along with ten dollars for her own first-edition copy. Almost a year later, she received her copy in the mail. Galleon had *Little Pearl* in a collection of stories called *The American Scene*, a book of semi-fictional stories and character sketches designed to reveal a cross-section of American life. Maggie was ecstatic. Abigail had charged her to leave no stone unturned until she was published by a major house. Well, Galleon was not exactly a major house, but Maggie had achieved her purpose—she'd been published.

—

After *Little Pearl* was published, Tate attempted to help out with Yancey more. He did it partially to help Maggie so she could spend more of her time writing, but even more to get Yancey out from under his mother's skirts. Yancey was almost five years old now and it made Tate sick to see how pale his son was. Maggie's column in *The Wilmington Star* required several days each week when she and Yancey would visit up and down the road gathering news, but it wasn't enough to put any color in his cheeks.

Every now and then, Tate stopped by the house to see if he couldn't persuade Maggie to let go a little. "The boy needs to spend some time out in the field with me. He can ride in the sled while I haul tobacco."

"No, Tate, he might fall. Besides, he's perfectly happy right here with me."

"Well, I don't want him growing up to be a sissy. I need my little boy to keep me company." He picked Yancey up and sat him atop his shoulders. "What do you say, little man? You want to go ride in the sled with Daddy?"

Before Yancey could answer, Maggie slammed a book on the table and reached out for her son. "No, Tate. He's too frail. You know what

Dr. Bayard said. He might catch cold out there in the damp."

Tate lifted Yancey down off his shoulders and stood him on the floor. "Maybe later, son." He looked at Maggie. "It's not right, you coddling him like this, Maggie Lorena."

"I wanna go, Mama. Please," Yancey said.

Maggie looked surprised. "No, honey, you don't. There are snakes and things out there and Mama wants you to stay here with me where you're safe." She gave Tate a harsh look. "Come on now, we'll go gather the eggs and Daddy can get back out in the field." She took the child's hand and maneuvered him towards the back of the house. Tate stood in the center of the room until they had gone outside. He knew that Maggie protected Yancey too much, but he didn't know how to change it.

CHAPTER 47
1921

When he was six years old Yancey started his first year at the school in Colly, riding the new yellow schoolbus with his brothers. Senators Evans and Yancey had pushed the public transportation bill through in 1920, but it had taken another year for the county to get the buses. Maggie liked to think Reece had done this for her, for his son. Of course, Reece had no way of knowing he might have a son. Maggie had been tempted to write to him and tell him. But how could she be sure? At times she thought she could see Reece in Yancey's eyes.

The thought of Yancey being out of her sight in school all day long frightened Maggie. If she was overprotective, she felt that she had good reason. William and Lenny had one cold after the other, passed to them by their classmates.

Maggie had an idea, but she knew it wouldn't set well with Tate. He was always after her to let Yancey be like the other boys. When she told him she was going to offer to help out at school, Tate looked at her like he thought she was crazy. "I'll just ride the bus up there with the children and ask the new principal if she could use my help in the library," she said.

"Maggie, I declare! You'll embarrass that young'un to death, not to mention William and Lenny." He'd been thinking how nice it would be for Yancey to ride the bus with his brothers and meet some other children.

"No, I won't. My boys are proud of the fact that I used to be a schoolteacher. You wait and see."

Lenny and William knew better than to protest when Maggie got on the schoolbus. They filed to the rear of the bus, leaving Yancey to sit with her in the front row. "He's just a little baby," William mocked.

"Hush up, Willie. Mama don't like it when you make fun of him being little. She'll come back here and make a fuss. Just be quiet and maybe nobody will notice."

Maggie held Yancey's hand as the bus wobbled down the dirt road, stopping every mile or so to pick up children. She'd made lunches for all three boys and put an extra piece of chicken in Yancey's lunch pail for herself. "Mama's going to get you all settled in school and she's going to go talk to the principal about helping in the library," she said.

"Why can't I go by myself, Mama?"

"Oh, you can and you are, son. You don't mind if Mama goes along to see about getting a job, do you?"

"No ma'am, but Willie said I was a sissy 'cause you had to go with me."

"Well, I'm going to spank William when we get home. Just you wait and see."

Maggie walked the hallways of the new brick school proudly. It had been built when the legislature consolidated school districts, closing down the last of the one-room schoolhouses. G. W.'s picture hung near the principal's office, right beside Governor Charles B. Aycock's. As a county commissioner, G. W. had pushed for consolidation and been an advocate of building school libraries and establishing courses in science and foreign languages. Maggie stood before his picture. It was a painting, really, from an old photograph taken just after he came home from the War. When she walked away, his gaze seemed to follow her.

"Let's go find the new principal, Yancey. I heard she was a real nice lady and I want to meet her."

A stately woman about Maggie's age, wearing a starched blue dress with a white collar and cuffs, came towards them down the hall. "Good morning. May I help you?"

"Yes, ma'am. I'm Maggie Ryan. I have three boys in school here."

The principal studied Maggie a moment. "Oh, that's your father's picture next to the auditorium, isn't it?"

"Yes, ma'am."

"Well, I'm Lucy Potter, the new principal." She turned to Yancey. "Hello, young man. You must be one of our new first-graders."

"Yes'm. I guess so," Yancey said timidly.

"Well, welcome to school, Yancey. Come and I'll show you where the first-grade room is." Mrs. Potter took Yancey's hand and Maggie followed close behind, feeling a little left out. Yancey glanced back at her a time or two, and she smiled and nodded as if to say Mama's right here. But before she knew it, Yancey was whisked away by the first-grade teacher without a goodbye hug, and she was left alone with Mrs. Potter.

"Well, it's always hard to see our children go off to school, Mrs. Ryan, but I believe your other boys have adjusted nicely," the principal said.

"Yes, they have," Maggie said, feeling exposed. "It's just that Yancey is my baby. He's a little frail and all."

"Don't worry about him being small. I've seen so many little fellows start school like that and when they graduate, they're these great big strapping boys."

"Mrs. Potter, I used to teach school over in Onslow County and I was wondering if you could use some help in the library."

The principal studied her for a moment. "I could certainly use some help in the library, but what I really need is an eleventh-grade teacher. Are you certified?"

"No, I'm not. I just wanted to volunteer to help in the library—or maybe help the first-grade teacher," Maggie said.

"Oh, I see. You want to be near Yancey?"

Maggie blushed. "Well, yes. Yancey is my last one at home and I thought maybe I could help."

"Of course, I understand. We'll work something out." She started towards her office. "I have to keep an eye out for some legislators who'll be here with the superintendent this morning to tour the school." She stopped suddenly and Maggie almost walked into her. "Say, you probably know the school better than I do. Could you help me out, maybe show them around? I'd really appreciate it."

"Why, yes, I'd be delighted," Maggie said.

"Good. I'll put you to work in the library shelving some new books until they get here."

It was all Maggie could do not to browse through each book before putting it on the shelf. She was excited about working in the library. Every evening she could take books home to read to the children.

About eleven o'clock, Mrs. Potter came for her. "The legislators are here, Maggie. I want them to observe some of our students in the library. I'll have the first-grade teacher bring in her class. After the gentlemen have looked around in here, you can take them on a tour of the rest of the school."

Senator Yancey took her hand when he was introduced, a puzzled look on his face. Maggie would have known him anywhere. It hadn't dawned on her that she might know any of the legislators. She blushed to think Reece might have been part of the entourage, but he was not among the group. "Yes, Mrs. Ryan. Have we met? Your face is familiar," the senator said.

She had to steady herself against the doorjamb. "Why, no, Senator, I don't believe so."

He held her hand a moment longer. "I'll think of it—never forget a face. I pride myself on that."

Talmadge Yancey was noticeably older, his salt-and-pepper hair now solid white. Their brief encounter in the Andrew Johnson Hotel dining room was vivid in Maggie's mind—and he was likely to remember before the day was over. When she chose Yancey's name, the idea that her path would ever cross the senator's again had been the furthest thing from her mind.

Maggie could feel Senator Yancey's eyes on her as she led the legislators from room to room and down the long hallway. She had worn her corset under a simple green frock, a bit faded but stylish. Her red hair had darkened slightly over the years, but she still wore it parted in the middle and rolled back on either side into a knot at the back of her head. In William's room, and again in Lenny's, she went to her son's desk, patted him on the shoulder, and introduced him directly to the senator while the other legislators socialized with the teacher and students. It was a matter of pride, gave some credibility to the fact that she was a married woman despite what he might have thought about her presence in Raleigh—should he ever remember it.

In the hall, Maggie purposely didn't point out G. W.'s portrait, not wanting to call more attention to herself than necessary, but the senator stopped her directly in front of it.

"Mrs. Potter told me that you were a Corbinn, Mrs. Ryan," he said. "I believe I met your father once. Fine man. This is his portrait, isn't it?"

"Yes, it is, Senator. Thank you." A little flustered, Maggie turned to the group. "Now, I'll leave you to Mrs. Potter. I believe some of the mothers have prepared a picnic for you under the trees."

She struck out for the library, where Yancey was eating his lunch at a table with several first-graders. He was so much smaller than the other children that he looked out of place. Maggie sat down in a chair next to him and whispered, "How's my darling boy? Do you like school?"

"Yes ma'am." He got up from his chair and ran his hand over a shelf of books. "Look at all these books! I'm going to learn to read them all, Mama. Every one of them."

"And what you can't read, Mama will read to you," Maggie said. "Oh, what fun we'll have in school!" She stood and reached for his hand. "Come over here, Mama wants to tell you something." They sat down at another table away from the other children. "Guess what? Mrs.

Potter said Mama could have a job helping in the library. What do you think of that?"

"It's all right, Mama, but Papa said you should be at home."

"Oh, he did? He talked to you about that?"

"He just said he hoped you didn't get a job, 'cause if you did, you'd be riding the bus every day with me and my brothers."

"Well, now, what's wrong with that, son? Mama loves her children and she wants to ride the bus with them."

"I don't know. Papa just said you ought to be at home," Yancey said.

Home was right where Maggie wished she was when Talmadge Yancey came into the library. "Mrs. Ryan, may I have a word with you?"

"Yes, of course," she said, trying not to show her apprehension.

The senator stooped down to speak to Yancey. "Hello, little fellow. What's your name?"

Yancey slipped out of the low chair and stood proudly before the senator. "My name is Tate Yancey Ryan. My mama calls me Yancey."

"Well, how about that! My name is Yancey, too, but it's my last name like yours is Ryan." He stood, pulled his watch from his pocket, and checked the time. "I don't have long. Could we step out into the hall a moment?" Aghast, Maggie followed him. "It took me awhile, but I remembered," he said. Maggie turned away, unable to meet his eyes. "Please, don't be embarrassed. It would be difficult to forget such a lovely face. Reece would be most unhappy with me." He paused. "You've heard, I'm sure..."

Maggie touched his arm. "Heard what?"

Senator Yancey looked shocked. "Oh, forgive me. You didn't know?"

"Know what? Has something happened to him?"

"Reece died of a heart attack a month ago."

Maggie leaned against the wall, her knees trembling. Unable to speak, she stared past him, across the hall, out an open window. There were children on the playground, running about in slow motion, their shrill voices pantomimed on the September air.

"I'm sorry. I would've thought..."

"No, I didn't know. I haven't seen or heard from him in over seven years."

"Oh, I see. Yes, he said you had agreed." He took her arm and led her further down the hall, away from the library. "Mrs. Ryan...Maggie...you can count on my discretion. Reece kept to himself, didn't have many friends. I was fortunate enough to be one of them. We got drunk one night—it gets awful lonely up there in Raleigh. He told me..."

"We were friends, that's all," Maggie interrupted.

"No, I think it was more. Actually, at the funeral, I asked Emily McAllister if she knew what had become of you. She said you were married and lived in Bladen County. I'm sorry. He was a good man." He reached for his watch again, checked the time, and snapped it shut. Unhooking the watch from the chain, he handed it to Maggie. "Reece left this to me in his will. Here, I want you to have it."

"No, I couldn't," Maggie said. "You must keep it—I have other keepsakes."

"The boy? Yes, that occurred to me. He's a little different from your other boys, but let's just say it's because he's my namesake. Maybe there will come a time when you can give it to him. Whatever, I want you to have it." He turned to leave, then reconsidered. "Reece said you both agreed that you had missed your chance for a life together. It's so sad when lovers are not free to marry, but I hope your choice was a good one."

"Senator Yancey, you have no right to assume..."

"Yes, forgive me, my dear. You are quite right."

She watched him go down the hall, wanting to go after him, ask him what had happened in the intervening years, but she couldn't. Trembling, she turned the gold watch over in her hand. In her mind's eye, she saw Reece tug gently on the chain, lift it from his watch pocket, snap it open, glance, then snap it closed. Engraved on the back beneath his initials, in ornate script, were the words *Tempus Fugit.*

The news of Reece's death devastated Maggie at first. It had been so difficult not to think of him—not to wish for his presence in her life. As much as she denied it, she'd always had a glimmer of hope that someday circumstances might bring them together again. She had wanted to write to Emily McAllister many times, but had resisted the urge. A bond had existed between them, a respect centering around their mutual love for Reece. Perhaps she should write to Emily now. A note of sympathy would be appropriate.

Bill Ryan had brought Tate the news of Reece's death shortly after it happened, but he had never told Maggie. Since Sally Catherine had passed on, Bill had taken to visiting Tate and Maggie every month or so. "Reece Evans just dropped dead on the porch of that big old house. Served the son-of-a-bitch right!" Bill had said. It was not like his pa to use profanity, especially in reference to the dead.

"Who found him, Pa?"

"The mailman. He said Reece must've been there a day and a half, said the stench was terrible. If he hadn't of come up to the house with a package, Reece would probably still be there, rotting on that porch."

"My God, Pa! Where was everybody?"

"I'll be damned if I know. They say Homer's crowd was off to a funeral over in Sampson County or someplace. Reece's girls were up yonder in Philadelphia. Miss Emily never stayed at the new house."

"Can't help but feel sorry for him, Pa. I never wished that on him."

"Me neither, son, but you can't help how you feel about somebody who tried to do you harm. I didn't even go to the funeral—all those big shots from Raleigh come down here. I'm surprised you didn't see something about it in the paper."

Tate decided not to tell Maggie. It wouldn't do any good to bring up the past. Besides, he hadn't thought much about Reece for a long time. The letter from him in Maggie's trunk said he'd found his true love. Well, hell, Reece might have *thought* he'd found her, but he'd been a married man back then and there was no way he could have kept her.

———

Maggie would have given anything to talk with Emily McAllister in person. There was so much she had wanted to say to her besides the few kind words she'd included in her note of sympathy. Emily had loved her brother dearly, but she'd tried to protect Maggie from him. Had he told her about their liaison in Raleigh? In a way, Maggie hoped that he had.

Emily replied right away. *I wanted to tell you the news myself, but I didn't think it proper under the circumstances. There are some things here that he left to you, but I think they would only cause problems in your marriage. Marriage is difficult enough without old ghosts coming back to haunt us. He left your house to the girls, but I doubt they will ever live there.*

Emily had called it *her* house. Maggie closed herself up in her room and pulled out the plans. Yes, there it was, *The Residence of Miss Maggie Lorena Corbinn.* Had he called it that, *Maggie's house?*

———

Reece's death released Maggie from her hope that someday, somewhere they might meet again. With him no longer a vessel for her thoughts and dreams, she had more energy for her writing. After *Little Pearl* was published she'd written a series of pieces for the *Progressive Farmer*, but Abigail's edited copy of *Evangeline* had lain untouched on her desk. It was time to take the manuscript up again, complete it.

Amazed at the way the words came pouring out, she pounded the typewriter day and night. All along she'd modeled the female protagonist after herself; now she felt free to develop the male protagonist in Reece's image. She raised him from the dead, gave him all the things she had never been able to give him in life—most importantly, a son he could know and be proud of.

Maggie mailed the manuscript to Abigail Adams knowing that she might see through the story. Abigail had accepted Maggie's note explaining her urgent need to get home to the children. She'd never had the right opportunity to tell Abigail differently, and Abigail had never asked. If Joella had told her about Reece, then she'd figure it out. What difference would that make now?

Abigail had left Raleigh at the end of the school year as she had planned. When Mrs. Burchart died less than a year later, she'd stayed in Boston, teaching at Radcliffe College in Cambridge. *It's a rather snooty girls' school—nothing like BFU, but then nothing could ever be quite like BFU.* Abigail was probably close to fifty now, though Maggie had never known her age for sure. It had been almost eight years since she'd seen her. Maggie began to think of how wonderful it would be to go to Boston on the train. Maybe she would if Abigail found a publisher for her. She enclosed a letter with the manuscript.

...I ask for your discretion. You'll see my heart and soul laid bare, but I hope others will not. If you think the manuscript worthy of publication, please suggest where I might send it...

Chapter 48

Tate's dream of building a new house had been set back even further when some of the crops didn't make good several years in a row. With three growing boys, there was hardly enough room to turn around in the little cottage that Uncle Archie had built. When G. W. died, they should've moved into the old homeplace with Aunt Mag. But what he really wanted to do was build them a new house.

He and Maggie were on the porch talking after supper when he tried to bring the subject up again. She was in a pretty good mood after getting paid for a story in *The Progressive Farmer* and he thought it was the right time. "I want to build a real house with high ceilings and a big front porch," he said. "The boys could each have a room. They're growing up, in case you hadn't noticed."

"I've noticed," she said, watching William and Lenny trying to catch an old rooster who was trying his best to get to the hen house. William had grown four inches since his last birthday and Lenny was not far behind.

"Well, don't you want a bigger house?"

"Not really. When the boys are grown up, it will just be a big old house to ramble around in and we'd wish we had this precious little cottage again."

"Precious to you, but not very comfortable for me and the boys."

Maggie didn't intend to give an inch. She couldn't bear the thought of moving into another house that Tate built. She knew what it would be like—half-finished, and her having to nag him all the time. "Well, you go ahead and build it," she said. "I'm staying right here in Aunt Mag's house."

She knew she was being unfair to Tate, but his idea of a 'real house' and hers were not the same. From time to time she got the plans that Reece had given her out of her trunk, running her finger over the rooms as he had done. She imagined the house built on a little knoll over near the old Croom place. Tate had even talked about that location one time, but he'd want to do it all himself and he would never do it right. Besides, even if they had all the money in the world, he'd die before he built a house that Reece Evans had designed for her.

When Yancey took sick, Tate dropped the subject of building a new house completely. Heeding Dr. Bayard's warning, Maggie always yanked Yancey out of school at the first sign of sickness going around. But this time Yancey was the first to get a sore throat. The weather had warmed, then suddenly turned cold and wet as it was inclined to do in early spring. On the bus, Yancey complained to Maggie that he was tired and his throat hurt. Before the bus had reached their house, he vomited all over himself and Maggie.

When the bus came to a stop, she wrapped him in her skirts and carried him to the house as fast as she could. "Mama's going to get you warmed up and give you a dose of quinine to settle your stomach. William, you go get Lizzie and tell her to come right away."

"But Mama, it's raining!"

"I know, honey. Just put Papa's oilskin jacket over your head and you'll be all right. Hurry, now!"

Lizzie was almost as protective of Yancey as Maggie was. She was at the house before Maggie even had his clothes off. Lizzie said that once red throat set in it had to run its course, but she brought her bag of folk medicine and made up a mustard plaster. No one was surprised when William and Lenny got sick a few days later. For a week or so, Maggie and Lizzie had all they could do to nurse the three children.

The older boys threw their sickness off fairly quickly, but little Yancey developed rheumatic fever and became sicker day by day. The pain in his joints was so bad that he cried when he tried to move. Even the weight of the bedclothes or the slightest jolt to the bed would cause him to cry out in agony. One day his knees would be the most painful; the next, his shoulders. Even his hands and feet were red and swollen. At night his fever went up and he poured sweat, soaking his bedclothes every hour or so.

Maggie was beside herself, staying up through the night, bathing him with cool water to bring his fever down. All Tate could do was sit and watch. She wouldn't let him touch Yancey. Aunt Mag came over almost every day to spell Maggie while she rested. Yancey was too sick to listen to her read or tell him stories, so she just sat by his bed and bathed his swollen joints with a mixture of black cohosh and lobelia that Uncle Archie had used for his rheumatism.

Dr. Bayard brought essence of ginger and bicarbonate of potash to add to the liniment, recommending that they cover the joints with loose strips of soft cotton bandages. He came almost every day to listen to Yancey's heart.

At one point, the fever subsided and Yancey began to look about as if seeing them all for the first time. "Have I been very sick, Mama?"

Maggie tried to pick him up as tenderly as possible. "Yes, you have, son, but I think you're getting over it. Look, Papa, Yancey's feeling better."

Tate had sat by the bed every night for over a week and he was overcome with emotion. "That's my boy. I knew you would," he said, wiping the tears from his eyes.

"Papa, tell me about Dancin' Daniel."

Tate began a tale he had told Yancey many times about taking Daniel to a Fourth of July parade in Jacksonville when he was a boy. He was just getting wound up when he realized that Yancey had closed his eyes and was resting peacefully for the first time in two weeks.

The weather warmed and spring dressed the trees and fields in a fresh shade of green. Tate got back to work planting corn and setting out tobacco plants, and Aunt Mag cut her visits back to every other day or so. Katie came with her three little girls, Sadie, Geraldine and Katherine, and they played on the floor at the foot of Yancey's bed while

Katie and Maggie caught up on the news.

"I was afraid to come while Yancey was so sick," Katie said, "but it looks as if he's on the road to recovery now."

"Come to the kitchen with me a minute, Katie. I'll get Lizzie to watch the children."

Katie followed Maggie into the kitchen, thinking she might have a choice piece of news that was inappropriate for the children's ears, but the look on Maggie's face told her otherwise.

"Katie, I'm scared to death. Dr. Bayard said that Yancey might have a relapse any time. His heart is inflamed." She began to cry and Katie drew her into her arms.

"But he's better. I can see that."

"No," Maggie sobbed. "He's not in as much pain in his joints, but Dr. Bayard says his fever might spike at any time and he doesn't think his heart can take another flareup."

"Isn't there something he can do?"

"No, he says all we can do is pray for time. The longer he goes without a relapse, the better off he'll be." Maggie lifted her apron to wipe her eyes. "Katie, if anything happens to Yancey, I'll go mad, I know I will."

"Oh, honey, don't talk like that. Nothing's going to happen."

Maggie tried to convince herself that Katie was right, but she never left Yancey's bedside. All day long, she sat and read to him. Sometimes he would fall asleep in the middle of a story, but he never forgot the place and he would wake and beg her to finish it.

"I dreamed I had a white horse with wings, Mama. Like the one in the story. Is it true, did horses really have wings long ago?"

"Only in fairytales, son."

"Could Daniel really dance?"

"Well, now, I knew Daniel, but I don't remember him dancing. I think your daddy is just making that up."

"You write stories, Mama. Is everything you write in your stories true?"

"No, not everything, son."

School was out and summer had hardly begun when Maggie noticed Yancey was sleeping more and more. She stayed by his bed day and night, ready when he woke to give him sips of water or rub him down with alcohol. But when he could no longer be roused, Tate went to fetch the doctor.

"I'm afraid this is what we've been dreading," Doctor Bayard said. "His temperature is 106 degrees." He grimaced, listening to Yancey's heart. "There's not much hope if this keeps up."

Maggie grabbed Dr. Bayard's arm. "There must be something you can do!"

"I'm afraid that it's out of my hands now, Maggie. All we can do is pray."

They all knelt by Yancey's bed and said their silent prayers. His breath was labored, just as Mary Ellen's had been, and Maggie knew what to expect. She sobbed over and over, "Please God, please God," refusing to believe that He would take this child from her.

William began to cry, louder and louder. "Don't, son," Dr. Bayard said. "We can't keep him here if the Lord is ready for him. Just let the angels take him."

Lenny looked around. "Are they here now?"

"Close by," Dr. Bayard said.

Just before dawn, Yancey stopped breathing. William and Lenny were sound asleep on the floor, but Maggie and Tate lay on either side of the bed, holding Yancey's hands. Dr. Bayard leaned over Maggie and listened to Yancey's heart. He touched Maggie's arm. "He's gone," he said, putting his stethoscope in his bag.

"He was such a good little boy," Tate said, tears streaming down his face.

"I don't know if I can go on," Maggie wailed.

Dr. Bayard tried to comfort her. "Of course you can, Maggie Lorena. You've got these other two boys—and Tate. They need you."

She shook her head. "God's punishing me. I'm not a good mother—not a good wife. He took Yancey away from me."

"Now, Maggie, I don't want to hear you talking like that. You're as good a mother as ever was," Tate said.

"You don't know, Tate," she sobbed. "I should have been better. I didn't deserve this child."

"C'mon, now, Maggie. That's no way to be talking," Dr. Bayard said. He turned to Tate. "I'll give her some laudanum. It'll help her sleep."

Maggie buried her face in the bedcovers, one hand still holding her child's. "Just leave me alone with my son, all of you. I want to be alone with him."

When they buried Yancey the next day, Maggie looked like she was in a trance. Aunt Mag and Katie had washed and dressed Yancey in his best suit of clothes, despite Maggie's insistence that she be the only one to touch him. Tate had to drag her into the other room and keep her there until she calmed down. After that she had gone into the trance and not spoken a word since.

Preacher Mizelle kept the service brief, seeing what a state she was in. Tate and Zeb half-carried her to the graveside and sat her in a chair. Tate stood at her side, wiping his tears with a handkerchief. Lenny and William were at her other side, their faces contorted in grief. The only other funerals that they'd been to were for older folks whose time had come.

Vases of baby's breath and yellow jasmine were at the foot and the head of the grave. Just to the left was Ellen's tombstone and next to that G. W.'s. A tarp hid the fresh earth that would soon cover the small casket. When they were all gathered, Maggie's brothers brought the casket and placed it on the rack above the grave. Preacher Mizelle said a few words, then nodded to Katie to start the singing.

Shall we gather at the river, where bright angel feet have trod;
With its crystal tide forever flowing by the throne of God?

Yes, we'll gather at the river, the beautiful, beautiful river;
Gather with the saints at the river that flows by the throne of God.

Before the song was over, Maggie began to moan and rock back and forth. At first Tate was moved by it, but when the song was finished, she wailed louder and louder and nothing he did or said could quiet her. Finally Katie and Aunt Mag got her up and dragged her to the buggy to take her home. William and Lenny stayed with Tate until the grave was covered.

"She's taking it mighty hard, Tate," Zeb said, standing with him as the gravediggers threw dirt on the small coffin. "Maggie was high-strung before, but this might push her off the deep end. She sure doted over that child."

"She'll get over it, Zeb. We all will. Yancey meant just as much to me as these here boys," he said, indicating William and Lenny. "But we all have to go on, don't we, boys?"

Both of the boys nodded, but William walked away while Lenny questioned his pa. "Do you think he's in heaven yet, Papa?"

"I imagine so, son. If we could see those angels, I'll bet they'd be right about there by now," he said, pointing to a place high above the tallest pine tree. "Where'd William go?" He looked around and saw William sitting with his back against G. W.'s headstone. "Go tell your brother we better go see about Mama."

"He said he was gonna run away if Yancey died."

"What?

"He said he was gonna run away if Yancey died because Mama would likely die too."

"Well, let's go get him 'cause Mama needs us all to help her get over this. She needs all of her boys, including me."

Zeb took Tate's arm and pulled him aside. "Don't count on her getting over it too soon, Tate. I saw another woman break down like that when her husband died. She went all to pieces and never did come out of it."

Chapter 49

After Yancey died, Maggie took to her little room more and more. She kept the door closed whether she was in or out. At times Tate could hear her moving about like she was going through her things. If she'd been doing her writing he would've been glad, but he never heard the clickety-clack of the typewriter.

"You ought not to close yourself up like that, Maggie Lorena," he said. "Now that school's out, the boys need you. Maybe you could all go down to visit Katie."

"I don't need to go see Katie."

"How come you're not writing articles anymore? Mr. Bell told me the other day how much he missed them in *The Progressive Farmer*." The sun was streaming in through the high windows on either side of the chimney, and dust was visible on all the little knickknacks that Tate detested.

"I don't feel like writing stories anymore. There's nothing I want to write about." She sat down in one of the upholstered rocking chairs and picked at the frayed cloth on the armrest. "I don't feel like doing much of anything. I just want to be left alone, Tate."

"What about your children? What about me?"

Maggie looked down at her feet. "You just don't understand how I'm grieving."

"Maggie, it's time you thought about the living, including yourself. Grieving's not gonna bring Yancey back. We did all we could for him," Tate said, choking up. He tried to take her in his arms, but she pushed him aside. "Maggie, he's gone. Grieving ain't going to change that."

"What do you know about grieving, Tate Ryan? You never lost much in your life except your mama, and she was old and had lived a good

life. Everything I ever loved has been taken from me. Poor little Yancey
was barely eight years old, and when he died, you just kept right on
going like nothing had happened."

Tate hung his head. Her hateful words were like stabs to his heart.
"You better start counting your blessings, getting on with your life." He
meant it kindly, but she didn't take it that way.

"My life? Yancey was my life!"

"It's a sin to talk like that when you have two other children, Maggie
Lorena. What about William and Lenny?"

She began to wring her hands and weep and wail. "Leave me alone.
Nobody knows how I'm suffering," she cried. "Nobody but God knows.
Just leave me alone!"

Tate decided to talk to Zeb. In the years after G. W. died, Zeb Corbinn
and Tate had gotten as close as brothers. Both were hard workers, providing for a family, making ends meet. Their farms joined in several
places, and it wasn't unusual for Tate to plow on over into Zeb's field or
vice-versa, just to get the work done. Tate's favorite time of the day was
the evening, when they'd meet at Miss Maybelle's store down at the
crossroad and sit around on the empty crates, jawing and chewing tobacco—a habit they'd both picked up from G. W.

"I know Yancey was special to her, Zeb. Probably because he was
sickly. She thinks she's the only one that has a right to grieve. But he
was my son too. What if I was to act like that? Where would she be
then?"

"You'd both be up in Raleigh in the loony bin, I guess," Zeb said.
He put his arm around Tate's shoulders. "But listen, I hear the best way
to get over the loss of a child is to have another one."

"Well, I can guarantee you that's not likely to happen. We don't
even sleep in the same room anymore."

"What?"

"Maggie hasn't let me near her since Yancey was a baby."

"That's probably what's wrong with her mind, Tate. Women have their needs, just like men, only they don't recognize them like we do."

"Hmmph! She won't even..."

"Look, Tate, just go crawl into bed one night with her. You'll see."

"It'd be a cold day in hell before she'd allow that."

"I 'spect I need to have a word with her," Zeb said. "Papa always said Maggie needed a strong hand. Not that you can't handle her, but she might listen to me."

Zeb bided his time, tried to think how his pa would have handled Maggie Lorena. G. W. had doted over all three girls. There was a time when he would go to Wilmington with his cotton and come back with a dress for each one. They doted over him, too, especially Maggie Lorena. But Pa wouldn't have put up with her behavior for very long.

Zeb knew the time had come when Maggie accepted Reverend Mizelle's call for sinners to come forth and tell their sins if they expected salvation. She stood up there in front of the congregation weeping and wailing, saying she wasn't a good mother, that the Lord had taken away her child because of it. Everyone in the family was mortified, but their friends and neighbors said they knew it wasn't true. Maggie wasn't herself. The Lord would understand.

After services, Zeb jerked her by the arm, steering her away from the crowd. Maggie was bewildered. "What is it? Where are you taking me?"

"I need to talk to you, sister," he said, coming to a stop in front of their father's tombstone. Look at this—your pa's grave. He probably rolled over in it when he heard you carrying on like that." Zeb's face was stern and he shook a long finger at her. "Why, you didn't let that young'un out of your sight, day or night. I'm ashamed of you, feeling sorry for yourself, getting up there in front of everybody saying you were a bad mama! What ails you, woman? You better straighten yourself out, now. Tate's not going to put up with much more of this mess."

Maggie tossed her head back and glared at him. "What would you know about it? You never lost a child."

"Well, if I did, I don't believe I'd be blaming myself for it."

Aunt Mag tried a different tactic. Being a woman herself, she knew these things took time. She had tried to be as much comfort as possible, visiting with Maggie every day or so, bringing her collards and sweet potatoes from her garden and seeing to it that she had papers and magazines to read. Some folks just took more time than others to get over things. Maggie would come around sooner or later, she was sure of it. What she didn't understand was why Maggie continued to blame herself, to feel so guilty about Yancey's death when there was absolutely nothing she could have done to prevent it.

When almost a year had gone by and Maggie was still moping around, Aunt Mag decided it was time to take another tack. "Why don't you go up to Boston and see Abigail Adams? You could take the train out of Burgaw. You don't even have to switch trains in Raleigh. Not until you get to New York. I hear it only takes about four days." They were sitting on the back porch while Aunt Mag shelled some late butterbeans for supper. Maggie didn't answer her. "Shouldn't you be getting back to writing that book you were working on? I thought Abigail was going to find you a publisher. I'd like to read it before I die."

Maggie rocked slowly in her chair. "I mailed it to Abigail before Yancey died. I've never heard from her since. I think something's happened to her."

"Oh, don't be so morbid. She might've gotten married or something."

"No, it's not like Abigail not to keep in touch. Not for this long," Maggie said. She looked out at the grape arbor where the scuppernongs hung in heavy bronze clusters. "Yancey loved to play under there. He used to hide from me and wait for me to come and find him." She sighed, tears spilling down her cheeks. "I keep expecting him to call out any minute."

Aunt Mag stood up, placing the pan of beans on a table and brushing off her skirt. "Listen here, it's perfectly natural for a woman to grieve over a dead child, but it's been long enough. You should have accepted it by now."

Maggie pulled her apron up over her face. "You don't understand, Aunt Mag. No one could ever understand. Please just leave me be."

When her heart was the heaviest, Maggie thought of going down to the river, tying a towsack filled with rocks to her feet, and jumping off the bridge. She was convinced now that Yancey was Reece's child and God had taken him away because she'd fornicated. That's how the preacher would put it. She'd never be happy again. God wouldn't let her be, not after she'd had another man's child and let Tate believe that it was his. That was the biggest sin. Maybe that's why God had taken Yancey away, so Tate wouldn't have to know.

But there was something else she worried about. Something that had seemed so logical at the time. God would know, God would blame her for the fire even if no one else did. It was all so confusing.

Katie tried her hand at helping. "Maggie, you've got to pull your-self together. Each child is precious in the sight of a mother, but you've got to go on for Tate, for William and Lenny's sake."

"Kate, there's more to it."

"I know, Maggie, but..."

"No, you don't know. Tate doesn't know either."

Katie could only guess at the truth, and she didn't like it one bit. From time to time, Maggie had made remarks to her, little innuendoes about how Yancey resolved the past. Katie had seen Reece's obituary in the *Wilmington Star* and was sure that Maggie had seen it too. But when she mentioned it to Aunt Mag, Aunt Mag said she herself had cut it out of the paper and burned it in the stove. "I told Maggie Lorena that the obituary was a friend of mine that died and I cut it out to send up North to some of her family. She asked me who and I made up a name. It was back before Yancey got sick and she was so wrapped up in him she didn't protest much."

Katie decided that Maggie's mind was beyond reason. "Look, I don't want to know. Whatever the truth is, you'd best leave it buried with Yancey and get on with your life."

Chapter 50

Aunt Mag heard a different story from Tate every time she saw him. "You know those colored boys I hired to help me barn the tobacco?" Tate asked her. "Well, Maggie said I needn't bring a bunch of mouths for her to feed, she wasn't going to cook for them. I sent for Lizzie and she said Maggie didn't say a word until those poor boys came up to the house to dinner. When Maggie saw them, she went around to the back of the house and climbed up the ladder. When I got there, she was on the roof like a madwoman with two butcher knives in her hands, ranting and screaming like a banshee. Every one of them ran off."

The situation would have been downright funny if Aunt Mag hadn't realized that Maggie's mind was at stake. "I keep thinking she'll snap out of it, Tate. I declare, I can't believe she's still acting so crazy. It's been almost two years now since Yancey died. Have you talked to Dr. Bayard? He knows a lot about melancholia."

"Doc says she's just wallowing in her misery, but he can't figure out why she feels like Yancey dying was her fault. What bothers me is her meanness."

"How's that?"

"She shut me and Troy up in the tobacco barn because I forgot to bring in her firewood."

"When did she do that?"

"About two weeks ago. We were in the barn one evening moving the tobacco around to get a better cure and she shut the door. I knew it was her and I called out and asked her what in the hell she was doing."

"What did she say?"

"She got down and yelled through a crack in the logs, 'I'm teaching you a lesson, Tate Ryan! You didn't get my wood in!'" Aunt Mag put her hand up to her mouth to stifle a laugh. "It's not funny," Tate said, wiping his brow. "Me and Troy, we almost suffocated in there!"

Aunt Mag sobered up quickly. "It's pitiful. I talked to Dr. Bayard, too, and he said she needed something to take her mind off Yancey. I've been hoping she'd hear from Miss Abigail, but Maggie thinks something's happened to her and she might be right."

"What on earth could Miss Abigail do?"

"You know Maggie wrote that book just before Yancey died. She said it was the best thing she'd ever written and it was going to make her famous. Miss Abigail was going to try and get it published."

"No, she didn't tell me. I don't see how anything like that could clear up her mind anyhow."

"Well, I have another idea. Why don't you start building that new house like it doesn't matter one bit if she wants it or not? I'll bet you can get her interested."

"I've been wanting to do that for a long time, but she won't hear of it. I wasn't sure how you'd feel about it either."

"Oh, pshaw, Tate! I don't care nothing about that house anymore. It's served its purpose. Besides, it's way old-fashioned. Jasper's putting an indoor bathroom in that new house he's building down the road. It has a sink with running water in the kitchen. You let me work on Maggie."

The next day, Aunt Mag helped Uncle Freddy hitch up the cart to Millie, the old mule. "You're worse off than me, old girl, but we can still get up and go, can't we?" she said to the mule. She had gotten an early start that morning, stirring coffee into a pot of boiling water before going to the garden to dig a bushel of new red potatoes. Uncle Freddy, the old colored man who had been one of her father's slaves, still came to see about her every day. He had helped her load the potatoes in the cart, then sat down on the back porch and waited for her to bring him his breakfast. He wasn't more than ten years older than she was, but she had called him "Uncle Freddy" all her life—since she was a little child.

She walked out on the porch and handed him a plate of ham and eggs with a big dollop of grits.

"You eat your breakfast, Uncle Freddy, and go on home. I'll be going down to Maggie Lorena's, carrying her some potatoes."

"You want me to go with you, Miss Mag?"

"No, I've got some business to tend to with Maggie. She hasn't acted right since Yancey died."

"Lizzie'll take care of her. The Capt'n made her promise to look after Miss Maggie Lorena," he said, nodding his head and sopping up the ham gravy with a biscuit.

"Lizzie can't help her any more than I can. I'm going to jerk a knot in her if I have to."

"Lizzie say Miss Maggie Lorena's mind snapped when her boy died. Won't do no good to jerk a knot in her."

"Well, I'm going to try and straighten her out anyway." She pulled her apron off and hung it on a nail by the kitchen door.

"Lizzie say they's mo' to it."

"More to what?"

"Lizzie say Mastuh Yancey won't Mr. Tate's chile."

"What on earth are you saying, Uncle Freddy? How would she know?"

"Lizzie jus' got sense 'bout things like dat."

"Why haven't you told me this before?"

"I tries to mind my own business, Miss Mag."

Aunt Mag pulled a worn straw hat down low over her face and eased Millie and the cart out into the sandy road. *So there is more to it. But who? Tate worshiped the ground that child walked on. He would have known. Besides, who on earth?*

She pulled into the lane and let the long tendrils of Spanish moss brush across her face as she passed under the live oak trees. Archie planted those trees—every one of them—because she'd asked him to. She pulled the cart up near the porch. "Maggie Lorena, come on out here! I brought you some new potatoes," she called.

Maggie appeared on the front porch in an old pink nightgown that had been one of Ellen's. Her hair was tousled and unbrushed. "What ails you, girl, are you sick?" Aunt Mag climbed down off the cart and walked up onto the porch.

Maggie reached out to hug her. "Morning, Aunt Mag. I guess I am feeling poorly. Tate and the boys have gone to Burgaw. I told him to bring me some of Dr. Pierce's Remedy. I've been out of it for over a week now."

Aunt Mag pulled a chair up and sat down. "No tonic is going to cure what ails you, Maggie Lorena. I came up here to tell you that Tate wants to build you a new modern house and I want my house back." This was spiteful, but she was provoked by what Uncle Freddy had just told her. Besides, the only way to get Maggie out of her house was to give it to somebody else.

"You don't mean that!"

Aunt Mag rocked back in the chair and set her jaw. "Yes, I do. I want to give it to Lizzie."

"What? You can't, Aunt Mag. You gave it to me. You wouldn't do that!"

The old woman stood up and looked directly at Maggie. "Yes, I would. This house isn't fit for anything now. You've let it go to rack and ruin. Why, I'm pure ashamed of how you've let it go down."

"But Aunt Mag, Tate is supposed to keep up with things. The boys are supposed to..." She straightened up, smoothed her gown and brushed her hair back from her face. "I do the best I can."

"What? Piled up in the bed all day? Maggie, you might as well stop wishing your life away. Wishing you was somebody else. If you didn't want to be a farmer's wife, you should've thought about that before you married Tate Ryan."

Maggie's look was sharp and cutting. Her eyes bore a strong resemblance to G. W.'s. "I could have married somebody else."

Aunt Mag got right up in Maggie's face. "Could have, but didn't!"

Maggie was frightened. She had never seen Aunt Mag like this. She opened the screen door, stepping inside before her aunt could follow. "Go away. Leave me alone. This is my house. You gave it to me! I'm not ever going to give it up."

———

Tate bought a keg of nails and a new hammer in Burgaw. On the way home he talked with his sons about building a new house. "I'm not sure Mama's ready yet, but Aunt Mag thinks it might take her mind off Yancey."

William looked straight ahead. "I d-d-don't think anything in the world c-c-could take her mind off Yancey. She wants to h-h-hold on to him t-t-too bad. She didn't even re-m-m-member that it was my b-b-birthday last week until you t-t-told her."

Tate wanted to cry when William stuttered. "She would have remembered before the day was over, William. You know she would."

"Maybe we could start building it somewhere out of sight and surprise her," Lenny said. "It would be so much fun. Remember how we surprised her with the new kitchen stove?"

"That's what I was thinking, too," Tate said. "I'll take you boys over and show you a little piece of land on Colly Creek that I'm thinking about. It's near the old Croom place."

"Is it on Aunt M-m-mag's land, Pa? Cause if it's n-n-not, Uncle Zeb and Uncle Jasper m-m-might put up a f-f-fuss," William said. Tate smiled. His boys were already figuring things out for themselves. They were smart boys.

"I'm gonna stop by Aunt Mag's. How 'bout you boys visiting with her a little bit and doing a few chores to help her out while I get on back to the house? I need to talk private with Mama. You can eat supper with Aunt Mag if she asks you."

Tate pulled the wagon around to the back door of the old homeplace where Aunt Mag was sitting on the screened-in porch. "Well, look who's here," she said. "Evenin', Tate. How're my boys doing? I've been missing you." William and Lenny hopped off the wagon and stepped inside to hug Aunt Mag.

"'Evenin,' Aunt Mag," Tate said. "We been over to Burgaw. Just stopped by a minute."

"Pa said we could stay if you need some chores done," Lenny said.

"He n-n-needs to t-t-talk to Mama 'bout s-s-something," William said.

Aunt Mag had an arm around each of the boys' shoulders. "Now that you mention it, I could use a load of wood up here on the porch where I could get to it," she said. "Might have some cookies on the table for whoever did."

After the boys had scampered off to the wood lot, Tate turned to Aunt Mag. "Did you talk to her about the house?"

"I tried to. But she's not right, Tate. Her mind's just not right." Naturally, she left out the part about what Freddy had told her. That was something she never intended to repeat.

"Well, if you couldn't make her see things differently, I know I can't," Tate said. "I might as well chuck these nails off Colly Creek bridge. It's no use, Aunt Mag. It's no use a'tall."

"Now, don't go giving up so easily, Tate Ryan. I declare, I've never seen the likes of you young folks. Go on home now. I'll feed the boys and send them on home before dark." She put her hand on his arm. "Maybe what I said got her to thinking. You go and talk to her."

When Tate got home, he pulled the wagon around to the barn, unhitched the horse and put the cart away. He'd likely find Maggie in the kitchen this time of day. She didn't cook much anymore, but she always managed some kind of supper. He walked over to the hand pump behind the house and pumped a dipper full of cold water. Looking up to swallow, something caught his eye. The back door to Maggie's little room was standing wide open. Shooing two chickens off the steps, he reached to pull the door closed and saw Maggie's trunk and her things scattered about on the floor.

"Maggie!" he called. She didn't answer. Walking across the little room and into the main part of the house, he called again, louder this time. "Maggie!" Still, there was no answer.

It disturbed him, he had to admit. She hadn't told him that she planned to go anywhere. He'd have seen her if she'd been out in the garden or gathering eggs. He called again, but the house was empty. Careful not to step on anything, he stood in the middle of her room and looked at the memorabilia strewn about on the floor. There were little piles here and there, as if she had been sorting things out. He spied the letter from Reece Evans that he had seen long ago. He lifted it up and saw another. This one had no postmark. It was in Maggie's hand. He opened it and began to read... *and after what you said, I realized that I might never change your mind...it would be fruitless for me to wait...I'll marry Tate, tho my heart will always belong to you.* He dropped the letter and picked up a scarab bracelet and the pin he had seen Maggie wear the day after the fire. *He gave her gifts!* There was a small box with a man's watch—a pocket watch, wound and ticking. Turning it over, he read the inscription. *Those would be Reece's initials!*

Tate's jaw tightened. His temples throbbed. Beside the box was a pile of carefully cut-out newspaper clippings. He picked them up and shuffled through them. *Legislators Assemble In Capitol, Senate Leaders Ask For Vote On Education Bill, Evans Re-elected In Onslow.* On the bottom of the stack was a picture captioned *Senators Evans and Yancey Sponsor Legislation for Public School Buses.* There was Reece Evans smiling, his arm draped across the shoulders of a Senator Yancey from Columbus County.

Tate dropped the clippings on the floor where he had found them. Maggie had betrayed him, sure as the world. He now knew why he had been so relieved when he'd heard that Reece was dead. As long as that son-of-a-bitch had been alive, he knew he couldn't trust him. But Maggie? He'd always trusted Maggie. What had been going on all these years? And why had she named his son after that senator and not told him? "Damn!" he said, slamming his forehead against the doorjamb. "I've been a fool, a pure fool."

When she returned from Katie's, Maggie found Tate in the barn oiling harnesses. He was sitting on a keg, several straps and harnesses laid out on the floor in front of him. He didn't look up. "Where are the boys?" she asked.

"At your Aunt Mag's. Where've you been?"

"I went down to see about Katie. She was having some pain. It's too early, but she wanted me to come. Roy won't be back until next week."

"She all right?"

"I think so. Dr. Bayard came. He said he thought she'd go another couple of weeks, but she has to stay off her feet." Maggie was pacing back and forth. Ill at ease, he guessed, because she had left her things spread out on the floor. "I don't know how she's going to do that with the children and all."

He didn't look up, just watched the hem of her blue print dress. "Looked like you got off in a hurry," he said, wiping his hands on a rag.

"What do you mean?"

"You left the door standing open."

"Oh." She walked to the barn door and looked over at the house. "You closed it?"

"I did."

"Did you go in there, in my room?" She was directly in front of him now.

He hesitated, studying her dusty shoes. "What if I did? You left it open."

"What on earth is the matter with you? I was upset, if you want to know. Look at me!" she demanded. When he did, she looked startled. "What's wrong with your head?"

Tate reached up and felt a knot on his forehead where he had banged his head. The blood was sticky on his fingertips. "Nothing. I bumped it."

"Was that while you were in there messing with my things?"

"What if I did?" he said again, but this time a little more defiantly.

"What ails you, Tate Ryan? I was upset and needed to go to Katie's. That's why I left my things out, but that didn't give you the right to go in there."

"What were you upset about?" he asked in a dull tone.

"Aunt Mag came down here telling me that she was going to take her house back and give it to Lizzie."

Tate glanced up at her, then back to the harness. "I guess that means we'll have to find someplace else to live."

"It means nothing of the kind. She was just being mean. It's not like her. I think maybe her mind is starting to go."

"Your Aunt Mag's got more sense than the rest of us put together. You're the one that's..."

"Hush up, Tate. You don't know anything about me. After all these years, you still don't know!" She stomped out of the barn.

Back in her room, Maggie put her things away. So he had seen it all—the letters, the clippings—everything. Flinching each time she picked up something he'd seen or read, she wondered how she could ever face him again. He'd know now that she'd married him because the man she really loved—a man Tate considered his mortal enemy— couldn't marry her. But he would never know that Yancey was...unless... She picked up the newspaper clippings and saw the picture of Reece and Senator Yancey. He might've figured it out. She locked the trunk and tied the string with the key on it around her neck.

Remembering she'd brought the mail in and put it on the kitchen table, she hurried to retrieve it before Tate came in. There had been a letter from Emily McAllister among the newspapers and magazines. The large vellum envelope reminded Maggie of the invitation to the soirée. It was addressed in the same heavy black ink and ornate script.

Dearest Maggie,

I have only recently learned of the tragic loss of your son, Yancey. My dear husband, Duncan, passed away only two weeks ago, following a short illness. At his funeral, Bill Ryan paid his respects, and I inquired about you. He told me about your precious son, how he had suffered, and how you continue to suffer. I can only imagine what it would be like to lose Darcy or Jeanne. They are my life—even more so with Duncan's death. Both are back in college now, and I miss them so.

I know that Tate and your other two sons have suffered this loss also, but a mother's love goes so much deeper. I hope that you have never regretted your decision...there is no greater bond between a man and a woman than a child of their own flesh and blood. You could never have had this with Reece. I will not go into detail. Let it suffice for me to say how determined he was to always have things his way.

What was Emily saying? That Reece had had the operation? Yes, that was it, pure and simple...*their own flesh...you could never have had this.* All those years of believing, of hoping even, that Yancey was Reece's child—all the guilt—was for naught. She had wished her life away, and on top of that, she had destroyed her peace of mind and what little chance she and Tate might've had.

Outside, the pump began to squawk. Tate was washing up, coming inside. She stuffed the letter into the envelope and reached to take the trunk key from around her neck, but there wasn't enough time. He was coming inside. Slipping into the parlor in the next room, she lifted the lid on the piano and tossed the letter inside.

Tate ate a sweet potato and some cold biscuits for supper and waited for the boys to come home. When they did, he told them their mama wasn't feeling well and to go and wash up and get to bed. Maggie never came out of her little room.

When he thought the boys were asleep, he went to the barn and picked up a can of kerosene, shifting it from one broad callused hand to the other. The wind had picked up and there was rain in the air, much as there had been the night their house in Onslow County burned. Sooner or later, she'd likely go out into the gazebo as was her habit after he'd gone to bed. He'd gotten up many a night and found her asleep in the swing, a quilt pulled up under her chin.

Around midnight he woke up, remembering his plan. He didn't feel good about it, but he was convinced that it was the only way to erase the past, the only way to start over. He looked through the house, making sure she was outside before he crumpled up several newspapers under her desk and doused them and her trunk with kerosene. Then he turned a lamp over on the desk and watched the oily liquid saturate the books and papers. Lighting a long wooden match from the kitchen, he watched the flames begin to spread before he went to roust the sleeping boys out of their warm beds. As much as he loved Aunt Mag, he knew what he had to do.

Epilogue

Four months after the fire, Tate could still smell the smoke. It was in the sand, in the trees and the curly moss that drug the ground. Maybe it was his imagination, but sometimes the smell was so strong that it burned his nose and watered his eyes. Sometimes he wished he'd built over by the old Croom place on Colly Creek like he planned, but he'd thought it would please Maggie to build a house here. As it was, she didn't seem one bit interested in where or what he built.

He lifted his brogans one at a time, shaking out the fine black sand that seemed to work its way through the leather into the cracks between his toes. As usual, he had gotten up before daybreak to split some kindling for the stove and light the fire before Maggie and the boys stirred in the camphouse. He sat on the stump of the magnolia tree that had once shaded the kitchen window. The yellow flames had licked the leaves off in great slurps and sent boiling sap throughout the tree's branches, killing it dead as a doornail.

Tate had sawed the tree's charred skeleton off at the base, but by mid-summer it had begun to sprout, struggling like the rest of them to get going again. Maggie said Uncle Archie used to point at the tree and brag about how he had brought it back in an envelope from a trip to Georgia. He'd planted it in that very spot because Aunt Mag wanted to look out her kitchen window at the creamy white blossoms and smell their sweet fragrance while she was washing the dishes.

At first, Aunt Mag had insisted that they come and live with her at the old homeplace until Tate could build the new house, but he wouldn't hear of it. "I'm much obliged for all you've done for us, but it's not right for you to have to put up with young'uns and all. Besides, we're a family and we need our own place."

"Suit yourself, but I don't think Maggie Lorena will like the inconvenience of being laid up in a camphouse. My idea was that you'd have a new house built when you moved out of mine, but I guess that's not what the Lord intended."

"Some things happen for the best. You just have to look hard for the good sometimes. Maggie might as well be laid up in a camphouse as laid up in your house. The only difference is she'll have me waiting on her instead of you," Tate said.

The camphouse was a one-room shelter, not much more than a shed with a dirt floor and a tin roof. It had a door and two windows that Tate had nailed screening over to satisfy Maggie. He built some bunk beds for the boys on one long side and a double bed for him and Maggie on the other. Freddie had brought back an old cookstove that Archie'd given the colored folks when he bought Aunt Mag a new Home Comfort range. They'd never even used it.

A dirt floor camphouse wasn't much to brag about, but at least they were all under the same roof. Sure, they were starting over from scratch, but Aunt Mag's house had been like a millstone tied around his neck, pulling him and his family down. Maggie'd been so wrapped up in herself she couldn't see that. She didn't think of her family anymore. All she cared about was that little room where she did her writing and that damn trunk. Yes, he'd been jealous of what that trunk held, what it meant to her. *But not anymore!* Everybody that had anything to do with what was in the trunk was dead and gone. Except for her.

Looking at the stacks of yellow pine curing out in the sun, he calculated how far they would go. It would take one or two more loads of pine to finish the framing before he could put the split cypress shingles on the roof. Maggie said he couldn't build a house as good as Aunt Mag's, but he'd show her. He slipped his feet into the worn brogans, laced them up, and stood looking at the partially-framed house. What mattered more than anything now was getting Maggie and the boys into a new house before cold weather. Things would be different then.

She said she didn't want a new house—that there was nothing in Colly for her anymore. But she would love this house when he got it finished. She'd settle down and start making curtains. Next spring she'd plant her garden and some flowers in little beds around the new house. That's what the fire had been about.

Gradually Maggie put things together until she was positive Tate had set the fire. He'd tried to get rid of the trunk for sure. The kerosene smell hadn't aroused her curiosity at first—there'd been so much commotion the night of the fire—but she'd smelled it for certain the next day when she'd walked into G. W.'s old room at the homeplace. She'd asked her sons to put her trunk there, where she'd be able to get to it. It smelled like kerosene had been spilled on it. The reason *why* hadn't occurred to her until later. At the time, she'd just wondered how she'd ever get the odor out. A number of times she'd wanted to confront him, but what could she say? Hadn't she done the same thing to him— to get out of Onslow County? She decided she'd just bide her time and save her egg money and the little bit she got from the newspaper. One of these days she'd get on the train and leave them all behind. Her heart hurt when she thought of leaving her sons, but already Lenny was talking about going to work next summer with his Uncle Roy drilling wells in South Carolina. And William, her dear William who might always stutter, had written off for a mechanics course and was working on cars for the few neighbors who had them. He'd set up a small shop in the shed next to the barn.

Aunt Mag was another story. Since the house had burned, she'd lost some of her starch. Maybe the fire had nothing to do with it, but Maggie suspected that she felt hard towards her—even towards Tate because he had allowed her old place to burn. Maggie couldn't tell Aunt Mag why Tate had done what he did. If she told her, she'd have to explain a lot of other things that were best left unsaid.

On the last Sunday in September, Maggie set up her typewriter outside, her back towards the new house Tate was building. She couldn't bear to look at it. He was trying his best to get her involved, but as far as she was concerned the camphouse would do just fine until she found a way out. She was glad Tate had taken the boys down to Jasper's. Maybe he would satisfy some of his building urge on Jasper's new place and she wouldn't have to listen to all that hammering.

A light breeze was enough to keep the yellow flies away where she sat out under the trees composing her article for the *Bladen Journal*. She was writing about Jasper coming back home after a year in Florida picking fruit. *Fortunately for the community, Mr. Jasper Corbinn says this time he has returned for good. He is presently building a new home just down the road from where he was born, convenient to the tables of his two sisters, this writer and Mrs. Katie Hill.*

Maggie was just putting the finishing touches on the article when she heard the low roar of an automobile engine and looked up to see a long yellow car turning into the lane, followed by a cloud of dust. *Who in the world?* She knew it wasn't Jasper. He'd driven a new black Oldsmobile up from Florida and she'd ridden in it just a few days ago. *Maybe someone looking for William?* She brushed her hair back from her face and wondered if she looked as haggard as she felt.

The car stopped in front of the house. The driver opened his door, stood and stretched, looking about at the moss-draped trees. He was wearing an expensive-looking navy pinstriped suit. Settling a matching hat on his head, he went around the car to open the other door. Abigail Adams stepped out and kissed the man on the cheek. She looked up at the trees, laughing. "You've never seen Spanish moss like this in Boston, Henry."

The gentleman reached up to a low branch, pulling off a handful of the moss, holding it up to his chin. "How'd I look with a beard, darling?" He wiggled his eyebrows and laughed.

"Henry, you fool." She glanced over his shoulder. "Wait a minute. The house... They're building a new house."

Maggie wanted to run and hide, embarrassed because she had let herself go. But Abigail saw her and called out, "Maggie, is that you?"

Barefooted, Maggie ran to meet her, so glad to see her that she no longer cared how she looked. "I can't believe it. What in the world are you doing here?"

"Oh, my dear Maggie. It's been so long." Abigail was wearing a white suit with a shorter skirt in the new style. Her hair was completely gray now, but she looked more feminine in makeup and bright red lipstick. As they embraced, Maggie thought she smelled faintly of cigarettes. Abigail held her until Maggie began to sob. "What is it, dear?" Abigail asked. "What's wrong?"

Maggie looked in the direction of the new house Tate was building and Abigail followed her gaze. "Your house? That precious little house Aunt Mag gave you, what happened to it?"

"It's gone. Burned to the ground this past spring." Maggie tried to recover, but the tears kept coming.

"Tate and the children—they did get out?"

"Yes, but..."

"But what?" Abigail looked distressed, as if imagining the worst.

Maggie stared at her, tears streaming down her face. "They're all right, it's just that..."

"Don't tell me any more now. I know it must have been awful." Abigail pulled a handkerchief out of her sleeve. "Dry your eyes and come meet my new husband."

Maggie refused the handkerchief and wiped her eyes on her apron, wishing she had put on a clean one. "Your husband?"

"Yes, dear, my husband, Henry." The portly, distinguished-looking gentleman walked towards Maggie, his hat in his hand, and she saw that he was bald except for a fringe of white hair over his ears. Abigail beamed. "Maggie, this is Henry Montgomery. Henry, this is the author of your new novel."

Maggie looked from one to the other. "What?"

"Mrs. Ryan, how nice to meet you at last. Abby has told me so much about you." He bowed deeply and kissed Maggie's hand.

Maggie was bewildered. She looked at Abigail. "How about running through that again? I don't think I understand."

"Come, sit here," Abigail said, pointing to the unfinished porch. "First, tell me what happened to Aunt Mag's house. Did anyone get hurt?"

"Not so you can tell it."

"What do you mean?"

"Oh, it's a long story."

"Something's not right. What is it, Maggie?"

"You don't even know about my baby Yancey." Maggie put her hands up to cover her face.

"What happened to Yancey?"

"He died of a leaking heart—just two years ago."

"Oh, no! Why didn't someone tell me?"

"I didn't know where you were. I hadn't heard from you and...I was all to pieces for a long time. The rest...oh, it wouldn't be fair to Tate to go telling it." Maggie wiped her eyes and sniffed. "But listen, when did you two get married?"

Abigail put her arm around her husband. "Just a month ago," she said, smiling up at Henry.

"You were teasing about the novel, weren't you?" Maggie asked.

Henry stepped forward and took Maggie's hands in his. "No, no, my dear," he said. "Abigail brought it to me a year ago, but I didn't get around to reading it until just before the wedding. It's wonderful. We're prepared to offer you a contract."

"We?"

"Yes, 'we.' I'm working with Henry now," Abigail said. "I hated Radcliffe. In fact, after Mother died, I hated everything and everybody it seems." She looked at Henry. "Until Henry came along, I was a lost soul, but we met at a literary festival in Boston and *voila!*"

"I wondered why I hadn't heard from you. I was worried," Maggie said.

"I know I should've written, but after Mother died...I think they call it depression."

"Yes, I know about that, too."

"Maggie, this sounds crazy, but we want you to come to Boston, stay with us in the brownstone. We have plenty of room and you would love the city. There are some revisions that need to be made. We could work together." She stroked Henry's arm. "Henry thinks it's a wonderful idea. You'd be right there with us and we could get the job done in no time." She paused. "You look like you need to get away for awhile."

Maggie started to cry again. "I can't believe it, but I don't know. I don't have clothes for the city and Tate and the boys..."

"Look. You'll get an advance. We'll go shopping—just you and I. We'll have a ball," Abigail said, hugging her again. "As for the boys and Tate, they can take care of themselves for awhile. Aunt Mag will keep them straight."

"Oh Abigail, it sounds too good to be true. I think I'm dreaming."

"Not this time, dear. As soon as I get back to Boston, I'm sending you a train ticket. You tell Tate if he isn't nice, you might not ever come back."

Maggie took a deep breath and smiled. "Thank you, Abigail."

"Where is Tate? I'll tell him myself," Abigail said.

"He's down at my brother Jasper's helping him build a new house."

"Henry, put the top down and we'll all go."

—

Tate could hardly believe his eyes when Henry Montgomery pulled his Buick touring car into the lane that led to Jasper's house. Maggie and another woman were sitting on the back laughing and waving like two silly schoolgirls.

"Look Papa, that's Mama," William said, starting to run towards the car.

"Come back here, William, before you get run over."

"Aw, Pa. I want to see the car."

"Just wait a minute. Let's see who it is."

Maggie hopped out of the car and ran towards Tate. He didn't recognize Abigail, nor the man who was with her. "Tate, come here. It's Abigail and her husband. They've come to see us."

Abigail strode towards him, her arm linked with her husband's. "Don't panic, Tate. We're just passing through." She started to hug him, but Tate backed away.

"I'm sopping wet with sweat, Miss Abigail, but I'm mighty pleased to see you."

"This is my husband, Henry."

Tate reached out his hand and the older man shook it. "Pleased to meet you."

Maggie looked around for Jasper, but he and both boys had zeroed in on the yellow car. She called out to them, "Jasper, boys, come over here. I want you to meet Abigail and Henry," but they paid no attention to her. "Look at that, they're more interested in that car, Tate," she said.

"Oh, let them enjoy it," Henry admonished. "Say, why don't I take them for a ride while you tell Tate what we're here for?" He kissed Abigail on the cheek.

"All right, darling," Abigail said. "Do you mind, Maggie?"

Maggie laughed. "They'd kill me if I did." Jasper and the boys climbed into the automobile and Henry revved up the engine. They roared down the lane and out onto the dirt road, Henry blowing the horn and the boys waving. "I declare, we'll never hear the end of this," Maggie said.

Abigail had taken Tate's arm and was walking towards the house. Maggie strolled along behind them, letting Abigail do the talking. "Tate, I want Maggie to come up to Boston for awhile. Henry's going to publish her novel."

"What novel?"

Abigail turned around and looked at Maggie. "Didn't you tell him that you sent me a manuscript?"

Maggie was uneasy. "It was so long ago. I think I did."

"No, you never told me you sent Abigail a book. I know you didn't," Tate said. He wanted her to know that she hadn't been the one who told him. It hurt him even more now.

"Look, it doesn't matter," Abigail said. "What matters is that Henry wants to publish it. He's one of the best editors in the country. Tate, what that means is Maggie needs to come to Boston for awhile. You wouldn't mind, would you?"

Tate hesitated, looking out across the treeless field that Jasper had chosen for his homesite. "No, not a'tall. It'd give me time to finish my house. Maybe Jasper's, too."

"I wouldn't be gone that long, Tate," she said.

But somehow he knew she would and right now he didn't care. Maybe she'd come back a different person.

———

Ham Hinson took Maggie's bags and loaded them into a two-wheel cart. "I'll meet you up on the platform, Miss Maggie."

"Do y'all want to go speak to Mr. Narley?" Tate asked. "I could pull the wagon around to the other side."

Aunt Mag sat primly in the delivery wagon, wearing the same outfit she had worn the day Maggie went off to college. "No, don't do that. I hear the train and I want to tell Maggie something." She watched Tate go around the station to give their regards to the stationmaster. "I can't believe that old coot Narley Hinson is still alive. He's older than I am, with one foot in the grave and the other on a banana peel."

"He seemed old when I was a little girl," Maggie said.

Aunt Mag set her mouth and shifted in her seat. "Tate thinks you're coming back, you know."

"What in the world, Aunt Mag? Of course I'm coming back. Why would you say such a thing?"

"Methinks she doth protest too much," Aunt Mag quipped under her breath.

Maggie stared at the train barreling down the track, brakes squealing, spewing like a dragon. It was a new 'Big Boy' steam locomotive, the first they'd seen on the Cape Fear-Yadkin Valley Line. Looking across the tracks at the old house where Dr. Bayard had his office, she saw some boarders standing on the third-floor porch watching the train. She wished the boys had come to see her off, but she hadn't wanted them to miss school. With her advance, maybe she could send for them. Someday, they might even go to college in Boston.

The wagon was so close to the track Aunt Mag had to hold her hands over her ears. "You better go on," she shouted. "They run a tight schedule. Give me a hug and promise me you'll write."

Maggie hugged her quickly and hopped down off the wagon. "I will," she called out.

Tate met her at the platform and lifted her up, holding her in his arms until the conductor shouted, "All aboard that's comin' aboard."

She pulled away from him and started up the steps of the train car, looking back over her shoulder. He looked so dejected, so lonely. She smiled at him. "I love you, Tate." The words startled her.

He grinned and held up his hand. If he said anything she couldn't hear it. Settling herself in a seat by the window, she watched him climb back into the wagon beside Aunt Mag. What was he thinking?

She removed her hat and took a deep breath. This was it, the leavetaking she'd longed for, and like always, Aunt Mag was right. Just like she'd been right when she said the burden of caring for her in her old age would fall on Tate. *You can't even take care of yourself,* Aunt Mag had said. Well, she'd show them all that she could, and someday she might return to her place between the rivers. Then again, she might not.

THE END

Carolyn Rawls Booth

Carolyn Rawls Booth was born in Bladen County, North Carolina, in 1936, on a wedge of woodland called Colly between the Cape Fear and Black Rivers. Her family moved to Raleigh when she was five years old, but she often returned to her birthplace, spending weekends and summers with her grandparents. The rich oral tradition in which she grew up provided the background for *Between the Rivers*, her first novel.

Elements in the novel reflect not only Carolyn's love of the landscape between the rivers, but an abiding interest in Southern food traditions, rural architecture, historical fact, medicine and mental health. Carolyn has also written a handbook for parents of children with cerebral palsy and holds a patent for a medical surgical pad. A freelance food and garden writer and photographer, she lives with her husband Dick in Cary, North Carolina, near their three children and six grandchildren.